# HEART *of the* COUNTRY

# HEART
## *of the*
# COUNTRY

*Bland Simpson*

Seaview/Putnam
New York

The author gratefully acknowledges permission from the following
sources to reprint material in their control:

Belwin Mills Publishing Corp., 1776 Broadway, New York, N.Y. 10019,
for "Lovesick Blues" by I. Mills and C. Friend, copyright © 1922 by Mills
Music, Inc. Used with permission. All rights reserved.

April Music Inc., a division of CBS Songs, 1350 Avenue of the
Americas, New York, N.Y. 10019, for "Long Day's Journey into Night" by
Bland Simpson, copyright © 1971 by April Music Inc., & Gadfly Music.
Rights administered by April Music Inc. Used by permission. All rights
reserved.

Bland Simpson and James C. Wann, Jr., for "Wayfarer in Your Heart"
by Bland Simpson and James C. Wann, Jr., copyright © 1982 by Bland
Simpson and James C. Wann, Jr.

Library of Congress Cataloging in Publication Data

Simpson, Bland.
Heart of the country.

I. Title.
PS3569.I4877H4   1983        813'.54        82-19236
ISBN 0-399-31007-X

Printed in the United States of America

For Anne

*Oh, who's gonna shoe your pretty foot?*
*Who's gonna glove your hand?*
*Who will kiss your sweet rosy cheek*
*When I'm in that far-off land?*

In the beginning, country music was tied to the land, and to all the landsounds, the wind and rain, the shriek of the raven and the coo of the dove, the turning of millwheels, the jangle of trace chains as men and women sang to each other and to their children and to the animals that worked the land with them. They took hornpipes and ballads of the British Isles, airs of love and violence from centuries past, took these and changed the names of the heroes and villains and places, and out of the deep dark mountains came songs of hardscrabbling frustration and wildhog sin and lonely guilt but also of simple delight and faith and love. And they mixed these with country hymns of the brush-arbor camp-meeters, and they played the music on the fiddle, the Devil's box, and on the banjo, the African's hide-covered gourd, and, later, on cheap guitars and foot-pumped organs. Theirs were tunes of eerie simplicity and full blood, tunes of people born to win and born to lose, of those bound for glory and those with hellhounds on their trails, of loving women, of murdering men, of farmers, miners, dancehall girls, gamblers, of city slickers and country boys who wished they'd a got em a half pint and stayed in the wagonyard, of homebodies lured away by rumbling trains and geargrinding trucks, of ramblers far away dreaming of home. Out of the great mountains and off of the redhill farms the songs came, from the hollows and bayous and deltas and coves, out into the grooves of cylinders and discs and onto the airways, out of the South and into the world, on three hundred thousand jukeboxes, on assembly lines in defense-plant towns Baltimore, Chi, Cincinnati, Detroit City. Boys with names like Oaty Smathers from places like Gatlinburg carried their daddies' mail-order guitars from the mountain hollows to the barracks at Bragg, Benning and Lakeland. Four chords and a sock rhythm and before long Oaty is a star in Nashville, the town of dreams, and before long a people who once entertained themselves to beat the band listen to someone else's music on mortgaged televisions and radios. But some old heads persist, and younger hands have caught the fiddles and the banjos before they hit the ground and crumbled, and these hands have learnt the notes and styles, the feel of it all, and then lent their own invaluable spirits. With them, even now there is heart in the singing and playing, and a power and truth, and ties to the beginning, and to the everlasting dust.

> *Your papa will shoe your pretty little foot*
> *Your mama will glove your hand*
> *And I will kiss your sweet rosy cheek*
> *When I come back again. . . .*

# PART ONE

# BONNIE MONTREAT
Summer, 1949

The car smelled good and rich as the hot air off the road blended with the greasy smell from the shoeboxes of fried chicken. Every so often, Daddy Montreat would pull into one of the soda-and-gas joints that had sprung up all along U.S. 70 since the war and fill up the tank with twenty-cent gas. Ivy refused to use the bathrooms in these grimy stations, nor would she let Bonnie, so Daddy had to keep pulling over onto the shoulder of the road while mother and daughter went and squatted out of sight in broomsedge fields.

The Montreats rolled west into late afternoon. Bonnie and her elder brother sang through all the old Carter Family songs they knew and started over again. Ivy had a headache from the motion and the noise and the heat, but she didn't complain, just kept her nose in her camphor handkerchief. Along about dusk, they passed a sign which Bonnie read aloud: "Nashville, 10."

Once in the city, they headed for the Sevier Hotel, where Daddy and Ivy used to stay when their band, the Tennessee Bumblebees, played the Opry. The neighborhood had gone

down. When they came upon it, the Sevier was all dark and
boarded up and looked like it had been for years. In the dim
hotel arcade an old bum was yanking at something, pulling it
apart.

"Oh, Franklin," Ivy said, disgusted. "Don't look!"

Daddy spoke sharply to the children. He hit the gas and
drove on.

A policeman on foot near the State Capitol building told
them about Mrs. Foil's boardinghouse across the river. "Turn
left over Victory Bridge, it's after you cross the L & N tracks.
It's a Christian household and a cheap rate."

Bumper made a wisecrack as they drove away, and Ivy
chided him, "You oughtn't to forget your teachings, Hubert.
It'll come back on you if you do."

Wisteria and grapevine tangled all over the high iron fence
around Mrs. Foil's place. They trudged up onto the porch,
worn out from the long trip driving into the sun. An old man
let them in and took them upstairs to two rooms with a bath
between.

Ivy put Bonnie and Bumper in one and told them to eat
their chicken and go on to bed. The boy and girl faced away
from each other like always at home and undressed and
slipped into their beds. Bumper got back up in a few minutes
and got him another drumstick. Bonnie listened to him
eating the chicken and sucking his fingers.

"Bumper? What was that man doing there at that old
hotel?" Bumper didn't answer, so she spoke again. "Do you
remember?"

"Sister," he said, "he was skinning a cat."

Next morning Bonnie Montreat sat up on her bed, her
legs crossed Indian style, and combed the sleep tangles from
her copper curls. "Are you really gonna come live here in
Nashville?"

"Someday," he said. "*If* I can get a job."

"How old do you have to be?" the nine-year-old girl asked.

"It's not how old you got to be, Sister—it's how *good*."

"Oh. Well, as good a picker as you are, I bet you won't have no trouble."

"We'll see," the boy said. "You got to be good and then some. Let me tell you something, Bonnie. Daddy says this town's on the boom with the music business and all. It's different from when he was going around with the Bumble-bees. I mean, they did all right, I reckon, but he says people get paid a lot better now and some of em even get rich. Old Acuff, he made all his money and bought hisself a *cave*."

"A cave?"

"Yeah, for charging tourists ticket money to go in. You take Daddy and Mama, they were just getting by. They never made enough money to buy no cave. They should of kept on going and come to Nashville instead of breaking up the Bees like that." The hawk-face boy sat on the edge of his rumpled bed and carefully polished his daddy's banjo. "I remember when you was a new baby and I was still little they'd take us along with em places, to barn dances and such. Mama'd set me to holding you off in a corner near where the band was, and when they'd stop and rest a spell Daddy'd come over and set with us and plop his banjo down in my lap. I was just starting to pick some and people'd stop and make a fuss. We'd have a real good time."

"And then there was the fire?"

"Yeah. And Mama started with her headaches and all. Anyway there won't never enough money in it to take care of us all."

Bonnie would remember walking and walking and seeing a big woman in a checkered apron tending an upstairs flower box as they came down the hill of Second Avenue. They were looking for a shop Daddy knew about where stringed instruments were bought and sold and traded. You could still read the sign on the shop window, though the *U* and the *N* and the *O* had fallen away from the inside of the glass. Each had left enough yellowed decal cement for the phantoms of the letters to be legible: YULANOV'S.

Bumper walked into the shop ahead of Daddy and Ivy and accidentally hit a low-hanging bell over the door that was supposed to ring when the door opened and trade walked through—only the door was already open now on account of the June heat and the overpowering smell of collards boiling down. Daddy lagged outside a moment, and he and his wife and his little girl looked at the left-hand window full of strange dusty instruments: a doublenecked guitar, a ukelele-sized hybrid of a banjo and a mandolin that Daddy called a banjolin, a regular guitar studded with chips of glass dazzling like diamonds in the morning sun. When Daddy walked on in, Ivy leaned over to Bonnie and said, "Put your hands behind you and don't touch nothing." Bumper pulled down an old Vega Tubaphone banjo like Daddy's hanging from a big wooden peg on the wall. He fooled with the tuning and plucked on it some.

Daddy retrieved a small six-string guitar from the dusty instrument window, a lovely little Martin ought-forty-five, one of the smallest they made. He turned it over thisaway and that. "How much?"

Yulanov was putting the banjo back up on the wall. "That? I ain't had a offer on it in so long, I don't know. Nobody wants em that small anymore. They want em cowboy size, jumbo, you seen em, I bet. But that little one's a sweetheart when she's all dusted off and polished nice."

Daddy Montreat held out the little flat-top and stared up the neck at Ivy and Bonnie. "Miracle it ain't warped to hell settin in the sun like that." He checked the registration of the frets and then ran his forefinger over a small rough spot on the hollow body. "What's this patched-up place here?"

"Bullet hole," Yulanov said, and when they heard that Bumper and Bonnie crowded around to look closer. "Old boy's wife got mad at all the attention he give that guitar. Kept telling him she was going to take steps and by damn she did."

Daddy held the guitar up to himself like you would playing it. "Looks like she probably put a hole clear through his right kidney, too."

"Naw," the shopkeeper said. "She waited till he was sleeping and blasted it with his horse pistol. He was all broke up when he brang it in here. I fixed it best I could. I reckon fifty dollars oughtta bout do it."

"Um-hmm," Daddy said and craned his neck looking up at the tin ceiling. "You know, you might can work a horse to death, but a mule's too smart for that. Let's go, children."

The Montreats started out to the street, but Daddy paused by the shop window and nodded at it and said, "You ought to clean this up sometime. People'll get the idea you don't care about what you sell."

Bumper reached up and slapped the hanging doorbell as they left. Bonnie heard the shopkeeper follow them to the door and mutter after them, "Damn hillbillies. Don't never buy nothing."

An old friend of Daddy's was stage manager at the Ryman, and he'd held out tickets for them to that evening's *Grand Ole Opry* show. Daddy took them out to watch the Saturday afternoon baseball game at Sulphur Dell, and they feasted on ballpark food: hot just-roasted peanuts and spun candy all colors and hot dogs and the children's favorite, "Cocama-colas." Daddy and Ivy drank big cups of beer. Bonnie fell asleep and missed most of the game. Daddy piggybacked his drowsy girl out to the dusty parking lot, a sea of stepside pickup trucks and squashy convertibles with wide whitewall tires. They drove back downtown and strolled around killing time till the Ryman opened.

On Church Street they stopped in the Candyland Sundries and Confectioneries shop. Bumper had a tall chocolate sundae, and Bonnie got some fresh made-on-the-spot pecan-and-caramel candy. Pretty soon Candyland started emptying out; it was time to get on over to the show.

The Ryman was a great red-brick tabernacle built by a reformed rakehell riverboater back in the nineties. It was big as the house of God, its bricks the color of oxblood and its windows and buttresses stark and bright like chalk. Hundreds of people were milling around and lining up on the sidewalk. Ivy hollered at Bumper to come on from where he'd strayed into a parking lot counting license plates from all the different states and Canadian provinces. An ice-cream truck slowly trundled up the street, and a couple dozen children broke for it as their parents cried after them in the mob. Bonnie held tight to Daddy's hand.

Inside it was stifling June hot. Three thousand people were crammed into the big curved auditorium: plain ruddy-faced hard-working folks got up in the best they could wear in this heat not to be going to church. The men were dressed in clean white or checkered pressed shirts and dark creased work pants, and the women wore party dresses with sashes and ruffled hems.

The air was thick as cotton. Children wilted in the heat, and old people just looked tired, though Bonnie saw that if you caught their eye they'd smile. Everyone had come a long way, it seemed like, and was glad to be there. Bonnie had no idea it took so many people sitting watching for them to have a *Opry* show. For her, it was always just her family taking turns at the earphone of their battery-powered Philco, and more recently listening around the big brown plug-in Motorola with its electric smells of warm wires and hot tubes.

There were chairs and chairs up on the stage and lines of microphones across the front and big double basses over on their sides. People moved busily back and forth from one wing to the other. Bonnie could see barrels and haybales and a real wagon and behind everything great tall backdrops painted up to look like a big open barn door with a yellow moon coming up outside. Bonnie thought they must have the make-believe farm things up there to make everybody feel at home who'd just come to Nashville from their real farms. All those backdrop things looked familiar to her—but there were others, too, that they rolled down from out of the top of the theater somewhere upstage of the singers, posters advertising flour or salt or car oil or tobacco or denim clothes. It was as if all those times around the radio she'd been right here at the Grand Ole Opry listening with her eyes closed.

As soon as the show got under way Bonnie quit squirming all around in her seat trying to see everything. She let go the funeral-parlor fan she'd been trying to cool herself with when she heard the black-suited man's voice. "Daddy," she said excitedly. "Daddy, ain't that the Judge?" Six people shushed her.

It took the audience a good half hour to loosen up and get over their amazement—after all these years of *Opry* worship from a distance, here they were, Really Here. It was a fine audience, presently bonded and strong as good steel, bonded by the familiar names and voices onstage and the style of humor and the singing and playing and all of it.

Suddenly Bonnie could hear their name over the loud-speakers. "And now we at the *Opry* want to take this opportunity," the Judge was saying, "to recognize those fine talents from the early years of country and mountain music and radio, all the way from Honey Run, Tennessee, Franklin and Ivy Montreat—two of the original Tennessee Bumblebees—and their children!"

Bonnie got tugged to her feet by Ivy, and they all stood in the bright white spotlight and looked around and waved at the cheering handclapping people in the great swooping hall. When they settled back down and the show rolled on, Daddy studied his program card a bit and slapped his knee with the palm of his hand.

"I'll swear and be damned." He leaned over Bumper and Bonnie to Ivy and pointed, and Ivy raised her eyebrows and smiled.

"What?" Bumper asked, and Daddy showed him.

"That Alabama boy up from the *Louisiana Hayride*," Daddy spoke low. "I had no idea on earth he'd be here tonight. No idea at all."

Lord! it was a moment when the young man with the thin blue voice stepped out and sang that song. It was a haunted moment, a coronation. Nothing had felt quite like this to the little girl, not church at its Eastermost holy nor school at its Christmastide-pageant best—nothing in Bonnie Montreat's brief nine years could compare with this. The crowd was on its feet waving and hollering for more. The show was stopped. She couldn't see and Daddy lifted her up like scores of other children there were lifted onto parents' shoulders. People there that night would never forget how Red Foley had to plead over and over again for the folks to please let the show go on after Hank Williams came back and sang six times:

> *"I got the lo-o-onesome*
> *I got the Lovesick Blues . . ."*

Backstage after the show, Daddy was shaking hands all around and introducing Bumper. He thanked his old friend Greer for the complimentary tickets and cussed him for putting the spotlight on them during the show. Bumper picked a little because after all he was thirteen and growing up fast and always talking about coming on to Nashville and looking for work. Ivy fell asleep in a chair by the light box and Bonnie leaned up against a wall off to one side. People were packing things up and clearing out.

When he came out a dressing-room door not ten feet from the little girl, Hank Williams was still wearing his pinstripe cowboy suit, and his hat was tilted back in a lighthearted way. "You lost, child?" he asked.

"No, sir. Waiting on Daddy and Bumper," she said.

Hank glanced at the two men and the boy with the banjo. "What's your name?"

"Bonnie Montreat."

"Oh." Hank smiled and nodded at hearing her last name. She was bright as a candle. "You gonna play autoharp like your mama?"

"No. I want to sing like you, Mr. Williams."

He frowned a moment, then winked solemnly at her and picked up his guitar. "Well, maybe you just will."

"Night, Hank," Greer called over to him. "And welcome aboard."

"Night," the singer called back, then turned and spoke softly so only the little girl could hear. "Now, Bonnie, don't forget old Hank Williams, you hear?" And before she'd even gotten her hand high enough to wave he was gone.

"I won't," she whispered. "Not ever."

The Montreats piled into the Dodge next morning early and headed out of town. But instead Daddy Montreat kept straight after the bridge and headed back downtown, turning onto Second Avenue. He stopped the car at the curb in front of Yulanov's shop and left the engine idling. He called up toward the second-story window, and a minute later the shopkeeper unlocked the door downstairs.

"What do you want now?"

"The little Martin," Daddy said, thrusting twenty-five dollars into Yulanov's hand. "And get the case too."

"This is only half what I told you."

"It's enough."

"I can't sell you anything on Sunday anyways—the blue laws."

"That's all right," Daddy answered. "Let's just say I bought it in my mind yesterday and I'm taking delivery today."

Yulanov picked up his Sunday paper from the shop's doormat and closed the door. Daddy Montreat looked back at his family in the idling Dodge. An arm reached into the dusty instrument window on the left and lifted out the Martin ought-forty-five. Yulanov opened the shop door just long enough to shove the guitar and its case out at Daddy Montreat.

"You'll have to put new strings on her yourself, hillbilly."

Smiling, Daddy Montreat put the guitar in its case, whose bullet hole had not been repaired, and walked back to the Dodge. He reached it over the back seat and set it on Bonnie's lap. "I told Bumper last night I'd give him my banjo. So this guitar—it's for you, little one."

# JOHNNY REX PACKARD
1946

After a gang of the other boys at the Nashville home had
got the albino Johnny Rex down and beat him bloody on
account of he looked funny and acted smart, the home's
director figured enough was enough. The Packard boy was
shipped across the state to another orphanage in Memphis,
where he kept to himself and did right. When a shot came
along at a kind of juvenile work release, hustling newspapers
in the afternoons, Johnny Rex raised his hand and volun-
teered. It got him out of the orphanage from three till eight
and saved the state feeding him his evening meal.

The afternoon *Memphis Truth-Sabre* gave thirteen-year-old
Johnny Rex a wide straw sunbrimmer and a canvas bag
stuffed with papers and put him to working the sidewalks
and street corners of Forrest Park out Union Avenue at
Manassas. He was teamed up with a black boy a year older
named Eck, short for Alexander. The first couple of weeks
they acted tough and watched each other with suspicious
over-the-shoulder looks. Then one particularly hot thick
Memphis afternoon Johnny Rex was setting over in the
shade of the statue in the park counting his money and Eck
wandered up with two Old Gold cigarets. He offered one.

"Where'd you get em?" Johnny Rex said.

"That lady yonder, Miss Violet." Eck motioned toward a
pretty young white woman standing in the shade of a pin oak
over at the corner. She was all dolled up, half looking at a
newspaper and half watching the traffic like she was waiting
on somebody or had someplace she needed to be.

"She just give em away like that?"

"Naw. Sometimes I trades her a paper for some smokes."

The two boys sat and sweltered, smoking by the statue,
and got to be fast friends. They found that by working
together, dancing around in traffic and rushing cars stopped

at red lights, making a sort of show for folks, they could sell papers faster. Eck and Johnny Rex were always seeing the young woman Violet around the park or at Harlow's Sundry-Confectionery next door to the Hotel Bedford Forrest where she lived. Sometimes about when they were through selling papers they'd see her leaving the hotel with one of her men friends. She'd wave, but the caller would look sideways up and down the street and hail a taxicab or else hurry her off to his own car round the corner.

"Them's busy fellows Violet goes to riding with," Johnny Rex said to Eck one afternoon.

"Yeah, man," Eck said. "Busy little white men."

"Someday when I got me some money, I'll take her out and it won't be no hurry. I hope she'll wait on me."

"Wait on you?" Eck said. "Wait on you for *what?*"

"Marrying, I guess. I'd as soon live there at the hotel with her as about anyplace else in Memphis."

"You dummy. Violet ain't studying no marriage. Not with you or nobody. She's a hooker, man."

Johnny Rex's pink albino hands were dark and grimy from the printer's ink off the day's newspapers. He wiped them along the sides of his pants and said kind of low, "What do you mean?" Eck and Johnny Rex had been together selling the *Truth-Sabre* around the park for several months now, but they had never talked about her or women or anything. Violet had took to them and always had cigarets and small bottles of whiskey and she never seemed to mind treating the paperboys or wasting a little money on them, either.

Eck laughed. "Ain't nobody told you about cool fun?"

"No." Johnny Rex felt himself getting red and hot and sweat breaking out under his white silk hair. It must be pretty important from the way Eck was talking. If it's that important, he thought, how come a nigger boy knows it and not me?

Eck laughed some more and said, "Come on, now. Ain't no call to get in a huff. Cool fun's when a girl takes off her clothes and you do, too, and then you kind of mess around."

Johnny Rex felt even hotter. He couldn't picture it in his mind. He thought of times they'd gone skinnydipping on camping trips from the home and tried to imagine it if there'd been girls mixed in instead of just all boys like it was. "What kind of messing around?"

"Rolling *all* around, man."

"Well, what about Violet, then?"

"I'm telling you that's what she does with them men. Gets with em and gives em cool fun." Eck shrugged his shoulders and they walked back to the newspaper building without saying much.

Johnny Rex felt funny talking about Violet without any clothes on. At the pressroom Eck asked one of the men to show Johnny Rex his pictures. He did, and Johnny Rex saw.

One day there was a headline story on the front page about a gypsy wife-killing down in Mississippi, and the boys sold their papers out by six. Johnny Rex had almost two hours before he had to be at the orphanage, so Eck rode him on the handlebars of his bicycle back to turn in their money at the *Truth-Sabre* plant down Union and then they rode on down to the river. All those weeks he'd been on the loose selling papers, and it was the first time the albino had got to see the Mississippi.

Where the Wolf River came down and ran into the big river there were a batch of run-down-looking flatboats and houseboats tied up at the cobblestone levee. Eck bumped his bicycle along, walking it over the stones, and Johnny Rex tripped on a foot-wide iron ring set into the levee itself, an old hitch-loop from steamboat days. They messed around awhile and then wandered up to Front Street and Johnny Rex saw a girl in a purple calico dress sitting still as a mannequin in the second-story window of a cotton merchant's building.

"Come on," Eck said. "I'll take you round Beale Street."

Beale was the liveliest place Johnny Rex had ever seen. A loud evangelist on a street corner was waving a copy of today's newspaper and shouting out how the headlines proved that the Bible's prophecies were coming true. A fellow Eck called "JoJo" leaned against a lamppost and flailed away like all get-out on a cigarbox guitar that looked to have screen-door wire for strings. The two boys passed swinging-door poolhalls and hot catfish cafés, and everywhere there were blind men and women—Eck told Johnny Rex they got that way from drinking canned heat and shoe polish they strained through bread trying to get the alcohol without the poison. Music from jug-band horns and bullfiddle basses and bluesy pianos sounded out from smoky hole-in-the-wall clubs.

"Know when these joints close down at night, Johnny Rex?" Eck said.

"No."

"They don't—till somebody gets shot or cut."

It was dusky dark now. The sun had gone down behind them, beyond the great green floodplain flat of Arkansas over the river, and the fire was gone out of the looming gray-clouded western sky. Eck rode Johnny Rex on the handle-bars again back up Union and dropped him off where he could still make it to the orphanage in time. Then he wheeled away from the albino, disappearing toward South Memphis in the dark.

When Violet took sick, Johnny Rex and Eck did what all they could for her. They checked on her at her room, knocking at the door and calling through it asking how was she doing, and she always called back saying fine but never got up to open the door. After a few days the boys decided she must be starving to death. They got a cousin of Eck's who cooked at a merchants' café to give them a mess of chicken and beans left over from lunch. When they came around to her hotel room with all the foil-wrapped food and called through the door about it, there was a silence and then she appeared.

She was like a ghost, all white and waxy, but she smiled her smile and they gave her the food. Then they took to coming back and hanging about in the hotel lobby after they'd gone and turned in their newspaper money.

The Bedford Forrest Hotel, where Violet stayed, had been a big showplace at one time. Around the molding up top of the lobby wall was a border of green-painted plaster relief decorations made in shape and size to look like watermelons. Eck spent his time pitching coins at a borderline in the fancy pattern of the tiled floor. Johnny Rex plunked around on an old player piano that'd been shunted off into a far corner of the room. He'd picked up a little piano from a Sunday school where he used to go, and there was more he'd learned from a pal at the first home that had an upright in its chapel. Eck and Johnny Rex weren't sure whether they were doing Violet any good, but at least they were where they *could* help her if she somehow let them know she needed it.

One afternoon a couple of weeks after she'd took sick, she walked out in front of the hotel and waved to Eck, who was selling right across the street. He ran over and brought her to a bench at the edge of the park. She was dressed nice and smelled of powder, but Johnny Rex could tell when he came up that she was still weak and didn't have all her color back. She thanked them for all they'd done for her and said she was going to go down and visit some of her people in Mississippi. She had a plan she'd been studying these two weeks. Maybe they could help her with it or maybe not, but anyway she'd look for them when she got back.

"You paperboys do right, now," Violet said and walked a bit unsteady back over to the hotel.

They watched her cross the street that day and had no idea then that she had almost died from a botched abortion or that she was thinking on tent revivaling as a better way than hooking to make her way in the world. That was the summer after the Second War ended; it was almost three years before either of the boys saw her again.

# BONNIE MONTREAT
Fall, 1949

Pity the father retelling a favorite story to his children and leaving out a detail, an aside, a color—the children will clamor and insist on getting the forgotten scrap back in the story where it belongs. Bonnie and Bumper loved the stories about Daddy and Ivy traipsing all over hill and dale and faraway city, stories of music, of Buck and Mary Liza and the banjo that came from the steamboat, Black Charlie and the railroad, the herd of mules, even Bonnie's own contribution, her stand-off with the blue-tusked boar.

For years Bonnie and her family lived with her great-grandmother Mary Liza, who had raised Daddy, in the old Montreat place those three miles up Welsh Girl's Creek above Honey Run. And Mary Liza was so ancient and so possessed of the wisdom of the race that she seemed to the children to have stepped forth from wondrous Time itself.

In 1875, a minstrel showboat lay aground on Tennessee River shoals awaiting higher water. Two of the troupers rowed a skiff into the riverbend town of London to pass the time and got caught with the tanner's daughter. The London sheriff, a spindly thirty-year-old named Buckhannon Montreat, locked the troupers up for their own protection in his rock-and-sod jailhouse while the tanner went off to drum up a lynch mob. Montreat sent word to the steamboat that he'd bond the troupers back to their show if they could make bail, which he set at one banjo.

The exchange took place at the landing ten minutes before the tanner returned alone—no one had reckoned the carryings-on of a young woman of age reason enough to take on the county law. The tanner cursed and leveled his hogkiller at Montreat, who dove sidewise and shot the tanner in the leg with his forty-four. While someone went for the liveryman-doctor, Buck Montreat studied the buxom young woman, Mary Liza. She had lain with him like a wife before. "You want to marry me for a husband?" he asked. She looked down at her father and smiled back at the sheriff.

"All right, then." Buckhannon Montreat walked twenty yards down the rutted mud street and emptied his pistol up into the air, to announce to London, God and everybody he'd quit sheriffing and got a bride. That evening the ex-sheriff, who'd come trudging home from the war with nothing but that pistol and a saddleblanket, set out to the east driving his buckboard. He held the reins to a big cotton mule in one hand and the waist of his new wife in the other. On the floor beneath their seat lay the banjo wrapped in a gunny sack. Full of peach brandy, they sang drunkenly and spiritedly as they made for Tammabowee County, Tennessee, on the Carolina border below Maryville. A big moon rose before them from behind a high spiny ridge. The musical Montreat clan was under way.

The waters of the Tammabowee country come out of the high hills in the shape of a crooked chicken's foot or of the top of a great hickory which has had light and space enough to spread. For almost twenty miles, the Tammabowee roared down that gorge like a waterfall tilted over on its back, and where it hit the Tennessee was a dangerous snarl of whirlpools and eddies and wild currents.

When Buckhannon and Mary Liza Montreat first ventured up the valley, there were no more than a half a dozen settlers up in the coves above the falls. They cleared a large creek bottom for farmstead and pasture, Montreat's Cove, about three miles above where their creek joined two others to form the Tammabowee. They had children. In time Buck got a roan mare and a jack stud and set to breeding mules. He went off trading them on both sides of the Great Smokies—from Cleveland to Knoxville in Tennessee, and back through Love's Gap into North Carolina as far as Murphy and Waynesville. Buck learned songs from all over the mountains and taught them to his wife, but neither of them could play a lick on the minstrel instrument that hung on their wall.

Once Buckhannon returned from Knoxville with another young couple looking to farm in the high country away from river life and river people. The man and his wife were Welsh and had a name they'd modified in America to Spangler. The Montreats helped Spangler and his wife and children get set up a ways down the hollow toward the Tammabowee. Spangler's wife taught Mary Liza to play guitar and for several years the two families worked and sang alongside each other.

Then one morning, crossing the creek to fetch honey from a storm-toppled bee tree, Spangler's wife was swept away by a freshet and drowned and lost. In his grief Spangler gave his wife's guitar to Mary Liza and disappeared with his children down the Tammabowee Valley back to Knoxville. There being no grave for the lost woman, the Montreats and what few others lived in those hills began to call the drowning creek Welsh Girl's after her memory.

In 1898 the Louisville & Nashville Railroad Company built a rail line up as far as the confluence of the three creeks, and named the other two Big Fishing and Honey Run. A settlement sprang up called Honey Run after the largest creek; it was a caldron of railroad men and timber men. The railroad was laid in there so the great timber could be torn off the mountainsides and gotten down to the nearest place flat enough to house a mill and convert it to boards and ship it away. What timber it was.

On the riverbanks elms and gums and willows and persimmons and chinquapins sprouted forth, and then up the slopes came basswood and buckeye, beech and birch, ash and cucumber, butternut and chestnut, holly and hemlock and sourwood and box elder and locust. Oaks on northy land grew to six feet in diameter. Cove chestnuts grew to nine feet, and tulip poplars there to eleven. Building the railroad up the rivergorge had been a mighty task—dynamite blasts and the roar of the rock slides echoed up and down the valley like sounds of war. But getting these mammoth trees down to the mills that married the forest and the flatcar was brute work for the toughest men and mules and oxen. Many of Buck Montreat's drafter mules were sold into this work.

With the railroad and the big timbering going on, small operators with broadaxes and whipsaws filled the hills. Ball-hooters, they were called, and tiehackers.

Black Charlie was one of these.

With a bundle of timber money and a desire to stay on, Charlie bought a patch of dirt up Welsh Girl's near the Montreats'. Buck stood for him against those who feared or hated his color, and in time Charlie worked alongside him as a partner trading mules.

Many was the time Buck and Mary Liza and Black Charlie watched the timber brought down out of the mountains, at first only the choicest, biggest timber but as years went by lesser grades and smaller trees. So it was the vast forests came down and went away from the mountains and the mountain people, who sold it for a song, to be owned and used and lived in and walked over and eaten upon by faraway peoples who would never know what kind of country it took to grow such wood or what kind of effort it took to harvest it like a crop.

There was prosperity in Honey Run and music up Montreat's Cove. Black Charlie knew all about playing that five-string banjo hung on the wall, and he taught Buck and Mary Liza both. The fifth Montreat child, Parris, married and stayed on in Honey Run and gradually took over the mule hostling business. He lost his first wife Independence Day, 1911, when she died delivering the boy Franklin Montreat. His second wife was widowed seven years later when Parris was killed in action with the 165th Infantry, 8th Tennessee, A.E.F., near Ourcy, France. She took their daughter Darcy back over the mountain to where she had blood kin, leaving the boy Franklin with his grandparents.

Mary Liza taught the boy his first banjo song in a down-stroking knockdown style called clawhammer. She said it was his birthsong:

> *Oh, the cuckoo, she's a pretty bird*
> *And she warbles as she flies . . .*

Black Charlie would bend over him, grinning and slapping his hand on his pants leg keeping time and saying, "Cock your thumb, drop it now, that's it, that's the boy! Once your hands get grown, you gon flat out *play* clawhammer banjo."

A great pestilence swept across the land. Influenza laid Buckhannon and Black Charlie in graves up on the hill not five days apart. A circuit rider finally got around and a funeral at the graves was held a month or so after the buryings. Somewhere away over the ridge a timber crew armed with crosscut saws was taking down the massive poplars from the slopes. A steam engine clacking up the valley blew its deep whistle. A span of mules brayed hard against the day. Mary Liza bade the boy to play his birthsong. "Buck'd like that, Franklin. Charlie too." He held the banjo that'd come from the steamboat and played a bit awkwardly in front of the preacher and the others there and sang in his little-boy voice:

> *". . . but the cuckoo never warbles*
> *Till the fourth day of July."*

Bonnie Montreat grew up studying the black-and-white photographs on the wall at home and the yellowed newspaper clippings from all over that Mary Liza had pasted into one scrapbook after another. There were twoscore of seventy-eights that the Tennessee Bumblebees had recorded over the ten years the band had worked. There were even a few never-played fifteen-inch disc transcriptions of their radio appearances, not just in Knoxville but on the *Opry* in Nashville and the *Barn Dance* in Chicago and late in the 1930s on the half-million-watt unregulated border stations just below the Rio Grande in Mexico.

Bonnie was most taken with the pictures.

There were the Bumblebees onstage with people at a ballfield in Asheville, people who'd traveled a long, long way to show off their skills, not just on guitars and mandolins and banjos and fiddles, but on all kinds of old dinner horns, whistles, psalters and zithers, on dulcimers, on mouth harps, French harps, on Jew's harps and spoons, even on bones. There they were on stage at the great national folk festivals held in St. Louis and Washington and Chicago, at the White Top Festival in southwestern Virginia and at the dedication of the Norris Dam, where FDR himself spoke. There they were in schools and barns and halls all over the South, touring eight days a week with a buck-and-wing dance team and putting on shows where folks came and paid a quarter in the days when nobody had a dime.

There was one photograph that Bonnie treasured over all the others. It showed all the singers and musicians and storytellers who'd been on the *Knoxville Jamboree Radio Show* one night. They were strung out in a long line on the big curved-front wood stage, holding their instruments and taking a bow all together. There was Daddy with his banjo standing between her uncles Fate and Soonzy McVaine, all of them smiling big and looking real pleased. And then a little farther down the line, about nine people away, was Ivy her mother in a long white gown hugging her autoharp to her breast and smiling a quiet smile, her head just a little bowed.

It was the night and the place her parents had first met.

Bonnie would hang on every word as Daddy told it over and over how Ivy Swann's eyes were blue as a country-fair prize ribbon and her hair as brown-red as deepwoods honey and how when she sang "Barbry Ellen" he knew before the first verse was up that he would have to marry the Pride of New Market, Tennessee.

Right after the wedding Franklin took Ivy back to Honey Run to show her off to Mary Liza. They set out for the big hills in the Bees' touring car which had on each side a painted sign advertising the band. The signs were in the shape of the state of Tennessee, and they carried the name of the band as well as the fact that they were REGULARS ON WBBL, KNOXVILLE. On the back of the long car was a paper sign that Fate and Soonzy had worked up. It read in crayon: JUST MARRIED.

Carson's Store in Honey Run was as far as they could go in the touring car, since there was no road up to the Montreat place outside of a sledge path and the creek bed. They walked.

Mary Liza was setting on the porch shelling beans when the four of them came across the footbridge over the rill and walked up the path between the Rose of Sharon bushes. It'd been the better part of a year since Franklin had been back, and he took in all the familiar sights of home in summertime. Sweet-pea vines and poison ivy covered the fence on the rill side of the house, and the ground was a riot of galax and rattleweed and timothy. The old 1880 boxwoods were high as the second story.

The old woman scarcely looked up from her beanshelling to say, "Now, which one of you boys has gone and got hisself a bride?"

Franklin looked down at his feet. "I reckon it's me, Grandma."

"Well, ain't you your grandpa's boy? Time we had another Montreat to cuss at and fuss over. Come up here, girl, to where I can get a good look at you."

Ivy climbed the porch steps to Mary Liza and made her manners, while the three men stood in the clover yard and waited. Mary Liza stared into the young woman's clear blue eyes and touched her red hair.

"Bless your heart, child," she said.

The generations embraced.

Mary Liza brushed a tear from her eye and called out,

"You McVaines go kill us a chicken while I get to know my family. Best kill two. And you, Franklin, fetch in some more water from the creek."

They had a feast that night. Ivy helped Mary Liza scald-fry the chickens in a black pot while the beans cooked down with slivers of ham and yellow onions. There were mustard greens and turnip greens, good for the soul, and big baked soda biscuits with sweetening of sorghum molasses. They left the door wide open for light and air, and sat inside at the big oak table with the panther's-claw feet that had balls inside so the table would roll. Mary Liza let the young folks spoil her. After supper she thought she'd like to have her a smooch of coffee, so they got some of the green beans that'd come to Carson's Store all the way from Brazil in great jute bags and roasted them and ground them in the little hand mill and fixed her some.

Franklin presently went out to the springhouse over the rill and got a jug of quality corn liquor, and they sat on the broad porch sipping and watching the constellations slowly wheel and turn in the mountain sky. As the cool evening draw poured down the hollow, Mary Liza fanned herself with the tail of a wild turkey and spoke to her near and distant kin of ghosts and days gone by.

Ivy Swann was lighthearted. She had married into the Montreats and the Tennessee Bumblebees too. The band's popularity grew, and, with it, Ivy's love for Franklin and his Montreat clan and the life they led, the rollicking and balladeering music they sang and played.

Franklin and Ivy had a son, Hubert, and four years later a daughter, Bonnie. In between time Soonzy had married Franklin's half-sister Darcy and they'd had a boy, Montreat. Franklin and Ivy's third child, Parris, was born six months into the Second World War. Ivy and all around her throve, but, as there is no unalloyed good in this world, it only seemed like it would last forever.

The Bumblebees signed up for a Lucky Strike-sponsored

Opry tour for the armed forces set to begin early in 1943. Just a few more performances in dancehalls and roadhouses around Tennessee and North Georgia before they would be off.

*The Moneywasters' Club was just a big puncheon-floored road-house made of unbarked uneven sawmill slabs nailed up over a stud frame inside and out. It was halfway between Cash Point and Pulaski, too long a trip to bring the children. All except for the nursing baby Parris had been left home with Mary Liza.*

*A ginger-bearded man with a hipsheath Bowie knife took money at the door as young and old couples and whole families poured in to hear the Tennessee Bumblebees. It was between Thanksgiving and Christmas, and for decorations they had pine boughs and garlands of play paper money tacked up all around the walls. There was a drink box full of bottle beer and soda pop on ice and somebody'd brought a keg of corn beer to sell for a nickel a cup. A good-sized tin heater roared away. The place was hot and cheerful.*

*Ivy left her baby Parris with the wife of the ginger-bearded man and fetched up her autoharp out of its case. People crowded around the bandstand—there were no microphones.*

*The way they figured it later, somebody must have opened the tin stove to put in some more wood just when somebody else opened the back door to go to the bushes. There was a great wintry gust through the room, and the reddened pipe jumped loose from the back of the stove. Sparks showered out onto the floor and against the walls, and the dry pine boughs nearest the stove burst aflame.*

*The splintery dry-barked wood on the walls caught next and spread, all in a matter of seconds. People panicked. On the far side of the bandstand Soonzy snatched his infant nephew from the terror-struck woman.*

*The Moneywasters' Club had doors that opened inward. After the first few lucky ones squeezed out, the crush of bodies forced the doors shut and sealed them. Of the two hundred and some that had come that night to hear the Bumblebees, a hundred and seventy-eight died in the fire. When the rescue workers and the firemen sorted through the victims by the light of a sad Sunday morning, they found among the burned dead a man with an infant cradled in his arms.*

*The Montreats buried Soonzy and Parris together like that, back
on the hillside up Welsh Girl's Creek under the juneapple by Buck
and Black Charlie. Beautiful Ivy Swann, Queen of the Autoharp,
took to camphor by degrees, and Franklin hung his banjo on the wall
and went down in the mica mine. The season of the Bumblebees was
past.*

At her great-grandmother's knee, Bonnie learned who she
was. In one room of the Montreat house, Mary Liza had a
large frame built and strung. With Bonnie's help Mary Liza
turned out enormous, beautiful quilts of the old patterns,
her favorite half dozen or so. At the very sounds of the
names of the coverlet patterns, a faraway feeling never failed
to settle over the young girl: Pine Bloom, Rose in the
Wilderness, Wheels of Time, Flying Geese, Radiant Stars,
and the Rising and Setting Sun.

While helping on these quilts, she learned of the building
of the Montreat farm and of the wealth that came from
growing great quantities of fruits and vegetables and knowing how to set them by to see you through harsh winters. She
learned the names of sawtooth mountains and spiny ridges
near and far, the names of the plants and what order they
grew up in after lightning set a woods on fire and cleared it
out, what trees grew starting how far up a slope and then
what picked up growing after the others left off as you got
higher and higher, and where the wildlife hid and what it
ate.

Her own family—Mary Liza, Daddy, Mama and
Bumper—seemed large to her, but she heard the names of
many, many others in talk there at the coverlet frame until
she thought it must be a much larger family than she could
ever imagine. She learned all these names, and then she
discovered that every one of them belonged to a dead
person. And Bonnie knew from the way Mary Liza spoke of
death that she did not fear it, only the surprise of it, and that
if it came when it was supposed to and you were prepared, it
wouldn't be nothing more than an expected visitor or a train
on time.

Mary Liza would often tell of Bonnie's own brush with death, how on the afternoon of the Japanese Surrender she'd got lost up the mountain and spent the night in a hollow oak. Bonnie could just remember the moonlight flashing and dancing as it struck the mica in the mountaintop high above her. When they found her next morning she was standing in a clearing holding a tusked blue boar at bay. She had been singing "Beautiful Dreamer" to it in her little bell voice, over and over again since sunup.

Mary Liza would cradle the small copper-curled head in her wizened hands and say, "I tell you things for good reason, child. Luck turns for you, and it'll turn against you, and you got to have some thoughts to back you up whichever way it goes. These old stories and lessons are like clues that might help you cipher something out sometime. Little one, you done had a miracle happen to you up on that mountain and it just could be you been marked for another. If it comes I aim to see you're *prepared* for it. Now fetch me that light blue thread there."

Bonnie and Bumper hiked the three miles down Welsh Girl's to Honey Run and had their lessons at the Log School. From Montreat's Cove they had to cross and recross the creek eight times as it cut from one side of the hollow to the other. They crossed on plank-and-stump footbridges where the water was deep, or in warmer weather they took off shoes and socks and tiptoed through the shallow water sliding over the shale at the fords—wadey-places, they called them. Sometimes in the dead of summer the creek bed would be dry as bones with only a few pools left here and there where snakes easily helped themselves to the small trapped fish. In winter these deep waters would freeze over but Bonnie and Bumper knew from Mary Liza never to try the ice.

About halfway down the steep trail they usually met up with their half-first-cousin, Montreat McVaine, where his family's hollow joined theirs and the bottom opened up wider. Treat was exactly halfway between the other two in age, two years younger than Bumper, two years older than Bonnie.

Inside the Log School it was dark. Long unpainted planks both floor and ceiling joined chinked log walls, and all the wood of the building was checked and cracked from the dry heat of the woodstove. Springtimes they opened the door and all the windows and the room sounded practically like a sawmill with all the mud-dobblers and carpenter bees coming and going.

All twelve grades sat together in one room. The children read from old worn McGuffeys and spelled from blueback spellers, books they got from wherever they could—every teacher had a few to lend out but mostly you had to find a friend or relative who'd let you use one till the next who needed it came along. Books were precious and rare in these hills. The children learned reading and spelling as best they could.

Mornings the children went straight down to school, but afternoons, especially when it was warm and the light lasted, it might take hours to get back home again. They most always stopped at the big willow crook in Welsh Girl's, where the two boys built a fort that they added to and improved over the years. Here in an old potato chip tin the children kept their supplies: string, nails, old candle ends, an Uncle Henry knife with a broken little blade, some flint, a bottle of pokeberry ink, and a Hohner harmonica for the key of G. On two shelves at the back of their mud-chinked lean-to was their collection of odd rocks and arrowheads, feathers, birds' and wasps' nests, seed pods and puff balls, turtle shells, bones and snakeskins.

Bumper was always boss of the three. He was the oldest, lean and tense and quick-tempered, and things mattered most to him. Had he been less iron-handed, the two boys might have paired off and ignored the younger girl; as it was, Bonnie and easy-going eye-rolling Treat grew to be a sort of team that either did Bumper's bidding or cut the fool thwarting him.

The old Log School was operated by a big Protestant church settlement foundation in Chicago. It'd been built by a man who ran a bearhunt camp out of it until his business was ruined by the timber trade. The settlement people bought it from him and sponsored its patching up. It was a public school, such as the Tennessee treasury allowed, and much more besides: a meeting place when politicians came through stumping, a music and dance hall when fiddlers and pickers swarmed down from the ridges to face off, and the home base for the operation of the community canning club at laying-by time.

At the front of the classroom was the unfinished picture of George Washington, and a rolldown American map hung over the long thin blackboard. All of the children sat on long hard benches—floor puncheons on fat pegs—except for the best spellers in the class, who got to sit at the handful of inkwell-style wood-topped and metal-bottomed desks whose shellac was chipping and whose carved-in initials were filling with dirt and eraser dust. When she was eight Bonnie earned one of those special desk seats for spelling a big word.

"Bonnie Montreat," the teacher said.

"Yes'm."

"Spell 'impossible.' "

The little redhead girl stood and thought. She could see Bumper out of the corner of her eyes and he was trying to mouth out the letters for her. Treat was sitting behind Bumper crossing his eyes and rolling his head back and forth like he was sick or dizzy. She looked away from them both.

"I-M, *im,* P-O-S-S, *poss, imposs,* I-B-L-E, *ibble,* impossible."

All the children near her whispered, "Ibble, ibble, ibble, ibble, ibble" when she got to that part, and she thought she'd messed up.

"Very nice," the teacher said. "Now, Bonnie, can you tell your classmates what's impossible?"

"Nothin," Bonnie said.

"What?"

"My great-grandma Mary Liza says nothin's impossible if

you put your mind to it and work hard and clean up after yourself and don't leave no mess."

The class laughed, but the teacher whapped a yardstick across her desk blotter and made them hush. "Do you children want to see me *hit the ceiling?*"

Treat muttered, "Yes'm."

The class laughed again, and again the teacher whapped the blotter. "Now, Bonnie, that's just a *saying*. What I mean is do you know what 'impossible' means to begin with?"

"Isn't it something you are not supposed to be able to do?"

"Just so," the teacher said. "That's it exactly."

Mary Liza never would move out of the old farmstead up Welsh Girl's and come live at the new house down in Honey Run where they had running water and electric. Daddy and Bumper built it in the spring of 1949 with the savings Daddy'd laid by from all his overtime at the booming post-war mica mine. "No ma'am, no sir," Mary Liza answered when Daddy and Ivy brought it up on the porch one night not long before the new house was finished. "I lived in this old house since Buck and I put it up near seventy-five years ago. Farmed and raised them cussed mules here. Loved here—all my children and some of their children been born on this land. Buck and Black Charlie are buried here and here I'll lay a corpse."

There was nothing to do but what she wanted done. In early September Daddy moved his family down to Honey Run. Plenty of food and preserves were laid by, and Bonnie and Bumper took turns going up Welsh Girl's after school to keep Mary Liza company and help with milking. She was slowing down almost every day, but she laughed as much as ever and told tale after tale about all the folks she'd known or heard of or been kin to. "Jedgematically," she would say and then tell Bonnie or Bumper what lesson was to be learned from the mistake of this person or the good ways of that.

Then one evening a week before Thanksgiving, Mary Liza gathered Bonnie up in her arms and said: "Child, I want to go over things with you tonight." They sat in the living room of the old house before an oak fire, and the coals deepened by the hour as Mary Liza questioned Bonnie about the herbs and the sayings and legends. They talked through true tales and yarns, and they sang. They sang the old ballads, the songs with little nonsense lines that made the rhythms sparkle:

*Rum tumma diddle e oh, e oh*
*Rum tumma diddle e oh*

until Mary Liza had gone through her third cob pipeful of scrip tobacco. She had Bonnie put the screen in front of the fire and she let the girl lead her to bed carrying a kerosene lamp.

Next morning, bundled in a quilt, the old woman came down the steps out front with Bonnie to see her off to school.

"Tell Franklin he'd best come up here himself and see to me this evening."

"Why, Miss Mary?"

"You just tell him, child, you hear?"

"Yes'm."

"And you, child, you go forward for me as best you can."

"Go forward?" Bonnie looked down the frosted path toward Honey Run.

Mary Liza laughed and held her sides against the cold. "Forward in this life, in this world, till we meet again in the next." The old woman kissed the girl on the forehead. "Run on to school, now, but remember what I said this morning."

"I will, Miss Mary."

"Bless you, child. I've not seen many as had your heart. You've been a little candle to me these last years."

Daddy reached the old farmplace in the early evening after the last trace of sunset pink had left the gray winter sky. He clambered upstairs and found his grandmother setting by her bed in the little oak rocker Buckhannon had made for her seventy years before. She looked right at him, and the faint sad smile on her face remained unchanged. In her right hand she grasped a faded tintype of her and Buck Montreat in their youth, in her left a silver spoon. She held these out in front of her like she wanted him to take them, but he instead sat down on the featherbed by her side and looked at her watching for him and waiting for him to appear at the door.

Mary Liza was dead as a stone.


# JOHNNY REX PACKARD
Fall, 1949


Their eyes is on the snakes, he thought, but they're listening to me. They're watching them snakes bend and writhe and they're taking to it themselves, but they're moaning along in time to my piano.

Through a flap in the Holiness tent, Johnny Rex could see a piece of harvest moon coming up yellow as the paint on a pencil over the West Tennessee flatwoods. The show was set up in what had been a cornfield up to six hours ago. It was still in stubble and furrows when they got there with the truck full of canvas and poles and lectern and piano all trussed in with quarter-inch hemp. Near about lost the whole damn mess, he thought, at that bad slough in the road. Then to get here and have to hunt up somebody that had a mule team and put em to drag-harrowing and flattening out the ground so we could have a revival tonight after all . . .

Violet Leadon was moving her arms up and down just slightly so the snakes would appear to be moving more than they really were if you were out in the crowd. There wasn't much light anyway, just a half a dozen bulbs strung around the inside of the tent on a wire they were tapping into the rural electric line. She's moving to my time, too, the boy thought as he kept up hammering out a regular octave bass. The snakes has got em all by the eyes, but I got em by the gut and that's the way this show works every time. The crowd had started into it, with aimless arm movements and waving of flat palms and closed fists alike. The men rolled their heads about like they were snapped loose at their necks, and the women's eyes all seemed to be rolled back up in their heads. Then the murmuring picked up and the closed and half-closed eyes came open and faced the front because, Lord, look what the snakes was doing now.

This was where Missus Leadon would pull her loose cotton dress back between her legs, baring her thighs, and she'd fall to her knees weaving back and forth with the snakes. It was the part of the show where Johnny Rex went from eighth to sixteenth notes on the octave bass, doubled his time and rode it like hagwitches ride men in dreams of the country nights.

"In the Lamb, in the Lamb, in the Lamb . . ." they chanted and moaned with her, sank with her to the cornfield dust and leaned forward following the snakes. This was what Johnny Rex liked, this part of it, the roaring and hitting the piano hard as you could. And he was so young, just fifteen, and so strange-looking and played so wild they always looked at him like he was some kind of miracle of God, too, and him not even having to fuck around with them snakes like Missus Leadon.

She was drenched with sweat and her dress was clinging on her and she reached just slightly under it in the front as if to hold her breast in and keep it from exploding from all the love of the Lamb that was heaving around in there. Men from the crowd reached toward her shouting, "Comfort" and "His love" and "Jay-sus," and she seemed to smile and cry at the same time but held out her other hand to ward them off and out of distance of her and the snakes. She was getting there, getting to it. Johnny Rex slammed on and his own bellowing started turning into a song. Violet Leadon on her knees arched slowly back till her tangled brown hair was dragging in the dust. The whole tentful, men and women both, was swooning. She rolled her head like the men and held her arms out to the sides not even looking and the snakes wrapped around her wrists and writhed up her arms toward her head.

A woman screamed and fainted.

A horse-faced man down front reached out to her and shouted with joy, "No pain in death, the Lamb, the Lamb!" Johnny Rex rocked from side to side and sang above the weird din:

> *"Misery and pain I fear no more*
> *Jesus will open that golden door . . ."*

He was joined by two voices at first, one a high nasal whine and the other a gargly strangled-up lower voice, and then others not so much singing as shrieking and howling in praise of the Lord's glory and in fear of the snakes on that woman. As more joined in the song, Violet lifted her torso back up, crossing her arms as she did and gingerly plucking the snakes from her upper arms. She raised herself onto one knee and then stood before the screaming singing hysterical worshipers. She beamed at them like sunrise over an ocean.

Johnny Rex's sopping shirt clammed to his chest as he eased up on the tune, no longer singing himself because they had a show every night but one this week. Missus Leadon dropped the two water snakes back into their box and raised her arms high above her head as the "Amens" rolled forth.

Anytime the show went this well and this far, Johnny Rex knew, it was a good money night.

"So now it's the churching business," Eck had said as he walked up to them that afternoon.

Johnny Rex and Violet had the tent all spread out in the stubbly dust and were drawing the lines out to stake it. The farmer who'd drag-harrowed the field was standing back off to one side with his two mules wondering whether he oughtn't go up and help or just stand back and watch that good-looking healer woman all straddled out working on them poles and stakes. He could see she and the albino were glad to see the black boy and climbed back up on his buckboard. "Reckon you don't need me no more now the nigger's showed up." They ignored the farmer and he rode off with the team.

"What took you so long, you son of a bitch?" Johnny Rex whooped. He dropped his mallet and ran to Eck and threw his arms around his shoulders. Eck and his sister Karintha had been good about hiding him out from the Juvenile Court people after he'd run off from the Memphis home, but he got tired of hiding out like a damn criminal. He'd left Memphis without saying goodbye, just scrawled a note that said he'd took up playing piano for Violet Leadon's traveling revival show. Then Eck and Karintha too had to pick and clear out of town when their uncle's heart got him down and running his flatwoods farm fell to them. Johnny Rex figured Eck might show up when the revival got up his way.

Violet smiled and called out, "Hey, paperboy."

Eck had on a torn maroon sweater over a blue denim workshirt and overhauls. Sweat was beading up over and around his wideset eyes and he blinked some like it was stinging. He had a soft-featured round open face with a doubting look. Solid-built black boys like him a generation later would be much sought after for the white college football teams, but not yet, not now. He answered Violet, "Ain't no paperboy no more, Miss Violet. Me nor Johnny Rex neither one. Here I'm a farmer and you got Johnny Rex playing gospel piano."

"I took you for a city boy, Eck." Violet slammed another stake down into the cornfield dirt.

"Used to be," he said. "Just like you and him, I guess, till some kind of change come along. You ain't gone and married my buddy, have you?"

Violet Leadon threw back her head and laughed.

"Goddamn you," Johnny Rex said, and then they were all three laughing. Johnny Rex made like he was going to slug

Eck, who said, "Pass me that hammer and let me hep you get this tent up right. Everything comes out of Memphis black or white is least half crazy. Got to be."

The young piano-playing albino met Eck out back behind the tent after the show that night, and they sat on the running board of the truck's cab, smoking. Johnny Rex stared up at the stars over Tennessee and rolled his head around trying to untense his neck and shoulders from all that banging on the piano. His ears were roaring. It was his heart gone crazy on him again. The home's doctor called it arrhythmia, told him these spells would come over him whenever he got too wound up. Johnny Rex was used to it.

Through the tent flap the boys could see the men and women coming up and embracing Violet Leadon—Sister Vi—and with some struggle regaining their composure and talking of weather and crops, talk that would carry them back to the cookstoves and the furrows and the portable sawmills of a deep woods ever pulling in on itself. Dust hung in the bulb-light inside the tent, and a baby coughed on it and cried.

The black boy Eck exhaled and spoke. "Why you do this shit, Johnny Rex?"

The albino laughed. "I reckon cause I'm the boss of what I do."

"You ain't no boss," Eck said. He nodded at the tent. "*She* the boss."

"Not of the music," Johnny Rex said. "I choose the tunes out of the book and I already made up three more of my own. We been singing all three and teaching em to people and selling printed sheets. I wasted enough damn time in that orphan home—now I'm making *money*."

"Hunh. If that's what you want you make more at one of them Beale Street joints."

"Get my ass busted, too, Eck. Where's your brain? Wish that woman'd get out here so I can speak to her."

"You coming with me for tonight?"

"Thought I would," Johnny Rex said. "What about your uncle?"

"He be drunk time we get back."

"Karintha?"

"She's looking to see you," Eck said.

Johnny Rex smiled and felt that good turn in the pit of his stomach. He hadn't been with Eck's sister in many months.

The Holiness worshipers straggled out of the tent, making their ways to wagons and pickups and battered Chevrolets that had lasted through the Japanese war and would have to last a while yet. Eck and Johnny Rex sat and smoked and listened to the old flathead eights turning over one more time, the dust hanging in the headlight beams and the lights themselves brightening as the engines raced and the clutches sprang back and the gears engaged.

The tent darkened.

"Where she get all this mess?" Eck asked.

"You mean the tent?" Johnny Rex said.

"I mean the tent, that upright you play, this hauling truck, all of it. She rob a bank down in Mississippi?"

"It took her a long time to put all this together," Johnny Rex said. "She was two years writing folks and making contacts so she'd know where to be going when she got the show out around the country."

Eck shook his black head. "You mean there's some *plan* to this? I thought you pulled over when you found a field that had enough crackers living near it to get gas money off of and keep going."

"More to it than that, Eck." Johnny Rex lit another Lucky and drew the smoke in. He gestured toward the tent. "Plus she ain't exactly give up from what she was doing before. There's always one that needs some private healing after the service's done."

Eck said, "Damn. She has it both ways." They sat a quiet moment in the cool dark October night. There were little tobacco clouds around both their heads.

"The tent, now," Johnny Rex said after a while, "it was

stuffed into some little shed behind her grandfather's house just there in Mississippi. She got her aunt to give it to her just for the carting away of it. Plus Vi she had to get it fixed up, you know it was full of holes and all. She was working days at a truck-stop café and weekends at this beer joint. They had live bands there and she said it was a right good time but she missed Memphis and all her friends there."

"What friends?" Eck snorted. "That woman laid up in that hotel two weeks and nothing between her and Old Master but a couple paperboys and some leftover chicken. You think about it, Johnny—what friends?"

"Well, people she knew, I guess."

"Customers."

"Yeah. Anyway, she'd heard somewhere on the radio about how all these people kept turning out to these tent revivals in different places around Florida and what was special about em was they had snakes. She told me she thought 'Hell' when she heard cause she never was afraid of snakes or handling em. And she remembered this big tent down at her granddaddy's from when he used to put on family reunion Fourth of Julys when she was little. Music and ice cream and all the works. He had it from when he was in a traveling medicine show."

"What'd her granddaddy play?"

"A nigger."

"Goddammit, Johnny Rex."

"I mean it. She said he had all these blackface routines and he'd run all around Mississippi and Alabama with some medicine outfit. That's how the tent got into her family. Well, Violet figured she'd get aholt of that tent and get her some snakes and a truck—"

"And a white boy piano player."

"—and me and we'd go around preaching and praising and see couldn't we make some money at it. Hell, Eck, she wrote ever Church of God preacher in three states that she could get the name of. Even sent em those little pictures you get four for a quarter. She got three dozen letters back inside of two weeks and you know what they said? Ever one of em: Sister Vi, snake-handling preacher woman? Goddamn, girl, get up here to East Jesus, Tennessee, and raise hell for us one time in the name of the Lord!"

They laughed, and Eck jabbed Johnny Rex in the side. "Come on, let's go."

"No. I got to wait and tell her so she don't get scared."

A man came out of the tent and shuffled toward them mumbling, "No pain in death, the Lamb, the Lamb." He went past them not ten feet away but never noticed the little red cigaret glows in the dark. So, Johnny Rex thought, it was the horse-faced man this time.

A small spot of light appeared on the tent from the inside. Eck shivered and said, "This tent thing's all right maybe during the summer, but, man, it's getting cold out here. What you gon do when it's freezing every night?"

"She's done thought of that already," Johnny Rex said as the Rayovac light joggled their way. Johnny Rex gave his friend a squeeze on the back of the neck. "Florida."

Violet reached the truck, and Johnny Rex told her he was going on back with Eck for the night. She shrugged.

"Where is it from here, case I have to come after you?"

"You won't have to, Vi," Johnny Rex said. "I'll be back time to get the tent in. Where is it we're off to tomorrow anyway?"

"Dyersburg."

Why did he even bother to ask? It would be the same, some out-of-the-way field near some peckerwood settlement that would turn out in a big way for her act. He could live with it, though. It beat hell out of reform school like they'd tried to put him in. Here he was traveling all around with a pretty damn good-looking woman even if she was damaged goods and a lot older. They got on fine. Who else was going to pay him to be his own boss and see some country and all he'd got to do was wild hog on the piano and bellow?

It was all right being sixteen and a half getting better on the eighty-eights all the time and getting paid good money and not to even have to fuck with them snakes. Violet and

Johnny Rex were about as free as you could be, shed of real jobs and school. Only one place, down in Georgia, in the whole time they'd been tenting around had the people gotten on them about snakes and sacrilege and had the sheriff and a couple of deputies run em out. Called em snake chunkers. Mostly they never got in any trouble. If you didn't look like a niggerlover or a labor agitator from outside, you had to be a pretty rank white person to run afoul of the law in 1949.

Johnny Rex and Eck left Violet to sleep on the little pallet bunk in back of the cab of the truck and went on off toward the uncle's farm. "Ain't you afraid to leave her like that, Johnny? She's tough, but—"

"She'll do all right. She gots a sawed-off shotgun beside her there, and that'll slow most anybody down. We been doing this awhile now, Eck. Kind of got it down by now."

"Yeah, but you usually with her."

"Not up front I ain't. I sleep in the trailer in back."

"Come on, now. All the time?"

"Yeah."

"You mean you been riding around like this all this time and you never once crawled up in there with her?"

"Well," Johnny Rex said, "every once in a while she asts me to come rub her neck."

Eck popped him on the back and went off in gales of laughter. "What's it like?"

The boys turned on the road that went off along the branch. In the middle-October night chill there was a faint oily odor from the spent crankcase lube the county sprayed on the roads to keep the dust down. They padded along, Orion and Hercules and Aquarius staring down on them from their corners in the Tennessee sky.

Johnny Rex spoke. "She gots a lot of energy."

Low firelight showed here and there through the chinked log house at Perse's farm when they got to it. The door

opened straight into the big room where Eck's sister Karintha was stooped at the hearth fussing with a pot. The room
smelled of woodsmoke and coffee. When she stood to greet
them, she was silhouetted against the quiet fire, and the
outer line of her hair shone from the light.

"Religion keeping you up past your bedtimes, Johnny
Rex." She was several years older than the both of them and
her voice was husky.

"A little," Johnny Rex said. He touched the black girl's
hand.

"I heated up these grounds again, Aleck, so if you all
wanted some coffee."

"Not me," Eck said. "I'm turning in. You talk to this fool
that's escaped out of Memphis."

He walked across the room and poked the fire, threw an
oak stick on it and stretched his hands out to warm himself.
Karintha reached in to the open hearth and got the pot and
poured Johnny Rex a cup.

"You got a little something for it?" Johnny Rex said.

She looked sideways at him and grinned and reached up
for a jar on the mantel. He unscrewed the cap and tasted and
added a couple ounces of clear whiskey to the coffee. From
upstairs there was a troubled snoring coming from the old
man Perse. Eck said good night and ambled back into the
shedroofed lean-to that was the hind section of the house.

Johnny Rex sipped from the hot cup and reached in his
pocket for the Luckies. The smells mixed and decayed into
each other the way things do in the fall: the tobacco and the
coffee and the burning wood and the husky-voiced girl in
her old bedcover robe. Even on a still night there was some
air moving, some cool air that the fire dragged in through
the broken chinking. He moved closer to the fire and the
black girl Karintha.

Johnny Rex would tell her about his flight with Violet
Leadon from the city that was Ed Crump's fief, about their
exhilarating depressing pilgrimage across Tennessee and
Georgia and Mississippi and Alabama and parts of Arkansas,

about the music he'd learned and the music he'd written. He would tell her again that but for her and Eck, he would of been caught and slammed into that reform school where he would have done bad and been bound for bigger, worser things. He would tell her that but for her easy initiation he wouldn't of known what was what the first time Violet Leadon asked him to come up in the cab of the truck and rub her neck and take his rest there with her.

If there was a piano here, he thought, I could explain it all that way. It would all be in the music, the country I seen, the times I had, the things I heard people say out of meanness and desperation, things men say to women or women to men, that hit the people they're saying em to like a gut full of buckshot. I could put that into the music I been learning since I seen her last, since her and Eck hid me. If there was a piano here I could explain all I seen and learned that way or at least I could try. She'd know what I meant anyway by the sound of it. I'd hit a big octave G with my left hand and a G with the seventh below and above and roll off from the B-flat onto the B with my right and just sing it as it came into my head and she'd know what I meant by it.

The alcohol and the coffee had set him up. The fire was dying down and she rustled with it so as to leave it for the night. They smoked more cigarets, and the roar in his ears from before had quieted till it felt like just a warm stream of air inside his head, like a thick warm breeze coming off a summer field late in the day. The breeze was weighted with tobacco scent, and Johnny Rex felt a power in him. He dragged on the cigaret and felt as if he could absorb desire and tomorrow. Ideas kept coming to him, and he thought, if there was a piano here I could play this what I'm thinking. Play it for her.

Karintha laid a hand on his leg and reached her fingers round underneath and back of his knee and gripped that thin muscle there. She said, "Go on and tell me where all you been since I seen you. I gots all night long."

It wasn't yet seven when he woke, but Eck was already gone. There was new coffee made, he could tell, and now there was the smell of frying sidemeat, popping in a skillet on the cookstove. He heard Karintha, outside, coming toward the cabin humming. He dressed.

From the loft there came an occasional wheezing cough. Johnny Rex sat at the kitchen table cleaning his fingernails with a paring knife while Karintha cracked the eggs she'd brought in from the coop. "When you gon make some real money, boy," she said, "and come carry me round the countryside and show me something?"

"I will, Karintha. You'll see. Only it won't be in no old furniture-moving truck full up with snakes and a tent."

"Snakes?"

"Eck didn't tell you?"

"Nobody told me nothing about no snakes."

"Hmm."

"All's I knowed was a preaching show that Leadon woman cooked up. Here. Eat this." She set the two wooden plates laden with breakfast down on the splintery table and sat with him. Inside his head it was all quiet now. Even when it all roared with him, she alone of those whose lives he touched would remain unfrightened. They both knew it, and it was one of those things never spoken or heard, but felt like rumblings from deep in the earth. She didn't ask him where he was going or for how long or when he might be back, nor did he say. Neither doubted they'd see each other again. They were outside the bounds of fear and dread.

He kissed her goodbye and left.

The chill October morning slapped him wide awake as he took great deep cold breaths and bounded along down the ruddy red-brown road. The good tobacco-and-whiskey taste from last night had gone sour on him, and his tongue was thick with it. He wished he could taste the fresh and crisp of the air, but all he could get was the cold of it.

Frost crystals on the truck windshield had melted by the time he got back. Johnny Rex felt the pocket of his worn corduroy jeans for the truck key and unlocked the door. "It's me," he said. Violet was still mostly asleep on the pallet up there back of the seat behind the drawn curtains. Johnny Rex cranked the starter. He put his heel on top of the accelerator and his toe on a springy button above it, except in this old heap the accelerator was gone and there was only the thin metal shaft left. He had to wedge it up in the treaded sole of his boot when he was driving. Sometimes when the truck was going along good at fifty or so the shaft would get loose of his sole, and he'd have to reach down and get it stuck back in and try not to run off into a ditch.

The engine turned over and caught and he ran it some to warm it up. He flipped the air-driven windshield wipers on and cleared the water off and the sunlight danced all around the wet window and the nose of the truck. He drove slowly off the field and on down the road in the other direction from Eck's toward a feed mill he remembered passing. There'd be somebody there that'd help load up. Violet slept.

Grinding machines whined away and the albino's nostrils filled with the farmy smell of the fine grain dust. There was a knot of men around a space heater in a corner and they greeted Johnny Rex.

"Whoa, there. Yonder's that piano man."

"Lookit his hands, Gid. I bet they's as blistered from banging on that upright as yours is from farming."

He knew the best way to talk to them was to wait and shuffle around and be the butt of a handful of dumb-ass remarks. He'd done this before. You couldn't hurry these fellows.

"Get him a five-pound sack of feed, Jerry. A big boy like him's a trough feeder, likely."

"Well," Johnny Rex finally said, "ham and eggs stuck in my craw. A little slop might just wash it down." The men laughed and settled down and waited. He hired two of them at three dollars apiece to help him strike the tent and load the platform and poles and piano. One was twice his age, and the other almost tripled him in years. They wanted to see the money first, so he showed them. He expected it. He'd done this before.

Riding back to the tent site the men asked him how long he'd been doing this and where'd they come from and where was they headed.

"Where you hiding that preacher woman?"

"Right behind you," Johnny Rex said carelessly. "She's sleeping behind them curtains." They jerked around excitedly to have a look. "She stays up there with her snakes." The men faced forward again like cold water'd been throwed on em. Johnny Rex drove on and Violet slept.

The two farmers turned out to be good-natured and worked pretty good with Johnny Rex. While they were at it, the farmer who'd dragged the field came by to take a look-see, and not long after him the horse-faced man drove up in a Ford pickup that had a rusting-out bed to it. These two pitched in some, rolling up ropes and such. By late morning the gear was loaded and secured and in the trailer and the brown canvas tied down over top. Johnny Rex paid off the two farmers and got an Esso road map out of the passenger-side tool compartment and leaned against the front of the truck studying it.

Violet crawled out of the cab bunk and climbed down, and the men stood back and mumbled some good mornings. She'd fixed herself up some behind the curtain, because after all she was what they'd come to get more of. She had that nice hourglass shape with a deep chest and wide hips that they could look at and see she'd be a armful for sure. She looked up. "The Lord sure give us a clear blue sky and nice traveling weather today, didn't he?"

"Yes'm."

"Sure did."

"Mr. Packard," she said. "You about figured out the roads to our next meeting?"

Johnny Rex nodded soberly.

"Well, I reckon I owe you gentlemen for troubling yourselves and coming out this morning to help see us off in good order," Violet said.

"Don't you worry about us."

"It's all took care of."

"Well, then," she said, stretching her arms out to each of the four countrymen, one at a time, staring each deeply and benignly in the eyes till each in turn looked down or away. "Sister Vi'll be back again at planting time," she said. "The Lord bless you and keep you and make His face to shine upon you and give you peace now and forever more."

The men all said, "Amen."

Johnny Rex took the warm black Bakelite steering wheel in hand and drove the truck off the empty field, leaving the men behind. He watched them in the big side mirrors as they waved glumly to Violet Leadon. The truck rolled away and a field grown up in slash pine cut them off from view.

To pick up the Dyersburg road they had to turn up the county road that ran by the branch and by Perse's farm. A laundry kettle was set to boiling out in the treeless yard. Johnny Rex saw Karintha struggling through the doorway with a heaping basket of clothes. He saw her notice the passing truck and felt her follow it on up the ridge with her eyes. The day was heating up from where it had been in the thirties early that morning, getting up toward seventy now, and the oiled county road getting grimy and soft under the weight of the truck. What with the bad springs and the piano, they could only make five or ten miles an hour till they hit the blacktop.

Violet slid out of the rumpled floweredy print dress, stripping back down to her slip. "It's getting hot as blazes in here," she said, climbing back up into the cab bunk. Johnny Rex's head felt dull at the sides and he punched the lighter in and shook a Lucky out of the pack. He cracked the front breeze window and opened the air vent that lifted up out of the dash.

They came up on another flatwoods, higher than where they'd had the revival and much of it timbered so he could see back behind and below. The way the road turned, he could make out where all they'd just been. He was thinking, We're headed north but we're bound for Florida. The red road began dropping away to the north and west, and in the side mirrors Johnny Rex watched the feed mill and the tent field and Perse's farm fall away out of sight behind him.

"You find a pullover place fore too long," Violet said. "My neck's still sore from last night."

# PART TWO

# BONNIE MONTREAT
1953

"It ain't no place for a little girl," Ivy complained.

"She's thirteen, Ivy," Daddy said.

"Oh, Franklin, the way they go on! Jerking and dancing and falling down and there's never been one of em here that handles snakes like this woman does. It's common."

Bonnie looked down at her plate and messed with her roast chicken and shucky beans.

"You've just heard talk is all," Daddy said.

Ivy lifted the handkerchief with the white waxy camphor in it to her face and shook her head. "You ever think when enough folks tell you the same thing there might be something to it?" Daddy chuckled at her. "Well, laugh, then," she said, "but I still think it ain't something that child ought to see or be at."

Daddy tried to soothe Ivy there at the supper table. "I'd just be taking her for the music—I'll see she don't convert."

Ivy sighed. Pretty soon Bonnie and Daddy were shambling down the hill toward the tent set up in Honey Run.

"Sounds like quite a crowd," Daddy said.

Bonnie listened to the voices pouring forth in song, the

April voices that'd been snowed in and pent up all winter
now singing loud and rough versions of "O for a Faith That
Will Not Shrink" and "When I Survey That Wondrous
Cross." As they reached the big tent, the revivalers were
beaking into "Joyful," a shape-note hymn the little girl knew
better as "Who'll Give Me Some More Peanuts When My
Peanuts Are Gone?" She remembered how the first time
she'd heard "Wondrous Love" at her church she'd gone right
into the lines Daddy'd taught her to that same tune about
"My name is Captain Kidd, Captain Kidd, Captain Kidd."
Daddy told her then, "Some of those old tunes are like a
mule or a workhorse—one day he might ride you to a wild
fiddling dance, the next he might take you to church; either
way it's the same mule. It's up to you to get your bearings."

Inside the tent were a good seventy or eighty people. She
thought she knew most of the folks in and around Honey
Run, but a lot of these people here were strangers. Many of
em, Daddy said, were from the farthest-back reaches of
Chiselfinger hollow, people who lived ten or fifteen miles
back up there and hardly ever came out. Others were big
solitary-looking men who worked in the logwoods and whose
eyes would settle on you hard and wouldn't shift or blink till
you looked away. Bonnie stayed close to Daddy and
stretched her neck to see down front.

A pretty brown-haired woman with a fine hourglass shape
was carrying on about something called the acrostolic succes-
sion and saying how predictions from Scripture were being
lived out in things you'd read about in the newspapers. She
was standing, sometimes speaking quietly, other times practically shouting and not making much sense to Bonnie—
though it *was* pretty entertaining the way she whipped her
arms around over her head. There was a crate on a little
table next to her, and behind her, swaying together in chairs
next to each other, were a young black man and woman, he
with a little drum and she with a tambourine. Near them
pounding on an upright piano was the palest man she'd ever
seen, with beautiful silk white hair. They must of gone all

around with this traveling church, because the sermon the woman was giving was sprinkled with mentions of people "living in Hell down in Mississippi" or other people "cleansed by His Blood" where they'd just come from in southwest Virginia. And the woman went on about how a little bit of money kept em going a long way with their work, and then a tin cup and a paper plate circulated through the throng. When Daddy dropped a quarter noisily into the cup, the old storekeeper Carson made a screwed-up face at him. It all seemed to Bonnie like something at a carnival that you only paid money if you wanted a chance to win a prize. They're just paying money so she'll show her snakes, Bonnie thought.

When the money plate and the money cup made it back down front, the woman stepped up her talk, and the black people went to swaying more and the strange pale man at the piano started banging on it harder than she'd ever heard anybody do. Pretty soon the black people were rising up out of their chairs and singing along with the white preacher woman, and the crowd was getting all worked up too. Except Daddy didn't seem caught up in it at all. He was just nodding his head and tapping his foot in time to the music. Bonnie Montreat had never heard anything like it—it was a lot of music, but it was more of a rhythm than a song. She held tight to Daddy. The woman reached over in time to the piano music and opened a lid of the crate on the table next to her and reached into it and pulled out a snake bigger than the biggest chicken snake Bonnie had ever seen. She felt her eyes bugging out as the preacher woman sang about Praising the Lamb and about Dying in the Lamb and Not Dying at All! as she let the big snake coil all around her arms and neck and then what'd she do but Lord! reach in that crate and pull out another one. And then she sank to her knees as the music got louder and the crowd pressed forward.

Down a crowded center aisle the worshipers handed, pushed a game-legged girl not two years older than Bonnie, and the preacher woman, putting her right hand up on the girl's head, forced the girl into a kneel. The girl fell over on her back, almost keeping the rhythm, and arched her hips skyward in an unmistakable motion as she moaned and the preacher woman moaned and the crowd, especially the men, leaned in and gurgled their voices appreciatively, encouragingly.

"I reckon you and me best go on now," Daddy said. They slipped out through a flap in the tent and walked homeward, Daddy with his arm around her shoulder. They could hear the singing and moaning and crying rise and rise till it finally crashed down and stopped. By the time they'd crossed the bridge and started up the hill for home, there was more singing coming from the glowing tent, but it was calmer now.

" 'The Old-Fashioned Bible,' " she said.

" 'Fisher's Hornpipe,' " Daddy answered.

The little girl and her father stopped once more, at the foot of their yard. They listened as the revivalers sang the old song "Parting Hand." Then there came the turning and rumbling of the motors of the trucks and cars that'd brought the people. The lights came on, brightening and dimming as the engines revved and slowed and drew slowly up the other hollows. The April night was taking on a chill. As Daddy and Bonnie strode up the drive, she pointed at a pattern of stars and said, "Look!" Daddy squeezed her hand and together, slowly, they said, "Job's Coffin in the Sky."

She wasn't at all sorry they'd gone. It was exciting even if it was some other church than theirs, because it was spring and there was always a spirit of revival in the air, in the land then. She glanced again at the patch of stars sinking behind the ridge above them. "Why they call it Job's Coffin, Daddy?"

"I don't know, child. Them stars is gone when it's fully warm. Maybe it means if you're patient like Job through winter the cold'll be gone and spring'll come. But I don't know." So Orion the Hunter is buried with winter by the people of the East Tennessee mountains.

Bonnie awoke and looked out her upstairs bedroom window next morning, through the muslin curtains with the colorful tatting Mary Liza had made, to see what was going on down by the revival tent. But the tent and the truck that brought it and all signs of the night before were gone, like the ghost deer of legend that pauses just long enough for you to see it and then vanishes.

# JOHNNY REX PACKARD
## 1954

He drifted through Knoxville dissatisfied, but with real money in the pockets of his two-pants suit. The call for the show wasn't until four that afternoon, so he had time to kill and by damn that was exactly what he was doing. He was lean and loose from the five years of roaming and sleeping in trucks and sweating over a piano. Now that they were good and well known he could demand and get a piano with even action and in tune. Yet he got aggravated and bothered easier than he used to.

It was a sweltering hazy day in August. Downtown was busy with shoppers and bargain-hunters, all bustling about amid the prosperity and fear of the time. Johnny Rex moved along down Gay Street sharing in the prosperity but not the fear. He knew what McCarthy was all about, hell, he recognized him. Not that he'd met the Senator or anything like that, but he knew the look and the sound of the voice. It was something about it that told you something else was going on in the man's head than what he was telling you. Like a man getting riled at you about one thing but you know that's not it, it's something else like his wife ain't sleeping with him. Johnny Rex'd seen that look plenty times.

I even get like that, he thought, but, hell, I know how to blow off steam. Sit down with a bottle when there's no show and no driving to be done and drink to get drunk, goddammit. With a bottle and a woman if you're lucky, and most times I am. Who'd of thought a gospel show would deliver up women to you on a regular basis like it did?

"Mr. Packard? You Mr. Packard?" A woman in pedalpushers was stopping him there on Gay Street and calling him "Mister."

"I'm him," Johnny Rex said. She was a pretty-looking brunette, and a man that must be her husband was hanging back leaning against a parking meter.

"Could you autograph this for me?" She thrust a brown paper bag into his hands.

Johnny Rex glanced at the husband. He too had a suit on and he looked a bit like a showroom car salesman. Johnny Rex sized the woman up. She had a warm friendly look, a little flushed from the August heat and from speaking to a big name like him. She'd scarcely even miss that husband, he thought. He glanced caustically at the auto salesman and in his mind made him vanish. Then he and the brunette stepped into the nearest car, a deep green '53 Chevrolet convertible with the top already down, and they drove off together across the Tennessee River toward Gatlinburg. She laughed and stretched and arched her back and unbuttoned her blouse and tossed it to the wind. She moved over to him on the car seat and let him wrap his arm around her and lay his big piano hand on her breast. Johnny Rex squeezed his eyes shut tight and ground his teeth.

"We went to the first night of the Crusade," the husband said, "and we're coming again tonight. Can't wait to tell the boys back at the bottling plant I got to pull your paw." Johnny Rex felt a cracked smile come onto his face. He scribbled something on the bag and redressed the woman mentally as she and the husband walked off and into an appliance store.

"Shame, ain't it?"

Johnny Rex wheeled around and faced an old man who was talking past an unlit cigar butt clenched in the corner of his mouth. "What?" Johnny Rex said.

"About the streetcars. I seen you staring at them old tracks there ashining in the sun. No, sir, there ain't no more streetcars and I say it's a damn shame. Got to where decent people, white women and all, just couldn't ride em, the way they was getting bothered. Said when they cut em out they was interfering with the ve-hicular traffic, ran them last cars down Gay Street all covered with flags. Nineteen and forty-seven, I was over there watching on that corner but you think I believe that ve-hicular crap? It was niggers and Commonists why they had to cut it out. Read your paper, am I right? You a veteran?"

Johnny Rex yanked a lungful of the steamy August Knox-ville air. "Where can I get a drink, old man?"

There were only a couple of people in the tavern that early in the afternoon, and the place smelled of stale smoke and beer and this morning's mopping. It was about two o'clock.

Johnny Rex had made a rule for himself that he'd kept pretty well: he wouldn't drink the day of a show. Which kept him sober a lot, considering how heavily booked the Crusade was. What had happened about a year or so back was that he and Violet were invited by the evangelist Wilbur Parham to join his Holiness Crusade Caravan.

"Sunny Wilbur" he was called. He put together his crusades like political candidates put together campaign organizations. Because that's what it is, he told Violet and Johnny Rex when he finally caught up with them at a fairgrounds in northern Alabama: it is a campaign for the Lord and against the *sub*version of our way of life. Parham was McCarthy with a Bible in his hand.

He was started out just a small-time Texarkana preacher with no particular gifts other than a near-photographic recollection of the Book of Ecclesiastes and a booming bassy voice. Then that letter of General MacArthur's got read to the Congress, and Truman fired him. "He oughtn't to of done that," Wilbur Parham told his wife when he heard. "Best damn general we got and lookit what's come of him. I don't care if I am a preacher, some things needs cussing." He preached on it in church about Truman and the General and Inchon and "I shall return" and "Christ shall return." He was news and entertainment all rolled into one for the little

Texarkana television station. All of a sudden Wilbur Parham had him a TV show, a whole hour on Sunday and then short sermonette sections here and there on the weekdays.

Pretty soon the Texarkana program was selling to a handful of other stations in Louisiana and Arkansas and Texas. Plenty of people would watch him to laugh. His talks made no sense half the time. They were the ravings of a man whose brain was seething in headlines and Ecclesiastes. So the folks who thought him a fool at first watched him and got to know and like him and before long got caught up in America according to Wilbur Parham. An audience of a few thousand grew into one of hundreds of thousands, and Sunny Wilbur took his show on the road.

People who'd gone to so much trouble to beat back the Krauts and the Japs, Wilbur said, people who'd now got to be so rightfully rewarded with automobiles and new roads to drive them on and frozen foods and freezers to store them in, people like the Americans that were so blessed by the Lord *ought* to get het up with Wilbur Parham and fear the Russkies and the Chinamen and all the Communists who'd take it all away and separate men from their women and women from their children and pay everybody the same no matter what. And, friends, breadlines from twenty years ago'll look good compared to what they got in mind if they take us over. And how they going to take us over, Wilbur asked, how they gonna do it?

*From within,* came the answer.

Johnny Rex nursed a beer and sat in the blast of a tall shiny chrome standup fan which blew the stale air about the tavern. I ain't getting drunk, he was thinking, but I am getting ready. I've had it up to here with that son of a bitch and his Jesus this and McCarthy that. How'd we get hooked up with this guy, anyway? Money. Better money and clothes and tourist cabins and motels instead of sleeping in the truck.

Wilbur Parham had come and sought out Sister Violet Leadon to join his Crusade because everywhere he went around the Deep South people would ask why he didn't have *her* in the show. Sunny Wilbur decided to see for himself. He caught up with Sister Vi when she was preaching to soldiers near Huntsville. He came in all wound up after getting held up in traffic that stalled while they moved several enormous missiles around town on huge Army flatbeds. Violet just knocked him back, with her proclaiming and her snakes and her hands upon the crowd. He was impressed by her raw religious energy and her good sinner-born-again looks. He met her after the meeting broke up and explained to her that America was just getting too damn prosperous and well-dressed to go to these old tent shows much longer and she needed what he called a shift in focus. He said she ought to get with his crowd on television and play the big halls and reach more people and make some real money.

Sunny Wilbur wasn't interested in Johnny Rex Packard and the rolling flourishes of his gospel piano. Nor was he interested in the colored couple, the young man with the odd assortment of rhythm instruments and an electric guitar, or the young woman who played tambourine and handed out the hymnals and collection plates. Nor the snakes. But Violet, now, dressed different and delivering personal testimony that he'd write for her, she could be a real addition to the Crusade. Sister Violet would up the ante and increase the draw, but she'd have to cut the rest of them loose.

Violet compromised.

She insisted on bringing Johnny Rex with her, cause he'd been with her from the beginning. As for the rest, well, she was pretty damn tired of fooling around with the snakes and of having to lay hands on whatever washed up at her tent. The black couple? They were a brother and sister who'd joined up with Violet and Johnny Rex when the attendance at her revivals got bigger than just the two of them could handle. But if the folks who sought the Lord with Sunny Wilbur Parham only wanted to see white faces up there on the stage and over the television, Eck and Karintha would have to go.

Johnny Rex blew up at her and disappeared with Eck and Karintha for two full days and nights. He came back all stubble-cheeked and stinking and broke and not saying anything about them or where they'd been, just that he'd do it. That he'd go on the Wilbur Parham show with her for the money but he wanted her to know there was something about the son of a bitch he really couldn't stand.

Now in Knoxville, the lanky young piano player sipped and thought, There's a hell of a lot of things about him I can't stand. The way he talks down to you, and his audience of dumb white shits afraid their own shadows might be out to steal their cars and rape their wives or cut their men. And that whole McCarthy line. If the country's overrun with Communists, why the hell ain't I ever seen one? All I seen in six years of rambling around is the same old greedy Americans scrapping for everything they can get and that's including me. Who'd go along with some damn scheme to take all your stuff from you? Communism might work over there where they's used to getting pushed around, but it ain't got a snowball's chance here in the U. S. of A. Johnny Rex finished his beer and drained a glass of water on top of that and crunched the ice.

"Hey," he said to the bartender. "You ever seen a Communist?"

"You damn right I have. They's a whole nest of em not two counties away. Sometimes they send em down to stand in front of the post office with signs and things."

"What?"

"I ain't shittin you. It's over at Skyliner, they got a center for em to get together and do whatever it is Communists do—make Molotov cocktails, I reckon."

"Skyliner's a damn music school or something," Johnny Rex said.

"Music my ass. It's a den of em. Niggerlovers. That's how they figure to work this takeover, through the niggers."

"Go to hell."

"Now, just a goddamn minute, you. This is my place you're drinking in."

Johnny Rex glared at him and stretched his big piano hands and clenched them and unclenched them. He got a quarter out of his pocket for his last beer and slapped it down on the bar.

"You're as crazy as Wilbur Parham," Johnny Rex said, "so you can both go straight to hell." He stalked out, and the bartender called after him as he slammed through the door and back out into the steaming August afternoon:

"What's the matter with you, buddy? You want to get your ass kicked?"

It was the last and biggest night of Sunny Wilbur Parham's Mid-South Holiness Crusade in Knoxville. Johnny Rex hadn't gotten drunk, but he'd kept a buzz on all afternoon to keep him going now that he knew what he was going to do. He stayed away from the hotel—he wasn't about to let Violet talk him out of it, *if* she guessed, and she probably would. Might even go to bed with me to get me not to, he thought. But likely not. She'd gone so bejesus since they'd took up with Parham that she took all he wrote for her to say and actually seemed to believe it by now. She didn't have her sense of humor about preaching anymore.

He'd kept loose, anyway. Especially this day now that he'd made up his mind. He was already wearing his suit, that dark drab thing Wilbur had him buy when they joined up with the Crusade. He'd go straight to the Civic Center and just let em wonder where he'd been all day. And not only that: he'd skip Sunny Wilbur's little prayer meeting he always held right before the show started. Why couldn't the rest of them see what a pile of crap Parham was?

Sunny Wilbur's Mid-South Crusade had sold well, and now at the last show they'd sold out the five thousand seats and then papered the Civic Center with standing room tickets, so everywhere the cameras panned there would be people sharing seats, sitting in each other's laps, hanging from the rafters. Too many people: fire marshals had to be rewarded for letting the stepped aisles turn into seating.

Men and women came wanting to hear Sunny Wilbur say

in his rolling bass that it wouldn't be easy but their prayers and concentration and donations could stem the godless red tide and their children could grow up healthy and free in an America strong and proud like the one they knew and loved as children. There was something wrong with this—these people had suffered through a great depression, but now they were willing to extend this vision of the new boom and prosperity as far back into the past as need be to keep their enthusiasm for quelling the red tide high and mighty. It was as if a whole people could come off the land and purchase enough automobiles and thick white-enameled machines, and the passions of Gastonia textile workers and Kentucky coal miners and Alabama tenant-farmer unionizers would be smoothed out and forgotten beneath the easy-to-clean enamel. Sunny Wilbur could put that vision into words and make them forget the other and spread the new vision out among them. Trust me, he said, me and Tailgunner Joe, for together we *can,* together we *can,* together we *CAN* "beat back ah the red tide that even now would ah drown us you and me and the children who must not forsake Jesus ah and lead us on to Glory . . ."

Fans and blowers whirred and whooshed all over the hall. Sweat dropped from mothers' brows and trickled down the scalps and faces of the babies in their laps. Men worked plugs of tobacco and spat the oily smelly brown juice into dixiecups. Boys and girls fell asleep only to be jerked awake by the shouts of approval from their parents.

"And the Lord says to me his servant Wilbur Parham he says, 'Shine your lantern, Wilbur, shine your lantern on Evil wherever it may be and expose it to My sight and I will destroy it as I am the Lord thy God—shine your lantern!' "

The Civic Center went black.

Women and children screamed, but Wilbur Parham settled them as he swept a shaft of white light over the audience from a two-hundred-watt electrified railroad lamp. He rolled on with his speech, and around the hall the cameras rolled with him. He hoped they were picking this up, that it would turn out. It was costing him plenty, but the networks were interested. In the dark, Johnny Rex shook his head.

"My light shines for the Lord. And what does it shine on, what does it il-lu-mi-*nate?*"

*What, what?*

"I see Lust in Hollywood and Communists right behind it. I see Treason in the Pentagon and Communists there too. I see Mongrelization in the judgment of the Supreme Court, and are they not there as well, these agents of the Red Tide?"

*Yes, they're everywhere.*

The lights came back up and Parham changed his tone. "They will use temptation, sin in any shape, to subvert this Christian nation. We must remain strong and clean or our future is Bondage." He went in a turn from exhortative to confidential. "My friends, I want you to hear someone to-night, someone with oral testimony, someone who has sinned, who has known the degradations of Lust and Free Love." This was what the men wanted to hear, came to hear: the story of the Memphis hooker who had found Christ and been born anew.

Violet Leadon stepped up beside Sunny Wilbur. Except now instead of being Sister Vi she was Mrs. Leadon. Sunny Wilbur had created for her a husband who died in combat in Europe. She was all done up in a nice suit and her hair fixed. Johnny Rex stared at her rear from his seat at the piano on stage and had to laugh. Wilbur had made her look like a housewife and talk like a Sunday school teacher.

"Friends," Sunny Wilbur said, "what kind of a country is it that'll let a soldier's widow turn to the streets for her daily bread? A troubled country . . ."

Violet spoke. Her voice quavered. Wilbur had taught her to do that, telling her that folks wanted to hear a woman like that—especially a fallen angel like her. She told about the first time. It was after she'd got the news about her husband and just couldn't seem to get over it. Then the benefits ran out and she had no savings. Things got bad. She didn't know what made her do it, but she was so hungry she went into the

restaurant at the Hotel Peabody in Memphis wearing her
best dress and a doublestring of paste pearls and ordered a
big Kansas City sirloin with all the trimmings even though
she didn't have a nickel to pay for it. When she was finished
she started to cry, not real loud or anything, just sniffling,
the way she was doing now, the way Wilbur Parham had
taught her.

And then there he was. A man, well-dressed and comfort-
ing, a businessman from Anniston or Birmingham, she
couldn't remember. He spoke softly to her: Are you all right?
Are you ill? No, she said, she was just real lonely, her
husband being killed in France and her in a big city like
Memphis and no family to lean on or go to. And then there
we were, him paying the check and holding her arm and
leading her outside where she could get some air. He could
see she won't a bad girl or anything like that, just a lonely
young war widow not much over twenty.

And then it was morning.

It never failed. First you could hear a pin drop. Then the
hall would be all full of the sound of sniffling. Violet'd go on
about spending all her times with strange men till that one
special day when she was in a room with a radio and a
Gideon Bible and Sunny Wilbur Parham was on the air and
he said, Look, friends, at the Book of Mark, seventh chapter,
where He cast out the spirit of Satan from the daughter of
the Syrophoenician woman, look there and you shall find
hope even in these times no matter how desperate how
unclean you are: hope in Christ Jesus! Her life was changed
in a moment. She sought out Sunny Wilbur and they prayed
together and Violet offered to accept the shame and humilia-
tion and to put herself on display as a testament to the
wonders that the love of Jesus could work on a fallen sinner
woman like her. Use me, she'd say to Sunny Wilbur. Use me
for God to make up for the way the Devil has used me. And
here I am today to tell you about the miracle of Christ in my
life and how glad I am to of lived through it all to come
before you and testify.

The audience stood and clapped and shouted its approval and encouragement, and Johnny Rex thought, Yeah, and to be making about ten times what you was when you was fucking with them damn snakes.

Sunny Wilbur raised his hand high, hers in it, and beamed and nodded and said, "Praise the Lord" till there was complete silence and he turned her loose and her moment in the show was past. "My blessed friends," he began, "this is indeed a wonderful night, and because it is so special we are filming this meeting so millions more can experience through the miracle of television what you are experiencing in the flesh, millions more all over America and the free world, and our boys in Korea too."

Back to the Communists.

"For this special occasion we are honored to welcome to the Lord's stage here with us to sing an old country hymn a fine Christian family. You will remember the great bandleader Franklin Montreat"—the applause started up again—"so please let the love flow and welcome Brother Franklin and his children Hubert and Bonnie and his nephew Montreat."

The little family choir stepped up to the microphone. Johnny Rex couldn't have even told you what song they sang. His own number was coming up next and he was to have the spotlight as he led the Sunny Singers on into "Rock of Ages" for a big rousing finale. Johnny Rex went through it in his mind, rearranging it for this particular evening even as he stared lewdly at the little Montreat girl. Get if off your mind. Goddamn jailbait.

"And now won't you all join," Wilbur Parham was saying, "our own Brother John Packard and the Sunny Singers in a hymn we all need to sing from time to time . . ."

" 'Rock of Ages,' " Johnny Rex began, " 'cleft for me . . .' "

It was the same as always. He'd given no indication what he was about to do. But then he started weaving just a little, and swaying during the breaths, swaying into and almost lipping the carbon microphone during the lines. At the end of the first verse Sunny Wilbur would motion the audience to stand, and after a great collective gathering of breath they and the Sunny Singers would hit the last verse with Johnny Rex. But not tonight. Johnny Rex thrust his left hand high above him and exhorted:

"Good people, I *am* Johnny Rex Packard and I *am* from Memphis, Tennessee, and this *is* the way we like to sing this song back home. Sing it with me one time!

" 'When I rise to worlds unknown . . .' "

He cut the time and was looping round the notes with his bluesy gravely voice. Wilbur Parham ground his teeth—Packard was screwing up the damn film.

" 'And behold thee on thy throne,' " the choir wobbled uneasily. It sounded like hell. Good, Johnny Rex thought, just the way I wanted it—good and raw.

" 'Rock of Ages, Good God Amighty! . . .

" 'Cl heft for me!' "

Men in the crowd started to boo him. One stood and shouted, "Quit singing like a nigger!" Johnny Rex didn't give a damn. The booing stepped up.

" 'Let me hide,' *I want to hear you now,* 'myself in thee!' "

"Amen!" Parham snapped at the choir. They cut in immediately, singing over Johnny Rex's last "thee" and into the face of the booing. Now Sunny Wilbur opened his arms wide and boomed out a benediction, venom fairly dripping from the words "bless" and "face" and "shine" and "peace." The hall lights came up. There was an ugly muttering tone among the Christian throng. Onstage, his fellow Crusaders gave Johnny Rex about six feet of clearance in all directions as he sat at the piano rolling out the flourishes. Parham with small jerky waving motions attempted to clear the stage in some orderly fashion. The cameras were still rolling.

Johnny Rex segued easily into Joplin's "Magnetic Rag," having the time of his life. "Come on, Wilbur," he called, "you know the words."

There are no words.

Sunny Wilbur Parham, co-conspirator and drinking

buddy of Tailgunner Joe McCarthy, stepped over to Johnny Rex and leaned in and said real low, "Soon's you get done with that nigger whorehouse music and come backstage, Packard, I intend to kill you."

Johnny Rex Packard tossed his head back and sang out, "Whooaahh, Lord, forgive thy servant Brother Wilbur who don't know his ass from a hole in the ground!"

Violet tried to stop him, but Wilbur slung her aside and dove at Johnny Rex, who leaned back while Wilbur Parham, messenger of God, slammed into the keyboard with a twelve-tone crash across several octaves. What happened next became one of the best-known moments in the whole of country music.

Somewhere in the first section of most any metropolitan daily from August, 1954, three stills from the film can be found. In the first, the silk-haired albino has the evangelist by the collar of his shirt and the seat of his pants. In the second, the evangelist is sailing forward off the stage. And in the third, he has fallen into a knot of worshipers who hold him up as he shakes his fist and rages at the albino, who is smiling broadly and maybe even beginning to laugh. Off to the left in this last, two policemen with nightsticks raised are already lunging toward the stage; behind them, a man with a banjo in his left hand is restraining with his right a wide-eyed girl.

The photos ran all over the world. They ran on the slick-paper covers of the first half-dozen singles he recorded. A star was born in Knoxville that night.

"Wild Man" is what folks called him.

Violet vouched for him at the precinct house where the leading lights of the Mid-South Holiness Crusade spent much of that night. She convinced Sunny Wilbur to drop any notion of pressing assault charges against Johnny Rex. The publicity would hurt Wilbur, who cared, and not Johnny Rex, who didn't. She also figured that witnesses and the film would have to report that Wilbur Parham was the initial assailant, though Johnny Rex did get in the last best lick. She even got the Crusade to pay him for the last week he was due.

After the magistrate worked through the papers, Violet rode with Johnny Rex in a Checker cab to the bus station and waited with him for the next westbound. They'd got a half pint from the cabbie and nipped at it while they waited and necked some in the kiosk booth where you got four pictures for a quarter. They got a set for her and a set for him. When the red-and-silver Trailways came Violet cried and they had a few salty kisses at the bus door.

"I don't know why you done this," she said.

"Aw, come on, Violet. I'm through with this shit. I'm going home." He took what was left of the half pint and boarded the bus.

He took a window seat near the back and nuzzled his head into the greasy plastic headrest and smoked and drank from the little flask and felt at peace for one moment in his stormy life. Johnny Rex had two hundred dollars cash in his pocket and a reclining seat and somebody else to do the driving. He listened to the big bus tires as they heated up and sang along U.S. 70, and let the tobacco and the whiskey wash Wilbur Parham and this last year away.

The silver bullet shot west. The small white beacon at the top in front read: MEMPHIS. This bus was an express.


# BONNIE MONTREAT
## 1954


All the way back home from the Knoxville Crusade, the warm air blew in through the hood vent of their maroon humpback Dodge, carrying the smells of engine grime and gasoline. Daddy drove and Ivy sat up front between him and a uniformed Bumper, who was home on a furlough. The

Army had transferred him from Texas to Korea. Bonnie stretched out warm and drowsy in the back seat with her head pillowed on a sweater in her cousin Treat's lap. No one said much about Johnny Rex Packard, but she got the feeling that Bumper was as peeved about it as Daddy seemed to be amused.

Next day in Honey Run, Bonnie and Ivy worked in the kitchen stringing the crowder peas that would hang and dry in their pods, and the hot peppers they'd use later in relishes and chowchows. Daddy came in with a basket of big almost-to-bursting sweet German tomatoes. Bumper, slamming the screen door as he ran in, tossed a scant handful of cress and bear's lettuce into the deep enamel sink.

Daddy said, "Why, that ain't enough to feed a rabbit."

"Rain's startin," Bumper said. "I'll pick the rest after the storm." It would rain good and hard and steady like it did every summer afternoon for a half hour or so and everything would be cleansed of the summer day's dust. Then there would be that eerie cast to the brilliant evening light as the sun set far away beyond the steamy valley. As the rain trailed off, Treat showed up sopping wet and grinning.

"Thought you had a real job," Bumper kidded.

"Hell, sojer boy, it's four o'clock. Number Three broke down and I got the boy that runs the saw off that one to finish up for me—we only got one carload going down today anyway."

"Can't you keep them boilers running any better'n you do?" Daddy said. "Seems like one's always down for repair."

"They're just like people, Uncle Franklin," Treat said. "You take Number Three—she went months nothing wrong and then all of a sudden she just gets uppity and says, 'I ain't gon strike a lick more.' You never know which one's gon kick out on you." Treat winked over at Bonnie.

"Let's go walk up the hollow," Bumper said.

Ivy reckoned it was all right. They were having a few others to come in for singing and music later and probably wouldn't serve up dinner till dark. "Get on back a little fore that," she said. Bonnie couldn't go till she finished with the peppers, and they'd got a good ten minutes on her before she set out.

It was a beautiful late afternoon. Even with running after them and breathing hard, she could hear a faraway call and stopped to listen. It was a tugboat horn way down the valley, out on the Tennessee, but she liked to imagine it was the whistle of a paddlewheeler river packet docking down at Indian Point at the mouth of the Tammabowee. She'd ride away on it to New Orleans or St. Lou or some other place she'd read about in geography.

When she caught up to Bumper and Treat they were wading through a huckleberry patch thick as tomato vines that had taken hold on the sledge path up to the old Montreat homestead. They reached the big willow crook in Welsh Girl's where they had their fort in schooldays. A mixed stand of pitch pines and hickory grew up the banks on either side. Here the hills pinched in and the creek narrowed and roared over great flat rock plates below the fifty-acre cove Buckhannon and Mary Liza Montreat had tamed. They hadn't much gone up there these five years since Mary Liza died, but Bumper seemed to want to go over everything on his visit home. Bonnie trailed along behind as he spoke of the burying.

Bumper could remember Daddy's getting Ivy to keep water boiling so he could pour it over and over the headboards to soften them. He was making a casket with a curved end, something special, he said. And Bumper remembered being sent to Carson's Store to buy a special package of screws and tacks—coffin hardware—with floweredy decorated heads on the screws, and Daddy whacking away all night with a borried bending hammer to get that coffin right, while Mary Liza lay out on the bed upstairs. Bumper's going on about all this made Bonnie's stomach churn. What she remembered was Ivy fetching her out of the hayloft where she hid crying and taking her in to see Mary Liza just one last time.

"Look," Bumper said, pointing up to the hillside grave-yard. The last rays of the sinking summer sun lit up the four piles of white quartz that marked the graves of Buck and Mary Liza and Black Charlie and Treat's father Soonzy with the baby Parris. The light climbed the hill some more and left the graves in shadow. It would be bright another hour or more in Honey Run, the way the sun went straight down the Tammabowee making the river look like a golden ribbon, but Montreat's Cove was behind a bend in the ridge and out of the sun now at six o'clock. Steam rose out of the rank untended bottom, not two hours since the cool cleansing rain, and the air was hot and thick again. They had reached the deep pool at the lower end of the cove where they all used to swim naked.

Treat nodded over at the creek. He was tugging at the laces on his thick-soled brogans. "I'm cooling off."

Bumper looked at Bonnie and shrugged. "I reckon we got time."

Treat said, "Hell, we ain't got time *not* to."

Bonnie Montreat had enough modesty about her that she wouldn't just strip down right in front of the boys. She made them look the other way while she went over behind a chinquapin tree and slipped out of her jeans and blouse. She swam out to the big rock where she could stand and still be under water from her waist, except now she stayed up to her neck and kept her new little breasts hid. Then Bumper and Treat kidded her about not looking at them as they got in, and that made her feel silly.

Treat had a plastic pint flask somebody'd brought him back from a UT football game over in Knoxville, full of some kind of berry wine. They took turns sipping the thick sweet stuff and pretty soon they were all three laid half in half out of the water on the little beach at the inside of the curved swimming hole. The wine wasn't all that good, but it wasn't all that weak either. It made them feel loose and giddy and more like the times before Bumper'd gone into the service. Bumper got out saying, "Don't look, don't look!" and

laughed all the way over to his clothes to get them some
smokes. He brought them back and they lay there snickering
and smoking on the soft silt and smooth pebbles.

Bonnie got sassy after a while and cut her eyes at Bumper
and said, "I looked."

"You did? You didn't, did you, Bonn? Damn it."

"Seen it all before," she said, and Treat laughed.

"No you hadn't."

"What?" Treat said.

"All right, then—you ast for it." Bumper har-harred, and
stood up with his bare rear to them and waited.

"What the hell?" Treat said.

"What in the world you got all on your hiny, Bump?"
Bonnie said.

They held their laughing long enough for Bumper to
explain how he'd seen another soldier in the shower with this
same tattoo and how he thought he needed one himself and
so he went on down Bragg Boulevard and got him one.
There on his left cheek were three hounds chasing a fox
right over toward the crack. "You with me so far?" Bumper
said. Then he clenched his buttocks and the fox disappeared, the hounds appearing to have chased it *zoop* right up
Bumper's ass. It about did them in, Bonnie and Treat
laughing till they cried. Bumper chuckled along till suddenly
he remembered something and jumped up.

"Those goddamn greens!"

Bonnie offered to help, but he said, "Naw, naw, it's my job.
I'll run up where all that pokeweed grows this side the barn
and break off some stalks and we can all leaf em going back
down the hollow." He grabbed his clothes and ran off.

Bonnie and Treat settled back down on the beach and a
shy feeling came over her about being there naked all alone
with just him. Maybe he felt it, too. "You want another
smoke?" he said and she nodded, sliding herself back down
into the water a bit. He lit the cigarets over by his clothes and
caught her peeking at his lanky loosejointed body. She
looked down and crossed her arms to hide her little breasts.

"Aw, Bonn," he said, slipping down easily into the water beside her. "It's just old Treat." She glanced at him and looked away. "Here," he said, "have a smoke and stunt your growth." That made her laugh. "You know," he rattled on in his easy way, "everybody's so damn busy this summer," he paused, "that you and me ain't played no kissin games like we used to."

Now, that made her nervous. "Treat, Mama says—"

"Aw, mamas're always saying you're getting too old for that kind of thing or else you ain't old enough. It can't be both, so I reckon it's neither one." Boy, she thought, Treat's always twisting things around and fooling you like that. But she wasn't prepared for what he did next. He slid on down in the water beside her and slipped his hand up under her wet hair and scritched the back of her neck and then ran his hand on down her backbone and over her bottom.

"Tre-e-eat."

He leaned around and kissed her real slow on the lips. Then he smiled at her and drew away and said, "Well, you tell me, one of these days." He pulled himself out of the water and said, "Getting-back time, I reckon. Don't look."

He'd given her a turn down deep with all that, and she didn't look as he got out and went over to his clothes. Bonnie pushed herself off the beach into the deeper water and swam back to the chinquapin tree. She got out and dressed. Tell him what?

Bumper came running back, and all the way down the hollow they plucked the poke leaves off the red stems. Her face and neck felt all burny and she knew she must be blushing up a storm. She thought about Treat all that evening as the living room and the kitchen filled up with a dozen or more people come to see Bumper home from the service and to sing and pick a little. She thought about how Treat had touched her and whenever he'd look right at her it would make her stomach butterfly cause it was like he was secretly winking at her and the both of them were thinking about the same thing, remembering. Bumper would nudge her every once in a while and whisper in her ear, "Now, don't you tell nobody bout that fox chase you seen." He would snicker some, but truth to tell, that and the Knoxville Crusade the night before and this party, all of it paled beside remembering Treat laying naked beside her in the swimming hole on Welsh Girl's Creek. And it was two years later almost to the day, in the hayloft at the farmstead where she'd hid out crying the day they'd buried Mary Liza, with excitement and a little fear but also with ease and no regret, Bonnie and her half-first-cousin Treat were each other's first.

# JOHNNY REX PACKARD
## 1954–55

When Johnny Rex got back to Memphis, he stayed with Eck and Karintha in a one-and-a-half-story unpainted frame house on the south side of the city.

They'd come into some money selling their uncle Perse's farm after he died, and used it to set up a little store in the black neighborhood where they lived. It was called a "grab" and they kept it open from seven in the morning till nine at night selling cold drinks and bread and potted meats and fishbait.

Eck had moved a high-yellow woman in with him, an East Texas woman named Sallybet with a shrill cascading laugh. Her giddiness made the quiet-mannered Karintha seem staid, but Johnny Rex's taste for her had never diminished.

One morning for old times' sake Johnny Rex rambled around to the Hotel Bedford Forrest and when he came back that afternoon he announced he had his own place now. The Bed Forrest had run down even more since their paperboy days. The manager said he'd be willing to rent Johnny Rex the three-room "Governor's Suite" by the month; Johnny Rex said he'd be willing to take it if he could have that old

Aeolian player piano from the lobby up in his rooms. The manager made a couple of phone calls. It was a deal.

The day Johnny Rex moved, Karintha put a "Closed" sign on the door of the grab and shut down early. Johnny Rex and Karintha and Eck and Sallybet took a bus over town to the Bed Forrest. When they opened the door his suite smelled like roses. Johnny Rex had put a couple paper roses in a jelly jar on his dining table and bought some rose-scented smellum to cut the musty air. He'd throwed open the windows and a light September breeze moved through the flat.

The sink was full of ice and beer. He opened them each a longneck bottle and sat down at the piano and started rolling out his big country gospel chords. He could catch almost an octave and a half with each hand. The piano was way out of tune and you could hear that there were some broken hammers and buzzing damper felts. But Johnny Rex had wiped off the outside and polished it up some and he was proud of his piano and his place.

"Somebody been busy," Karintha said.

"Somebody gon stay busy," Johnny Rex said.

They drank up the beer and went out looking for more. It was only nine or so now, but there wasn't much in that neighborhood and the places they did pass had all closed up tight. Anytime Johnny Rex would point down a side street Eck would say, "No, I think down this way."

A squad car pulled up alongside of them and slowed down to their walking pace. Some guitar instrumental music was coming out of the tinny dash speaker with a tom-tomming beat behind it. The officer riding shotgun spoke. "You folks lost?" There was menace in his voice.

"Just out walking is all," Eck said.

"Gon be curfew before long and you look a long ways from home. What about you, white boy?"

Johnny Rex seethed. "No problem—just walking with my friends, that's all," he said.

The police nodded and looked back to Eck. He said, "What's your name?"

"Eck de Graffenreid."

"Eck de Graffenreid. Eck?" the police said, excited. "The goddamn paperboy?"

Eck looked like he felt funny. "Used to be," he said. "Me and him both." He pointed at Johnny Rex.

"Son of a bitch," the police said. "I know you. I'm Eddie Ricketts used to pull drinks and sell stuff at my daddy's drugstore back at the hotel there."

"Yeah?"

"Yeah. I'm a city cop now."

"No shit."

The police poked a finger mock accusingly at the albino. "You was there, too, hunh?"

The women were frightened. Johnny Rex was obliged. "Yeah. I member you too."

"Sure, sure," the police said. "Mmm-hmm." Then there was a stupid silence till Eddie Ricketts thought of something to say. He looked the black girls up and down with a gleaming eye. "I bet you paperboys really know how to have a good time."

"Mmm-hmm, mmm-hmm," Eck and Johnny Rex both answered.

"Well, we got to go find us some bank robbers. You all see any more police you tell em I said you was OK." The '54 Ford squad car cruised away and with it the sodajerk policeman and the junglebeat drums.

"What the hell was that all about?" Johnny Rex said. Inside his head was roaring.

"Just messin with us is all," Eck said.

"You never told me about no *curfew* since I got home."

"It ain't a law, honey," Karintha said. "It's a attitude. They just don't want niggers out late roaming around causing trouble."

"Cept on Saturday night," Eck said. "Then they look the other way."

They strolled on, spirits dampened and out of sorts. Johnny Rex said the way he remembered it there was noth-

ing but warehouses and no beer stores down where they
were headed. Eck said not exactly, and the women laughed
some. Johnny Rex all of a sudden caught the drift of what
Eck was doing and he stopped them all in the patch of light
cast by a greencapped streetlamp.

"Goddamn it, Eck, I ain't *ready.*"

"Aw, come on, Johnny."

"I told you before: not till I'm *ready.*"

Eck drew a breath. "You was ready soon's you made up
your mind to toss that preacher off that stage. Won't no
shillly-shallying around about that, was they? All right, then.
All's I want you to do is *meet* the man. He ain't half's big as
Karintha and you ain't ascared of her."

Karintha stroked the small of his back and Sallybet giggled
and Johnny Rex felt foolish. He'd been back some weeks
now and managed to run through most of the wad of cash
Violet had got for him. He hadn't took a job or even looked
for one. Hell, for all he knew he might have trouble getting
one after that scrape back in Knoxville. But still it seemed
like the wrong time, them roaming around full of beer and it
pushing ten o'clock.

"Trust me, boy," Eck said winningly.

A dim forty-watt bulb in a wire cage illuminated the sign
on the green door:

RANGE MAGNETIC RECORDING/
MOON PHONOGRAPHIC RECORDS
Large Deliveries in Rear. Ring Bell After 8 PM.

The building was smaller than most of the other warehouses
they'd passed, brick repositories with large white letters on
black fields advertising NEW RAGS FOR OLD and PILLORY'S
PAPER BOX and SOUTHERN WINDINGS. Eck pushed the button
and waited. There was no sound, but soon a boy younger
than them opened the door a crack and said, "Yeah?" He had
bad skin and greased hair boxcarred around the side and

ducktailed in back. The boy must not have seen many albinos, because he gave Johnny Rex a twice over before he said wait a minute he'd get Phelps.

They stood shuffling in the little reception room. It's kind of nice, Johnny Rex thought. The walls were knotty-pine paneled and there were a pair of matching table lamps with ceramic guitar-shaped bases set on endtables by the sofa. *Variety* and some trade magazines were heaped on a coffee table. Johnny Rex lit him a Lucky and watched the smoke get sucked up into a vent and felt goosebumps on his arms. Hell, this place was air-conditioned.

The boy came back and with a head nod motioned them deeper into the building. They followed him down a narrow hall and up a step into another room. It was an engineer's booth, with several different tape recorders and a control board and a power amp with red lights on it. It reminded Johnny Rex of the radio and television studios he'd been in during his stint with Sunny Wilbur. But this was an honest-to-God record plant. The studio beyond the glass booth was dark except for an exit sign shining off at the back.

"Hey, Eck!" a voice called from underneath the control board. The room smelt of solder smoke.

A small man slipped out into view, a wiry man with black slicked-back hair and white bucks and a toothpick. He smiled and nodded to Eck and the others and said to the boy, "Skibo, call Chi-Tech and have em put a dozen more of these 3810 VU meters on the bus tonight." Then to Eck: "This whole building's gon blow up the way damn board's behaving. How you folks doin?"

"You know my sister and Sallybet," Eck said. "This here is Johnny Rex Packard."

Phelps Range stuck out his hand. "Yeah, *yeah*. The piano player wrassled the preacher in Knoxville. Eck told me about you. Hell, I seen it in the paper my own damn self. You just hit town?"

"About a month ago."

"A *month*? Where you been hiding him, Eck? Ain't this the

man gon make us all *rich?* What kind of material you got, Packard?"

Johnny Rex wasn't sure what to make of it. He knew Eck and Karintha did percussion and backup vocals at this studio to pick up a little extra change, and Eck had told him that Range always had his eye open for talent. He'd meant to get around to the Range studio sooner or later. Eck sprung it on him tonight.

"Material?"

"Tunes, songs. You write you own stuff, don't you?" Range asked.

Johnny Rex glanced at Eck. He had a bad aftertaste from Wilbur Parham and his fast talking. Range picked up on his uncertainty and practically yanked him into the studio.

"Come on over here," he said. "Grab that side." The two of them pulled the brown canvas cover off of the grand piano. "It's a Chickering," Range said. "Just got it a couple months ago, and I've tuned it once a week since." Range pulled out the heavy padded adjustable piano stool and gestured to the albino. "Take it away."

Johnny Rex felt flushed. Eck and Karintha and Sallybet were watching through the glass window. He wasn't sure what he was supposed to do. He looked down at the floor and tried to think what to say. Damn, he thought, I told Eck I won't ready.

"Look, Mr. Range," he began, looking back up. But Phelps Range was across the studio grabbing some bottles of beer from a small Frigidaire behind a baffle separation.

"I hope you like Blue Ribbon."

Johnny Rex held out his hand and took a bottle.

"Smoke?" Range said.

Goddamn, Johnny Rex thought, he smokes Luckies. A broad grin spread across his face and he sat down. "What do you want to hear?"

"Any damn thing you want to play. And this ain't no audition. You're hired to do session work if you want to at twenty-five dollars a three-hour session. I know you're hot,

Johnny Rex, cause I heard you on one of the TV shows
Sunny Wilbur did. I doubt if you've gotten any worse."

"No, I ain't."

"What I want to hear now is what you sound like when
you're setting around with your friends drinking Blue
Ribbons and smoking Luckies, cause that's what folks're
doing when they're listening to songs on the radios and the
jukeboxes."

Johnny Rex drew in a lungful of the heavy smoke. Who in
the world are you, little man? he thought.

Range was a sometime drummer from Kentucky—some
said he'd played with Ernest Tubb, but none knew where or
when. He'd started out making jingles and radio spots with a
two-track tape recorder he set up in an old Airstream trailer
just north of Memphis. When a shouting Acrostolic church
left him a 1922 Estey upright to cover an unpaid-for session,
Phelps Range was owner of a music studio. He sold the
Airstream and mortgaged the instruments and equipment to
move down to the warehouse near Union where he worked
out of now. He was betting that the Hank Williams legend
would spur scores of dreaming textile workers and tenant
farmers and returning Korean War vets to traipse into what
few Southern cities there were and find the man with the
studio and cut em a hit. In Memphis, Phelps Range intended
to be that man.

"You take old Hank howling over that old wooden Indian
with those tomtoms rolling along behind. What would you
call *that*?" he said to Johnny Rex.

"Jungly beat, I guess."

"But on a country song, now."

"Well, that was Hank."

"There you go," said Phelps Range. "That's what I'm
looking for."

"The next Hank Williams?" said Johnny Rex.

Range laughed. "No. The man who'll pick up where Hank
left off and go him one or two better."

Eck and Karintha too and Sallybet had moved into the

studio itself as Phelps talked on about music and Memphis. He said it was no mystery why things like that happened in Hank's music, when you thought about how Hank came up and all, learning his guitar from that old black man Tee Tot down in the Montgomery streets. There was that side to Nashville, but there was that side to Memphis and more. Like the radio show with the DJ named King that everybody called B.B. for Beale Street Blues Boy. Eck knew B.B. at least to say hello and he knew all the places where B.B. played around Memphis and north Mississippi and west Arkansas. He'd taken Johnny Rex along and Johnny Rex had marveled as the people called out "Lucille" as if it was a real woman and not a guitar B.B. was making come to life and sing like that. He remembered sitting up late with Karintha years before way off there in the Tennessee flatwoods. That was the feeling, he thought. That I could make a piano sing like this, come to life and sing.

"There are all kinds of things in the air," Phelps said, "you just got to give em a place where they can mix together and *congeal*." That word he kept using: *"congeal."*

Several hours of talking and drinking and rolling out the tunes convinced Johnny Rex that Phelps was on the level. This man Range seemed to have been *waiting* on him, preparing for him somehow. Or maybe, Johnny Rex thought, he does this every night, or is prepared to, until he does find the right one or ones who'll put his dream together for him.

It hit him fully just how much Range was looking for. "You mean to put me on records under my own name and send me out to play in auditoriums and all?" he said. "All's I ever done is be off to the side of things, never the one up front. Who's gon pay to see a albino anyway?"

Phelps brought out a vinyl bag from a cabinet and tossed it over to Johnny Rex. "If it worries you, see what you can come up with."

Johnny Rex opened the bag and rummaged through it. Just what I was afraid of, he thought. A bag of makeup. This shit's for queers. He'd barely let em put any powder on him the different times they were filming Sunny Wilbur's Crusades.

He laughed and tossed the bag back to Phelps. "I ain't even gon tell you what I think of this shit. You need some piano played you can find me at the Bed Forrest. We got to go now." He stretched and ambled over to the studio refrigerator and grabbed him a couple beers. "Taking some beer to get us home. It's what we was out hunting anyway. See you, cat."

At the front door, the foursome stopped and Johnny Rex opened the bottles on the door catch. Foam ran down the jamb. Phelps heard them stopped there as he pulled the cover back over the piano and cut the studio lights. He went to the door and watched his albino discovery and the three Negroes ramble on off down the brick side street. Johnny Rex and Eck and Karintha were singing something, and the girl Sallybet was laughing and making remarks whenever they left an open spot. We gon do just fine, Mr. Packard, Phelps Range thought; just fine, thank you. And then he hollered as the scrambled melodies glided off along the walls of the great warehouses and back to him:

"Go, Stacker Lee!"

It wasn't two days later that Phelps Range called him in to do his first sessions—a black gospel quartet singing a slow "Roll, Jordan, Roll," a white quartet right after, and then a lone country crooner with an old Bradley Kincaid Houn' Dog Guitar where one of the dog's legs and half his tail had flaked away from the hound decal. "One more cowbilly," Phelps said, "flogging his way to the Opry or the Hayride, whichever'll take him."

The work came regular after that. All in all, Johnny Rex had a big time doing these sessions. He never failed to impress whoever he was playing for, because for one thing an albino is never *not* noticed and for the other he was a quick study and his playing was never stale. Word spread about that crazy albino Phelps had working for him, but Johnny Rex never actually acted crazy in any of these sessions. They just all assumed he acted crazy at some time or another. That affair of pitching Sunny Wilbur off the stage in Knoxville was recent enough that his name and his personality even acquired a certain weird luster that he enjoyed.

He got to living pretty high, working steady and drinking beer and sleeping only with Karintha, who came and went freely to and from the hotel. For a time the roaring in his temples left him. It all made him feel more or less normal after the years of roaming around with Violet and the snakes and doing it in the back of a truck cab.

Before long he had him a suite of rooms, he liked to say, and enough money to keep him going. White-man paycheck in one hand, he thought, and black-woman belly in the other. You doing all right, Johnny Rex.

Phelps Range kept after him to come up with material of his own to record, but Johnny Rex for the time being couldn't seem to be bothered to come up with anything. Every once in a while Phelps would get on the drums after a session and he'd talk Johnny Rex and the bass player into staying around and they'd mess around with different beats and different tunes. By the spring, though, what Phelps Range wanted was starting to happen. Johnny Rex grew tired of giving away his flatted-third and slip-note piano tricks to, as he put it, any son of a bitch who came through the door with enough jack to book a session, and him only making enough to pay his way and nothing much left over. Karintha started having to tend the store more often on account of there being a big highway construction crew moved into that neighborhood, building Boss Crump Boulevard. The little grab store on the edge of all the construction suddenly was making twice what it had been. So Johnny Rex frequently did without his woman and fooled around on the piano and thought about his situation.

He remembered the times he and Violet Leadon used to write those gospel songs and print em up and sell em at the tent shows. I can do that again, he thought. But nothing much came. He remembered back to the night he met Phelps Range and what they'd talked about. What the hell kind of music was he trying to invent, anyway? All that talk about Hank Williams and the rolling tomtoms on "Kawliga." He started to get edgy in the studio. He began to screw up regularly. Phelps found an empty bottle of triple peach in the bathroom in back of the echo room. Finally Johnny Rex blew a session. Phelps came around to the hotel later and asked Johnny Rex to level with him. "What is it?" he asked. "You need money or what?" His eye caught the scraps of papers, scribbled on and crumpled laying about the front of the piano and on top and on the floor by the pedals. So . . . he thought. Good. Phelps Range left.

Phelps picked up from Eck that Karintha's time was getting more and more taken up with the store. Johnny Rex came and hung out, moping and even getting surly from time to time. "Sits around in back—and you know how small the damn sto' is—eatin sardines with his fingers and drinkin beer out a paper cup even when Karintha tells him the law'll shut her down if they catch him at it." Again Phelps thought, So . . . I can't help what's between him and her. But I got to look after my man. Find him some strange.

The record man knew where to look. There was a white gospel trio, a father, mother and daughter, who came in from time to time to cut a side or two. The parents seemed to believe that the girl, who was sixteen or so, had hung the moon, and the girl in turn acted like they were right about that. Phelps knew she had a thing for Johnny Rex even though Johnny Rex couldn't have cared less. After all, she was just a little girl with a little-girl body and the piano man was used to something a bit different from that. Phelps called her in for a session, just her, no parents, and left her working with Johnny Rex on a song, saying he had to run across town and they'd put it down after he got back.

The girl Lee Anne and Johnny Rex were pushovers for each other. She got all up behind him and leaned over his shoulder to study the music and rubbed her breasts against his back and he leaned his head back against her shoulder and she whispered something about his poor neck must be awful sore and it was echoes and shades of Violet. Phelps Range hadn't been gone ten minutes before they were on the couch behind the echo-chamber room. It was easy as puffing to make a pinwheel turn.

They were back at the piano, though, when Phelps returned, and Johnny Rex took him aside and suggested they might step it up because he kind of wanted to borrow Phelps's ragtop and take Lee Anne out riding. So Phelps ran down a quick vocal level on her and put down only one take, saying he just wanted to demo the tune and thanks for coming in, Johnny, Lee Anne. "Sorry I had to run out and hold you all up." And so much for appearances.

She'd never been in the Bed Forrest before, but she'd ridden by it lots and who was he anyhow the man they'd named it after? Some old crow, she bet. She talked a lot without having much to say, but that made it all the easier on Johnny Rex, who didn't want to have to think. They did it again in the bed where Karintha hadn't been for six weeks and they smoked Luckies and sipped whiskey and did it some more.

After he carried her home he drove around Memphis awhile smoking and sipping at a bottle of beer he held between his legs. It was almost April, and the smell of the river's mud was on the spring breezes. He felt pretty damn good and he decided to run by the Big Ant Club, where the rhythm-and-blues crowd hung out. Eck might be there. Hell, I'll buy him a beer, he thought. What kind of music was it anyway that Phelps Range was driving at? Hillbilly rhythm and blues was all he could think of. It seemed hilarious, the thought of a string band standing up and singing some Big Mama Thornton tune, or of B.B. and his crowd singing "The Wreck of the Old 97." He had to laugh out loud. Yeah, I feel pretty good. That Lee Anne, what a little piece she is. Barely noticed her those other times, but whoa now, I ain't forgettin that number. Eck was at the club, but things were winding down, so they had a beer or two and went with the house band drummer back to a house over in Orange Mound where somebody had some reefer. They all got pretty drunk and stoned and Eck drove Johnny Rex home to the hotel and told him he'd get the car back to Phelps the next day sometime.

The two words "hellfire" and "firepower" were jostling around his brain when Johnny Rex awoke. Outside in the sweet cool early spring came the sound of the garbage trucks clattering around the square. He tried to remember what all had happened the night before, but it was too hazy. He did remember Lee Anne. He went to his refrigerator and got him a slice of bread and a cold Blue Ribbon and sat down at his piano. He felt like his old self again, like when there was some excitement and risk to his life where lately it'd been steady and full. How'd it take me so long to notice? he thought. In a quarter hour he'd got the better part of a driving blues written, one of several he'd take in to show Phelps inside of a week. This one was about a woman who'd got the Devil on her side and in her body so she could make men do bad things and they'd love it. It was rougher than anything on the radio at that time, but Johnny Rex wasn't thinking about markets—he was thinking about how he felt right then after a night like last night.

It would be his first hit, the song that established him as the "Wild Man." He called it "Hell Power."

After the introduction of Johnny Rex to Lee Anne, there was an air around the studio of something about to happen. When the albino came in to do his session work that week there was something intense in his manner, in his attack on the piano, and the edge of his playing.

"What's up?" or "What's new?" Phelps asked him each day. Johnny Rex just raised his eyebrows and shrugged.

It was a day early in the second week in April when Johnny Rex brought in the sheaf of lyrics and chord charts. Even before he'd heard anything, Phelps was stunned by what he saw: Johnny Rex had got hold of some makeup and blacked his eyebrows and lashes. It made him look devilish, striking, as if in some uncanny way Jolson had returned in whiteface instead of black.

"Think I could go on the road like this and not scare hell out of them?" Johnny Rex said.

Phelps rocked back and forth on his feet from heel to ball. "You ain't gon scare nobody. You gon drive em wild. Jesus, Packard, there's nobody in the business looks like you."

The cosmeticized albino strode into the studio and let out a musical war whoop. That's what it was, a war cry, a declaration of intent to commit sacrilege against the Sunny Wilburs of the world and to commit passion in favor of the Lee Annes and the Karinthas.

"Phelps, get Dace down here on bass and you handle the drums and let Skibo run the board. I bet we can lay two or three of these down this evening unless you got somebody coming in."

"No problem," Range said. "We got the time. But don't you want me to hear it first?"

"Book it on faith."

"Whoa, god*damn!*" Range dashed back out to the telephone. This was what he'd been waiting for: the impulse, the fire that raged in Johnny Rex Packard when he played. It took a little while to dig up the engineer and the bass player, so while they waited Phelps and Johnny Rex ran through the first song. Phelps made mental notes, crucial adjustments in the way the beat would be played and perceived. He would use an eighth-note ride and push the "and" of beats two and four with his largest tom. There would be no cymbal rides, just one great crash on the sizzle cymbal at the end of the tune.

And above it all Johnny Rex would be wailing and hammering on that Chickering piano, delivering by both force and insinuation a new unsettling sound in country music.

That session took three hours. They didn't even try to

back the song "Hell Power" with another one of Johnny Rex's originals. Phelps was too excited: "This has got to be released yesterday!" He flew to the Chi-Tech Mastering Labs in Chicago the next day with tapes of "Hell Power" and a hopped-up version of "Tennessee Waltz."

By the end of the month the first five thousand 45-rpm singles arrived back at Phelps's studio from a stamping plant in Kentucky, all in sleeves with pictures of Johnny Rex tossing Sunny Wilbur off the stage and with the words "Wild Man" under his name. Phelps invited every disc jockey in Memphis he thought might play the record to an occasion at the studio. He invited the press. They got photographs of Phelps and Johnny Rex drinking champagne right out of the bottle and dancing on a table top in the studio as "Hell Power" played through the speakers time and time again, photos of Johnny Rex playing the piano with his hands crisscrossed, upside down, with his elbows. He was wearing his makeup. And they got pictures of crates and crates of records being loaded into a sleek black '54 station wagon by the fellow who functioned as Phelps's main distributor in the states of Tennessee, Arkansas, Louisiana, Mississippi and Alabama. He was a heavyset young man in his late twenties up from Bay St. Louis on the Gulf. His name was Joseph Quill.

At first, all of the white country stations played the tune and about half the black rhythm-and-blues stations. Then the balance shifted as pressure mounted to have the record banned and people argued about whether "Hell Power" was a country record or a race record. In churches all over Memphis, they said it was a crime and a sin for such a record to exist. But you couldn't find the record anywhere in the riverport city. It was sold out in all the stores.

From out on the road, Joe Quill was calling in daily with reports from Shreveport, Texarkana, Montgomery. Phelps got word it was getting played as far north as Detroit. He told Johnny Rex, "I thought you might like to know they've come up with a word for our record, I mean a word they're calling your music. Been saying it all day whenever they play 'Hell Power' on the radio, and I bet you a five-dollar goldpiece it'll stick."

"What?"

"Rockabilly" was the word.

Phelps canceled recording sessions with the bread-and-butter gospel groups and ground out more of the next Johnny Rex Packard songs to have them ready when "Hell Power" died down. *If* it died down. He ordered larger pressings. Joe Quill came back to Memphis and bought a truck. They had to hire a secretary to handle the telephones at Moon Records.

Money started to pour in and women hung around the Bed Forrest lobby. Johnny Rex hid out at his suite of rooms and ripped out his newly installed telephone and drank gin fizzes and longed for Karintha. She was too alarmed by all the uproar to come by. She was frightened by it. She'll come around, Johnny Rex thought. Meantime he hired a Pinkerton to keep all but the most luscious young girls away from his room. He was amazed at his appeal and his power.

The Pinkerton drove him to Phelps's studio at odd times to record. Johnny Rex and the trio readied "You Blew the Roof Right Offa My Heart." Phelps manned the board and there was a new drummer. Eck played percussion and sang along with Johnny Rex. It became clear as the "Hell Power" record sold and sold and sold through the summer of 1955 that the tour they were mounting for the fall would not be limited to the country circuit. Many of those country dancehalls and honkytonks would simply not be big enough to hold the throng that promoters saw building to attend Johnny Rex Packard concert dates. It wouldn't matter if he had a nigger in his band. And all because of one record, he thought. Hell, why didn't I come across with this when Phelps first asked for it—this could of been happening months ago. He forgot the comfort and the calm and the Karintha of those worka-day six or seven months. Johnny Rex sat by the corner window at his suite of rooms at the Hotel Bedford Forrest and drank gin fizzes deep into the night. He heard the roaring inside his head and he encouraged it.

# PRESTON HEWITT
## 1958

It was between Preston Hewitt's junior and senior years of high school in Knoxville that he got involved for a short spell with the Skyliner Folk School off in the hills. The plan was that he would spend the first two months of the summer doing research work for his father, a history professor at the University of Tennessee; then he'd have the family's second car and could spend August at Skyliner helping with three one-week conferences.

It would all look terrific on Preston's record. It'd better— he had a shot at a scholarship to Harvard and everything was aimed at that bull's-eye. His father knew the director at Skyliner and had set it all up. In fact, there was almost a whole chapter in Professor Hewitt's book devoted to Hal Milton's labor-organizing efforts from three decades ago. The book was tentatively titled *Crisis in the Cotton Mill: The Southern Textile Labor Movement 1919–1941*. Professor Hewitt was sympathetic with Milton's work then and now, when it was much more involved with the integration movement, but the book was basically a noncommittal reporting of votes at various mills, of attendance on picket lines, of crowd sizes in different marches and riots. The way Professor Hewitt could thank Hal Milton for all his information and input was to donate Pres to work for room and board at the August conferences. It would be very quiet. No one in Knoxville would need to know, but it was exactly the sort of thing that would appeal to Harvard when they sent the scholarship package in.

Preston found Skyliner pleasant. The main building was a

great rock lodge with a gable roof and two dormers, and a dormitory wing off one of the gable ends. It was way up on top of the mountain, shaded by one great spreading oak and overlooking a lake down the mountainside a ways. When Pres first drove up the cedar-lined drive in the '55 Chevrolet, Hal Milton was out on the lawn under the oak serving punch to the other assistants who'd be helping with the August round of conferences.

"Young Hewitt, eh?" Milton stepped back after shaking hands with the boy and took stock of him. Preston had a fresh, open face and clear gray eyes, and his spare frame marked him as a basketball or track athlete. "Here's your name tag, Pres. You play sports?"

"Just tennis." Preston laughed. "Too small for football and can't hit a baseball far enough."

Milton nodded. "We've got volleyball and a lake here. I expect you'll do all right with them. Come on, let me introduce you to your partners in crime."

Preston met his cohorts, half of whom were black. He'd known black people came there to Skyliner, but he was surprised he was actually going to be working with some his own age. Wonder where they sleep and eat, he thought.

Downstairs the lodge had a kitchen and a library and a large central room with an enormous log footrest before a stone fireplace for the cool mountain nights. Hal Milton and his wife lived in an apartment upstairs, and the conferees stayed out in the dormitory wing. The Skyliner staff stayed in three-sided camp huts with bunk beds that were tucked here and there about the school's hilly grounds.

They had dinner family style and Hal Milton told stories and put everyone at ease while they helped themselves to fried chicken and mashed potatoes and mustard greens and iced tea in tall plastic glasses. After supper Preston washed dishes with a white boy from Nashville and a black girl from Charleston, South Carolina, who was there with her brother.

At one point Milton bounded into the kitchen and collared Preston. "You play guitar, don't you?"

Dad must have mentioned it. "A little."

"Did you bring it up here with you?"

Preston nodded yes. More than a few times he'd been the center of attention when his church group went on retreats—of course he'd brought it along.

"Good, *good!*" Milton smiled. "You all hurry up and finish and we'll do some singing."

Well, Pres thought on the way down to his car to get the guitar, this is all right. I like this. He was pretty clearly about to be the leading light among the staff crowd. As he hit the porch he was chagrined to hear the sounds of another guitar being tuned at the other end of the hall where they were all gathered.

"Ah, Pres, wonderful! The more the better." Milton plunked Preston down in a chair beside his right-hand man, the permanent staff director, a trim earnest-looking fellow in his early twenties named Gary Owwens.

Owwens looked up from his tuning and gave Preston a broad inclusive smile and asked if he knew "Rockabye My Saro Jane," but Preston said no.

"Just follow me in open G," Owwens said.

"Open G?" Preston asked.

Without a second's hesitation, Owwens traded his own guitar, already tuned open, with Preston's and proceeded to tune Preston's down. He spoke out to the little band: "Give us a minute to get straight here and we'll be good for all night."

Everyone laughed, and Hal Milton and some others got a fire going in the big fireplace. Then Owwens cranked up and led—he seemed to know every song anyone named or thought of. Preston followed him, and the bunch sang before the open fire for an hour or more with increasing spirit and a sense of belonging together here. After they finished, Hal Milton stood up and said a few words about Skyliner, how he and his wife had established the school along the lines of the Danish folk schools where people gathered to try and figure out solutions to their common problems. They lived together and sang the songs of their fathers and mothers and tried to understand who they were as a people,

as a community, and how they could resolve their differences. Milton said that was what Skyliner was all about
"except that where we live is the South and our problems are
about labor and race. Unfortunately the Southern people
are not only *not* agreed about how to deal with these problems but many of them won't even recognize that they exist."
The fire was dying down and they sang a benediction before
setting out with flashlights to the three-sided cabins.

> *Kum ba ya, my Lord, Kum ba ya*
> *Oh, Lord, Kum ba ya*

At what seemed like the crack of dawn Gary Owwens was
waking Preston and the brother of the black girl from
Charleston. "Let's roll," he exhorted. "They'll be thirty people here by noon."

They trudged up the hill through the tall wet grass.
Breakfast was eggs and hominy and bacon and wholewheat
toast and plum preserves from last year's Skyliner harvest.
Everyone ate together and drank pots of hot coffee, with
thick milk from the little Jersey the Miltons kept, until they
were steaming.

After breakfast they got their assignments for the day.
This one would work in the library and keep track of books
that conferees checked out and file the pamphlets and news-
letters that had come in since the last group of assistants.
Another would man the mimeograph machine with its blue-
purple ink and run off the handouts and newssheets they
would need in the conference classes. Another would work
with Mrs. Milton in the kitchen and in the Skyliner garden.
And so on. Preston's first job was the library, but Hal Milton
let on that he hoped Preston would continue to play guitar
and help lead singing—Gary Owwens had done it so often he
appreciated the help that made it all fresh again.

So it went, from dawn till lights out, the whole time
Preston was there. Big family meals, staff and conferees all
together, and then a bunch piling in to wash dishes, and

always interesting helpful earnest people coming into the library maybe looking for something in particular, maybe just poking around looking through the materials stashed on the board-and-brick shelves. When it was hot before the afternoon thunderstorm there was swimming in the Skyliner lake and hiking along the mountain trails. And then those beautiful cool summer nights with the open-tuned guitars ringing and the sound of three dozen voices uplifted making a joyful noise, united in song and the belief that the evils of two and three centuries could be eradicated not just in their lifetimes but soon, next year or the year after, but soon . . .

It was heady stuff. A lot of sincere notions were sifted in with the available facts about how best to create pressure on employers, school administrators, lunch-counter operators, and then maintain that pressure within the limits of the law. The absurdity and impracticality and economic inadvisability of segregation would become so obvious and painful under the force of a concerted movement that it would fall away. School districts were targeted. Sit-ins at restaurants were discussed. They were creating a network of church people and educators and journalists sympathetic to the movement, the sort of people who would stand up and be heard and file suit and risk their jobs to help create a New Society.

The last week was the most exciting. There were small delegations from Greensboro, North Carolina, and from Charleston and Montgomery and Little Rock. Their sessions were led by a thin compelling black man who wore dark pants and a white short-sleeve shirt and dark thin tie even in the heat. He had been all over the South helping build the network of support and contacts and courage that everyone knew it was going to take.

His name was Reverend King.

He spoke out under the spreading oak tree, and Pres thought how the three weeks up on the mountain had flown. He'd never once gone down the mountain to the nearest town, Heuvil, though he'd wanted to—but Hal Milton advised against it, so Pres and the others had stayed away. "It's too rough down there. Don't push it."

Reverend King was earnest and full of fire. He was troubled, he said, at hearing of friends and allies being roughed up, or even at the emotional violence caused by discourtesy and insult. He was exhilarated, though, by the support and sympathy that he encountered on his travels, at the eagerness and hope he found right here at Skyliner in the black and white youths on the staff.

"Here is living proof," he said. "Proof that we *can* sing together. Let us stand together now, and join hands in a great circle and pledge once again here on this Tennessee mountain that in the years to come we shall work and we shall pray and we shall *see* the scourge of racism steadily blotted out across this land. This is the dream I have!" They sang:

> *"We are climbing Jacob's ladder*
> *Soldiers of the Cross."*

The conference broke up and Preston and the other assistants drifted back into the library to talk with Gary Owwens about their fieldwork projects for the Skyliner Folk School. The projects turned on a folklore and oral-history collection Gary Owwens had been putting together for several years now. As a reward for their unpaid work at the school, the young people would be given a small amount of gas and food money to finance a short trip to collect songs and stories. Gary Owwens had helped the assistants figure out where they'd most like to go, trying as he did to see that a broad cross section of Southern folk music was covered. The tapes they brought back would be edited down to album length, pressed, and distributed by a New York record label interested in Southern folkways. One of the assistants was off to witness and record a shape-note singing convention in Alabama, and one to seek out an old blind blues singer in Mississippi. Another would be recording a church group that sang ancient black spirituals in the Gullah dialect in the Georgia Sea Islands.

Preston's choice, urged on him by Owwens' interest in the link between black and white banjo playing, was in his own backyard, in the area of white mountain music. He chose a white banjo player living way back in the hills forty or fifty miles southeast of Knoxville, a man who'd led a string band back during the Depression.

Preston Hewitt chose Franklin Montreat of Honey Run. He signed out a high-grade two-track recorder from the Skyliner library, and came down off that mountain in his '55 Chevrolet with a hundred new songs in his head and a heartful of faith that he could be part of changing the world.

He made the trip from his home in Knoxville across the river and up the Tammabowee gorge into the high hills where the Montreats lived. It didn't occur to him to call ahead and set the session up; he never figured a real hillbilly would have a telephone. So he just drove up there and stopped at the white stucco building with the steep blue-tile roof and the Pure Oil sign just beyond the sign that read: HONEY RUN, UNINCORPORATED. He went into Carson's Store and asked where he might find Franklin Montreat.

"Depends on who wants to know," Carson said.

"I do, sir."

"And who are you when you're at home?"

"I'm Preston Hewitt from Knoxville."

"Look like a damn college boy to me."

Preston looked at his feet. "No, sir, not quite. I'm a senior at Crockett High School. I'm on a project to talk with Mr. Montreat about the old times when he had the Tennessee Bumblebees going."

"Old times, eh?" Carson laughed. "Son, that was just yesterday. He started that band right here in this store one Friday night, sure did. Right over there by that space heater's where they played their first tunes. Must of been thirty years ago, but it seems like a day."

"Twenty-nine," Preston said.

"What?"

"Twenty-nine years ago," Preston said. He'd done some digging and found out the band had officially formed in Honey Run in June of 1929. "According to my research."

"Do *what*?" Franklin Montreat stood in the cornfield up behind his house and looked sidewise at Preston like he'd said something crazy.

Pres squinted in the late-August sun and explained again about the Skyliner tape recorder and the New York record outfit and tried to sneak a little flattery in to make Mr. Montreat like the idea.

"I ain't made a record in twenty years, I reckon," Franklin Montreat said, smiling. "I'd be right rusty going back to it now."

Montreat didn't sound real firm, and Preston thought maybe if Montreat saw how disappointed he was there might be a chance for it. He was right.

"Well, thank you for your time, Mr. Montreat," Preston said. "I guess I'll be getting on home. Sorry to bother you."

"Whoa, now," Franklin said. "I don't want to send you away empty-handed. Come on, let me show you my dogs and we'll go on back to the house and have us some lemonade. It's getting hot out here."

Preston was surprised at how young Montreat was. He'd expected a real ancient, but here was this fellow who scarcely looked fifty, and out in an acre cornfield with no shirt on chopping weeds in this heat! Franklin Montreat carried him over to a batch of ramshackledy outbuildings, small pens and coops, that held chickens, a couple of pigs, a goat and two hounds.

"That's Penny Lee," Montreat said, "and the other's Little Man." The dogs came up to the chicken wire and lapped his fingers. "That's right, easy, now," he said to the dogs.

"They look like hounds," Preston said.

"Hell, they *are* hounds." Montreat laughed. "Black and tans, registered."

"They run deer?"

"No-o-o, boy—I broke em off deer and trash. These are coon dogs. A-number-one coon dogs, too."

"You eat raccoons, Mr. Montreat?"

"Barbecue one every now and again. But mostly not."

"But you hunt them and kill them."

"I didn't say that. If we do kill one we'll skin it and sell the pelt and eat the meat. Usually if the tree's small enough where the dogs have treed, we'll hold the dogs and shake it out and let it run off. Give it a good head start and then have another chase."

Preston shook his head a bit and reached his hand gingerly down to the chicken wire where the dogs were snuffling. "Guess I've just not been around it, being from Knoxville all my life. I don't get it."

"It's to hear the dogs' voices, to hear em giving tongue," Montreat said. "It's for the music, son."

Ivy made up a big batch of lemonade in the kitchen and brought it in two tall green-tint glasses to Franklin and Preston. The living room was wallpapered, improbably, with scenes of a society fox hunt whose hounds and hunters had grown dim with age and late-afternoon sun. Bookshelves along the side walls were full, not of books, but of magazines and old newspapers and scrapbooks. What brass remained on the firedogs was polished, and the hearth was swept clean. Over the mantel was a banjo-style pendulum clock, its glass door painted with a portrait of George Washington and a smaller view of Mount Vernon.

There was not much furniture in the room: a maroon-striped wing chair, a couple of plain ladderback wooden rockers and a big formal dark-wood sofa with scalloped antimacassars in three places along its back. To one side of the mantelpiece was an ornately carved sixty-six-key pump organ with a stack of hymnals on the floor beside. Off to the mantel's other side was a wall full of pictures. Franklin sat in his easy chair while Preston studied the old photographs. Preston had thought he was an expert on Franklin Montreat and the Bumblebees from reading old stories in the Knoxville papers, but he was wrong.

After a few minutes Franklin spoke: "Call yourself a folk song collector, eh?"

"Yes, sir," Preston said.

"I knew some others once."

"Collectors?"

"Yeah. Songcatchers, we called em. Young couple from England by the name of Stokes."

Good Lord, Preston thought, he knew Carter and Melissa Stokes. Gary Owwens had impressed upon Hewitt the importance of the British couple who forty years ago had begun their great work, crisscrossing the great eastern hump of Appalachia, prowling its dark corners, its plateaus, ridges, divides, for the old airs and love songs and ballads that linked their own islands with these wild lands and forgotten peoples.

"Did you know—?" Preston began.

"They said they were looking to write a book," Franklin Montreat said.

A book! After all the years of traipsing unguided along narrow unfamiliar mountainside paths, staring down many times upon ruined buggies and cars in treetops in ravines below, they'd ferried their scores of notebooks of music and lyrics back to England, where they had argued and compared and edited and then published. "It was called *Songs of the South: From Massanutten to Millbank, Georgia*," Preston said.

"Sounds like them," Montreat allowed.

"It won a Pulitzer Prize in 1932," Preston said.

"That may be," Montreat said, "but they never won no prize from me. They ate my grandmother up like a piece of cake, but they won't no more interested in me than a cow is in grazing on rocks. I tried, but they turned me down. Played em some string-band tunes I'd learned off my crystal set, but they said 'No, no, that's *radio music*—that's the last thing we come here for.' Yessir, they had it all divvied up in their heads between new music and old music and I tell you it hurt my pride that the music I wanted to play em somehow didn't count. 'Songcatchers'! I bet you five dollars I caught more songs than they ever did. No, sir, they don't get no prize from me. Music's music, that's all I say."

Preston looked respectful and waited.

"Now, what exactly was it they wanted me to put on this record you talking about?"

Ah, Preston thought, so he will do it. "Oh, I don't know—some stories maybe about what it was like traveling around in the old days, whatever songs you might want to do. Oh, and Gary Owwens said it might be nice to have a little bit of instruction on there, too, about different ways you can tune the banjo, and playing technique."

Montreat sipped his lemonade and tapped his foot on the rug for a minute while Preston Hewitt looked away, back at the pictures on the wall. "Ivy? Come in here a minute, honey." She appeared at the kitchen door with a handkerchief in her hand. "Ivy, you know what this young un aims to do?"

"I got no earthly idea, Franklin."

"He aims to make a record of me and my banjo, talking and singing about when we had the band. Be all right, wouldn't it, if my wife got on there, too? After all, she was in the band."

Preston grinned. "I don't see why not."

Ivy put the handkerchief to her face. "What's your name again, son?"

"Preston Hewitt."

"Well, Preston, I don't know as anybody'd buy a record of us anymore. We don't travel or go play anywhere cept Frank sometimes goes to a gathering somewhere with our daughter. That's who you ought to get on record now."

"Who? Your daughter?"

"That's right," Ivy Montreat said. "She's on the East Tennessee Country Jamboree Saturday evenings after wrassling, Channel Five right there in Knoxville. You ain't seen it? Seems like you would of, it's right in your own backyard."

Preston felt embarrassed and on the spot. How could he tell them he'd never once seen that show, never cared to or even thought about it? Never really even listened to a country-music radio station. Maybe Gary Owwens'd sent the wrong guy. What do I know about country music? he thought.

"That ain't what they're after, Ivy," Franklin said. "Sure, he's seen Bonnie, but—"

Preston had seen her all right. But only in the last few minutes in one of the pictures on the wall. "She's pretty," he said quickly.

"Thank you, son," Franklin Montreat said. "Takes after her mother."

Ivy said, "Oh, Franklin."

"Anyway," Franklin said, "it's one of those folk music groups from up New York wants some recollections from the old days, that's all."

*"New York?"* Ivy frowned. "Just seems like Bonnie or Bumper would make a record that'd sell more copies. They're more in touch, I guess you'd say."

"Bumper's our boy," Franklin explained, "a few years older'n Bonnie. He's going to Nashville soon's he saves him up some money, gon be what you call a sideman, a session man."

"But not Bonnie," Ivy Montreat said. "Knoxville's all right, but I'm not letting her go to Nashville. Not gon to have her following all that for a living."

Franklin Montreat looked up at his wife leaning in the doorway. "Maybe you need to lie down take a nap, Ivy," Franklin said.

She nodded. "Maybe so. Heat's kind of got to me this morning. Good luck with your record, Preston. I'll try and remember your name if you come back again."

"Thank you, ma'am," Preston said. "I'll do whatever you all want to do." Be cooperative, he thought. Be polite and cooperative as hell.

Ivy Montreat left the room.

"You say you got a tape recorder out in your car right now?" Franklin Montreat said. "Well, fetch it on up here and we'll talk a hour or two during the heat of the day, kind of get started here. Then I got to get back to my corn and I got to put some polish on a saddle for my girl fore she comes home from work."

"Bonnie?"

"She's a seckaterry down at the mica works."

"But you said she sang on television."

Franklin Montreat laughed. "That's just on weekends, in Knoxville. You can't make no living singing thirty minutes on TV once a week. Unless you do it in Nashville. Then you might can get rich. Go on, get your machine."

Preston started for the front door, and Franklin stood up out of the easy chair and stretched. He glanced out the front window down at the road. "Lord, Preston—that your automobile down there, that Chevrolet?"

"Yes, sir."

"Good thing my boy Bumper ain't here right now. He'd steal that car setting still."

Preston waited at the door like Franklin Montreat might have more to say to him. He wasn't sure if Montreat was bragging on Bumper or on Preston's car. That's my problem talking to these people, he thought. I'm never sure when you're supposed to laugh.

"Go on, now. Let's get going," Franklin Montreat said.

"Yes, sir."

Through no particular skill of his own, but rather due to his good fortune in having such a winning subject in Franklin Montreat—all of which Preston would freely admit to himself if to no one else—it would turn out to be a fine recording.

There were half a dozen sessions altogether, the last on a Saturday in October. Preston was just packing up the tape recorder when Bonnie and Treat drove back in from Knoxville. They had hurried back to Honey Run from the television show to attend some occasion, and it was the first time their paths had crossed.

"This your record man, Daddy?" Bonnie said when she and Treat got up the hill to the porch.

"Yep. Just finished up. It'll be on the *Hit Parade* next week," Daddy Montreat said. "Right, Preston?"

"Tomorrow evening," Preston said confidently. She's fetching as hell, he thought. Sourwood honey.

"Preston," Daddy Montreat said, "this here's Ivy's and my girl Bonnie and her cousin there Treat McVaine that plays fiddle. Soonzy was his daddy." A shaking of hands. "You going to the stir-off at Cottrell's?"

Treat held his fiddle case up high. "Wouldn't miss it, Uncle Frank."

"Well, now, whyn't you two take this Hewitt boy along and show him something real. He's been cooped up in Knoxville for about a hundred years near's I can tell and nobody's ever took him anywhere."

"Sure," Bonnie said, "if he don't mind walking."

Cottrell's was several miles up Chiselfinger Creek, up a hollow that got so steep near several of the falls that Preston had to grab the roots of trees above him to keep going. There was only one flashlight, Treat's, which worked steady. Preston had had one in his pocket, but the batteries were low. He decided to save it just in case. So Bonnie and Treat, who knew the way and were always some bit ahead of him, had to keep turning around and shining the light so he could keep up. Now he saw what she'd meant by "if he don't mind walking." He could feel blisters forming on his heels.

But it was worth it. Presently they heard a fiddle playing and some singing up the way. When it stopped, Treat got his fiddle out and played out a couple of choruses of the same tune by way of warning the crowd ahead that more was on the way.

"Whose bow is that, Treat?" Bonnie said.

"Lash Carruthers if I'm hearing right," Treat said.

How the hell can they tell? Preston thought.

"I'd a took it for Seth McVaine," Bonnie said.

"Aw, no—come on, honey. Fate ain't gon let his boy play slides that sloppy. Wait and see."

When they got closer to the sounds of the gathering, Treat repeated the practice of following the tune they heard with a brief reprise on his fiddle. A roar came from the distance, and a voice cried out in the moonlit night, "He-e-y, Treat!"

"Well, I'll be," Bonnie said.

Treat cupped his hands and called, "Ha-a-llo, Lash!"
There was another roar from up ahead.

Clouds of steam arose from a great vat over the fire in the
clearing. In the moonlight, which came and went behind the
rolling clouds, Preston could see a couple dozen people, and,
beyond, a house and a barn. There was a little mill powered
by a mule walking in circles, and two people fed stalks of
sorghum cane in between two cogged wheels. Juice ran into
the vat, where it boiled and bubbled, and a crowd was
gathered around dipping cane stalks into the thick, sweet
syrup.

Bonnie and Treat got much greeting. Preston hung back
till Bonnie said who he was, and then he too was welcomed
into the crowd. Treat and Lash played fiddle and they ran
several sets of dances, great-circle ocean's-way dances with
breaking into two couples at a time for the steps. Then there
came a call to play one game of Ollie Oxenfree, and the
crowd, ranging in age from eight to twenty, split apart and
everyone dashed into the woods except Lash and Cottrell
and Cottrell's wife. Preston went back down the hollow
toward where they'd come from, since he didn't know the lay
of the land. The moon disappeared again and the woods got
dark and he dashed for a big beech tree he'd seen. A low
limb slapped him in the face and he tripped on an exposed
root and fell.

His hands were scraped and stinging, but, worse, as he
pulled himself up, he was afraid he'd sprained his foot. He
stood and limped to the trunk of the tree he could barely
make out. He reached into his jacket pocket for the bum
flashlight, which he hit and made come on bright so he could
see what the damage was. Preston barely flashed it on before
he heard her.

"Cut it out fore they see!" Bonnie said.

He flipped it off and stuffed it back in his pocket and
forgot his throbbing foot for the moment. She reached him
and clutched his arm and said, "I didn't know as we'd have a

chance," and before he thought what to say back she put her hand up on the back of his neck and pulled his face down to hers and kissed him and kissed him more as she mumbled, "I love lassy-making time." God, he thought, she's fast. He ran his hand around under her wrap, up under her sweater and tugged her shirt loose so he could feel her back. She was leaning on him, his back against the tree, almost all her weight on him, and he about to slide his hand down into her jeans, when she spoke again.

"I'm sorry, I didn't know Daddy'd send that boy along with us."

Jesus! She thinks I'm her goddamn cousin. Her cousin? Tell her? Stop her? No . . . He leaned on the tree and couldn't believe this was happening to him as she worked to undo his belt buckle and couldn't, and before he knew it she had the flashlight out of his jacket pocket and was shining it to see what she was doing. She said, "When'd you get this belt bu—" and the bum flashlight started to go out. She shone it up just before it clicked out, and there was enough light on his face for her to see it was Preston Hewitt and not Treat McVaine. She gasped in terrified surprise a few times as if she was building up to a scream and Preston clapped his hand over her mouth and she resisted and started to struggle and he hissed at her, "Stop, stop it, Bonnie. I'm not going to hurt you. I thought you wanted to with me, that's all. That's all."

She slapped his hand away from over her mouth and whispered loudly and bitterly, "That's all, your ass. You heard me call his name. You *knew* I was mistook. You was gonna let me go right ahead, I know it." She sighed mightily in the dark.

Preston said, "I'm sorry, Bonnie, guess I got too exci—"

She knocked his head back against the tree, and then she pressed up against him before he recovered and spoke as stern to him as anyone ever had. "Don't you never say nothing about this to nobody or else no telling what kind of story I might have to tell. Now let's just forget about it."

Then, the moon still obscured, she ran off into the dark woods away from him.

For a few minutes he leaned against the tree with his foot throbbing and his loins tight and a headache coming on from that blow. *Get the hell out of Dodge, fool.*

Preston made it back down the hollow as best he could with a sprained foot. He found a stick for a cane and hobbled. He skipped and hopped and tripped on roots and slid down the steep places and fell and picked himself up again and kept going. If I can just get back to the car before they come, he thought. I got everything from Frank Montreat on tape, I don't have to come back—ever. And she can't tell about this any more than I can. It'll blow over—everything does. If I can just get back to the car and get gone before they come . . .

He did.


# JOHNNY REX PACKARD
1959


The albino was a star now.

Police were bound to give him a hard time and newsmen were bound to write him up and women were bound to make his loving a legend. It was "Get in that squad car, you pastyface son of a bitch, or I'll crack your head again . . ." or "MOBILE (API) Dec. 19—Bloodied and bruised following a brawl in Sykes' Tavern over who set fire to the jukebox, roughhousing country singing star Johnny Rex Packard of Tennessee apologized and 'made it right' with Sykes by pulling a 44-caliber pistol from his glove compartment and opening fire on his own Cadillac . . ." or ". . . won't quit talking about that week she spent with him at Muscle Shoals and him buying a hydroplane right there on the spot with cash and riding her all over Wheeler Lake in it and her coming back here and talking how his was bigger'n John Dillinger's ever was."

Enough of that and people got to thinking how he was cruising for a fall and a lot of them not just expecting it but hoping for it. But that it should happen *here*.

Poor Birmingham, for passion will not stay put. Johnny Rex had needs, he said, and when a man got needs . . . He never made a secret of it, but he was country shrewd enough to try and keep quiet as best he could when he was off that stage. But Jesus God, the man would get eat up with the very fires people were paying by the thousands to see burning through him, and sometimes those fires jumped the breaks and there'd be no telling where he'd wind up or what he'd do.

They gave him his one phone call after they booked him, and he tried to reach Phelps Range but it was no good. Phelps was still in Mexico on vacation. Nothing to do but wait till he hears about it, Johnny Rex thought. He'll know what to do.

He paced his stinking eight-by-ten cell till Range finally showed up the next night.

"God, Johnny. It don't get no worse than this."

Johnny Rex nodded and looked down and watched Phelps work his hands, closing his fist and then opening, stretching his fingers, rubbing his greasy fingers into his palms. The cellblock light was sickly and there was a hollow sound to his voice in there. Phelps talked hollow about tired and nervous and knots in his stomach and a long trip and lousy food and the fear that this time at last the Devil in Johnny Rex had set him up and walked out on him. Phelps Range emptied the pockets of his sport coat—he'd brought Johnny Rex packs of Lucky Strikes.

The albino lit one and inhaled the thick blue smoke. He thanked Phelps and offered him one and Phelps Range smoked for the first time in years.

"It was a accident, Phelps."

"What?"

"I mean maybe it was my finger on the trigger, but it was a accident like I said."

"Well, tell me how come it looks so goddamn bad, then?" Phelps snapped at him, and the albino's eyes filled with tears and his torso shook like he was having a hard time drawing a breath. "I'm sorry, Johnny Rex." In five years of music and work and business and money Phelps had never had cause to speak to him so rough and bleak and hopeless. He reached around and gripped Johnny Rex by the back of the neck and pulled the singer's head to his shoulder. "I'm sorry." Phelps smoked another Lucky while Johnny Rex wept.

After a bit Phelps stood and walked to the barred door and called to the guard. "Johnny Rex," he said, "I'm hiring the same fellow to defend you that got them Little Rock counterfeiters off. His name's Vance Garland. I'm gonna see him tonight and I expect he'll be around to talk to you tomorrow."

"He's good?"

"The best."

"Phelps? "

The guard came.

"Yeah?"

"Phelps, listen. Before you go, tell me how them charges read. I was so damn confused and hurting. One of em kneed me in the gut when they was pulling me out of the squad car. I hadn't talked to nobody."

"Johnny, tell the lawyer everything you can think of, everything you can remember, when he comes." Phelps Range glanced at the guard and drew a deep breath. "They're gon try and crucify you, son. They're gon make a example of you to get back at you and at ever hick and colored boy that's wandered into Nashville or Memphis and made more money than the good people of Birmingham approve of. You'll be guilty in the churches and the women's clubs of too much money and wild-ass living before you even get close to court, accident or not."

"But the charges, Phelps. What does it say?"

"It's bad, Johnny. First-degree murder. And just for good measure, miscegenation."

"Miscege — what the hell does *that* mean?"

Phelps Range motioned the guard to unlock the cell door and let him out. "You don't know?"

Johnny Rex shook his head.

"It means Karintha."

"This shit true?" Johnny Rex waved the newspaper through the bars at the guard who had smuggled it in. It was the first he'd heard about the vigil those girls had been keeping outside the Birmingham jail since the story of the shooting broke yesterday morning.

"They're down there all right," the skinny guard said. "I used to date one of em's older sister. Matter of fact, took her out to see you play one time." The guard ambled over and stopped before Johnny Rex's cell just out of reach.

Johnny Rex read the paper through the bars in the dim morning jail light. Ever damn one of em's under eighteen, he thought. Down at the bottom of the story it listed some of their names and said where they came from other than Birmingham. Their homes were towns that ringed the city: Dolomite and Irondale and Bessemer. Johnny Rex had a vision of himself being cast down into the mines that he imagined were in these places with ore and steel names. They would cast him down into the dark pits naked and with a pick. Evil laughter would cascade down at him from up above where judges and tormentors gathered to await his death. The pick would be too heavy, and yet each day they would replace it with yet a heavier pick till he would groan and collapse crushed beneath its weight. And he couldn't get the breath to sing one last line. He couldn't get the breath to—

"It was out at a tobacco warehouse toward Columbiana," the guard said.

"What?" Johnny Rex gasped. I'm afflicted, the albino thought. I can't think straight.

"Nemmine. I'll tell you later. I got to get back to work."

The guard walked away, calling back, "Hey, there's more stories about you inside."

What else could there be after the headlines and photographs of himself on page one? He flipped the paper open. Another whole story was called simply "His Women" and there were smaller pictures of Violet Leadon and Karintha de Graffenreid running with it. Where had they taken Karintha? No one had told him. Or Violet? Poor Violet.

A hot surge from his stomach came up the back of his throat as nausea and delirium advanced on him. He slipped down against the cell toilet and retched, then he pulled the pillow down from his cot onto the floor with him. He felt weak.

It was four years now since "Hell Power" came out and he'd got the letter from Violet. She'd come into some money and a eighty-five-acre dairy farm some miles northeast of Memphis—one of her old friends from her Hotel Bed Forrest days had left it all to her out of the blue, and though his family was contesting, her lawyer said she was in the clear. Violet said she'd got shed of Sunny Wilbur and was intending to come back to Memphis and start a permanent mission of her own on the farm, a retreat where worshipers from all faiths could come and pray together. She had heard his record and was proud of him, of course, but deeply disturbed about his message. She wanted to meet with him at length, alone, to talk about his soul. She would need his help with the dairy-farm mission.

Jesus God, he thought. Wilbur's got to her or something. This ain't Violet. It was a lot to think about all at once. Johnny Rex read Violet's letter in the studio office and looked up and shook his head goddamn as Phelps came back from the engineer's booth. How the hell do you turn a dairy into a mission? they both wondered.

"I'd sell the damn thing if it was me," Phelps said.

Johnny Rex nodded and only half paid attention. He thought of Violet with the snakes and the tent, then of Violet working for Sunny Wilbur all scrubbed and dolled up. He thought of necking with her in the bus-station photo booth and felt that little turn in his gut. She's after me, he thought, but not that way. It hadn't been that way since she'd let Wilbur Parham convert her or heal her or whatever the hell you'd call it he'd done to make her quit. She never said a damn thing about why she was giving it up for who knows how long right in the smackdab middle of her prime—and Johnny Rex knew it won't just him she was stopping with, cause she had the hungry eye. But she just went right on and suffered it. Some hold Wilbur had over her.

"What about this test pressing?" Phelps Range was saying, waving a lacquered disc before him to bring him back. "Want to give it a spin?"

Johnny Rex squinted tight and then opened his eyes wide and stretched his mouth. "Yeah, yeah, sure, I was just thinking." They wandered down the hall into the studio, where Skibo had rolled out the portable turntable and was fiddling with the board and already grinning because he'd given it a listen with Phelps and knew it was a killer. Johnny Rex smiled a half-cracked smile and nodded and listened. The song started out over the big speakers:

> *Slipping in the back door*
> *Of a big house on Bourbon Street . . .*

He wondered why this new Violet had never said anything to him when she knew damn well he was slipping off after Sunny Wilbur's extravaganzas. Hell, she knew about Karintha from way back. But then he guessed it was because he'd never gotten on her about her farmer boys. *We're just two gritty lowdown sinning—*

Phelps brought him back as the song was over. "Twenty-five thousand advance orders in Texas *alone*."

"I got to get some air, Phelps. I'll listen again in a while. This thing about Violet." He turned and left abruptly.

Outside in the street men from the warehouses were

eating sandwiches leaning against trucks, against the brick walls. They looked grimy and beaten as they emerged, but they got some life back in them at their lunch break. The white men stood in clusters and talked about whether it was better to hunt squirrels with a rifle and a dog or with a shotgun and no dog. Sideways and sometimes bitterly they mentioned to each other their lusts. The black men clustered, too, and tossed coins gambling on closest to the wall, joshing each other about poonbread and poontang and this girl or that. They were loud.

Johnny Rex scuffled down the steamy Memphis work street wondering what it was Violet wanted to work on him. Whatever it is, it won't work, he thought. Karintha hiding away from me all ascared of the fuss and money and good luck I'm having and Violet coming back inheriting a damn farm but all bejesus and not putting out. Hell, I got to get a band together and go out touring concerts and all this fall and get me more pussy than Frank Sinatra and make some real money. I can't be messing with these crazy women either of em.

There was so much dust caught in the humid air the sky was gone white. Johnny Rex was getting a headache. He stretched his mouth and pressed his forefingers to the sides of his head. He ducked into an alley and leaned against the bricks. The voices of crapshooters down at the alley's end echoed up toward him. He pulled the red ribbony strip loose from the package with the red ball inside the green and black circles and tossed the cellophane away. He smoked and calmed himself.

I'll talk to her sure, he thought, but I ain't going looking for her. Something weird about that letter. Dairy-farm missionary, hell. Wonder if it's gon be like a church. If that's it, she wants to hire me again for music. But she must of heard my record by now, said she had. I'm a rockabilly honky-tonker now—I ain't going back to gospel shouting. No money in it, for one thing. Even old Violet'll understand that. Maybe we could just be friends or talk to each other on the phone when I'm in town. In fact, he was flat-out afraid of her return. She'd got religion and abstinence, but each time he assured himself that that distance between them would keep them from starting up again, he'd remember the feel of her breasts that last time. In the bus station, Christ Lord, we could have, right there and then, he thought. And he'd feel that turn in his stomach and he would be flooded with all the sensate recollections of all the pleasures and comforts of her rocking hips. Goddammit, she can't just do me any old way, not now. I don't know what kind of scheming plan she's got for me, but whatever it is, it won't work.

But it was the age-old plan and he was wrong as all men are wrong, for it did.

"Well, why don't you start by telling me about it?"

The lawyer sat at the foot of the cellblock bunk in his shirtsleeves and loosened his tie. Johnny Rex lay propped up in the bunk. There was a cool moist sweat around his temples and below his eyes like that he got when he ate apples. The lawyer even with the coat of his blue serge suit off sweated heavily, curling out his lower lip and mopping his face like a field hand. Vance Garland had a head that seemed a little big for his body. Johnny Rex thought he had about him the look of a fast-talker con man. But Phelps wouldn't screw up at a time like this . . .

"Say?" Garland prodded him.

It seemed like forever ago, though it was only four years.

Violet and he were walking around on the farm she'd come into. It was sometime in Indian summer, so the day had the warm balminess of the dying season about it as well as the hint as evening came along of the cool and crispness of autumn. Violet was already living on the place in what she called the big house. It was nothing more than a common two-story frame farmhouse to which had been added a kitchen and pantry out back and four foolish columns in front.

He found the whole thing hard to swallow. Here they hadn't seen each other in more than a year and she was rattling on about dairying and Jesus and poets who lived off on a farm in New England a hundred years ago. And she'd only give him a little pecklike kiss on his cheek and squeezed his hand and give him a look full of meaning only he wasn't sure what it meant.

Has she lost her damn mind? he thought. Or forgot where she come from or what we been through together?

At the barn the stout, bearded manager was making ready for that afternoon's milking. At Violet's request he rattled off a line of talk about holding tanks and performance goals, and Johnny Rex could tell from the dull flat speech that he wasn't from anywhere around Tennessee. He spoke proudly about the farm's Ayrshires, and Johnny Rex let his mind drift, until the farmer asked, "And what do you do in the vineyards of the Lord, Mr. Packard?"

It was too much. He was either putting Johnny Rex on or hadn't heard of him, and either way it was too much. "I'm a liquor drinker and a niggerlover and I play honkytonk piano for a living is what I do for the Lord." Johnny Rex kicked once at the ground and with an ugly kind of leering look gave Violet a nod with his head for her to follow him. He stalked off toward a bunch of willow trees down by the branch.

Son of a bitch that don't know who I am.

When she caught up to him he was crouching on a big stretch of moss, cracking twigs and throwing them against the rocks in the creek. "Now, what'd you go talking to him that way for?" she said.

"You answer me first. What'd you get me out here for? I ain't no farmer and you know it. Or maybe you don't now that Jesus is running around your brain so bad. For God's sake, Violet, we ain't got much to do with each other anymore and it looks to me like it oughta stay that way."

"You dumb ox," she said, and slapped him with such a wallop it knocked him flat over. He was stunned. She knelt down by him and touched his forehead and ran her fingers lightly along in his hair and spoke quickly and directly like she'd thought about what she was saying before she ever said it. Like the old Violet.

"You got too much wild about you, Johnny Rex, so you got to take it from me. You and me always used to get together real easy in the flesh, but what we got to do now is get you to let me help you get your mind and soul right"—she took a breath and reached her right hand down and started in undoing his breeches and talking yet—"and if it takes the flesh to heal the soul, then God planned it thataway and I'm doing His work."

He reached a hand up to pull her face down to his, but she pushed his head back down against the moss like she meant it to stay there. "Not yet," she said, sliding her head down his chest and easing him out of his pants, and then, from the bidding of her lips and her tongue and her fingertips, he felt his eyes roll back in his head and he lost his rage in her.

When they came out of the willow grove a couple hours later, she had entranced him into taking just the deal she wanted him to: half the farm and mission operation she was setting up would be his, provided he'd help finance it with his concert earnings and record royalties. He would swear off drinking hard liquor around her and sleeping with other women anywhere. Incredibly, he agreed. The whole arrangement would remain secret until she determined it was the right time for people to know. And there was one other thing.

With all the papers in order, since she had arranged it, and with only the dairyman and his colored help there to witness, that day as the sun set beyond Memphis into Arkansas, Johnny Rex Packard and Violet Leadon were married on the front porch of what passed for the big house of the old dairy, newly renamed Trinity Farm.

Vance Garland brushed back his hair and ran his tongue along the inside of his teeth. Perhaps there is justice for Johnny Rex Packard, he thought, but it might not be till the other side of the great divide. The homicide laws in this case seem to be what the man and woman in the Birmingham streets say they are and that is, simply, whatever is necessary to conform with the singer's guilt.

"You would say, then, that you married Violet Leadon impulsively?" Garland asked.

Johnny Rex popped his hands together and cursed. "Goddammit, Lawyer, say it so I can understand what you're gettin at. You said, 'Tell it' and I told it, didn't I?"

The cornered beast, the caged bird. "I'm sorry," Garland said. "I mean on the spot, on the spur of the moment."

"Well, yeah. But it won't like we didn't *know* each other." He laughed shallowly. "It was just the way it turned out. It was kind of a crazy time."

"All right. Let me ask you another. How much did she know about you and Karintha de Graffenreid?"

"You kidding? All about it, from way back."

"But you swore off other women when you and Violet married?"

"Well, what was I supposed to do, out on the road half the time and the other half when I'd get back to the farm she'd be gone off running her crusades? Me paying a lot of the bills for that damned place and what was I getting out of it?"

"But when you hired Karintha and her brother—"

"Eck."

"—Eck, to join your band that fall, you didn't think that was like waving a red flag in front of Violet?"

"Maybe."

"Maybe? Johnny Rex, I've already got back in my office a copy of the *Memphis Truth-Sabre* of November twenty-second, 1958, with a photograph of Sister Violet Leadon, leading Southern evangelist, as she denounces her husband Johnny Rex Packard for his vile, mongrel music, disclaims any responsibility for his actions during his current tour, and in fact states she is considering divorce."

Johnny Rex said, "We made up. It's like with a lot of people, fight and fuck, fuck and fight. And if you're working for me, why're you badgering me so goddamn bad?"

The world just looks different to him, Vance Garland thought. He seems to have no idea how serious it is. He must think his self-righteous fury is somehow going to prove for him it was an accident. "I am trying to discover, my young friend, some way to get a jury of nine white men and three white women or some mix thereabouts on the side of a hard-living country-music singer who has for ten years, apparently, alternated between the beds of a popular white evangelist and an unknown black storemistress most recently employed as a member of the singer's chorus. And to get that jury *not* to believe that this same singer, widely known as 'Wild Man,' who with little more than a moment's notice married the white woman just when she'd come into something of a country estate, when she discovers him in a hotel love nest with his black concubine, could turn on his wife of four years and murder her."

*"It wasn't that way!"* Johnny Rex, who'd been leaning over against the opposite wall of the cell, lunged at lawyer Garland, his hands at Garland's throat.

"Jesus! Guard, *guard!*" Vance Garland's head cracked against the wall.

"Not that way, wasn't, not, wasn't like that, I'm tellin you . . ." Johnny Rex screamed as he pressed the lawyer down on the cot, not even hearing the sound of the guard's key ring against the metal of the door lock or the guard himself shouting at him, till the door swung open, banging back around against the bars, and the guard's billy cracked into the albino's roaring pounding skull and he went down.

The guard stood slack-jawed over the crumpled singer and listened to the lawyer draw shallow breaths past a rattle, a sucking gurgle in his throat. Vance Garland's face was a violent red, and his eyes were all flushed and tearing copiously. He said haltingly as best he could, "Don't you . . . dare . . . tell . . . a soul."

The guard looked amazed. "I *got* to. I got to report something like this."

Garland struggled to breathe and grasped at his pocket,

tugged at his wallet and pulled out a twenty-dollar bill and thrust it at the guard. "I'm filing . . . no . . . complaints."

The guard pocketed the twenty and escorted the lawyer out of the dim green corridor of the jail. Vance Garland got his breathing back and said again before putting his coat on and heading out into the street where the band of girls kept their vigil for Johnny Rex, "Not a word." The guard nodded.

Must have gone straight to the goddamn phone, Vance Garland thought later. The son of a bitch. There it was in that afternoon's paper:

WILD MAN' PACKARD ASSAULTS
OWN LAWYER IN CELL
Guard's Story; Trial Date Set

Vance Garland stood furiously and read the story, looking up and watching the weak-minded forty-year-old newsboy Jordie who delivered in his building walk away. Garland called his wife, Emmy, and told her he wanted them to get away, for her to pack some things, that he'd be home for her in an hour. If he hurried he could beat the traffic and they'd be at the lake before seven. Garland left his suite on the fourth floor of the Alabama Building and went to a store where records were sold. A man helped him. "I want to buy a Johnny Rex Packard recording," Vance Garland said.

The man raised his eyebrows. "You and half of Birmingham," he said. "They might be a couple left, but none of his latest, you know. Folks want the last ones, the ones that've got that colored gal on there, too." He pointed the lawyer toward the record bins.

Johnny Rex had his own individual bin, "Packard," after the *P*s in general. There were only a handful of long-playing records in the section, a Moon Records combination of Johnny Rex's big successes: " 'Hell Power' and Other Hits." The singer in the cover photograph was seated at a piano with his left elbow leaned on the music rack and his head cocked against his left hand. He wore a gold-lamé tuxedo coat and an open, even optimistic expression. His eyes were heavily made up.

"Now, that's one of your early 1958 releases," the man said. "And he's a damn sight more country there than he's been since he's got the niggers involved. But you know it really *is* the records he made with that mongrel band that people's bought: we must of sold four, five dozen the day after the killing, and we got easy a hundred on the waiting list. It's like that all over town. Damnedest thing. You want to get on the waiting list?"

Vance Garland shook his head and pulled his wallet out. "No. This will do."

The man made change. "Ain't it amazing, a fellow with all his money just going and screwing up his life so damn bad?"

The lawyer slammed out the door. God, what a city. He drove his Buick eight to a package store and bought a bottle of Jack Black. His wife was ready at home with a suitcase and two bags of groceries. By then she had seen the afternoon papers.

When they arrived at the lake, Emmy set about making dinner, and Garland poured a stiff bourbon over ice. He put his new Johnny Rex LP on the small Motorola.

"Vance!" his wife said, startled, when she heard it. "What're you doing playing that music?"

"It's my client."

"That's *him*? Horrid man." She marched out of the kitchen and over toward the record player. "After what he did to you—"

"It's all right, it's all right," he said. "I want to hear him."

She sulked through dinner as they listened to Johnny Rex pound away. Finally, when Garland was in a faraway state, she slipped away from the table and turned it off. She served caffeineless coffee laced with Kahlua and they opened the sliding door out to the deck and listened to the crickets. His mind drifted, and the next thing he knew they were lying in bed in the dark and silence. He thought aloud:

"There are probably only three people who believe it really was an accident: Phelps Range, the black girl, and me. He's violent as hell, but I don't think he's a murderer."

"Vance," she said, "I want you to refer this case to someone else, get it out of your firm. John Rather, or Gibb Smythe, what about one of them?"

He exhaled. "No. This case is mine."

"Vance, he tried to *strangle* you today. He tried to *kill* you."

"He just wanted me to shut up. I do believe he loves both those women, and now they're lost to him. I've never had a case quite like this."

"And him sleeping with a colored girl, uuhhhh," she said, revulsed. "You wouldn't ever, would you, Vance, ever?"

"Emmy, Emmy." He kissed her on the forehead and reached beneath the cover and rubbed her soft belly. The cry of a heron came forth from the lake.

Vance Garland got out of bed and pulled on a robe. He went to the kitchen, piled a half-dozen or more ice cubes into an old jelly jar and splashed the liquor over the ice liberally. He closed the door to the bedroom so she wouldn't be bothered by the light and the record player, which he turned on but lower than before. He listened and thought. The ice in his drink sizzled quietly and he got up and replenished it. He was down to "Liège Belgium 1905" in the bottle of bourbon by now. The lawyer drank deeply and well and felt bonds between himself and the powerful caged man who'd attacked him twelve hours before.

He felt the power to defend rising in him.

Once the trial started, Johnny Rex sat sullenly, hands flat on the defense table in front of him. He wore no makeup. Under the fluorescent lights of the Birmingham courtroom the albino looked ashen and unreal. Each day during the trial as he left the courtroom he was showered with lights of the newsreel film boys and the popping and flashing of the press photographers' cameras. Phelps brought Johnny Rex pictures that appeared in the newspapers, and Johnny Rex had to agree that the record man was right: it looked like Johnny Rex Packard, young and wild and vibrant country rockabilly performer, was subdued and aged by the shooting incident and incarceration, that he was old and beaten. One other impression that Phelps said Johnny Rex's ashen albino appearance gave:

That he was guilty.

But all Johnny Rex would say was, "I told you, Phelps, and I'll tell the court, the papers, anybody—it was a accident."

State's Evidence A was the bullet that passed through Violet Leadon Packard's brain, and State's B was the pistol that fired it. State's C was a sales ticket:

Wave Schelling's Gunshop, Memphis, Tennessee. July 5, 1957. One Iver-Johnson owlhead pistol, #1517, w/new firing pin. $95.00. Ten boxes .32 caliber cartridges @ $4.00. Total $135.00. Sold to: J. R. Packard, Trinity Farm, RFD 1, Millington, Tennessee.

There was no question whose gun it was killed her.

"Your witness," the prosecutor said after his first round of questioning Karintha.

"Didn't seem so bad," Johnny Rex whispered to Vance Garland. "All's he got from her was how long I'd been knowing her and about how they once worked in the tent revival but got fired when Violet took me and went to work for Sunny Wilbur."

"He's not finished, Johnny."

"Your witness."

"Mr. Garland?"

Vance Garland approached Karintha. She sat withdrawn into the witness box like a widow threatened by a bank. The women's jail had allowed her a plain shift, a dark dress of such deep maroon it was nearly brown.

"Miss de Graffenreid, how long had you and your brother

been working for Johnny Rex Packard in Mr. Packard's touring concert band?"

"Since fall of 1958."

"A year. Would you say it was a common thing for Johnny Rex to come in person to wherever you and your brother were staying to talk about a new song or something to do with the show?"

"I reckon so."

"You reckon? Would you say yes or no?"

"Yes."

"And you testified earlier that when Johnny Rex Packard came to your hotel room that night before the shooting, that all he was carrying was some music—do you recall telling the court that?"

"I said it was all I could *see* he had."

"Yes. Now, when Mrs. Packard knocked on the hotel room door that night, did Mr. Packard make any attempt to hide or get out that front window onto the fire escape, anything like that?"

"No."

"He didn't try to hide. What *did* he do?"

"Johnny Rex he got right up and opened the door and it was her and he said, 'Hello, Vi,' and she came right in."

*If there was a piano here,* Johnny Rex thought, *I could explain it all that way. It would all be in the music: the country I seen, the women I had, the things I heard people say out of meanness and desperation, wild mean things men say to women or women to men, things that hit the people they're saying em to like a gutful of buckshot . . .*

Violet was wearing a flowered print dress with big pearl buttons and the top one undone so it opened and showed a hint of that deep chest of hers. She had her hand tight on a little purse, though she usually never carried one. She seemed to look beyond him as he opened the door, to look across the room at Karintha lying back in the bed, the sheet pulled up and just her head and her brown burnished shoulders showing.

"Hello, Vi." He stepped back as she shifted that harsh crazed glare onto him and came slowly into the room. The door swung back on a badly hung hinge but didn't close all the way.

"I'm sick of this," she said. "I've had enough. I'm sick of it," and Johnny Rex said, "Violet? Violet?" both of them speaking at once, and Karintha from the bed didn't say a word but already started to whimper. And then they gripped each other like they were grabbing at each other's belt, but Karintha couldn't really see because Johnny Rex's back was to her and Violet was right beyond him. They were grappling about their wrists and hands because Violet must have unzipped that little bag and he must have seen what she had inside, and he started saying, "No! Violet, no, *no!*" and they grabbed and shook at each other some more, harder now, and that was all there was to it, just a few seconds, that was all.

The gun sounded like a bomb going off in the room.

Violet fell back against the nearly shut door and slammed it and slid to a heap on the floor. She stared straight up at Johnny Rex. The little hole was near the top of her cheek just below her eye. Blood pumped from another hole in the back of her head and pooled on the floorboards. The pistol had fallen away beside her.

"Jesus blessed God!" Johnny Rex said, looking around at Karintha, who was moaning, choking in the bed. He knelt and put his right hand around back of Violet's head but jerked back when he felt the thick warm blood. He gasped as he looked at his hand. It was thick on the back of his hand and was lightly in the hairs of the first joints of his fingers like paint that has been brushed against. He grasped the doorknob but couldn't turn it because the blood from his hand greased it. He yanked a handkerchief from the pocket of his sport coat thrown over a chair and turned the knob and opened the door, shifting Violet to the side as he pulled it open. There was already a knot of people in the hall.

"There's been a accident," he cried. "Somebody find a phone and get a ambulance."

It was a second before anybody moved. They were all Negroes. It was a Negro hotel. A white man waving his blood-covered right hand was ordering them to get involved in trouble. There might just be one telephone in the whole place. At last a woman in the back of the throng said the word "Law" and raced off toward the stairs. An ancient wizened black man said, "Is they hurt bad?" Johnny Rex shook his head no and retreated back in the room.

When the Birmingham police arrived a few minutes later, they found Violet slumped on the floor staring up, bleeding, Johnny Rex in a trance, Karintha sobbing. The ancient black man poked his head around the door behind the two policemen, saying, "He say they won't hurt bad but I knowed they was. I knowed, cause they was just too much blood on his hands."

Violet was already dead.

*If there was just a piano I could explain. I could roll out the big chords and shout it to you how far back this thing goes and how mixed around it all got. You know me. You know my voice. I'd sing it out straight for you people to understand. Karintha, she can't tell it. Violet, she should of never got to messing with that gun of mine. If I just had a piano, I'd fill this courtroom with the truth.*

Prosecutor Wilson in his redirect asked Karintha only four questions.

"Under solemn oath, Miss de Graffenreid, can you swear that this pistol did *not* get into your hotel room on the person of the defendant Johnny Rex Packard?"

"No."

"During the struggle between Mr. and Mrs. Packard, when your view was blocked because Mr. Packard's back was to you, can you swear that Mr. Packard did *not* produce the pistol and cause it to be fired?"

"No."

"You could not. Miss de Graffenreid, had you at any time

during the past ever engaged in sexual relations with Johnny Rex Packard?"

This was what Birmingham had come for, to savor, to brood over and condemn.

"Objection," said the defense. "This is irrelevant, your honor."

"Overruled."

"Yes," Karintha said. "I had."

*Why,* he thought, *is she telling the real, whole truth just like they ask you for when they put you up there?* But what did Johnny Rex know of the depths of a woman's hurt? She had felt for him for years, from the time he was old enough for her to see a man she could love in his strange young eyes. *If I could just sing to them, play em on the piano what I know and feel, they'd see how it was, how it couldn't be any other way.*

"And had you, Miss de Graffenreid, engaged in sexual relations with Johnny Rex Packard earlier that very evening in the very room where Violet Leadon died?"

Objection. Objection overruled.

Karintha lifted her chin. She'd been there for Johnny Rex all the time, right back to the beginning, and nothing was so right as telling now that it was Violet who was intruding on *them,* her and Johnny Rex, and not the other way around.

"Yes," Karintha said. "I had."

There the state of Alabama rested its case.

The Birmingham jury in only an hour and a half the next morning found Johnny Rex Packard guilty as charged.

The State Appeals Court would find no error in the Packard case and would deny Vance Garland either a mistrial or a new trial with change of venue on account of prejudicial pretrial publicity in the superheated atmosphere in Birmingham.

Johnny Rex Packard, reviled wife-killer, would be packed off to Caldonia Prison in southern Alabama, where he would sit awaiting execution, death in the chair.

They could of let me have some sunglasses for the ride, bright as it is, Johnny Rex thought. You get down here and

even if it is November the leaves ain't hardly turned. Hand-
cuffing me to Garland, and the sheriff of Jefferson County
setting there with his gun drawn in case me and Garland do
what? Break out here in the middle of no goddamn where
with the car doing eighty?

Vance Garland said, "It's hard on him, Sheriff, on account
of he's so fair."

"I *said* we'd fix him up, Lawyer, but there's only going to be
one stop made between Birmingham and Caldonia and I say
when and where it is, clear?"

"Very."

"All right, then. Enjoy the scenery."

Cotton fields flew by, picked over and stubbly. It was a blue
late-fall morning that got hazy as the day drew on. There was
a mix of dust and smoke in the air, dust from the tractors
turning under the stubble and smoke from control-burning
of the underbrush in some of the woodlands they passed.
From a cut cornfield where the farmer had turned out his
hogs, a flock of redwing blackbirds lifted up and flew all atilt,
wings catching the sun, across the white concrete road.

Johnny Rex had been surprised to see his lawyer show up
at the city jail to ride with him and the county police all the
way, a hundred twenty miles south to Caldonia. By now he
knew Garland well enough to realize Garland's wife would of
given him pluperfect hell about it, about how bad it'd look
when the newsphotos ran with Johnny Rex and Garland
handcuffed together coming out of the jail that morning.
But the albino was grateful for the lawyer's having stuck with
him after how all he'd been to Garland.

The sheriff spoke to the deputy. "It'll be a store up there
on the right at a Y after that stand of pines."

Goddamn, Johnny Rex thought, it's about time.

The cruiser pulled up at the station with the high-peaked
roof, an Esso place, and the car made clicking sounds as it
rolled slowly over the countless flattened bottlecaps that
served for paving for the station's drive.

"Go get him some shades," the sheriff said to the deputy.

"Lawyer, you pay. This ain't a state expense." Garland forked over some cash. When the deputy reemerged from the station with the glasses, a knot of men followed.

"I done told em to get back away, Sheriff, but they'd got to see who it is."

The sheriff rolled down his window and cussed the men. "Get on back, you men, all of you. I got a prisoner here's dangerous."

The deputy was having trouble getting the car started. The men came closer, slowly and not threatening, just curious. They leaned down, craning their necks, squinting in the white midday November light. The lawyer in the back seat helped the prisoner get the yellow wraparound sunglasses on.

"Go on back inside," the sheriff said again. He ordered the deputy, "Hit it, Norris."

"It's flooded," Norris said.

"Goddammit."

One of the men moved around to the deputy's side of the car and peered in close and saw. "It's that Packard boy!"

"Niggerlover."

Johnny Rex heard it. He looked at the gaptooth through his sleek new glasses and nodded without expression. The men from the station backed off some as the cruiser started with a roar. Johnny Rex knew these men, knew thousands like them, for they were the body and soul of it when he and Violet had run the tent revival all over: crackers come in from the flatwoods and hill country to get a look at the healer woman working them snakes. The cruiser spun out over the bottlecaps.

Johnny Rex woke up at the Caldonia Prison gate.

After they checked him in, Vance Garland spoke to him one last time through the rigid wire that made it seem like they were on opposite sides of a henhouse fence. He handed him a pack of Luckies and told him it was one of the hardest things he'd ever had to do, to tell him this.

"Phelps left a message and I called. Karintha got on a boat bound upriver this morning, and someone said she had a suitcase that was too heavy for her, so he helped her."

*The roar echoed at him from somewhere away off, but he pulled hard on the cigaret and pushed the flat tops of his clenched fists as hard as he could against his temples.*

"When he saw her again, she had the suitcase tied tight to her wrist, and she was outside the railing."

*Inside his head it was like a thick warm breeze coming off a summer field late in the day, a breeze weighted with tobacco scent. It was blowing over him and Karintha and all the boats out on the Mississippi that were sailing and steaming off into the boiling sunset, off the western edge of the world.*

"She was shaking her head crying and pushed herself off from the railing. He couldn't hold her."

*Johnny Rex felt a power in him as he stood up on the bluff and led the singing. He could hear the cannons firing trying to make the body rise. The singers were tiring, weakening, but he kept them going. If they kept at it they could catch her, bring her back before she slipped away over the edge beyond the Mississippi.*

*He heard his own piano playing fiercely away somewhere, and it gave him the strength to revive the chorus there on the bluff. They were firing the cannons more now, and clouds of black powder mingled with the tobacco smoke. Someone was leading him—to rest, he thought—but the singers stayed in place. He kept looking back at them over his shoulder, hoping madly they could keep it up. Then he heard the roaring again, the roaring of a fierce wind bearing down on him, snatching him away and casting him westerly off the bluff, far out into the Mississippi, out to its spilling edge side. And then he knew she was gone, but with the current ripping westward like it was, mercifully, he would join her soon.*

# BONNIE MONTREAT
## 1955–1959

When Bonnie and Treat became lovers, he had already quit school and she was in her ninth and last year at the Log School in Honey Run, last because the Log School was on the verge of closing down. The next year Bonnie and her schoolmates would all be bused down the long valley to the new county consolidated school built in the overnight town of Indian Point.

Indian Point was a great sandbar and floodplain at the confluence of the Tammabowee and the Tennessee, a broad gently sloping flat that built up year by year as the Tammabowee dropped its sediment as it slowed to meet the Tennessee. It had gradually become several square miles of willows and water maples and cottonwoods that shed their white puffs in the spring. There was a railroad trestle bridge crossing the Tammabowee there, as well as a siding, and right after the Second World War a silver truss automobile bridge got built.

Then, in 1949, the Southtimco outfit which had been working the forests of the Tammabowee country for decades suddenly sold its entire operation, its timberlands and deeds, to the Triumph Paper Corporation. Triumph spent the next three years constructing a massive industrial complex at Indian Point, one of the largest pulp and paper mills anywhere in the South. In March of '52 they cut the ribbon and opened the doors and the great clouds of sulfurous smoke started belching from the tall stacks. The timber still came out of the hills, but it no longer went to the planing and saw mills in Honey Run. Instead it was chipped by a massive grinder and rushed straight down the valley eighteen miles to the waiting maw of Triumph Paper. Indian Point, as a town, went from zero to sixty in nothing flat.

So Bonnie Montreat went to high school three years in a building the county slapped up out of brick and steel and aluminum, a building that could of been anywhere, in Michigan or California or on an airbase overseas. There were not quite a hundred students in her class, many of whom were, like her, children of the hills and farms of the nearer reaches of the Tennessee Valley; but equally many were the children of city-dwellers who had come in to manage and supervise the vast Triumph paperworks. They dressed and talked different and listened to different music on the radio. And after Bonnie helped put together and perform the first of several East Tennessee pageants that her school sponsored, she knew that her crowd was thought of by the others as country and hillbilly.

But she didn't care, because she had Treat, a secret that was the source of all her satisfaction and her charm.

She was fresh and pretty and poised, and her musical gifts were obvious. She was leader of the soprano section of the high school's small chorus, which regularly presented programs of folk and popular patriotic songs; she was applauded as soloist time and again. But she and her up-the-valley family didn't have the money which dressed and decorated the daughters of the pulp mill managers, and she was invited neither to be a cheerleader nor to join a social club, the Indian Point Cotillion, which a dozen of those girls began. These were slights that Bonnie Montreat scarcely noticed.

The boys sought her company because of her unadorned good looks and her easy manner and because of the blithe unaffected way she swung her hips as she walked down the halls. But she turned them away one and all, never going out except on the activity bus to a football game or with the chorus. Her datelessness passed fairly unremarked that first year, but during her junior and senior years when more and more of her suitors got access to automobiles, which they must of thought would get them access to her, she heard from her faster girlfriends just what the boys were saying of her: that she was cold as ice, frigid, that she don't put out. She'd been nicknamed Stonewall. During her senior year, she was pretty much left alone by the boys who had found her such poor hunting.

Sometimes, but not enough that anybody had noticed, Bonnie would miss her bus up the valley and study in the library after school. Then she'd walk a half mile from the school grounds to the Triumph company canteen. Her copper curls flounced all over the brown fleece collar of a goatskin flight jacket Bumper had given her that she wore as her winter coat October through April. She'd meet Treat when he got off his shift at the mill, and he'd drive her home. Some of his fellows from the plant showed interest in his half-first-cousin, but Treat put them off, saying he was looking out for her while her brother was off in the Army. One guy whose wisecrack back that he was probably looking into her too got his nose broke.

Oftentimes Bonnie and Treat would slip off separate ways and meet and love at the old barn at the Montreat homestead where they kept an old plaid wool blanket stashed under the hay in the loft. Many Friday nights she sat in, singing and strumming guitar along with Daddy on banjo and Treat on his daddy's fiddle and the others who came into Carson's Pure Oil wearing denim coveralls and dusty mashed-in fedora hats and carrying battered instrument cases. These nights were special to her, because she and Treat had a sweet secret and a love they shared as they played music together. Old Carson always kept a hot pot of beans and fat meat set up on the kerosene space heater that had replaced the potbelly woodstove, and during the breaks in the playing the men would laugh and speak familiarly of the guns and the dogs of their fathers and grandfathers and recall long-ago hunts and hounds giving tongue. Sometimes Daddy would play alone, and she'd glance at Treat and a faint knowing smile would pass between them. Then she'd close her eyes and listen as her father's banjo imitated hounds on fox races and foxes running up trees and as it called up as only music can the deep sweet mysteries of the lives of those who had lived in these mountains—in coves, on knobs, up prongs and branches and forks and hollows—and shared the mountain ways for a very long time.

Saturday nights Bonnie and Treat would drive his old stepside Ford pickup way up an abandoned logging road on Chiselfinger Ridge and park on the mountain above the clouds and listen to the Opry on the radio and watch the moon if there was one and make love no matter what.

Between her junior and senior years, Daddy took her on a trip with him to Knoxville to deliver a batch of tunes they'd written. She and Daddy set to music poems people sent in to an odd little publisher who advertised in a farmers' almanac. In the city Daddy took her by a television station where his old friend Knoxie Marcum worked. Knoxie had been a radio announcer back when Daddy and Ivy were going around with the Bumblebees, and now he hosted a Saturday evening local music program. Bonnie had seen it more than once through the snowy reception on old Carson's television set at the store in Honey Run. Knoxie was taken with Bonnie. "I'd know whose child she was anywhere," he said, and auditioned her right there. He put her on his next Saturday night show as a special feature with her cousin Treat—"the children of the Bumblebees"—and they soon became regulars.

Knoxie paid her and Treat gas money and a little extra to drive to Knoxville and perform. He also provided her with a tiny budget to put together a getup for his show. She got herself a couple of secondhand prom dresses, chiffon pink and lime in color, and a collection of cheap cut-glass earrings and necklaces, a big red wig and some makeup. By the time Bumper came home from service that fall Bonnie had achieved no small amount of notoriety at the Indian Point High School on account of her dolled-up self on television. Bumper played a few programs with her and Treat but figured he'd best get on to Nashville before he ran through the money he'd saved up. He couldn't figure why Treat'd want to stay on around Honey Run and pressed him to come along, but there was nothing that could tear Treat away from his sweetheart.

Almost nothing.

One day Daddy Montreat hiked up to the old family place and mentioned that night at supper that it looked like somebody'd been staying up there, not in the house because it was tumbling down at the roof, but up in the barn. "They had em a place all cleared out in the hay on the loft where there ain't no leaks in the roof yet. Some ginseng digger, I reckon. Had em some candles and a blanket too. Wonder they ain't burnt the place down yet, living that way, but there ain't much you can do about that kind of thing once you abandon a old home. Better it get used than wasted."

It shook Bonnie, and Treat too when she told him. They knew it had to stop. Surprised and frightened, they saw how utterly without hope and future this love of theirs was in any society beyond their blessed own. They had been so happy and so wholly devoted to each other, so free and easy with each other in the flesh those three years, that they were unprepared to see their idyl ended. But end it they must. Treat would follow Bumper to Nashville after all, and after graduation Bonnie would find work as a secretary in the office of the mica mine, where her father was still foreman. Bumper and Treat would make regular appeals to the family to let Bonnie come to Nashville and try to break into country music with them, but Ivy wouldn't allow it. She would swear that Bonnie could never have any kind of a normal life performing; she would speak darkly of the dangers of the musician's life, and memories of the Moneywasters' fire would be in everyone's mind. And Bonnie Montreat for all these reasons would stay put in East Tennessee, before long even quitting Knoxie Marcum's television program, her ambitions blunted by nervousness and uncertainty. But Bonnie and Treat went one last time to their loving place.

It was late late fall when they held each other that last time in the hay, and ached and wept together there. After, in the chill of dusky dark they walked up the hillside across the high weedy meadow, up past the juneapple family graveyard and buried their old blanket in a pile of rocks. *Never no more,* they vowed, *never no more.* They kissed and swore their heavy burdensome farewell and then walked back down the trace toward Honey Run, not together hand in hand and side by side as before, but noiselessly and not touching, one after the other like two packhorses numb with weariness.

# PRESTON HEWITT
## 1959

Except for a couple of cards back and forth from Gary Owwens, Preston had no real communication with the Skyliner folks for some time. He and Gary had met in Knoxville and edited the Montreat record there at the Hewitt house. The two-track master was packed off to Folk Town Records, West Twenty-third Street, New York City, the week after Thanksgiving, 1958. Israel Palomar, the label's owner, promised an early spring release. Palomar was as good as his word.

Just before Easter, a dozen copies of the album came in the mail: *Franklin "Daddy" Montreat Remembers the Tennessee Bumblebees.* On the front cover was a snapshot of Daddy Montreat and Ivy on the front porch of their home in Honey Run, he with his banjo and she with her autoharp, and on the back some old Bumblebee photos and some notes that Gary Owwens and Izzy Palomar must have written. There at the bottom of the back cover was Preston's credit: "Recorded and Edited by Preston Hewitt; Technical Assistance Provided by Skyliner Folk School, Heuvil, Tennessee."

Then one afternoon in early May his father met him as he came off the high-school campus. Professor Hewitt was waiting in the family's Chrysler Imperial station wagon and waving at him impatiently. When he crossed the street and reached the car, his father said, "Hop in, Pres, we have to run out to UT and have a little talk with Dean Claiborne." The dean, it seemed, had been requested to provide information to the Tennessee Bureau of Investigation regarding UT students who had in the past five years participated in any workshops or programs at the Skyliner Folk School.

"The TBI?" Preston asked. "What's wrong?"

"Nothing, so far as I know," Professor Hewitt said as they drove crosstown. "Just routine. The TBI apparently is charged with investigating regularly all schools chartered by the state to see that there are no charter violations."

"Seems like it'd be left up to the Board of Higher Education or something," Preston said.

"Does seem like, but this *is* Tennessee. Anyhow, since Dean Claiborne has all but guaranteed that you'll receive a Rodanthe Scholarship, I wanted us to be quite cooperative with him, you see?"

"Yes, sir." Goddamn, that's great, Preston thought. I can't wait till it's official and I get the letter. High school would be over in three weeks, and the only question remaining there for Preston was whether he would deliver the valedictory or salutatory address, who would finish first, he or the girl bound for Swarthmore. His admission to Harvard had been locked up long since. The real tension for two months had been getting that scholarship, without which Preston's trip up to Cambridge would be beyond the means of the Hewitts—and Dr. Claiborne, Professor Hewitt's mentor in the history department and for eight years now dean of arts and sciences, sat on the board of the Rodanthe Foundation and represented the Southeastern United States. Claiborne was the key.

The high-pile bottle-green carpet in the anteroom of Dean Claiborne's office was spongy like moss under Preston's feet. He studied the dark oil portraits that hung about the paneled room. A buzzer buzzed discreetly, and the dean's secretary motioned the Hewitts in.

Dean Claiborne stood behind his desk and extended his long arm officially to shake each of their hands. He introduced them to a dark-suited man with owlish glasses and very closely cropped hair: "Dr. Hewitt, Preston, this is Mr.

Pendleton Lindy of the Tennessee Bureau of Investigation. Mr. Lindy is an attorney whose work involves charter integrity and tax status matters of our nonpublic state-chartered educational institutions. Mr. Lindy?"

"Yes. First let me say that you do not have to answer any question I might ask, but I assure you this procedure is quite routine. On a revolving basis we review the activities of every educational institution in Tennessee, usually every third or fourth year. I'm here in Knoxville completing a rundown on the Skyliner Folk School. I understand, Preston, that you participated in activities there last August, that is, August of 1958."

*Something about him.* "Yes, sir," Preston said.

"Good," Lindy said. "I have two questions of fact relating to complaints lodged by citizens in the county there where Skyliner is chartered."

"Yes, sir?"

"The first complaint alleges the unlicensed and illegal sale of alcoholic beverages on the Skyliner premises. Can you tell me anything about this?"

Preston laughed.

"Please, Preston," Dean Claiborn said.

"Yes, sir." Preston settled down. *Jesus.* "I know what you're talking about, but it wasn't like a *bar* or anything. It wasn't for sale either. Hal Milton would buy cases of beer and bring them up the mountain to Skyliner and put them in an old Kelvinator for the staff and conferees. There was a shoebox strapped to the inside of the refrigerator door and Mr. Milton asked that whenever you got a beer—or soda, there was Coca-Cola and all too—you contributed a quarter to the kitty to cover the cost. That was all there was to it."

Mr. Lindy scribbled shorthand notes furiously. "Thank you. My other question relates to the identity of a man attending the third August workshop. Here—I have his picture." Lindy handed Preston a photograph.

"Oh, yeah—that guy."

"You recognize him?"

"He was there, but he wasn't really a conferee, he was like a visitor, a writer, I think. His name was something Albert."

"Joseph?"

"Yes, Joseph Albert."

"And he was definitely there?"

"Definitely. Why, what's he done? Robbed a bank?"

Lindy ignored Preston's lighthearted question. "Do you recognize this photograph, Preston?" Lindy produced a snapshot that had been taken out under the great spreading oak the day Reverend King last spoke. Preston remembered and told how Joseph Albert wanted to be in all the photographs and how he even asked different ones to take pictures of him and Reverend King and Hal Milton with Albert's own camera—" 'So I can be in the picture,' " Preston quoted him as saying.

"Yes," Pres said. "That was the closing of the last conference at Skyliner."

"Thank you, Preston. That's all I need to ask you. Now I'd like to have Dr. Claiborne's secretary type up these notes and ask you to sign them, if that's all right." Lindy stood with his steno pad and strode toward the door to the anteroom.

"Sign the notes?"

"Well, I'll have them written up in the form of a statement."

*Something about him.* Preston felt all of a sudden like he was being pushed into something. "Mr. Lindy, I told you what you wanted to know. I don't understand why you need me to *sign* anything."

Lindy stopped at the door and looked up at the ceiling and spoke with his back to Preston and his father and the dean. "This is standard practice, Preston. This interview cannot serve as an official deposition unless it is typed and signed." He walked through the door.

"Deposition?" Preston said. "Dad, that's legal, like for court or something, isn't it? Why're they talking to me? Why don't they just go on up to Skyliner and talk to Hal and Gary? I think I ought to call Gary, at least before I sign any—"

"Dr. Hewitt," Dean Claiborne said tersely. "Please let me speak with Preston alone a moment."

The elder Hewitt left the room.

"Dean, I'm sorry to seem like an ignorant schoolboy, but I don't quite get what's going on here."

"Sit down, Preston." He did. The dean took great slow strides about the room and spelled it out for him. "Preston, the Skyliner Folk School is unpopular both in its home county and in Nashville. Extremely unpopular. I suspect that you, being your father's son, are well aware of this."

"Yes, sir."

"There is nothing happening now that has not happened many times in the past. The Governor and the Attorney General have responded to enormous political pressure to investigate the school top to bottom for the umpteenth time, and since Skyliner has always drawn heavily on UT and the Knoxville academic community for staff support, however quietly, we here are under pressure to cooperate fully with the state's investigation. And I mean fully. That is why Mr. Lindy is here, and that is why you are here. Hal Milton has weathered every storm they've visited on him, and I have no reason to believe he won't weather this one. However, when the state is requesting clear and objective fact, we must put the truth ahead of whatever feelings we might have for Skyliner, eh?"

"The truth," Preston said. "What if you don't cooperate? What if you sent Lindy away empty-handed?"

"That failure would be reflected rather significantly in my budget, and in many other ways, some subtle, some not so."

"I see," Preston said. "Well, I'd still like to talk to Gary before I actually sign anything for this guy."

Dean Claiborne stared out the great triple-hung window behind his desk at the campus statue of the scholar with its green bronze plaque. "I'm afraid I can't permit that, Preston."

"Sir?"

"Preston—may I ask you very simply to sign these statements for Mr. Lindy and have done with it?"

*Something.* Preston said, "I don't think so, Dean Claiborne. I think I'll do what I said."

"Young Hewitt," the dean said, "how I loathe bringing this to bear on you. It's a very simple matter. The pressure on me to provide the state help in this has been, frankly, intense. And I'm afraid I must pass some of it along to you. Were this a moral question, a question of ethics, I could fully appreciate your holding back. However, as it is, you are being called upon to describe a refrigerator and identify a man from his pictures, matters, as I have said, of clear and objective fact. You have done these things. All you are now requested to do is attest by your signature that what you have said is true. If you cannot cooperate to this extent, that is your decision. But let me tell you without a doubt that if you so decide, I will have no choice but to withdraw my support in pressing your case for a full four-year Rodanthe Scholarship. That, I am sorry to say, is what must hang in the balance."

Lindy came back into the dean's office with the typed statement, and Preston read it without saying anything. The part about the beer merely stated the existence of a refrigerator stocked with beer by Hal Milton and the fact of a shoebox into which conferees at Skyliner were expected to place twenty-five cents for every beer taken from the refrigerator. The part about Joseph Albert astonished him. The name was changed to Van Ludic, and the statement—Preston's statement—said he was a known member of the American Communist Party. "What in the world is this?"

" 'Joseph Albert' is an alias, a *nom de plume* for Van Ludic," Lindy said, "and Van Ludic *is* a known Communist. Even though you did not know him as such at Skyliner, I thought your statement should reflect the absolute truth of the matter, the real facts."

*No choice but to withdraw my support.*

Preston Hewitt borrowed a pen and signed the Skyliner deposition for the Tennessee Bureau of Investigation.

Preston didn't call Gary Owwens after all. Instead, he tried his level best to forget the incident, and his father seemed to

know better than to try and bring it up. After a couple of
weeks with no word, Pres figured the Skyliner investigator
must have checked everything out and left town. As far as he
could tell there was no real way either Hal or Gary would
even find out about the deposition.

He was wrong.

Less than a week before graduation, Preston was leaving
the high-school campus in the afternoon and there again was
his father in the station wagon waving at him. Again they
drove, but this time to no place in particular. "It was more
serious than I thought that day," Professor Hewitt said when
Preston first got in.

"What do you mean, Dad?" Preston said.

His father nodded back over his shoulder. "Paper in the
back seat. I'm sorry I let you do it, boy. I'm sorry as hell."
Preston reached for the paper and flipped it open. There on
the front page of Knoxville's afternoon daily was the big
news:

### Skyliner Raided for Illegal Alcohol
### Injunction Padlocks Communist Center
### Charter Trial Slated

Hal and his wife and Gary never knew what hit them.
Sheriff Alistair Webster of Wise County, Tennessee, led four
deputies and six TBI agents onto the Skyliner Folk School
grounds between the hours of six and seven o'clock that
morning. They took a roll of pictures of the refrigerator.
They appeared before a judge who was waiting on them
back at the county courthouse with an injunction already
drawn up by 9 A.M. They seized the Skyliner property and
padlocked the doors by noon, giving the Miltons and
Owwens less than three hours to clear out and only two
hours to prepare themselves for arraignment—Milton for
illegal alcohol sales and his wife and Owwens on related
conspiracy and accessory charges. Before the afternoon papers hit the streets, the Attorney General in Nashville had

announced to the state press corps the scheduling of a trial to challenge the Skyliner charter on moral and security grounds.

"I think," he added, "that we'll revoke the hell out of it."

At his father's insistence Preston spent the summer with relatives in San Francisco. He was back in Knoxville in September only long enough to collect his things and head north. At Harvard he read of the Skyliner trial, of the findings against the school, of the selling off of its equipment, its library, of the subdivision plans for the Skyliner mountain. Bit by bit Preston swallowed his self-loathing over his part in the case. There was nothing I could do, he thought. I had no choice. I didn't really do anything but tell the truth. I guess it was selling beer.

He well knew that the spirit of charity ran so high among his former fellows that he would have been forgiven if only he had gone back and faced them. He was too ashamed. Besides, a sentiment was growing in him that there was nothing to be gained by it. If he had acted like a Judas before, now he sought the loftier absolution of Pilate. What was the point of hanging himself? He washed his hands of it and began under full Rodanthe Scholarship to make his clever, above-average way through the nation's great university. He turned his eyes for the time being away from his beautiful and cruel and demanding native soil and looked instead toward a time when he might forget the moment he had stood young and weak in the dean's office and had been a knave and a fool.

# PART THREE

# BONNIE MONTREAT
## 1960–1963

A few months after Treat had gone to join Bumper in Nashville, the two of them made a visit home. Bumper left Treat off in Indian Point and told Daddy and Ivy and Bonnie he'd be up to visit later on. All during dinner Bumper kept up crowing about Nashville this and Nashville that and how big things'd happen if he could just get Bonnie out there to sing with him and Treat. Daddy laughed at his big talk, but Ivy glared at him for not dropping it. Then Bumper got going on Treat.

"Bet you thought all that boy could do was chaperone his cousin," Bumper said, nodding at Bonnie. "Weren't so— Treat's turned out to be a real ladies' man, yes ma'am yes sir."

Bonnie could feel her face go red. "What about you, Bump?"

"Oh, he lets me tag along with the extras." Bumper laughed. "But ain't no way I can keep up."

Ivy didn't like this line of talk, and she nodded at her daughter to clear the table. Bonnie carried the plates out to the kitchen and scraped the porkchop bones onto a pie tin. She was afraid she'd say something sharp to Bumper or, worse, start crying. "I'll just feed the dogs, Mama," she called and was out the back door and into the cold in a flash.

"What's wrong with her?" Bumper said.

Daddy's eyes narrowed a mite, but he didn't speak. Ivy slammed down a spurtle on the cutting board by the sink and said, "I'll tell you what's wrong with her, Hubert Montreat. It's all this talk about dates and picture shows and record studios—that child ain't old enough to buy whiskey and you come home getting her all riled up and wanting to be in Nashville roughhousing with you boys."

"No worse than her being a old maid in Honey Run, Mama."

"Stop this arguing," Daddy said flatly. "I don't want to hear any more tonight. Set us up three rounds, son, I hear your cousin's car. No more of it, Ivy—understand?"

Ivy drew the camphor-soaked handkerchief out of her pocket and pressed it over her face.

Out in the pen Bonnie fed Penny Lee and Little Man and shivered and huddled with them. When Treat's car pulled up the drive, she hid back of the dog hutch so he wouldn't see her when he came round to the back. She could just make him out as he knocked on the door and then saw him framed against the kitchen light as he opened it and went on in. She heard the big how-do Daddy gave him before the door shut. Penny Lee snuffled at her, and Bonnie stroked the crown of the dog's head. She was angry now and full of bitter resolve: I'll just stay out here till he's gone. But she'd run out of the kitchen with the dog scraps so fast she hadn't gotten a wrap, and it was freezing cold.

Maybe there was a tarp or an old quilt over in the tractor shed. Or a bottle of something, she wished. She went in the shed and knocked around, stumbling over empty oil cans, but all she found was a pile of burlap feed sacks. She got herself a half a dozen and wrapped them around her shoulders like a shawl and set up on the tractor seat and waited.

Her teeth were chattering loudly and she was tapping her

feet on the tractor so she didn't hear him come up. She about jumped out of her skin when he called to her from the open end of the shed. "You in there, sugar-britches?"

"*Treat,* you— Oh, you, *Jesus!*" Her voice was all shaky from the moment and the cold.

"What're you doing out here?" he said. "It don't take no twenty minutes to feed two dogs."

"I'm waiting for you to . . . *leave.*"

"Leave? Hell, I just got here. Come on down here and give me a hug, Bonn."

"Don't you 'Bonn' me, Treat McVaine. I ain't one of your Nashville girlfriends."

He was silent a few seconds. "Bonnie, let's go on in the house fore you freeze to death out here."

"I wish I *would* freeze to death," she cried out at him. "Be better for the both of us." Why had Bumper told em? And then gone on and on about it? It ate at her heart and she didn't mind Treat knowing, not at all.

"Your brother's a real loudmouth, Bonn."

"Well, I got a earful about you."

Treat walked on into the shed and leaned on the big rear wheel of the tractor and spoke sharply. "What am I supposed to do, a fellow my age and all? Never look at another woman same time I can't have the one I love with all my heart?"

She burst out crying and Treat reached up and helped her down off the tractor and held her to him. *Never no more.*

It would be a year before Bumper would write that he and Treat had landed a steady paying job at a club, a year before she was twenty-one and old enough to know her own mind, as Daddy said, and go on to Nashville to join them. A year before she had got used to the idea of Treat and other girls— maybe Treat would find a new love, but Bonnie knew better about herself. In time they would come to an understanding. Their hearts were broken but true, and even upon a rubble a beautiful city can be built. They would help each other in time—but it would be years before Bonnie Montreat got over the ache and hurt she felt in the tractor shed that night.

The Trailways bus whined west toward Nashville. Bonnie let her seat back and ignored her mother's warning to sit forward and not put her copper curls back against the greasy plastic headrest. The bus smelled of sweaty bodies pressed together and cigaret smoke and Negroes passing half pints of whiskey and cheapjack eight-day wine back and forth and folks eating chicken out of shoeboxes and sardines from shallow tins. A man stood in the aisle dead on his feet swaying as the bus tires sang them along into the night. It was tired air on this bus and tired people breathing it. Back behind her the washroom door swung free and slammed loudly every time the bus bore right. Why don't nobody close it? she thought.

*Nashville, the Hollywood the South had longed for and invented on its own soil and in its own image; Nashville, the wealthy tawdry sprawling city on the Cumberland River held by the landscape of central Tennessee the way two hands cupped together might hold a Monopoly house or hotel, held cupped in that bowl of middle Tennessee some call the dimple of the universe. The rim of hills that ring the city holds a blanket of smoke and fog over it, and the blanket is a long time unraveling and clearing away of a cold and damp winter's morning. You can call Chattanooga and Memphis just great big country towns, but not Nashville—wealth has been there a long time and it shows: timber wealth, trapping wealth, trading wealth, insurance-company and moneylender wealth, all of it that came before Nashville was the town of dreams, the Hollywood of the South.*

*Along lower Broadway coming up from the river were bars and pawnshops and Western-wear emporiums where cheap dreams were peddled, and are peddled yet, to the drifters and grifters and would-be cowboys who wrote their names on the walls at Trix's or who wandered into Ernest Tubb's Record Shop and stared at the pictures of the stars of hillbilly heaven on earth all up around the molding. There were the crowds of tourists who buy books of guitar instruction and song collections and who pose with enormous cardboard photo cutouts, life-sized, of Hank or Ernest or Kitty or Skeeter, and who carry the photographs back to show off to their friends and relatives in Texas or Illinois or Japan or anywhere.*

*Up the hill away from Broadway and Trix's and all the furniture companies that date back to the simple commercial era before Nashville was the town of dreams was the Hotel Sam Davis, twelve stories of dull red brick with its six yellow bands round the top. It towers over the Seventh Avenue Café where the cowboys and drifters sit on gold spinning stools and watch their fellows play at the hopeless twenty-five-cent Bahama Beach gambling machine while they themselves order the cheap food advertised in the signs painted on the plate-glass windows, silver and red letters with puffy red cloud lines around the words: "Ho-made Chili." And it towers over the Banner Café with its maroon-and-green striped awning and Budweiser sign, and over the squat Hotel Ross, where the windowsills are dotted with jars and canned goods and groceries.*

*Highest on the downtown hill before the coming of the New South skyscrapers is the Greek Revival Capitol building, where the legislature forced a cupola to be constructed and then apologized to the architect at his death by burying him in the building's wall. Out the ridge to the south is the other great public building, Union Station, of massive rocks, a great castle of transport built to ferry the sons of Tennessee to and from the wars of their nation.*

*Walking back down one of the named, not numbered, streets that slide off the hill toward the snaking green-brown river, a drifter might look out on the inexorable plying of the commercial boats, the barge traffic on the Cumberland. Across the river a crane might be unloading sand or fertilizer or coal from a barge and into a funnel onto a conveyor belt which carries it up the riverbank. Nearby two tugs wait with empty gray and rust-color barges to go back downstream for more. The sand in the barges is like the silt held in suspension in the murky river, slipping along, and also like the drifter, the would-be cowboy who watches, a mere particle in a flood of life's animate and inanimate. All particles that slip in and through and out of Nashville, the silt, the sand, the drifter with a few dollars in his boot and a pint of triple peach in his belly and the Silvertone guitar his daddy got mail order from Sears a generation before in his hand, but his heart as empty as the unloaded barge now*

*bound downriver to some stretch of shoals for more grains and
particles, like him forever moving about, like him unnoticed, unremarked, unrecorded, unmourned.*

*Nashville is Hollywood east of the Mississippi and south of the
Mason-Dixon Line; the town of dreams where he would find his if
time and chance would just allow.*

*The last barge in a train of three rounds a bend in the meandering
Cumberland and moves out of sight.*

When Bonnie got to Nashville, she found that Bumper
had been talking her up to Swag, the manager at the Hog
Locker, the joint where Bumper and Treat played. She was
willing to give it a try: singing with them, just doing old
country standards and a few current hits. She auditioned,
and Swag agreed to take her on and even bump the cover
charge up a little so they'd make enough to split three ways.
Treat told Bonnie the manager'd said, "Hell, a pretty redhead like her ought to make you mullets look right good."

They were popular all right, but it was with a pretty rough
crowd. A scarface man nightly ordered his steak "guitar big,
nigger lip thick, pussy tender, and lightning quick." And the
Hog Locker was too far out on the edge of Nashville for any
of the Music Row people to just casually wander by.

The sign hanging over the beer-joint door read: LI E MUS C
THE MO TRE TS. Once she'd started performing there Bonnie
kept after Swag to patch it up. "I'd like it better if folks could
at least get it right about what our name was," Bonnie said. It
wasn't a very large sign and it was angled wrong for folks on
the state road to get much more than a glance at it as folks
whizzed by on the state road. Most of the people who drank
beer there or ate the dollar-and-a-quarter strip and T-bone
steaks were regulars, though Bonnie's appearance on the bill
did increase the draw. "They all know your names," Swag
said. "Why bother about that sign?"

She bothered because she had ambition. As long as she'd
had Knoxville television to perform on and a nice little

secretary job right in Honey Run and Ivy to play on her fears, she'd resisted Bumper's pleas for her to come on and move to Music City. But now that she'd shaken loose from home, she was trying for real. When she started at the Hog Locker she said she'd give it a month or two and see what happened and who noticed.

After six months she started cussing the whole arrangement. She didn't think they were getting anywhere. "Hell, I can tell the difference between something happening and nothing happening," she'd say.

But Bumper was content to pick through forty songs a night and go home smelling like stale beer and cigarets. "Come on, Bonn, this is just rent and food money. Just to keep us going while we try and get other things lined up, that's all."

"It ain't enough for me."

"What about me?" Bumper said. "I come here to play banjo." It was true—after no time at all in Music City Bumper had realized that the only commercial demand for banjo anymore was in dogged low-pay touring with a bluegrass band. But Bumper could flatpick a guitar, too, so his second instrument became his first. He bought a chicken-picker's special off an old road dog and offered himself as a guitar man.

Every once and a while Bumper and Treat got session work, and whenever Bumper thought it was a good idea Bonnie would tag along. She met some folks and heard some right hot playing, but nothing opened up for her. The only reliable thing was four nights a week, Wednesday through Saturday, at the Hog Locker. After ten months Bonnie Montreat got fed up and packed her bags. Treat drove her to the bus station, but when the Knoxville bus was nearly through loading she turned and cried on his shoulder and said she'd give it just a little longer if he and Bumper would put up with her.

"Course we will, sugar-britches," Treat said. They shuffled

back across the bus terminal's terrazzo floor, Treat sliding around like he was skating where the black man had just dragged a wet mop.

"Quit trying to make me laugh," she said, shaking out her copper curls.

She sat over by him and let him put his arm around her as he drove her back. He felt like home to her. How could she stay mad or blue more than a couple of shakes? He was just too disarming and gentle with her—not protective like Bumper was, but not severe like Bumper could be, either. By the time Treat got her back to the tiny house, she was in pretty good spirits.

Bumper came to the door and said, "Well, well. And here I was a wondering what we was ever gon do without you." He would of gone on, but Treat made a warning face at him. "Well, come on in. But don't think you can lay around here whining and bitching about every little thing that don't happen just your way."

Bumper sat on the sofa across from her, looking like he had advice to give. Bonnie sat in the big worn maroon stuffed chair and looked at the floor and talked low. Treat hung back so as not to make trouble.

"I could sing backup vocals or chorus or something if you all'd introduce me a bit more, help me get some auditions."

"It ain't that easy, Bonn," Bumper said. She knew he wasn't kidding her. She'd seen both of them as they took different ones aside at the Quonset Hut and other studios and pointed her out. Nothing ever came of it.

Bumper spoke with a kinder voice. "Bonnie, what they really want for that work is vocal groups that're already together, that stay together, that can work up chorus parts quick, you know, like the Jordanaires or something."

"I know, I know."

"You know, but I don't see you trying to put anything together, form your own chorus group or nothing like that, now, do I?"

"No. I don't want no chorus group, anyway."

"All right, then, what do you expect?"

"Well, it may sound prideful, but I still say I could do just as well as Kitty Wells or Skeeter Davis or any of em if I got half the chance."

"Half the chance my ass. They all got songwriters turning out hits for em to sing—*that's* what you got to have. Me and Treat don't neither of us write. We pick. So until we find somebody to crank out a few hits for you, sister, and somebody else to back you going into the studio, it's the Montreats at the Hog Locker and damn glad we got the job, too. Ain't that right, Treat?"

Treat knelt down to where he could look at her, because she was staring down at the floor. "Bonnie, honey," he said, "there's a lot of girls like you, that's come to Nashville wanting and hoping to get a start. Now, if you're gon stay and try and follow this through, you got to quit thinking it's all gon be laid out on your doorstep some night while you're asleeping."

"Treat, this ain't *you* talking."

"Now, yes, it is," he said, "so you listen up and I'll tell you something: you probably wouldn't believe how much better you are now than you were when you first got here."

"What?"

"Your voice is stronger and you're more sure of yourself, and it's from all this singing you been doing. From handling yourself at a mike in front of people. Even if a lot of em *are* rednecks and clodhoppers, they're still people you got to sing to, to reach from the stage. Can't nobody give you that kind of experience or confidence, and you sure as hell can't *buy* it. You earn it is what you do. You earn it and you bide your time till something opens up for you. And *then,* when you stand up and open your mouth and sing, you got all the strength it takes to convince people what you're singing is the truth. How old are you, sweet pea?"

"Twenty-one," Bonnie said. "But when Daddy was twenty-one—"

Bumper started laughing.

"Lord God, Bonn," Treat said, "that was thirty years ago. Don't you think country music might of *changed some* since then?"

"Yes, but—"

"Now, how old was Hank Williams when he had his first hit, that's more like it, but, hell, *that* was better'n ten years ago."

"I don't know," she said.

"Twenty-five," Bumper said.

"There you go," Treat said. He put his opened palm against her flushed cheek, and smiled. "Let's try taking it a step at a time. It'll come to you. It'll come to all of us."

She nodded, but she was thinking about what Bumper said: *They all got songwriters turning out hits for em . . .*

"Come on, I'll buy us a beer," Bumper said. He stood before her working his tongue against his molars.

"You all go on without me," she said.

"You sure?"

She smiled and gave him a hug. "I reckon I got to get unpacked."

Suddenly it all seemed so obvious she almost laughed aloud at how she could of failed to think of it before: *I'll just have to write songs for myself.*

It was early evening. She lay back in the pillows of her bed and thought about it all—her ambitions, her disappointments, and what would satisfy her about staying indefinitely in Nashville. A plan would do that. A plan whose workings she could push along no matter what other people did or didn't do. Being her own songwriter, at least trying to be, was a plan that would satisfy. Once she had written enough songs, she would seek out a publisher. It all began to make sense. Songs are ideas, she thought, and folks with the ideas are the folks who're in on the beginning of things; if you wait around for somebody to bring the songs to you, you're no better off than a parked car just waiting to be started. She lay back in her pillows and liked her plan and relaxed and let her hand slide down and find the place and closed her eyes and satisfied herself and fell asleep.

A while later she awoke and got up and showered. She put
on her robe and got herself a tall glass of wine and stretched
out on the living-room sofa with her little Martin ought-
forty-five and some paper and a pencil. She strummed
bright and easy and came up with a tune she hummed over
and over till some words began to come to her.

"Don't Run Me Round in Circles" was her first Nashville
song. All in all it was a pretty fair start. She liked it and she
got comfortable with it so she'd be at ease singing it for
Bumper and Treat when they got back. How they will be
surprised, she thought. She figured on a pace she thought
she could keep: In three months if I make up one every week
I'll have twelve songs, an album's worth. She resolved to do
it, and before too many months were up, she would be able
to look back and say to herself, I was wrong about that, but I
wasn't far wrong.

Bonnie Montreat worked up a list of publishers—song
pluggers, Bumper called them—to call with her batch of new
songs. She got the names off record labels and album covers.
She steered clear of the big outfits, deciding instead to go
after a handful of smaller companies. "Ones, you know,
that'll really hustle for me," she told Bumper earnestly. So
began a period of learning who was who at what company
and then stalking him. If she was willing to wait long enough
at some given office, chances were she'd get in to see the
man—she was young and pretty, after all.

One song plugger she got in to see interrupted her halfway through her first song: "You cut any records yet?" She
shook her head. "Thought not. Got a tape of this you can
leave, a demo?" No again. "Well, sweetheart," he said, "you're
gon have to put something on tape if you want to find
yourself a publisher. It's just the way it works, these days. If
you were signed to my company and I had nothing of yours
on tape and here's, I don't know, say Ferlin Husky or
somebody setting in my office *desperate* for a tune—how the
hell am I gon get him to hear *yours*? I can't be calling all over
town for you. Somebody like Ferlin ain't gon set still but

fifteen, twenty minutes, and if I can't dredge something up to show him by *then,* well, I reckon it's just tough titty for you *and* me."

Bonnie bolted up and packed her guitar away.

"Hey, what're you doing?" He stood up as well, but she just glared at him.

"I come down here to Music Row to talk business, not trash."

"Listen here, Miss Montreat," the publisher said, amazed and sarcastic, "if you can't take it in Nashville, why don't you head on back to East Tennessee till you've grown up a bit?"

"You got no call to be so mean," Bonnie said, heading for the door.

"But if you *do* stick around, put your damn tunes on tape if you want anybody to do anything with them. *Or* you." As she slammed out the front door of the small brick block building, she heard him mutter after her, "*Girl* songwriter, my ass."

Bumper sat waiting for her in their '57 Chevrolet parked in the sun. He looked up almost uninterestedly from his Max Brand Western and spoke. "What'd this one have to say?"

"Same damn thing," Bonnie said. "Record the songs, make a tape, then we'll see."

"How many's this make now?"

"About a dozen."

"Think anybody's trying to tell you something, sister?"

"Yes, I do," she snapped. "They're telling me to go out and spend a couple hundred dollars I ain't got on studio time and not even know if anybody's interested enough to do any more than keep em on file."

She wasn't about to let on to Bumper or Treat or anyone else about the resistance she was meeting from publishers on account of being a woman, and a young one at that. It was like they didn't even hear her sing the songs, like they were just focusing on her looks. Sometimes she'd get a remark about how pretty she sang, but nobody seemed to be hearing her songs for what they were. She didn't believe it was because she hadn't put them down on tape—plenty of songs got pitched by the writer just strumming through it on guitar in somebody's office or motel room. What did these song pluggers think? That people wouldn't sing a song if they found out a woman had written it? Maybe she was reading too much into it. Maybe it was just easier for the publishers to take what their standard old hacks brought in, on tape, for them to work around town. Tired old songs that sounded like everybody else's, but at least the guys that had to go plug them were comfortable with the guys that wrote them. That made it kind of like a closed circle with her on the outside. There was something stale about the whole business, but she aimed to hold to her will and let it tow her on through.

All right, she thought as Bumper drove them home, if this is how it works, like they all keep telling me, then I'll work it that way. I'll record my tunes. Only they ain't gonna be these stale crying-in-the-beer songs I keep hearing. What they're gonna hear out of me they won't be hearing anywhere else.

"Bumper?"

"Yeah?"

"What's the hour rate down at that fellow Phil's garage studio?"

"Too much."

"Oh, come on."

"I don't know. Fifteen or twenty dollars an hour plus tape."

"Is it two-track or four-track?"

"Four-track? You got a symphony or something to record that I don't know about?"

"I'm gon make the best tape I can afford."

"Yeah? And when's that?"

"Sooner than later."

"Dream on, Bonnie."

She knew Bumper would a whole lot rather spend any spare money on repairing his car than on several hours of studio time and all the cost of extra tapes and reels and boxes for the dubs you had to make to leave all over town. But what else was going to get them anywhere? Their daddy's name had opened a few doors, but just long enough for old

whoever it was to have a cup of coffee with Bumper and
Bonnie and make them listen to him go on about Old Days in
Country Music and What Great Times They Were. Both the
children learned that folks' affection for the minor legend
Daddy Montreat was didn't really carry over in any workable
way into the contemporary Music City marketplace. People
seemed to think it quaint somehow, their carrying on in
Daddy's footsteps, but they were not only left to distinguish
themselves in their own rights, they were required to.

Treat McVaine, as sweet and encouraging as he could be,
was just too easily distracted by skirts switching by—he
couldn't be relied upon for any practical help in forging
ahead in this town. And here Bumper, as fine a picker as he
was, was just laying up waiting on fortune. It'll all come in
time. Something'll turn up. You'll see. All things come to him
who waits.

So, though they were both on her side, Bonnie was alone
at the fore. She discovered that much of what fired her
resolve also fueled her imagination. The songs came tumbling out of her. After she'd finish one, she would write the
lyrics out neatly in longhand and record the song at home on
a thirdhand pawnshop Wollensak she'd bought. She would
play the tapes back and criticize herself and polish the
performance against the time she and Bumper and Treat
would go into Phil's or some other hole-in-the-wall studio
and start to record her growing library of songs.

She set her own standards, and her rule to herself was no
*dull* songs. Tunes by Bonnie Montreat must be either heart-
breaking or high-spirited. She quickly discarded a song if the
lyric idea or the tune or the chord progression seemed
monotonous. If it entertains me, she thought, I'll know it,
because it'll be fun to sing time after time. And any song I
write that can make that cut is fit to go out of this living room
and into the world.

Bonnie and Bumper and Treat pulled up to Phil McCrack-
en's garage studio set up out back of one of the brick and

stucco bungalows down Sixteenth Avenue South, almost in
the shadow of the enormous Ward-Belmont finishing-school
mansion. Treat and Bumper unpacked their instruments,
and Bonnie went over the lyric and chord-chart sheets she
had neatly printed out and Thermofaxed. She was thrilled
and nervous.

"Why don't you let me hear some of em while I set up,"
Phil said.

She strummed and sang to him as he wrestled the sound-
separation baffles into place. Phil was a studio musician
himself, a drummer, and he told her to just let him know
what she wanted in the way of drums or other percussion,
like tambourine or rhythm sticks. Bonnie hadn't really given
it any thought. She'd figured she'd be playing a good, hard
sock rhythm on her little Martin while Bumper flatpicked
fills on his Gibson Dove. And Treat'd keep a drone going on
the fiddle. They'd trade off so the simple melody lead breaks
were evenly balanced between Bumper's guitar and Treat's
fiddle or mandolin. A little more variety that way, she
thought.

But now Phil McCracken was offering drums and such,
and she didn't know from I reckon how to talk drum talk.
They never worked with drums back in East Tennessee—just
string band or bluegrass configuration where the rhythm was
just, well, *there,* and a string bass was all anybody expected to
give a tune some bottom. The first thing that came into her
head was something simple that she knew from hanging
around sessions occasionally with the boys.

"High-hat ride'll be fine," she said.

"Which tune you want that on?"

Which one? Won't that suit for all of em? Bumper and
Treat looked up from tuning and picking and laughed as she
reddened.

"Come on, Phil," Treat said. "She ain't no drummer."

Phil turned to Bonnie. "You can't just come in here booking a session and not even know what you want. This ain't
somebody's living room, it's a studio."

Bonnie felt her cheeks flush even more, and a stinging in her eyes. She stepped outside and walked over to a large spreading oak, her hands jammed down in the pockets of her cowgirl culottes. Acorns rolled around like marbles underneath her feet. Why'd I bother to dress up like it was a date to the movies or something, just to come and get made fun of?

It was early on a September evening, a warm one with a waxing harvest moon rolling up in the sky over the house-tops of the old residential section. Bonnie found a patch of moss between the big gnarly roots and sat down. She could hear people visiting on a side porch nearby and there was the faint sound of someone playing an autoharp or psaltry. Or maybe it wasn't that at all. Maybe it was just the bugs whining and whirring together a few last desperate times before the chill and frost did them in. Her heart settled heavy in her breast, and she wanted a glass of wine and some sweet beau to hold her head in his lap and run his fingertips lightly over her brow.

The autoharp strains vanished, carried off by one of the light breezes that came by now and again and shook the oak leaves against each other. Soon all the leaves but these would be down and then these, stiffened and dead and waiting till spring to fall, would clack and rattle together all winter in the high and chill winds, stiff and noisy as a dried-out holly bough when you pitch it out after Christmas. She leaned back against the trunk of the oak and closed her eyes.

"Bonn," Treat said. He startled her.

"You go on."

"Not without you." He stood there beating his horsehair bow against his pantsleg like it was a riding crop and leaving a chalky line of resin there.

"Get on away from me," she said. "I ain't through thinking yet."

Treat flipped the fiddle up against his breastbone and started sawing away, with a lot of doublestopping:

> *Me and my wife and my wife's pap*
> *We all raise hell up at Cumberland Gap*

"You never could sing, Treat."

"Well, take over, cousin," he said, fiddling on as he crossed his legs and lowered himself Indian-style in front of her. She sang ahead:

> *Uncle Dan Tucker, he likes sin*
> *Any old shape that it comes in*
> *Me and my wife and my wife's pap*
> *We all raise hell up at Cumberland Gap*

They laughed and Bonnie marveled at how Treat could always touch her, find that sweet pure chord that tied and would always tie them. She leaned over to him. "Hold me a minute like you hold that fiddle," she said. Treat took her in his arms and kissed her hair. She could hear his heart like an old friend.

"How about let's go in and get to work?"

"Aw, what's the use, Treat? It's just always the same, getting yelled at or laughed at or pawed over till it kind of works on you. All it took was old Phil McCracken starting in like he did and I just lost my nerve."

"Bonnie, honey, you're taking this all too serious."

"No, I'm not. Think about it—outside of Mama and Daddy and you and Bump, who's really giving me much encouragement?"

"Come on—you knock that Hog Locker crowd flat back out on their ass when you cut loose."

"You're dreaming, Treat. Those old boys been flat on their ass three hours before we ever get started. I want to make something out of this little band. I ain't going back to Honey Run and have everybody say I rode the bus off to Nashville and got pushed around and had my heart broke, and then run on home to pick up where I left off at the damn mine office toting up figures."

Treat said, "Bonn, it won't be the Hog Locker forever. We just keep at it, there'll be a record someway."

"You think? I was all set to go sing for Bo Talley, left pictures at his office and his lawyer's office . . ." She broke off. "Oh, hell, Treat, you don't want to hear this mess."

"Yes, I do. I want to know what put you in this temper."

"Well, last Saturday morning, I won't even out of bed, and I got this call from Earl Viggery's office."

"Bomar Talley's lawyer?"

"Lawyer, manager, publisher, you name it. I been in to sing for him a couple times cause he scouts songs for Mr. Talley. His office ain't nothing for what all he must make. Old lumpy leather sofa and a couple of standup ashtrays. Anyway he nodded while I played and looked me over and I couldn't tell if I was getting through to him or if he was sizing me up for some *harem* he was putting together. He puts his hands on my shoulders, then fore I knew it he'd slipped em down to where he was cupping me, you know. I said 'I wish you'd just find you someplace else to put these hands of yours,' and he said 'No, I think this is the most comfortable place they been all day.' So I just hauled off and popped him hard. You getting some idea what my last week's been like?"

"Bonn, I was gonna say something about standing your ground and slinging it back but you don't need no lesson from me. Come on," Treat said. "Let's go on back in and have some fun with this, just let it rip like at the club. Word'll get around sooner or later, and when folks catch on to what a ball of fire you are, everybody and his brother's gonna want to work with Bonnie Montreat." Treat stood and pulled her up and they walked back to Phil McCracken's garage with their arms around each other like the young lovers they'd once been.

Inside, Bumper was flatpicking "Blackberry Blossom" and Phil was holed up in his tiny control booth reading a girlie magazine. Bonnie stepped toward him and patted his arm. "Okay, Phil. You want to show me what you can do on your drums?"

Bonnie's attitude about the Hog Locker changed. She quit thinking of it as time killed and effort thrown away. She began to try out different things and take note of what worked or didn't. She was concentrating.

She spent less time and more energy onstage, and the crowd wanted more of her. Between sets, instead of milling around the club and drinking beer with regulars, she took an unused office right next to the cold-storage locker and made it her dressing room and hid out from the crowd.

She quit singing in her cowgirl culottes and blouse and got herself instead three different outfits: a frilly dress, a slinky dress, and tight green satin pants and a shiny cowboy shirt to match. When she came out and did her section of the show, it *was* a show. She was singing only her own songs. Bumper and Treat let themselves be carried along on the strength of her enthusiasm and the increasing skill of her designs. New people were coming to the club, not just on weekends, but nearly filling it up on Wednesdays and Thursdays as well.

Outside the Hog Locker, Swag put up a new sign, lighted with three floodlights from below and angled so it was easy to see from the curve of the road no matter which way a car was coming or how fast it was going:

**BONNIE MONTREAT**
and the
**GREEN VALLEY BAND**

It was in the men's-room john that he and Joe Quill first spoke, the way Bumper told it back later. Quill peered at him through those hornrims and started up, even as they were both still spraying into the bottoms of the side-by-side urinals onto the wire-mesh screens and deodorant cakes. Bonnie had to laugh at the idea of such an important moment in her career beginning that way.

"Your sister," Quill said laconically, cocking his head back some.

"Yeah?" Bumper said. ("Somebody's always after you, Bonnie, that's what it looked like it was gonna be there at the first.")

"She could be big," Quill went on. "*Real* big."

"She'd like to think so," Bumper said. He shook himself and zipped up, stepping aside so whoever was waiting behind him could move up. The crowd drank so much during the band's sets that there was a line as much as six deep to each of the two wall urinals and the commode. There was suffocating smoke in the narrow bathroom, and soggy brown paper towels covered the floor. A few men, given all this, preferred to go outside and piss on each other's tires. But most crowded into the men's room, making crude remarks and carving refinements with buck penknives onto the rubber machines and their come-hither women.

Quill stayed right behind Bumper. "Now listen—I mean it."

"Mean what?"

"Here." Joe Quill pulled out an overstuffed billfold, the kind that convicts made at the prisons of the Southern outback, and he drew out a business card: JOSEPH QUILL, ARTISTS' MANAGER.

"You Quill?" Bumper said.

"That's right."

"I heard of you."

"Good," Quill said. "You all got representation?"

"What're you talking about?" Bumper chewed on the inside of his lower lip and eyed the manager with his sidewise suspicious look.

Quill gave a tired sigh. "Bonnie and you and the band— you all got a manager? Anybody booking you places?"

"No," Bumper said. "Mostly we take care of our own business."

"I see. Where all have you played, out of town, I mean? Memphis? Knoxville?"

"Naw," Bumper said. He was getting irritated at all the questions. He pretended to look out the bathroom door when it swung open one time to see what time it was on the beer company's hanging promotional clock, a small seaview diorama that endlessly fascinated the Hog Locker drinkers. "Listen, I got to get back to work. Uh, really we just play here, Quill. Like a steady gig, you know."

"Yeah," Quill said. "Radio?"

Bumper Montreat let go the half-open door and kicked the bottom edge of it with his boot toe as it shut. "What?"

Quill was smiling now. "Have you all done any radio?"

"Not exactly. But Bonnie's working on getting a audition with Bomar Talley to see about her and us getting on the Opry. I mean it, I really got to go. Maybe I'll talk to you later sometime."

"How about tonight—after the show?"

Bumper squnched up his face and said, "Naw, I don't know. Bonnie might be tired."

"Ha, ha." Quill laughed loudly and slapped his pudgy friendly hand on the guitar player's back. "Now that *is* rich, Montreat. After the show, then, I'll take you all out and get you something to eat." Quill shook his head and edged past Bumper out the men's-room door into the main room of the Hog Locker.

Bumper slipped up right after him and tapped his shoulder. "I don't think you heard me. I said—"

"Take me up on it, boy," Quill said. "I can help. And let me tell you something about your sister—that girl don't know the *meaning* of tired."

They followed Quill back into downtown Nashville, him driving a black Lincoln with a Continental kit, them in their Chevrolet nervous and laughing and wondering could this be *it*? They crossed the Cumberland on the truss bridge at Shelby Street and parked over near the Ryman and went to Linebaugh's twenty-four-hour restaurant on Broadway.

After they ordered chopped steak and wedges of meringue pie and coffee, Joe Quill leaned toward Bonnie. "Who writes these songs for you?"

Bonnie tilted her head and smiled wide as both Treat and Bumper pointed at her.

"Well, son of a gun," he said. "I heard that out at the Hog Locker, but I wanted to hear it from you. How long you been writing?"

"Six months or so," Bonnie said. "This batch you heard tonight, I mean. But I always used to be the one that wrote up things, you know, for programs we'd put on at school and such."

"No kidding?" Quill nodded encouragingly.

"And you seen those old ads in the farmers' almanacs, 'Your poems set to music'? We did that too, at home," Bonnie said.

"Not me." Bumper shook his head.

"Except Bumper. But my father and mother and me, the three of us did. We'd get all kinds of poems from this publisher Daddy knew in Knoxville, all kinds of things people'd send in to him—sweet old-fashioned things like sampler verses, and lots of religious ones. Didn't make us much money, a dollar a song, so it was more like a game, to see how many we could do. We'd work em out at the organ, and keep at it till we had a batch done. Then next time we went to Knoxville to shop we'd stop at the publisher's and swap the tunes for new poems to set."

It was that kind of evening, a getting-acquainted time, and later Quill would tell Bonnie how he'd come to the Hog Locker because he got stood up and needed something to do. How he thought she'd talk his ears off, she was so full of beans. How tickled he got thinking about that little Tin Pan Alley family out in the East Tennessee hills. How captivated he was, start to finish.

Quill made his pitch that night to captain their future for them. He had a vision of their career, and he laid it out to them over the beef and baked potatoes. The vision was neither wild nor unique. They would work together and tighten up the act. They would develop a look for the band. There would be rounds of auditioning for record people and publishers—

"But I been in and out of so many publishing houses by now it makes me *sick*," Bonnie said.

"Well, get set to do it all again, Bonnie," Quill said. "This time it'll work."

"I can't believe it."

"You will, Bonnie girl. We'll have you a good, reputable publisher within a month."

"A *month?*" she almost squealed. "Now, why on earth should that happen when here I been flogging away at it for ages?"

Quill smiled. "Cause I can make it happen. People all over this town know me and owe me favors, and there's plenty don't owe me a thing that'll be glad for a chance to work with me. Things ain't exactly like they was in the old days when they booked em straight off the Opry switchboard. Now you got to show em—record people, publishers, all of em—a good plan and a good planner pushing it along. That's what I do and I'm damn good at it. Take your time—think it over and check me out. This is a standing offer."

Quill went on and described how they would put tapes and pictures together, maybe try for a shot or two on the Opry, but mostly get out on the road and find out which songs really connected with all the folks back home. "Then we'll soon as it makes sense see if we can't cut us a hit single. If none of the major labels here in Nashville are interested, we'll start with an independent somewhere. Either way your name will of got around and you'll of built an audience— that's what really makes a record take off. See, you got to look at the big picture and put the whole battle plan together and then just work it and work it. Bang on that plan like a drum, or like a big bluetick hound tracking a boar coon. You just get that audience up a tree and surround it—and keep em there." Joe Quill had gotten kind of het up, Bonnie could see, and Bumper and Treat were slapping the table at his telling them the music business wasn't nothing but hunting. Quill laughed and rolled his eyes and said, "Something like that, anyway."

"What do you get out of it, Mr. Quill?" Bonnie asked.

"It's Joe, Bonnie girl, and what I get is a standard ten percent contract and the chance to have a big time and do business with crazy people like yourselves." They reacted all at once. "Sure you're crazy," Quill said. "We're *all* crazy to be in this business. It don't always show, though." Then, flattering Bonnie, he added, "Or if it does, it's in the nicest ways."

He called for the check and paid it and they left Linebaugh's. Out in the parking lot, with the Ryman Auditorium looming up over them as a great ship dwarfs travelers at a dock, Quill said a few last words and Bonnie knew he was speaking especially to her. "Like I said, it's a standing offer. Bumper's got my card. Call me soon, now, and let's get down to work." Then he got in his Lincoln and drove off into the Nashville night.

At first, after they signed, Quill sent them out in a couple of station wagons with a bass player and a drummer and some equipment. But in what seemed like no time, though it was months, he'd got them a mothballed old '48 GMC bus that'd once belonged to the singer and piano player Johnny Rex Packard. It took a scrubbing inside and out to get rid of the rust and mildew the bus had picked up sitting idle over in Memphis. Bonnie was amused as the mountain traits of helldriver and mechanic came forth in her brother and cousin. They refused to hire a mechanic, convinced as they were from the commingling of bravado and beer that the only differences between the new old bus and their '57 Chevrolet was diesel fuel and size. One of the other players nicknamed it accidentally when he made the remark "When we get out touring, this is sure gonna be Road Hog Heaven." His girl made and framed a sampler that said, "Road Hog Heaven" which they hung up above the driver's right.

Then began a kaleidoscopic year, a blur of touring "behind," or in support of, their first release on Cane Records of Indianapolis. Quill was confident that they could all make more money for the time being by sticking to a small regional label. Almost overnight, Bonnie Montreat would be identi-

fied with the song, the single and then the album which
followed carrying its name:

> *The Big Heart from the Little Valley*
> *Is here to see everything goes all right.*
> *The great big heart from the little old valley's*
> *Gonna love you tonight . . .*

It was a stretch of touring that no matter how hard she'd be
willing to work in the future she would never try to match.
Their killing season, she called it, two hundred and eighty
one-night stands winding all over the South and the upper
Midwest and the Lakes States. "Big Heart" had sold thirty-
some thousand copies by the time Joe Quill got ahold of the
bus and organized the tour—and he was convinced they
could push sales to a hundred thousand by just banging away
at it and not calling in the dogs and pissing on the fire and
going home early.

So bang away they did, in high-school and college gymna-
siums, dressing in the sweat-smelling locker rooms, and in
dark armories and small civic-center coliseums.

Sometimes they were the headline act and sometimes just
the incidental entertainment at a tractor pull or a Shriners'
fundraiser barbecue or a beauty pageant. A Homecoming
Queen would be crowned and Bonnie would watch her go
off with her football-captain date and her aluminum-foil
crown and scepter. Then Bonnie would appear in the follow
spot with her hair all teased out big and bouffant and her
face painted up and her tight strapless sequined dress.
There would be a dazzle and popping of flashbulbs as
different ones came down close to the stage to get their own
souvenir pictures of the rising star. Without fail, she would
upstage the young beauty just crowned, singing her "love
songs and dance tunes." Crowds were captivated.

"Your voice's got honey in it, Bonnie," Quill liked to say,
"but it's got a kick too. That's what got me when I heard you
out at the Hog Locker, and that's what'll get them out there

in America. Sort of a fantasy version of the girl next door, am I right?"

Bonnie laughed and laughed at Joe Quill's loose talk about how it was he would sell her, voice, body and soul. "Not my *soul*, Joe—I got to hold something back!"

Quill said she was getting going in country music at a real good time—it didn't bother him at all that the business had shrunk from its Hank Williams heyday to where now only around eighty radio stations were even playing country. "There's just too many folks out there that want it, *bad!*" And by that Joe Quill meant a hell of a lot of people. Bonnie and Bumper and Treat could see it coming back, because the longer their record was out, the more response they got when they worked the gyms and the armory shows. More and more people clapped at the opening bars of "Big Heart" and joined in on the choruses.

Bonnie came to see that to the women in her audiences she was a pretty doll who brought tears to their eyes when she sang her love songs. Maybe there's some who think it's a bad life I'm living out on the road, she thought, or some who'd call me a painted woman in this makeup and low-cut dress— well, they can all stay home. I'm working hard and giving a lot of myself and I want the women who come to be proud of me and proud of the idea of their daughters doing shows as good as I try to do em.

With the men, of course, she knew, it's completely differ-ent.

All along the tour's itinerary there were promotional ap-pearances at grand openings and rodeos and county fairs and there were publicity spots on the local radio and televi-sion stations. It all felt familiar to her because of the Knox-ville jamboree show years before, except now working and traveling and pushing hard, Bonnie had much less patience with hanging around waiting for this one to get back from lunch, or that one to repair some equipment. But these stops were something you had to do, even wanted to do when you were rested, like Huey Long stopping in at each and every country store to let em know he cared about em and that whatever they were mad about, by damn, he was mad about it, too. It was like that, this dropping in at the country radio station and jawing on the air with the reigning personality, only here you were campaigning for the commercial success of your music. Even if you were a big and longtime star, which Bonnie wasn't, you had to make yourself available and show you weren't putting on airs just because people were paying to see you, show that you just got lucky and tell how everywhere you went folks were so nice and put themselves out for you and gave you such warm receptions. And you admit life out on the road does get tiring, but you wouldn't want to be doing anything else because you love to sing and you love taking your music to the people.

Even when her patience wore thin, Bonnie threw herself into this offstage publicity campaign, making use of her good looks and her wide smile. It involved all kinds of appearances on local television talk shows or early-morning farm-news-and-weather programs, where she'd have to show up at 5:30 A.M.

Radio was more fun. She'd usually drop by a station in the late afternoon after they'd set up the stage and run a sound check. Sometimes, if they were staying over in a motel that night, she'd even drop in on someone's radio show not long after her concert was over. She had a knack for sizing up a situation and she'd be earnest or sassy and flirt just the right amount and butter them up and they'd know it and not mind at all because she had a lot of good spirit mixed in with her ambition.

And when she came back around the second time with her record for them to play she'd almost always find a warmer welcome and a stronger interest. I guess it goes like this, she thought, that you can see the progress from one time to the next, and the progress since I set my mind to it and started working up our show back at the Hog Locker.

It was working, first her plan and now Joe Quill's. Bonnie

Montreat would ride the upward spirals of fortune the way birds ride thermal winds, for as long and as high as the warm and rising air would carry her. Every day the Big Heart from the Little Valley was gaining scores of suitors and admirers. The old and ever-new story of success was becoming her own.

# JOHNNY REX PACKARD
1960

Caldonia Prison was a turn-of-the-century fortress, maximum security, a devil's island in a sea of scrub pines way down below Montgomery. The squared-off horseshoe faced due south, toward the Gulf and the sun. There was a large yard and a wall with a watchtower on each corner.

Johnny Rex Packard came to Caldonia a famous man and a rich man, though legal fees and back taxes and Phelps Range's bankruptcy finished that. For a while, he was the object of leering, jeering taunts about his case and his women. He never responded.

Then the Alabama Governor, to repay a political debt to the lawyer Vance Garland, had Packard's sentence commuted from death to life. The taunts got more bitter. Being albino, Johnny Rex could only bear the Deep-South light early or late, so they gave him a special time, after sunrise and just before sunset, summer and winter, to exercise. He walked the yard alone, and the cries rained down on him from the cellblocks above.

"What you gon do next, Packard, sing your way out?"

"Governor owes me a favor, too, Johnny Rex. I'll be getting the chair next week, chair you was supposed to get, white boy. You hear me?"

He heard them, every morning and night, but their voices

sounded flat and puny and faraway to him. His head ached more and more often and he just let it.

"Sing me out, too, niggerlover."

"I'll make it my last request, Johnny Rex. Tell the Governor I want to hear 'Hell Power'—I been in hell half my life but the only power I'll ever get'll be those last ten thousand volts."

Johnny Rex heard or imagined he heard blacks in his cellblock whispering among themselves at night that he was a conjure man, that he was hagridden by the ghost of that wife he'd killed and that was why he'd got no strength to do or say much of anything.

He thought his mind must be shutting down on him, the way his head ached and he couldn't concentrate or think straight for very long anymore. He ate his meals with the rest, but his eyes wouldn't focus on anyone whenever he looked up from his tin plate. They gave him a simple, repetitive job, punching license plates with the slogan BIG BEAUTIFUL ALABAMA beneath the numbers.

No one ever heard the first complaint from him. There were religious services in the prison, and there was a piano. The warden invited him to join them, to play, but he acted like he hadn't heard. He never came.

Johnny Rex lost the desire that had driven him, lost all sense of mission or message. His feet led him down corridors and his hands did his work; his eyes opened for him by morning and closed for him by night, and he slept deep and dreamless. Not a year before, he could of looked into any face in that prison and heard within him the song that told its story and sung it back. But now he knew no man and heard no music. There was nothing to say.

One day while working at his job in the industrial room his mind went all the way blank on him, as if a black curtain fell before his eyes. Reflexively he pulled the lever that dropped a press under hundreds of pounds of pressure on the top of his left index finger. He collapsed, but no one heard him cry out. Johnny Rex lost a joint, but when he was healed up and

ready to come out of the infirmary he made the longest
remark anyone would hear from him for years to come:
"I want my old job back."


# PRESTON HEWITT
1960–1965


At Harvard College, Preston began to get his nerve back.

He lined up with his classmates along Holyoke Street to eat
roast-beef sandwiches and lobster salad at Elsie's, bought
dollar-a-bottle wine at the Broadway Supermarket sales,
went to dinners at the Trowbridge Street apartment of one
of his tutors and became accustomed to halibut and sword-
fish steaks. He took part in the great Bogart revival at the
Brattle Theatre, and drank espresso at the Blue Parrot
coffeehouse or beer at the Casablanca bar, with its enormous
wall poster from the movie *Hell's Angels*. He learned to call a
drugstore with a soda fountain a "spa" and a milk shake a
"frappe." He skirted the little knots of dark-suited close-
cropped Black Muslims who hung around Harvard Square
hawking copies of *Muhammad Speaks* and playing on white
guilt—"Come on, man, you got plenty money or you
wouldn't *be* here!"

And he sang and played guitar, at first in his Parsons Entry
room for his own entertainment, but soon as his reputation
spread in various places around campus. He sang the folk
songs he'd first heard at Skyliner, though he let on that he'd
grown up on them, and ballads of peace and civil rights, and
popular songs he culled from the recordings of Seeger and
Baez and that new boy from upper Minnesota that everybody said sang like a pig in barbed wire, Bob Dylan. Preston
played in residence hall commons, at picnics and parties, and
by his second year he'd worked up enough of a repertoire
and following to play hoots, open nights at the Boston clubs.

Plenty of others were doing the same, and before long the clubs were glutted with solo folksingers. A handful, Preston included, decided to throw in together and formed the Baker's Dozen Jug Band, a hodgepodge modeling itself after the old Memphis jug bands of the '20s and '30s. By 1963, when Pres and the others were finishing up school, they were the house band on every fourth weekend at the Club 99½. And they'd made a record. Pres had renewed his contact with Israel Palomar at the Folk Town label in New York where the Skyliner field recordings had been pressed and promoted, and he'd been able to sell him on the jug band's bright, snappy act. They played dates at colleges and folk festivals around the Northeast and dates in coffeehouses down in the Village in New York where people lounged around in Levi's and denim workshirts and talked about Hemingway and Paris in the '20s or Ginsberg and the City Lights Bookstore out on the Coast.

Every now and then some political type would collar one of the band members in a dressing room or out on the street after a show and demand to know why the Baker's Dozen which was having such a field day with old-time black music didn't do more with its popularity and talent and money to help with the protest movement. Why indeed? He'd read in the *Crimson* about some of his fellow staff trainees from years ago at Skyliner; they were out on a retreat in the East Tennessee hills when local sheriff's deputies moved in on them and burned their camp. They themselves were beaten and arrested and charged with interracial sexual activity. That was only one of many such incidents in those years. Preston kept his own counsel.

But that day in August of 1963 when King and half a million astounded Washington and the world, he sat in his apartment in Boston watching television and burning with shame and fury. I should have been there, Pres thought. He felt like a nomad who had folded his tents in the night and spat over his shoulder as he retreated into the arid wastes of his spiritual desert.

Then the world changed. Oswald carried his long gun to
the high perch in Dallas and coolly did his gruesome work.
Preston Hewitt felt justified, even perspicacious, in his growing cynicism. He spoke to his friends after Dallas with an acid
cocky voice that all but said, I called that one right on the
money, didn't I, now? He began to affect country slang and
pass himself off as one Southerner who really understood
what was going on down there. He knew what he was doing.

"You see," Preston said to the singer Annalee before a club
date, "it don't matter what you do, or how good you might
be, they'll get you. Every time." Annalee shook her head and
said, "But who *are* they, Pres? Who could be so evil?" And
Preston, though he knew that the thinking was sloppy, was
applauded for quipping, "Ah, the Oswalds, the Klan, Bull
Connor's firehoses, Dade County's cops—Them."

The Baker's Dozen Jug Band played on. They made two
more records for Folk Town and developed a small, strong
following in the collegiate Northeast. But folk music got
harder and louder as Johnson grabbed the reins and jerked
them tight and bombarded the nation first with his Great
Society and then with his Vietnam. Pres and Annalee and the
others had scarcely gotten through their set that year at the
Rhode Island Folk Festival when the hero of folk music,
Dylan of Minnesota, strode out onto the stage with an
electric guitar and ended the innocence of the urban folk
revival.

Even before that Preston had seen the handwriting on the
wall. He was feeling restless and ready to try something
tougher than jug music. The right time to pull out of the
Baker's Dozen came along. Half the band's members turned
to a Boston bicycle mechanic who proclaimed himself a
spiritual leader and healer in the Eastern tradition; the other
half parlayed marijuana hobbies into serious flirtations with
heroin. They were all of them living in a enormous falling-
down rowhouse in Roxbury, panhandling by day for spare
change and by night attempting, in hastily assembled duos
and trios, to recapture even a fraction of their former
audience.

Preston Hewitt had too much a sense of self-preservation to hang around Boston in a scene that was slowly dying. He walked to a pay phone down the street late one afternoon and called Israel Palomar at Folk Town and told him he oughtn't expect anything more from the Baker's Dozen. He described the living situation of the band and the fixations of its members on religion and drugs.

"Jesus, Pres," Palomar said at the other end of the line, "I'd heard last month about you all not making the jobs in Rochester and Pittsburgh, but the impression I got was that it was illness both times."

"It was lies, Izzy. The band's gone to hell."

"Why're you telling me this? Why don't you get in there and straighten up the act and get another album out? Let's get back to work!"

"Shit, Izzy, they don't want to work. They've gotten into junk and crap religion. You can't go onstage drunk or high and expect anybody to pay attention. I'm telling you because they're going to hell and I ain't going with them. And because *I* for one might just want to come back and record for you again."

"Come back from where?" Palomar said. "You going back to Tennessee?"

"You kidding me, Izzy? I'm going to England for a while." *"England?"*

"You heard me right. I got almost fifteen thousand socked away and a brand-new passport."

"Well, goddamn, son." Israel Palomar laughed on the other end of the phone. "I think I'm catching on. Known you, what, five, six years, and I thought you were just one of the crowd." Then Izzy's voice turned serious. "I almost forgot—have you heard about Hal Milton?"

"No, what?" Pres said.

"He was down in Nashville last night leading a civil-rights march at the State Capitol. Had a massive stroke and died on the Capitol steps before they could get him to a doctor."

Preston Hewitt's throat clutched.

"Think you could fly down for the funeral? It'll be in

Knoxville and then they're burying him out near the old Skyliner place."

"No, I . . . got too much to square here before I take off. I'm sorry."

"I know it's a shock, Pres, very upsetting. He was a great American."

Pres mumbled something.

"Keep in touch, okay?"

"I will."

"Goodbye, son."

"Goodbye, Izzy."

They rang off. And Preston Hewitt's reserves of cynicism failed him now and the scar tissue that for years had protected him from his hurt over his part in the ruin of Skyliner fell away from him. He leaned his head against the Plexiglas wall of the Roxbury telephone booth and wept bitter, bitter tears.

# BONNIE MONTREAT
## 1964–1966

Joe Quill parked his Lincoln on Hawkins between Sixteenth and Seventeenth Avenues South and came around to open the door for Bonnie. He held his arm out to her and they strolled around the corner and on down Seventeenth not quite a block to a two-story ruddy-brick bungalow. Bonnie was wearing her cowgirl culottes and had her hair in two heavy braids. She looked like a redhead Annie Oakley.

"Remember," Quill said as they walked, "nobody said this was a sure thing."

"Yeah, Joe." Bonnie winked at him. "But it ain't shaping up half bad." Joe Quill had been angling for some time now to hook her up with the man waiting on them upstairs in the Music Row bungalow. She'd met the man a time or two doing guest spots on the *Opry,* and Quill had picked it up around town that he was interested in her and liked her music. When his longtime singing partner Sandra Gay announced her retirement, Quill had tried to place Bonnie on his road show going out, but she was still locked into her own touring schedule and missed the chance. It was a disappointment. Then there was the pressure of the other *Opry* women not to let her in. Every star's package tour had one slot, two at most, for a woman singer; a new girl in town, if allowed onto the *Opry* and thus into the pool of candidates for the "woman's slot," was a very real threat. There were women who'd been on the *Opry* almost since Hank Williams' day, waiting in line, waiting their turns, and now here comes this pretty young thing from East Tennessee who writes her own tunes and might get to go before them to the head of the class. Bonnie Montreat with her fiery copper hair and that odd distinctive curl to her high voice—the *Opry* women wanted none of her. There was backstabbing and it was fierce. But now Quill believed that with her touring experience, the exposure she'd gotten and the respectable hit she'd had with "Big Heart," there was no way Bonnie and the Green Valley Band could be denied becoming part of the *Opry* cast and part of a main-chance package show.

They stood at the leaded-glass swinging doors and read off the string of businesses: Talley Entertainment, Inc.; Talley Music Publishing, Inc.; Talley Enterprises, Inc. Bonnie said in a low bawdy tone she could get away with using on Quill, "Got his fingers in a lot of pies, Joe."

"Hell, he's got ten, ain't he?"

"Fingers, or pies?"

"Get on in there, girl."

Inside the door, the receptionist was fixing to unwrap a sandwich and have lunch at her desk. She reached for the intercom, but Bonnie saw Quill give her his thick-as-thieves look and the two of them breezed on by. Quill said over his shoulder, "He's expecting us. That's all right, I know the way," and up the stairs they went. Through the open door of the corner office down the hall, Bonnie could hear the man's voice as he worked somebody over on the telephone: "Hell, you tell that wedgeheaded buzzard it's *always* gonna cost a little more the next time than the last, and if he keeps on thinking our little more is too much, you tell him he just ain't thinking *big enough* for Bomar Talley. You hear? Fine. Do what now?"

Bonnie and Joe Quill walked into the office door and waited for the business call to end. There sat Bo Talley in a swivel captain's chair, his back to them, and his snakeskin cowboy-booted feet propped up on the sill of a big plate-glass window that looked out on an enormous walnut tree. The phone was cradled between his ear and his shoulder and he was all hunched forward working on a loose thread in his right boot with a letter opener. Between saying "No" and "Unh-hunh" and "Don't let em do you like that," Talley took the boot off and stood up and leaned into his work. Abruptly, he wheeled around and saw Quill and Bonnie. "What? Listen, Clyde, I'm getting confused and mad about this and there's a damn good-looking woman just come walking in here with that crazy man Joe Quill, so you work this out yourself and check me later, all right? All right." He hung up. "Well, hello, Red—where you been all my life?" The big man in the pastel denim cowboy suit stepped practically over his desk.

Quill said, "Bo, this is—"

"Hell, Joe, I know Bonnie Montreat when I see her. Yes, ma'am, met you at the Ryman, don't know if you remember. Bomar Talley at your service."

"Nice to see you again, Mr. Talley."

"Bomar, Bomar, call me Bomar." He turned around long enough to snatch a sheaf of papers off his desk.

"Bomar, then," she said.

"Listen—you all grab a seat. Just got to run these contracts down the hall and then I'll be right back and we'll just hold the calls and visit, how about it? Joe, how you doing? Why don't you come up here for a week and get this place *right*? I swear it's hellacious sometimes. Be right back." He lunged into the hall like a replacement in a tag team match.

"He's a pistol," Quill said. "I've known him a good many years now. When he first decided to try Nashville, I got some of his records around to make sure he didn't come into town a stranger."

"Hmm," she said. "A fellow like him ain't gonna stay a stranger anywhere very long."

Quill laughed. "No, but you know by now how far a little help can go in this town, and how much time you can kill without it."

"Yeah." She smiled. She was relaxed, sure of herself and comfortable with Quill's judgment in all this. He felt that there was no stronger career move she could make than to work in Bo Talley's road show, and that there was a strong possibility Bo would make her an offer. Bonnie stood up and put her hands on her rib cage just below her breasts and stretched. "Late session last night, Joe."

"I'd of liked to been there, but you know how it goes. All this running ragged don't seem to be hurting you none," Quill said, adding with genuine affection, "You look real good, Bonnie, real on top of things."

"Why, Joe." She was touched.

"I mean it, Bonnie girl. You look good and healthy and happy. That rubs off on me, you know—makes me feel like I'm doing a good job. This meeting today makes me feel good, too. You and Bo'd be real strong together, and I mean *real* strong. You ever caught one of his live shows?"

"One time years ago in Knoxville."

"Well, then you know. Bo can pure *T* take an audience and charm its ass off. You got that magic, too, but you can always learn something from somebody like Bo that's been out there ten years longer than you."

"I'd be proud. He's a old pro."

"He ain't so old, Bonnie. You like him?"

"Well, yeah, what I've seen. But besides, he's married, so don't go getting any ideas. Look at these pictures here." On the walls between framed posters and acetates and gold records there were gilt-frame snapshots, many of them of a woman and two children.

"Ida," Joe said. "*That's* a whole nother story. She ain't exactly what you'd call *around* anymore."

The lanky Texan strode back into his office, already talking. "I hate I kept you waiting. Did you get any coffee? Here, there's some cold drinks in this little frigerator under my desk, should of told you before I went down the way. Damn." He sat down all at once and grinned. "Joe, we fought em off long's we could, but now we might just have to roll over and let em get us. I'm telling you."

"What now, Bo?"

"Television, man, *TV*. Ain't quite got it worked out yet, but I'm getting there, running in circles and jumping through hoops, mmm, *mmm!*"

The two men talked fast and showy for a while, and when it settled down a hair Quill went straight to business. "Bo, since Sandra Gay's left the Opry and retired you've got quite a hole to fill. I've talked this road-show business over with you, and I've talked it over with Bonnie." Quill glanced at Bonnie and smiled sagely. "Now, she and I both know a slot like this don't open up every day, and that there's a lot of talented women in this town you owe it to yourself to consider. But I figured since you showed some interest when we talked last Monday that I ought to get her down here with you so you could talk straight to each other and see where things stood. It's one of these personal-chemistry things." Quill tilted back in his chair and folded his hands over his stomach. "Then there's that whole business about the *Opry* women and Bonnie getting on or not getting on. A few things to talk about, I reckon."

Bo Talley swung around in his captain's chair and studied Bonnie a moment, wide shirt collars with silvery points flying out over his coat lapels. He breathed deeply and spoke up. "Okay, last things first. As far as them gals ganging up on you, Bonnie, don't you worry. I can handle them. I have a pretty fair idea you'll be invited in the next week or two to join the *Opry* cast regular."

Could of knocked me over with a feather, she thought.

"But about the road show itself, now." Bo Talley swung back around to Quill. "Far's I'm concerned, Bonnie is a fine, coming talent, and I don't have one doubt in the world she'd be a great asset to the Bomar Talley Show. But now money, Joe, we touched on this a bit, and like I said then, the lions got to take the lion's share."

Quill nodded. "I think we can get together."

Bonnie Montreat looked back and forth between the men—they were way ahead of her. Bo mistook her puzzlement for censure of his money remark.

"What concerns me is your band, Bonnie, cost for one thing, cause it'll mean extra salaries and a extra bus. And keeping em in line for another, cause that's something I just can't be bothered with. So here's what I'd say: If you want to front for your own band, that's fine. But you got to absorb the cost—them and the bus—and make sure they don't get in my hair. I guess I couldn't say it any plainer."

"Bonnie?" Quill said.

"I got to take the Green Valley Band. It's my family—at least Bumper and Treat. I don't mind about the cost, but I need them, you understand?"

"Sure," Talley said. "If it's just the three of you, there'd be room on my bus. Good so far. Now the other thing: Would you be willing to work at least some with my band, to come out during my set and sing a duet or two with me?"

Bonnie's mouth dropped, and Quill's face stayed absolutely blank.

"Lord, Bomar, working with you that way, that's more than I ever thought might happen. I'd love to, of course."

"Wonderful," Bo Talley said. "That'd really juice the show up for me. I'll look forward to that."

There was a moment of silence.

"Is that it?" Bonnie said. "I mean, are we gonna *do* this?"

"Hell, yes!" Bo Talley said. "Life's easy when you know how

to say what you want. Joe, have we all said the same thing at the same time in the same place? Ain't that your rule?"

"Sounds like," Quill said.

"Well, that's just fine." Bomar Talley stretched out his West Texas arm and shook Bonnie's hand. "Looks like we got us a good old *country deal!* How bout dinner?"

She waited at her place for him to pick her up and went through all the stories she'd heard about him.

The line on Bo Talley was that he'd come out of panhandle Texas DJ-ing some small country station and moved on to the Texas equivalent of the *Louisiana Hayride* and then got a band going and started putting out records—that was where Quill came in. He had a hit in the mid-'50s and weathered the storm of rock 'n' roll, even cut a few songs that did all right on the rock-'n'-roll charts. Along about 1955 or 1956 he'd joined the *Opry,* and by now Bo Talley was a major star. He drove a race car and wore opal and turquoise necklaces with his cowboy suits and had a little replica of a steamboat that he'd ride his friends around on at his place out on the north shore of Old Hickory Lake.

She'd heard he was wild, at least when he was drinking, but she'd been around town long enough to know that nobody much cared so long as the records got cut and the jobs got played and the money got made. Stories about Bo's drinking and running women were famous. One time he'd been showing some old Texas buddies around town, and they ended up at the country-music bars down on Lower Broadway between the train station and the Cumberland. The friends took off and left Bomar drunk with no idea where he'd parked his car. After an hour or more of searching he'd gone into a souvenir shop and bought him a big straw hat and a pair of sunglasses and went to the Grayline there on Broadway and took the homes-of-the-stars tour. When they announced his house, he got off.

She'd heard how his wife, Ida Talley, had surprised him at a hotel room where he'd put on some girl's slip and was chasing her around. When he opened the door and saw his wife, he boomed at her boozily, "Look, honey—see what I bought you." And how not long after that Ida was going to have a hysterectomy and she called the Country Music Organization's Hall of Fame and offered in all seriousness to bronze her uterus and donate it to the museum. Not long after that Ida went around the bend.

Bomar Talley raised his glass and said, "Partners?"

Bonnie responded, "You're the boss."

They were at Ireland's near Music Row, sitting in a little alcove behind frosted-glass windows with shamrock and Irish cross etchings on them.

"Now listen to me, Bonnie," Bo Talley said. He put his glass down and loosened his string tie with its longhorn clasp. "I mean for us to be working together on this thing, cheek by jowl like it was for me and Sandra Gay. You can keep to yourself as much as you want, or you can kill time with me—I been working too much and too hard and I just want to get back out on the road and see some country, have a good time, do the show, drink whiskey and talk soft to a pretty girl—you get what I'm saying?" When she didn't answer right off, he said, "Oh, shut up, Bo," and slugged back a big gulp of beer.

Bonnie gave him a serious gentle smile and reached over and touched his hand. "It's all right, Bomar. I just got to feel my way a little slow, I guess. I ain't in quite the hurry I was when we hit town a few years back. Now we're getting it worked out to travel with your show, things are starting to really make sense. But you throw too much at a girl all at once and she's liable to get her head turned to where she can't keep her balance. My turn to shut up."

He pointed at her beer and she smiled and hoisted the glass.

"I guess we both said a mouthful," Bo Talley said.

"Well, we ain't neither of us the quiet type."

"Been here before?"

"A few times with the band."

"Good-looking gal like you ain't got no boyfriend knows how to show her a good time?"

"Busy as we been, there ain't much way to keep up with anybody. Anyhow, I don't much care about letting some fellow waste a lot of money trying to impress me."

Bomar Talley looked at her cockeyed.

"I don't mean *you*, Bo. Tonight, this is celebrating, ain't it?" Bonnie said. Talley looked down at the table like he was hurt. "You mad at me?" she said.

He kept looking down a moment, then broke into an enormous grin and said, "For *not* having a steady boyfriend, you kidding?"

She breathed out a deep noisy sigh. "That was *mean*, Bomar. Now you owe me. Tell me straight: Where's your wife I saw in all those pictures in your office?" He looked down at the table again the same way and she thought, He's joking me again. Now he's gonna look up and grin.

Instead he stood up abruptly. "I'm gonna go out to the car and have a smoke and see can't I figure out how to answer that without getting you and me both upset." He walked off, leaving her feeling foolish and rude, and was back in five minutes with a whiskey glow on his face. He leaned in close to her across the table like he was going to say something intimate or secret.

"I could tell you a story about every table in this room. Who was with who and wrote which country hit just setting there after dinner."

"What are you talking about? I thought you were mad at me for asking about your wife and now you're talking to me like I was a tourist."

"Hadn't you ever heard that saying about the truth being stranger than publicity?"

"I'm not sure we're working out so good."

"Don't you see, Bonnie? There's a million stories and you got to pick your way through em like a soldier in a minefield. I reckon you heard a tale or two about me and Ida already, but the truth is this." He told how his wife had an operation a few years back and came from the hospital a day early. Bo'd had a wild stag party going on, and something about it set her off—she'd gone to screaming and tearing up around the house, throwing things, almost talking in tongues. They called an ambulance, and the doctor told him later she'd had a combination nervous breakdown and stroke. "They's a big name for it. We put her in a special-care home in Franklin. I send her flowers, used to go see her, but she just stared at me. She might as well of been staring at a petrified ham for all she recognized me. I pretty much quit going. Doctor says she could come out of it tomorrow, or two years from now, or never. I take care of her fine, don't you worry about *that*, but I got a life to live and a business to run, so I push on."

The big heart from the little valley brushed a tear from her eye. "Do you still love her?"

"Well, sure, but it's real different. Not like being married at all. That woman out there at Franklin with the blank look just ain't Ida, just ain't the woman I married."

The waitress cruised in balancing a big tray with their steak platters, and the sight of the beef kicked Bomar Talley back into his earlier humor. "Medium?" said the waitress as she handed that platter to Bonnie. "And rare for you, Mr. Talley."

"Yes, ma'am, you know me," Bomar Talley said as he helped set the beef plate down in front of him. "I like to see the blood run."

It was breezy there at the flight service of the Nashville Metro Airport. Bonnie stepped into the hangar and studied the great Southeastern navigation map on the wall and slid the course-and-distance ruler from Texas to Alabama and back. Bo signed in with Crockett, the burly fellow who ran the flight service.

"We'll be back later on this afternoon," Bo said. "Come on, Bonnie Montreat, let's you and me get out there and bore some holes in the sky."

Bo Talley yelled, "Clear!" out the pilot's window and cranked the engine of his 172. He grinned at Bonnie. "Trust God and Pratt and Whitney." In moments they were hundreds of feet above Nashville.

She looked west at the downtown skyscrapers, the Life & Casualty Tower and the Capitol building, and there on the near side, big as the house of God, was their home place, the Ryman Auditorium.

Then she looked off into the distance of what Bo called a "seven-mile day." Even with that kind of visibility, she marveled at what all there was in the air. Everywhere was a white and gauzy haze, as if all the textile mills of the South had opened their vents and stacks and blown their lint-laden air skyward where the cotton dust hung together and created a white pall above the Southern lands.

But there was more to it than that. She saw in the patchworks and checkerboards of the landscape the little whirlwinds that blew the dust up out of the fields, and near highways she could see batteries of bulldozers and earthmovers kicking up clouds of dust. And more clouds steamed out of stacks and escape valves on the roofs of countless aluminum buildings.

Bonnie had got so wrapped up in the hustle of Nashville's commercial music scene that she'd scarcely noticed the sound and light and motion of the sky's-the-limit New South all around her. Everywhere there was Growth, the ravenous phoenix nesting this time in the South. In the country, especially in the country near the cities, the sign of it was the clods of earth tracked out of the vanishing forests on the tires of the massive sixteen-wheel dump trucks hauling away the trees and brush and rock from somewhere back off the hard road to make way for Briarcliff or Ridgefield or Kingswood. These were signs of a new plant locating, of jobs, of new homes for imported managers to live in. Bonnie Montreat gazed out from the airplane and realized that these tracks of spilled red clay on country roads marked the appearance of a new landscape, the passing of the old. It moved her.

Bo reached around behind the seat and tried to get something loose from under his guitar case, but he couldn't manage. "Bonnie, can you catch that folder under there with the plastic on it? I want you to see where we're heading."

They landed on a grass strip named Logan's, a high meadow rimmed by several Piedmont peaks about forty miles southeast of Nashville. The field was cut in half by a dirt road leading up from the blacktop through the airstrip past the only official structure at the field, a wind sock. "Family that keeps it up has a boy down at a base in South Carolina flies himself home from time to time, and no one much else uses it but me. I like to come down here and think."

They touched down and taxied and stopped. Beneath some metal flashing at the base of the wind-sock pole were a few dryrotting tire chocks. Bo secured the plane as best he could and reached in for his guitar. He and Bonnie walked down the road through a pine thicket and beyond to a little hillside pond.

She lay back in some clover along the pond's edge where there was a break in the reeds and cattails, and she stared up at the ever-whitening August sky. Bo sat in a tailor's crouch and tuned his guitar, and for the next hour or so they worked on the bridge of "Pride of the Valley." It had given them a lot of trouble. The song itself was in the key of G, but the bridge went to an F chord and had some half steps in it. The verse ended with Bomar singing melody on the tonic G note, and Bonnie harmonizing on the B a third above. On the bridge, Bo dropped a full step to the F while she went up a half to C but then slid down half steps to B, B-flat, A as he held the F, and then she went back up to the B, sliding through the B-flat as he slid up the G through F-sharp. It worked like that twice. Then on the third line of the bridge he was supposed to slide down to the D below while she went up an octave above him. There was nothing difficult about the idea. With the blend their voices enjoyed—his husky and burred, and hers high and curled—it was the kind of vocal work that would sound slick and effortless and would distinguish them as a duet team over the coming years. But right now they were just starting, just getting it down, and it only sounded good if it was pitch-perfect.

The air got still and stifling. They went up the bank in the deep blue-green shade of the pines, but even so they were each one sweating like they were in a steambath. They got the bridge of that tune to where it was just about right—it wasn't rough and out-sounding like it had been, but it was still tentative.

"I got an idea," Bo said.

"What's that?" Bonnie narrowed her green eyes.

"Let's just flat-out get this right a time or two, and take us a swim." He nodded over toward the pond.

Bonnie held the top button of her blouse away from her like she was airing her bosom. She decided she'd agree. "Okay, Bo."

After that bargain was struck, there wasn't much working. She went around behind a patch of cattails and shed her slacks and blouse and shoes, keeping on her pants and brassiere. And she remembered with a turn in her stomach all the times she and Treat swam naked in the deep hole at the big willow crook of Welsh Girl's Creek.

Bonnie made Bo Talley look away while she eased into the murky tepid water of the pond. "I'm keeping a eye on you, Bo," she said, then looked away while he stripped down. She padded around, trying to keep her feet out of the cool muck on the bottom of the pond, and heard him come on into the water. He sidestroked out to the middle of the acre-and-a-half pond and waved her to come on out.

"Can't do it, Bo. It'd mess my hair up."

"What's the matter? You got a date tonight?"

"Damn straight," Bonnie said. "With you."

He swam back in and from a distance of about ten feet splashed at her and she shrieked at him, "Don't *do* that, Bo!" But he splashed her again, so she retaliated. The water rolled off his pompidoo like his hair was the feathers of a duck's back. Then he dove under and came back up out in the middle of the pond where he'd been before. He went down again, and again, each time coming up someplace different from where she'd expected him to. Finally he surfaced about three or four feet behind her and she whirled around. She dove over at him and wrapped her good gammy legs around his waist, leaving him no choice but to hold her around her back with his big hands. She'd surprised him, she could tell, but she didn't care and spoke before he had a chance to:

"I got too many clothes on."

He reached up under her bra strap. "Yeah, I believe you do." Then he locked his fingers together and made a seat beneath her bottom and carried her out of the water that way. Her arms were around his neck and she kissed him lightly on his neck and ear. When they got to the clover, he let her down. She could feel that he was limp as he pressed against her.

"You not interested, Bo?" She wondered if she'd over-stepped her bounds.

He shook his head. "That's not it. You just got to bear with me a little." She sat in the clover and watched while he went over to his clothes and got something out of his wallet. Must be medicine, she thought, because he leaned his head back like when you take a pill. Well, you can't go all the way halfway. She quick got out of her bra and pants and tossed them away while he wasn't looking so when he strode back to her both of them were naked.

"I didn't mean this to be part of your job, Bonnie."

"Come on down here in this clover with me before I get my feelings hurt," she said. And so he did. She loved him with her eyes open, rocked with him easy in the grass with eyes wide open as she watched the great white steamy clouds roil up in the distance.

"I got to hand it to you, Joe," Bonnie said. "This sure beats what we *were* doing." She and Quill were having a drink in the hotel bar after a show at Stockyard Hall in Kansas City.

Bo Talley had been called away to deal with the problems a half a dozen business calls held in store for him. Poor Bo, she thought. Even out on the road, it never really lets up.

Quill said, "Well, Bonnie girl, you wouldn't be doing *this* if you hadn't of been doing *that* first."

Joe sure has a way of keeping you humble, she thought. Of reminding you that one thing leads to the next, step by weary step. The first eight or ten months had been pretty rough on her, what with Bo's audiences yelling like they'd half been betrayed, "Who's *she?* Where's Sandra Gay?" Then Bonnie and Bo's first duet, "Pride of the Valley," had been released and they'd gotten used to her high curly voice and quickly swung around to where now they loved her, just like that. And all those *Opry* women who'd voted against her and catted about her had come around, too, and now would invite her to the quilting bees and say, "Aw, honey, you *know* we always loved you." Now Joe sat with her in St. Lou sipping on a double shot of Old Crow and running his finger down a column of figures on a sheet of paper. "What you got there?" Bonnie asked.

"Oh, it's the breakdown for the expenses of the show tonight. The promoter's a old friend of mine. Gave me a Thermofax."

He handed it to her and she read down the column of itemized budget figures. The Montreats took two thousand dollars, the coliseum staff and rental of the hall itself took another two, tickets cost fifteen hundred to print up, and almost seven thousand dollars had gotten eaten up by advertising on radio and television and in the newspapers.

"That's almost as much for tickets as *we're* getting, Joe."

"Lot of people'll run through a lot of tickets."

Twelve hundred dollars or so got skimmed off to pay a variety of taxes and to cover the royalty to Broadcast Music, the song-licensing agency. "And goddamn, look a there," Bonnie said, "under 'Misc.,' they even spent a couple hundred bucks on a blurb in *TV Week*, for God's sakes."

"The place was sold out," Quill said.

"I know, I know."

"Okay, darling, let's see." Quill got out his yellow plastic mechanical pencil and started figuring. "Maximum gross was about thirty, and this batch of things, including you, takes it down to sixteen thousand. Talley has a guarantee of six. That leaves ten thousand he splits straight up with the promoter—nice work."

Bonnie looked off and thought a moment, her mouth just slightly open and her tongue resting against the roof of her mouth. "Be nice when we can get *our*selves in that position."

"Don't you worry," Quill said. "You're on the right track. There's a lot of talk about Bo's television show. What'd you all have coming out of the gate, two dozen stations? I'll lay you good money that the show'll be syndicated to double that by the end of the year."

"*Fifty* stations?"

"Yep. And double *that* over the next year."

Bonnie shook her head. "I know it's been doing real good, but that just sounds incredible, Joe. How can it happen so fast?"

"Think about it. First of all, it's cheap to make, which means you can sell it cheap to the individual station and still come out making good money. And then it's good old cornshucking, outhouse-humor programming. People want it, and the stations *know* they want it, but they can't get it from the networks. It's just about a surefire thing for an advertiser, if he wants to reach country people or blue-collar people, to have Bo Talley and Bonnie Montreat plugging his product every Saturday afternoon or Wednesday evening or whenever the local station plays it. I tell you, I'm glad Bo got in it early as he did, cause there's a half a dozen more either starting up their own shows or talking serious about it. It could get pretty damn hot out there."

Bonnie Montreat liked the down-to-earth feel of the *Bomar Talley Jamboree Show,* the half-hour program they taped right there in Nashville and shipped out to the local stations that syndicated it. They did it in color, even though it cost more. When Bonnie had reminded Bomar that most all their audience only had black-and-white televisions, he'd said, "You got to think bigger than that, Bonnie. Never can tell when the networks might get interested, and they'd want color. No, ma'am, you never know."

"Go on, Bo—networks?"

"You got to be prepared for anything. We're picking up a subscriber every other week or so. How bout let's just roll with it and see what happens."

On the show, they didn't use Bumper and Treat, they used Bo's band and that was it. The budget wouldn't allow otherwise. The boys seemed to enjoy the time off and usually spent it out on Old Hickory or Percy Priest roaring around in a bassboat drinking beer, but she knew it peeved Bumper for her to be up there in front of Talley's band without them—he'd told her so.

"Bo's band, Bonn, it don't sound like *we* do. I mean, it's country and all, but it's got that swing in it that he brings to about every song he does. Whole nother fiddle style, too."

Bo Talley was brought up on the West Texas swing sound. He was famous for a polished blend of roadhouse honky-tonk and upbeat Southwestern swing, and all his fiddlers over the years had played Texas longbow fiddle. It was a smooth elliptical style that bore almost no resemblance to the raw, driving, even scraping mountain sound, derived from dance tunes played with a shortbow, a "jiggy" bow, and a fiddle held not to the chin but slam against the fiddler's breastbone or cradled in the crook of his arm. This was Bonnie's heritage and this was the kind of playing she got from Treat. Bumper's minding about her being up there on the show without them grew partly from his feeling that the songs came out different somehow on television from the way they were on her records. He was right, but it didn't bother Bonnie considering the amount of exposure she got from the show.

She knew that another part of what ragged Bumper was

simply her independence. They weren't all in on things anymore like they were back at the Hog Locker. And something else about Bumper—he was jealous of Bo. Not cutting or shooting jealous, but jealous that bumped along and boiled up every now and then. When it did come out, she thought that if Bumper could work up such feelings about Bo Talley, to whom they all owed so much professionally, he'd probably kill her if he ever found out about Treat. It made her uneasy.

"You better watch your step, Bonn," Bumper would sneer, "cause half this town knows you're polishing Bo's knob regular—"

"You listen, Bumper. I don't go round flaunting nothing and neither does Bo, so whose business is it but his or mine anyway?"

"Hell, I'm your brother."

"Oh, quit, Bump—I'm twenty-six years old, ain't I?"

"Bonn, if you're old enough to slip around with Bo Talley, or anybody else for that matter, then you're old enough to get married and make it right."

"You know Bo's already married," she'd say.

"To a crazy woman. He could get a divorce in a heartbeat if he wanted to, or if you wanted him to."

"Bo'd never do that. What do you think people would say if he abandoned his wife? We're going all right things the way they are. You worry too much. You really do."

"Aw, Bonn. It's just I don't want you getting in no trouble."

"I'm doing all right, I said."

"Maybe. But I'm damned if you're ever going to make the Talley band sound like me and Treat are up there, too."

"The rate the show's catching on, Bumper, it ought to be able to afford you too before long. We just got to do like Joe says and take things one step at a time."

The *Bomar Talley Jamboree Show* always opened with Bo in one of his wild cowboy outfits, the red denim suit with the silver don't-tread-on-me snakes embroidered above each chest pocket or the green satin three-piece suit with the sequined alligator on the back. He'd be strumming his big Stramberg f-hole guitar, singing a musical advertisement for the show's sponsor, a high-alcohol Chattanooga purgative called Bastille Bitters. Bo would kick through a couple of numbers before bringing Bonnie out. She was no longer wearing prom-dress getups, but tight, form-fitting leather shirts and pants, cut cowboy style and with small silver stars studding every seam. Her copper hair was pulled back into a twirled ponytail under a light-tan Mississippi-gambler hat, the bead of its string drawn up tight underneath her chin. She'd sing a solo, then a duet with him. In between the songs there was a little talking, simple remarks and jokes and more ads for those electric bitters. Then they'd let the band show off instrumentally before a solo by Bo, and then another duet, this one a rouser to wind up the show. All that was packed into a taut half an hour.

To Bonnie, the informal program really took her home, home in her heart and memory to those times they'd all sat around and played at Carson's Store there in Honey Run. She knew there was a difference between the *Bomar Talley Jamboree Show* and the time-honored picking and singing sessions at the gas-and-grocery joints, but it didn't seem like such a bad one. What if you were sick or old or moved north to work assembly lines and couldn't get by that store in your little crossroads hometown? You could just flip on your television set wherever you found yourself and let the syndicated Bomar Talley show sing you back home to where you wished you were, where your best and dearest moments were had.

"Join us again next week now, you hear?" Bo Talley grinned broadly and healthily at the camera, signing off. "We'll be right back—right, Bonnie?"

"Right, Bomar!" They broke into their sign-off song, a spirited fare-you-well if ever there was one, and the credits rolled over "Travelin That Highway Home."

# PRESTON HEWITT
## 1965–1967

Preston Hewitt went off to England.

He picked up a second B.A. at Lincoln College, Oxford, and, when there was time, played solo or in pickup groups in clubs and at festivals. Pres found he didn't have to play at being the expatriate Southerner in England quite as he had done back in Cambridge. The young Brits liked to hear him talk—he was authentic simply because he was there. Through friends at Oxford he met musicians down in London, and found himself in touch with a couple of successful English rock groups. His new friends were interested in the wealth of old country-and-blues tunes he knew and in the country inflections in his singing and picking style. He taught them to tune and play bottleneck.

Preston began to write songs, but he didn't show them around. He was saving them for himself, biding his time. He had become shrewd like a stalking cat.

He got back to New York in the late fall of '67, after the Summer of Love, and took a room on an airshaft high up in the Manhattan Towers Hotel on Broadway at Seventy-seventh. The city was a jumble of memories to him from his college and jug-band days.

He'd been there many times, at first with crowds of school-mates to see a show or a concert and then to be plumped down safe and comfortable in someone's uncle's Park Avenue apartment. They rode in taxis to recommended places and were usually flat broke by the time they were bound back up the coastal railway toward Boston.

During the jug-band years there were rowdy evenings of performance in dark hole-in-the-wall Village clubs with church-pew seating and postage-stamp tables, followed by wild cavorting around the Central Park drive in Checker cabs with girls from all over hardened by four or five years in New York. The nicer girls were copy editors and editorial assistants on magazines or at publishing houses. They worked hard and didn't make much money and bunched up in threes in characterless apartments up on Lexington and Second Avenues and talked about vacations in the islands. The more interesting women wore denims and tie-dyed blouses and tank tops without bras and ran custom jewelry or leather-goods boutiques way downtown. They lived there or else in big scuzzy rent-controlled shotgun flats up on Amsterdam or Broadway right above shoe-repair shops or greasy walk-in chicken restaurants. These latter generally had more money and more appetites and laughed when he asked if they lived on a safe block and talked about the Coast or India where they went to buy trinkets for pennies to resell for dollars in the Village. They were tougher, used to being jilted and by now to being in charge of the jilting. He lay abed with dozens of young women and talked about no demands and no hassles and no jealousy and no strings, and the women who liked to talk that way liked him just fine.

Preston Hewitt sat up in his airshaft room at the Manhattan Towers and remembered New York from back then. He'd blown most of his savings on Oxford and bumming around Europe. It was time to get in touch with his old record-label friend, Israel Palomar, who had written him about a job.

"You know who Robert Harding is, don't you?" Izzy said when Preston called.

"Old blues producer, isn't he?"

"The original blues producer—he discovered Scrappin Dog and a whole mess of them," Palomar said. "Blues, jazz, you name it, he was there first. Harding's been over at Carpathian Records for some years now as a sort of folk archivist, and he's about to start on a project that'll be a joint release between Carpathian and the Library of Congress. He needs a production assistant. I saw him out at a ball game at Shea the other week and told him you were coming to town and that you knew something about the old stuff and had studio experience. He wants to talk with you—even remembered the Baker's Dozen and seemed to half like what you all did."

Preston's lack of enthusiasm for what sounded like a dull job showed through. "Well, I guess I ought to go talk with him."

"Now, come on, son. This'd be a feather in your cap, a real honor," Izzy said. "Seems to me you ought to cool your heels and take a look around before you try to jump back into the recording game, especially as a solo artist these days."

"What do you mean, Izzy?"

"I mean it's not what it was. Been down to the Village lately?"

"No." And he hadn't, but he'd gone to the Fillmore over on Second and seen the marble light show and been blown out by the volume and had gotten a notion of what a performer had to do to grab an audience these days.

"Well," Izzy said, "you'll still be able to find Folk Lair and the Lamplight and the Whiskey, but most of the others have closed down for good. Hell, I've got about half the staff I did when we were putting out the Baker's Dozen. When're you going to come by and play me some songs, anyway?"

"Pretty soon. Just let me get settled some and I'll be down. I'll call Harding tomorrow."

"Call him *Mister* Harding."

"Mr. Harding, then."

"Let me hear from you, Pres. Goodbye."


He went to see the old producer Harding the next day, walking down Broadway and picking up Sixth Avenue at the foot of the park. Crossing Fifty-seventh Street going south, he was suddenly astounded by the glass and steel canyon that loomed before him, and the mammoth towers that didn't seem to have been there last time he was in that neighborhood. One had panels of dark and light green. Another was a shaft of silver and chrome. The Carpathian Broadcasting

Company's fifty-story tower at Forty-ninth Street was made of something that looked like gray volcanic rock, with decorative pyramids in shallow relief running up the pilasters— the logo of the great radio and television and recording conglomerate.

The secretary at the front desk eleven floors up stared blankly at him. He saw he'd interrupted her reading of the *Billboard* Hot Soul 100 chart. Preston gave his name and explained he was there to see Robert Harding.

"Is he expecting you?"

Yes, Preston nodded, thinking, What would happen if he weren't? Would I be shot in the back before I could get to the elevator and make myself scarce? For breach of corporate peace.

"Wait over there," she said, pointing to an uncomfortable chrome-and-cushion sofa. She phoned Harding's secretary, who presently came forth to fetch him.

"I'm Fala," she said. She was an Italian-looking girl, short with dark ringlet curls and a purple minidress.

They walked down a bright hall of closed doors with multicolored album covers framed and hung between every two. "This is the pop and rock section," she said. "All these offices are either artists-and-repertoire men or in-house producers." In each of these small cubicle offices, snatches of demo tapes and dubs of yet-to-be-released albums were being checked out by these arbiters, listened to at extremely high volume for just a few seconds at a time. The walls shook.

"They spend a lot of time listening to dubs, testing new pressings," Fala shouted.

"Testing for what?" Pres barked. "Their effectiveness as munitions?"

The young woman left him without an introduction at the door to Harding's office at the end of the long corridor. "Go on in—he's in there." She turned and walked off.

The door to the office was open. Harding himself was wearing earphones and was hunched over fiddling with tone and volume controls on an amplifier. On the walls was a gallery of big glossy framed photographs, old black-and-whites, of a number of performers. Some he recognized and some he didn't. Bessie Smith. Duke Ellington. Scrappin Dog. Many were publicity-type shots, but many were unposed photographs of Robert Harding in conversation or at dinner or just standing around with one musical luminary or another. It was quite a collection. The Harding in the pictures was tall and trim, wearing a bow tie and a broad relaxed toothy smile. He looked like money—and he seemed to be enjoying the hell out of things.

Preston thought he'd best speak up. Harding was tapping out a quarter-note ride in the air.

"Mr. Harding?"

Harding wheeled around in his swivel chair with eyes afire and a mad grin, pulling the earphones down around his neck like a piece of jewelry.

"I'm—"

"Ah, yes, Preston. Been expecting you. Come around and listen to this—funny as hell!" They didn't even shake hands. Harding clapped Preston down into the chair and popped the earphones on him like a parent putting earmuffs on a child. A black woman was singing to a funky gliding piano accompaniment and there was a lot of static on the recording.

"Who is it?" Preston said loudly.

Harding motioned to him to take the earphones back off. "Bessie Smith and Jelly Roll—never been released."

That's unbelievable, Preston thought.

*I see you brought your pig, Daddy, I see he's all growed up.*
*Your pig he must be hungry now, so ain't it just his luck.*
*Bring him in my kitchen, let that porker walk across my floor.*
*If that pig don't feel like eatin, Daddy, don't bring him*
*Round my house no more.*

Preston started chuckling and looked back up at Harding, who said, "That's just the kid stuff." A new tune rolled on, with lyrics lewd as a second-story backstairs room on a Beale

Street Saturday night. Preston listened as the pornographic blues went from soft to hard, and he found himself impressed by the explicit simplicity of it all. After the third song, Preston took the earphones off and wondered what sort of comment would fit the moment. He needn't have. Harding spoke first.

"Want to help me produce some hits, Hewitt?"

"Beg your pardon?"

"Just kidding, son. Izzy told you what I'm up to here?"

"He said you had a series to put together out of the Library of Congress vaults."

"Something like that. That would describe maybe two thirds of it. The rest of it is material that belongs to me, old things on wire, cylinders, all sorts of stuff. Out takes, fragments, stuff I only thought enough about at the time to save, not worth releasing *then*. But now, looking back with the perspective of thirty-five or forty years, this sort of material has a lot of character, a lot of value for fleshing things out. What you were just listening to, for instance—that was just some noodling around a Chicago hotel one night, 'thirty, 'thirty-one. Bessie and Jelly Roll were by my room. There was a piano there and we got to drinking and laughing, singing those bawdy songs."

"They didn't mind your recording them?"

"You kidding? They knew there wasn't a damn thing I could do with them. We did it for fun. I was about your age then. Had a ball. There's a lot of other material, too much to go into now. You think you'd like the job?"

Preston was surprised. "I don't know what the job is, really."

"All right. I have enough budget to produce a series, between twelve and twenty albums, depending on how much attention and shall we say repair work has to go into each one. This material is very old, quite fragile, and poorly recorded by today's standards. Since the work is mostly assembling and editing from well-catalogued sources, it should go quickly. I want to put the albums together over the next six to eight months and release them in sequence over a two-year period. And I want to complete this project before Carpathian moves me even further down the hall."

"Further?"

"Exactly. Out in the air above Forty-eighth Street, Hewitt, not a healthy working environment for a man at my stage of life. I need an assistant to help me get it wrapped up before this place implodes." Harding motioned toward the rock artillery range. Then he lifted a stack of file folders off his desk, revealing several records. "I know from Izzy Palomar what your qualifications are." Harding thoughtfully lifted each of the Baker's Dozen Jug Band records, pausing long enough to nod or comment, "There's your prizewinner. Now this one, you'd have been better off without it."

Preston was taken aback at having his old band judged so summarily.

"By and large, you all did a fine job. Some of the most original and interesting recordings to come out of the folk revival. I'd be proud, overall, if I were you." Harding flashed his toothy grin: "Of course, you missed some of the very best of that old jug stuff."

"We did? I thought we listened through *everything*."

"I'm referring to my private stock, as yet unreleased."

Preston shook his head. Do I really want to work for Harding? he thought.

"Of course, there's no way you could have known about that. Quite seriously, one of the key reasons I'm interested in you is this." Harding held up the bottom record from the short stack on his desk. It was *Franklin "Daddy" Montreat Remembers the Tennessee Bumblebees*. I'll be damned, Preston thought. The things that come back to haunt you. Harding continued, "Several of the releases in this series are to be white mountain and hillbilly material, and I've never been long on that. Country music is more interesting to me socially than musically. Essentially, I consider it the music of an unmusical people."

Jesus, what a prig!

"Urban blues and early jazz are my meat. So, I'd make you the captain of the early hillbilly music, black country blues, and anything jug-related. If you took that on, we'd be able to knock this thing together in short order. The salary's twelve hundred a month for as long as it takes. Do we have a deal?"

Preston looked down for about ten seconds, thinking of his diminished capital and his plan to keep a low profile as he polished his material before making another push. He thought, too, about the prestige of working as Robert Harding's lieutenant. I'd be in the studio editing rooms most of the time, working alone, he reckoned. It's a short-term thing, no big commitment here. Like the man says, it won't do you no harm. He stood and reached across Harding's desk and offered his hand to the grand old man with the toothy grin.

"You're on."

# BONNIE MONTREAT
## Late 1967

Bonnie Montreat was worn out and it showed.

Bo had warned her not to squeeze in that last solo swing she'd taken down into Alabama and Mississippi between tapings, but Quill had pressed for it. Her last album, *Country Cruising with You,* was still moving in the deeper South after breaking fast and tapering off elsewhere. "You got to get in and push hard where and when they want you, Bonnie girl," Joe lectured her over the phone.

Five one-nighters and a couple thousand miles, and then on the way back up to Nashville the bus had broke down in the night. Bumper and a couple of the others had gone raging off in the darkness, 3 A.M., in Where-was-it, Alabama, looking for a GMC dealer they could wake up. Bonnie had tried to sleep, but knowing how close they were going to cut it getting back to Nashville kept her jumpy and nervous.

Bo didn't have the studio but for that one afternoon, and they'd already lost an hour and a half by the time she raced in full of apologies and No-Doz. She drank several cups of coffee, but that was a mistake. It made her stomach feel like it was all lined with hot roofing tin. They made her up in a hurry and raced her out onto the set, an old-timey '49 Ford pickup truck, its bed filled with hay and barrels, in front of a covered-bridge backdrop. Bonnie baked while they fiddled with the lights, and when they finally started to tape she was close to tears.

"You're not concentrating, Miss Montreat," the floor manager snapped. "Let's try it again."

Along about then Bo arrived and watched several more flubs. She'd seen him come in, though he hadn't meant her to. He spent all his time these days holed up with his lawyer and accountants working up plans for a franchise restaurant chain, Bomar Talley's Texas Eatin'. Each restaurant would have a big neon Bo on its roof and underneath a flashing motto saying: "That's Talley's, That's Texas!" Producer must of called him and told him the taping was going sour or some damn something to get him to come down here, she thought.

She watched Bo stop at the water fountain and take something out of his pocket. I knew it, she thought—the silver snuffbox he carries his white rockets around in. He knocked back a pill or two and took a drink to wash it down. She was going to have to have a talk with him. The trouble was, their business was going such great guns she never got half a chance. She barely had time to sleep with him anymore, between recording, the *Opry,* touring, taping the show. She thought of all those lucky beerhazy thousands who listened on six-inch car-dash speakers to her and Bo doing the *Ernest Tubb Midnight Record Shop Show,* lucky because they were pulled off on side roads all across the South while she and Bo worked their ass off. When they finished and finally could go home Bo'd be so jangled she'd have to drive and he'd sit drinking warm 7-Up with Rebel Yell in it all the way out to Gallatin. By the time they got there he had usually passed out. Bonnie watched him striding over from the water cooler.

He loomed over her. "Let's see can't we get it right this time, Bonn."

She burst into tears, and Bo called, "Take five," out into the studio and wrapped his big West Texas arms around her. He apologized and let her cry. When she was through she fixed her makeup and, her face all flushed from crying, did a beaming slambang version of the song on the next take.

After that last *Bomar Talley Jamboree Show* segment was done and the show could be packaged and sent out, they were supposed to have nearly two blessed weeks off to themselves. Then there would be the disc-jockey convention, or the *Grand Ole Opry Birthday Party* as they called it, when the country DJs from all over came to Nashville to be wined and dined by the name producers and to rub shoulders and maybe other parts with the stars. It was like a legislature pulling together from out of the sticks and hustings and coming to the capital. Bonnie Montreat and Bo Talley would be much in demand. She was looking forward to the two weeks of rest and quiet together to get ready.

But four days running Bo broke his promise to stay home with her. He was gone early till late working on the franchise restaurant plans, looking over artists' sketches, meeting potential regional directors.

"Why *you* got to do all that, Bo?" Bonnie asked him.

He shook his head and said earnestly, "It's my name on it and my big neon statue outside every one. It's natural the folks who're involved or thinking on getting involved want to deal with me, at least *see* me a little bit—makes em feel big-time to be in business with Bo Talley. I promise you, Bonn, tomorrow'll be our day. Won't be no more of this."

"I got to talk to you, Bo."

"I know, I know. We'll talk about everything. Take a good clear view of everything we're doing. Hell, I don't know, maybe even take a trip."

Toward the end of the first week, Bo quit coming home altogether, staying over in Nashville instead at the Andy Jackson Hotel. He called her regular, to tell her he loved her and was sorry about the way "this damned franchise bidness" had taken over their time off together. "It's just too damn important for me to let go the reins now and not make sure the horse comes out of the gate running like I want her to." Bonnie would hang up the phone and realize she was grinding her teeth. She spent those two weeks alone at Bo Talley's Old Hickory ranch.

During that time the ranch felt like a tomb. It bore down on her how overdone it all was. She drove in through rock pillars that held the massive spiked electric gate at the entrance. Iron cherubs held gas lamps all down the driveway, and there was wrought-iron furniture and statuary all about the lawn. The house itself was a hodgepodge of great modern flying angles that held a commanding position on a bluff that dropped away to a point on Old Hickory Lake. Beyond the boathouse right on the point, Bo's flagpole flew American and Texas Lone Star flags.

Inside, the house was like a museum. Everywhere were gifts from Bo's fans all over the world: a stuffed lynx, an English coaching horn, a moosehead from Canada, German beer steins, on one wall a giant shellacked manta ray from the Caribbean, Mexican tiles, a wagonwheel chandelier, a polar-bear throw rug and a zebra-skin chair, a coffee table with mother-of-pearl musical notes inlaid, a small cannon that would actually fire, and everywhere statuary of cherubs, angels and lute-strummers. Once it had been fascinating to her, now all she could think was that everywhere she looked was junk. It depressed her no end.

There was no one to visit with, either. Bumper had taken off on a fishing trip down to Louisiana with some session player friends. Quill was in Memphis looking over a local soul-music band he thought promising. And Treat had gone off to Cincinnati in hot pursuit of a woman he'd spent a little backstage time with there when the Bomar Talley show had last toured through. For the first time in five years she had a little time off, but she was alone without kin, lover or friend to spend it with. And, she thought, without the energy to do much of anything.

She took herself in hand after a couple days: I ain't gonna mope around this house no more. I'm gonna get out in the sunshine and get some fresh air.

Bonnie took a canoe out early and late, before and after the wind had whipped up a chop on the lake. And she went riding on one of the ranch's Tennessee walking horses, a sorrel that had foaled the spring before. One afternoon the overseer came and found her and told her that her cousin Treat was up at the house wanting to visit. She rode up and met him at the patio near the pool.

"What're you doing here, Treat?"

"Ah, I was wrong about Cincinnati."

"You were?"

"Or she was wrong about me, that's more like it. She thought I was rich, and it was pretty easy for her to see that I won't. Anyway, just thought I'd stop by and hit you all up for a drink before I head back into town. Where's Bo?"

"Town."

"Town? Hell, I'd of thought you'd be out here all holed up like a couple of doves."

"Yeah," Bonnie said bitterly, "that was the plan. But instead he's working day and night getting his restaurant chain all set up. He ain't been out here in a week."

"And you been out here by your lonesome?"

"Lonesome is right. Just me, and the overseer's been here during the day."

"Well, whyn't you get out and go somewhere, sugar-britches?"

"Don't much feel like it, Treat. Truth to tell, I don't feel so good."

Treat stepped over to her and put his arms around her. "What's wrong with you?"

"I don't know. Out of sorts, I guess. That damn DJ

convention starts tomorrow. Bo called before lunch and said he told all his franchise people they *had* to get out of his hair after today. He's supposed to come home and spend the day and take me back in to the big opening reception. Only I ain't going."

"You're not gonna go? Bo isn't gonna like that."

"I know, I know," Bonnie said. "But I just can't get my heart in it. I'll say I'm sick. Come on, let's us go inside and have that drink."

They sat and sipped from a small bottle of brandy and benedictine she brought out from the bar. After a few tots she slipped over close to Treat and lifted his arm and slid under it, and after a few tots more she turned toward him and smiled. "You know, cousin, this stuff makes your lips sweet for kissing."

Treat held her away from him. "Dammit, Bonnie, don't fool with me. What we swore off ought to *stay* swore off."

Bonnie poked his side and tickled him and before he recovered she leaned right in and kissed him. "You never was stingy with me, Treat. Look how things're off kilter around here. The Lord'll just have to forgive this lonesome girl. Tell me, now, where's my old sweetheart?"

"Setting right here loving you like he always has."

They opened their arms to each other and turned back the years.

Next day Bo called to say he was heading out—the business was out of his hands for a while and Lord was he ever in a partying mood and looking forward to tonight. Bonnie told him she didn't feel up to it and Bo blew up.

"Shit, woman. Here I been working my fool head off getting this mess all cleaned up and cleared out and you been out there at the ranch with two weeks of setting on your ass with nothing to do and now *you're* the one can't be bothered to get dressed up and go out to the reception. I'll be damned if I'm gon drive all the way out there just to turn around and drive all the way back in." He just about hung up on her.

That afternoon she went riding again out to the point. A powerboat roared by, and Bonnie waved. Its driver blasted out a greeting on a loud shrill airhorn. Her horse spooked and galloped off at a pace out of Bonnie's control. When she thought she had the sorrel reined in at last, the skittish animal reared back and threw her.

At first she couldn't move. She lay crumpled on the ground with the breath knocked out of her. Her left foot hurt, throbbed as if one second it was asleep and the next it was being stuck with a thousand pins. Her insides felt like they'd come loose. She was salivating mightily, but she was thirsty as a running dog in July. She lay there wondering if she'd broken some ribs or punctured a lung.

Presently her wind came back and she lifted herself up on her left arm. The overseer had gone off to Goodlettsville looking for a tractor part. Likely he'd not be back. She dragged herself ten feet or so and leaned against the trunk of a young black walnut. She figured her left foot must be sprained, but nothing else seemed broken. Still her stomach was killing her. The sorrel grazed nearby. Bonnie saw a dead branch, not too large, hanging above her. She worked her back up the tree trunk and stood dizzily a moment, then in one motion she reached for the branch and missed it and fell. She lay still as waves of heat washed over her, and the world seemed to tilt when she opened her eyes.

It was a couple of hours before she got the strength to try again. She got it this time, twisting the walnut branch till it broke off and then snapping the twigs and the end off so she had something to use for a cane. She was a good quarter mile from the house, and it took Bonnie a painful hour to limp back.

She collapsed onto the sofa where she and Treat had made love the day before. There was a cold sweat on her forehead, and her teeth were chattering. After a bit she gathered up enough strength to reach for the end-table telephone and call her doctor in Gallatin. He was out to the Talley ranch like a shot. He got her to a bed and undressed her and wrapped her foot with an Ace bandage. He gave her a needle of something that made her go limp and float. The doctor was sitting at her bedside not three feet away, but his voice when he spoke seemed to be coming through a long speaking tube.

"Do you want to call Mr. Talley?" he asked.

She shook her head no.

"Well, I can stay until someone can come," he said, "but we *do* need to find somebody to keep an eye on you tonight."

"Treat."

"Who?"

"Treat McVaine." She spoke very slowly now, as if to lift her tongue were a great effort and the words themselves were heavy weights. The doctor picked up the bedside telephone and waited for her to tell him the number to dial. She closed her eyes and saw the numbers floating before her large and clear in the dark—if only she could say them. She managed, and she heard the doctor's voice from far away down the speaking tube as he explained to Treat, "Your what?, cousin, then, has had a bad spill—thrown from a horse. No, nothing. A sprained ankle and some bruised ribs. But she's been shaken by the fall, and Mr. Talley isn't available—she needs someone to sit up with her. Half an hour? No, don't worry—she's hurt, but she'll mend. We'll see you shortly, then. Goodbye."

The doctor put his hand lightly on her forehead, and she tried to lift her heavy eyelids and speak. "Just rest," she heard him say. "You're full of Demerol and you're going to be pretty groggy for the next day or so. You're very lucky, Bonnie, your neck could have been broken." A broken neck, she thought as she floated.

She was out for almost a day drifting and dreaming, sometimes awakening and lifting her heavy eyelids. Treat was always there smiling and soothing her forehead and shushing her back to sleep. When she finally came around, the next afternoon, he told her there was bad news. He didn't mince any words.

After he'd got there to see to her the night before Treat had called around looking for Bo. He'd finally got hooked up with a reporter from one of the Nashville music trade papers who told him the story. It seemed there'd been too much drinking on empty stomachs at the reception and that a lot of em, DJs and a few musicians, Bo included, had ended up just skipping the dinner. They'd been around the pool at one of the downtown hotels and they'd got to pitching each other in the pool. Well, and what did Bo do after they tossed him in but come out cackling and saying he had to get inside and find some dry clothes before he caught pneumonia, and he'd be right back down. Next thing they knew there was Bo hollering down at them from a little balcony up on about the fourth or fifth floor. And after he'd got all their attention, which wasn't hard since he was up there stark naked raving at them, after they were all whooping and calling things out back to him damn if he didn't climb over the little balcony railing and turn back toward the hotel so it was like he was mooning them, but what he did next was even *better* (said the trade paper reporter)—Bo Talley rolled up a newspaper and stuffed it in his ass. "That's right, Bonnie, that's what the guy said, stuffed it in so it was sticking out just like a tailpipe. Then he reached around there with a butane lighter and set it afire and dove with his flaming ass five floors into the swimming pool. So help me God, my buddy said there was close to three dozen that saw him do it," Treat said. "And they ain't found the first scratch on him. You can't hurt a drunk."

Bonnie closed her eyes and leaned back in the pillows.

"How'd he get home, after all that?"

"Drove the Cadillac, I reckon. I hadn't been out to look. Anyway, he come in here all loud and boozy about eight o'clock this morning. I'd got that story not a hour after it happened, but I didn't say nothing about it—and he was down scrabbling around the liquor cabinet looking for some special bottle of something. I come out of the guest bedroom here and told him to quiet down and what all had happened, you being throwed from that horse. 'Which horse?' he hollers. 'Which goddamn horse threwed my Bonnie?' And I said I didn't know, but I reckoned it was still out loose somewhere cause there hadn't nobody gone to fetch it back to the stable that *I* knew of. And Bo said, 'Well, *I* will. I just goddamn *will.'* So just like that he forgot about looking for his special bottle and he goes upstairs and I heard him scrabbling around up *there* and then I heard the door to the upstairs deck slam and that was it for a while, about twenty, thirty minutes."

"And then what, Treat?"

"And then I heard a noise like a thunderclap echoing up from the woods or up from the lake and I thought what? just for a second because then I knew exactly what he'd gone and done."

"I don't get it. What?" It was almost more than she could take in, still in a haze as the Demerol wore off.

"He'd gone out and found where that horse was grazing at the edge of a pine thicket on the other side of the fence from where her foal was looking on, and I swear, Bonnie, if he didn't put a rifle to his shoulder and level it on that pretty critter that never meant you no harm and he shot her dead. Then he come back here and passed out."

# PRESTON HEWITT
## 1967–1968

A lot of Preston's job at Carpathian was paperwork. Preston spent his mornings drafting copy for album-liner notes, corresponding with the folk archive at the Library of Congress, and editing Harding's research papers. During the afternoons he'd listen through tape after tape and end up the day writing a terse memorandum on what he recommended for further consideration.

Harding's days were chopped up. He generated large

amounts of editorial material for Pres to look over, but he also spent a good bit of time sifting through other material for his memoirs; in the evenings he frequently had dinner and banquet dates and then jazz concerts or club dates to keep up with. Much fell to Preston that he would have expected Harding to do, and for the first three months he found himself going back to the office after supper. Occasionally he made copies of Harding's work dubs and took the tapes back to the Manhattan Towers; he'd smoke a joint and work on in his room.

Preston despised the New York City winter, the wind whipping in off the icy Hudson, the cruel wet-gray cold. It was bitter and depressing, this hunching of shoulders and leaning into the side-street winds that sliced through the canyon walls. About all he did was work at the Carpathian project and move toward the day when he could take his growing nest egg and go somewhere and get back into recording.

But where? If he wanted recording, real-money recording, there were only several cities to choose from. He'd been living in one of them, and he refused to stay on in New York. Nor did he have the slightest interest in the West Coast: he thought San Francisco effete, and Los Angeles downright repulsive. That left one recording center: Nashville, Tennessee.

It was too ridiculous, the idea of making his move in his own goddamn backwater state capital. But if there really were only three major choices—and he believed this to be the case—then there had to be *one* that didn't get ruled out. He thought and thought about it. And Nashville held out one promise for him that neither of the others could. In Nashville, he would stand out. As far as he knew, there was nobody with long hair and a beard who was hip to what had been going on in folk and rock music and making it work for them in that middle-Tennessee haven of saps and suckers. Nobody anything like me, he thought. Or like what he could be if he worked at it. He'd have to cut it pretty close. But even if he was the city-boy son of an academic, he had his folk and jug-band background. You didn't *have* to go around a place like Nashville wearing signs that told everybody you'd gone to Harvard and Oxford. And musically, the edge he had from hanging around with the English rock crowd might just make the combination work. Might just.

He took a break from the Harding project at Christmas and flew home to Knoxville to see his family. While he was there, he decided to ride over, hell, just three, four hours, to Nashville and take a look around. He phoned Harding back in New York and asked him to call ahead and get someone from Carpathian's outpost there to show him around. "What for? You're not bailing out on me, are you, Hewitt?" "Not a chance," Preston said. "Just thinking ahead."

The Sunday after Christmas Preston drove into town on U.S. 70. Carpathian wasn't especially big in the country music field, but it had acquired one of the best of the early Music Row studios—Omar Barclay's Quonset Hut on Sixteenth Avenue South. There was a fellow there to meet him. He was about Preston's age and introduced himself as Wayne Pynkham but said, "Everybody calls me Skibo." He was country as a mule with his bony frame and big cowlick, but Pres could tell as he talked that here was a real technical whiz, an electrician and tinkerer who'd grown up messing with recording equipment so that now his outward appearance disguised a sophisticated engineer.

"How long you been doing this?" Preston asked him.

"Hell, I don't know, since I was twelve or thirteen. See, I used to sweep up and do odd jobs for Phelps Range—to get him Coca-Colas and stuff—that was when he first come to Memphis with a little biddy tape recorder set up in a old Airstream trailer."

"Range? You mean Moon Records?"

"You got it, cat. I was there start to finish, the whole shooting match. When Phelps went bust and closed down, I just moved on over here to Nashville. You know how things're always breaking down in a studio—I can fix anything. Never had trouble getting work."

"Well, I'll be damned. You must have known Johnny Rex Packard, then."

"Shit. What you talking about? Damn right I known him, I remember the first time he come into Phelps's studio. Known him all the way through all that shit. Me and Phelps was setting there together in that courtroom in Birmingham the day they sentenced him. Crazy fucker."

"Damn."

"Yeah. Well, listen, I got to get back to work on that board, couple of pots to put in—we got a heavy week coming up. You go on look around all you want. What'd they tell me you were, a producer or something?"

"Assistant."

"From New York?"

"Well, I work for a fellow up there."

"So, you gonna cut some stuff down here—them fancy New York studios ain't good enough?"

"Ah—"

"Just kidding."

"No, I been thinking about moving down here to Nashville and making a go of it as a musician."

"Session player? Get in line and good luck."

"No, songwriter. Singer too if I could swing it."

"The way you look?" Skibo said. "They'll laugh your ass right down Broadway into the river. Who give you this idea, some fruit up North?"

"It's my own idea. Hell, Skibo." Try it out and see where it gets you. "I grew up on country music."

"Grew up on—? Shit. Where you from?"

"East Tennessee. Up around Knoxville."

"Well, goddamn, why didn't you say so, Hewitt? Don't know how the hell you gonna *prove* it."

"You want proof?" Preston said. He tugged the denim up from over his roughout cowboy boot and reached down inside and pulled out a half pint of Jack Daniel's. "How about ninety proof?" He unscrewed the cap and offered it to Skibo Pynkham.

"Convinces me ever time," Skibo said as he took a pull on the little bottle. "You know, Hewitt, I can put them pots in anytime between now and nine tomorrow morning. How bout you let me ride you around and show you a little bit of the town?"

"That," Preston said, "would be mighty fine."

Back in New York after New Year's, Preston hunched into the dead-of-winter winds and stepped up his pace on the Harding project. By the end of January, most of the selections for the different albums had been made. Harding made several trips to Washington and personally escorted a crate of original materials from the Library of Congress back to the Carpathian studios on East Fiftieth where Preston was holed up with an engineer.

The work was steady and the hours long, so much so that Preston never felt the urge to look for a woman. There'll be plenty time for that later, he thought. The only recreation he gave himself was to go down to the Village and play Monday evening open nights at the Lamplight. He didn't mind that there was no money or publicity—that wasn't why he was doing it. He wanted some time on stage to develop a new stage presence and work out the kinks. In Nashville there would be no limit to how country he could be, if he could talk and sing the audience past his hair and beard. The real question of the moment was how country he could be with an urban audience. The management at the Lamplight remembered the Baker's Dozen Band and gave him some Tuesday nights too, where he split sets with another act, three each. They billed him "Pres Hewitt, Formerly of Baker's Dozen Jug Band, Folk," but he made them change the last word in the sign to "Country."

He went over fine, his offhand folk-club personality melting easily into the laconic posture of a country boy just passing through. He talked slower than was his wont, and developed a gravelly burr at the lower end of his singing range. Whoever came up and introduced him onstage never said he was from Knoxville, but that he was from the hills of East Tennessee. If ever anyone from the audience called out for a Baker's Dozen tune, he'd say, "Naw, that was another lifetime. We got to get serious now. Vietnam and all. Lord, I wish I could write a tune that would stop the killing." And then he'd put them through a heavy elliptical ballad about a country boy a long way from home, in some far-off city or jungle camp. He'd hang his head over the guitar as he sang, and every once and a while he'd look up mournfully at the crowd as if to say, "You know, life's rough out on them streets"; then he'd smile wistfully as if to say, "But long as we can slow down and sing us a song, everything'll be all right." He could look out like that and just feel his act working. He knew it was hokum—ingratiating, captivating, hypnotic hokum—but it was putting him across as both sensitive and authentic. By the time Preston had played a half-dozen Tuesdays, his rustiness was gone, and he felt a genuine lift about going down to the Village and putting on "country boy from East Tennessee." But will it work in Nashville? he thought.

In early March, Preston and Robert Harding tied up loose ends and titled the twelve-volume set *Between the Wars: Music of the People During the Big Bubble and the New Deal: Blues, Rural & Urban; Country, Hillbilly & Western; Jazz, Dixieland & Swing.* The collection was superficial in many ways, but tight as a drum. There were no flat moments. The first release would be in May, 1968, and Harding planned to release the remaining eleven volumes at a clip of one every two or three months. Preston had no way of knowing the last afternoon, as he and Harding each uncorked a split of champagne, that this collection, as a companion to the early 1950s Library of Congress folk collections, would be cited for a special Grammy by the recording institute "for artistic merit, social value, and technical excellence—a landmark of American heritage." When that news came two years later, it took him by surprise. Should have known all along that Harding would pull off something sharp, he thought. It was just his luck, stumbling into that situation.

Preston poured out his champagne and relaxed. Harding took a healthy gulp of his own and then regarded Preston quizzically.

"Hewitt, I must say you've done a superior job here. You're bright and shrewd and quite obviously not afraid of long hours. I wouldn't hesitate to recommend you for this sort of work to anyone."

"Thank you, sir." Why, the old codger.

"Well, you might have guessed any of that. But I'm puzzled—I don't feel I know you one whit better than I did the day you first walked into this office last September."

"I don't understand, Mr. Harding." What the hell's he getting at?

"As I watch you head off to Nashville for reasons I must say escape me, it bothers me that for all your excellent discrimination among these different pieces of music, I still don't have a clear bead on where your *heart* is in all this. I have no idea what you truly value, what you *hold dear.*"

So that's it, Preston thought. He considered answering but realized he'd be getting into a long and convoluted statement. He didn't care to.

"Well, I'd appreciate it, Mr. Harding, if you'd speak well of me to whoever you think I ought to know in Nashville. I'm going there simply because that's where I think I can make a lot of money. And because it's warmer. About all that other, not knowing where my heart is and all, I wouldn't want you to take it personally. Nobody else knows, either."

He made his way down to Nashville in early March, not as Ivy League Preston Hewitt, but as Pres Hewitt from East Tennessee just in from doing a little production work up North. He'd wanted that known, that he wasn't just one more Boxcar Slim come to town with a cheap Harmony guitar and fifty dollars to his name who'd be broke and drunk and sleeping down at Union Mission before a month was out. That information plus the word that he was all right even if he was a longhair got around Carpathian in Nashville, thanks to his holiday driving and drinking with the engineer Skibo Pynkham.

Pres was quiet. He kept his own counsel and his mouth shut. He didn't put on airs. He dressed down but not grubby—it was one thing to come across as a country boy, but it would be a disaster to be thought a hippie, a "damn whoopie," as they said there. He took a room at the Parthenon Guests up West End a mile or two from Music Row. The woman who owned and ran the house told him he couldn't have any company, especially musicians. It was all right with him—he didn't want any.

He filled in as assistant engineer under Skibo a number of times. He learned where the songwriters hung out, especially the young ones, the hungry ones, the crazy ones. Pres was way out on the edge and he knew it. Just so long as I don't fall off, he thought. He saw that in time he could fit in, slip in the back door, just by virtue of hanging out and holding on. There just weren't that damn many people in Nashville trying to make it as songwriters and singers. Compared to what he knew of the pop and rock world back in New York, this was very small indeed. As far as the old boys coming in from the country with their guitars looking for big breaks, sure there were a lot of them, but they didn't figure into anything. Skibo'd go drinking with Pres and they'd sit down at the Sidewinder right on the edge of Centennial Park where the Parthenon was and watch the cowboy drifters come and go.

The Sidewinder—two dark rooms side by side, with a long bar connecting them at one end—had been a speakeasy, a gambling club. Nowadays one room was for pool shooting and gambling machines, and the other was where aspiring songwriters played for one another their newest tunes and talked shop together and tried to polish their rough diamonds into hits.

"The longer you stay, Pres," Skibo said, "you'll see how people hit town in waves, and one year is a kind of cut—after that most of em'll throw in the towel and go on home. Hardly any stick it out long enough to get a good shot. Here they are, tired of nothing happening and buying ten-dollar rolls of quarters for the gambling machines and the bartender's giving em free drinks to egg em on. Their dreams of the big time in country music, it's all just turned to shit. One guy'll stay on a machine all night till he's drunk and busted, banging on the glass and crying his heart out."

During the last week of March, Skibo sent Pres over to roll tape at an independent studio where a fading honkytonker was trying to cut a comeback single. Some of the honky-tonker's old buddies dropped in on the session to buck him up and encourage him, and one of them was the singer Bomar Talley.

Bo Talley seemed to take an interest in Pres, saying small talk things like "Don't recollect seeing you around, boy," and "How long you been in town?" At one point there was a long break while they waited around for a fiddle player to show up and play on the B side of the single. Pres drifted over into a corner of the studio and got his guitar out. He sat there picking and singing soft to himself while the others drank coffee and beer and gossiped. After a while Talley ambled over and started talking at him.

"They tell me you was in a jug band some years back."

"That's right."

"Still play them jug tunes?"

Pres shook his head no and kept playing. Talley was such a big name in the business it made him uneasy not knowing why he was getting special attention.

"Whose songs you doing now?" Talley said.

"Nobody else's but my own from here on out," Pres said.

Talley rocked back on his boot heels a bit and raised his eyebrows. Pres wondered if maybe he'd gone too far, humility being so highly valued here in Nashville. So he smiled sheepishly and shrugged his shoulders, adding, "Leastways that's my *plan*."

Bo Talley nodded solemnly and put his big hand on Preston's shoulder. "You stick to your guns, son. You're all right. And it looks like you know what you're doing in the booth there. Any of your songs down on tape?"

"No."

"Hell, if you're gonna get your songs cut in this town you better get started yesterday, know what I mean?, and keep em coming or somebody else'll steal your lunch."

Pres nodded and let him talk.

"Listen, I know how it is, fellow new in town, your money gets a little low and it's hard to scrape up what it takes to get you a good tape together. You got to eat before that."

"Yeah, that's right." Pres had four thousand in the bank.

"Now, I got me a little demo studio set up at my ranch. You let me know when and we'll get you a tape, just do it up right out at the house. It'd give me a chance to hear some of your songs."

The fiddler came into the studio to much horraw and catcalls, and Bo Talley held his hand out flat for Pres to shake. "But, listen now, if I don't like it, I'll be the first one to say so. Yessir, the first one. You just ask anybody, Pres, and they'll tell you: Bo Talley's straight as a damn arrow when it comes to leveling with a man." Then he cuffed Pres again and walked away.

Why in the world is a big gun like Bo Talley offering me the use of his home studio? Pres thought. He's been writing his own material for years. And living with Bonnie Montreat, who's one person that never wants to see me again. And Pres smiled as he thought, Just my luck again.

Pres worked on his songs in the mornings when there was no one around the Parthenon Guests house to be bothered.

And Skibo was seeing to it that Pres got around and that people in the industry—they didn't call it the business anymore—were getting used to his face. He sent Pres out to set up and break down the microphones and wires and cables at studios here and there along the Row. One afternoon about a week after he'd met Talley, Pres was over at the Carpathian studio talking to Skibo, who was splicing some tape at a cutting block. The phone rang.

"Catch that for me, will you?" Skibo said. "I'll call em back." But it was for Pres.

"Son, *son!* This's Bo calling, Bo Talley. Listen, I was afraid you might not of thought I was serious about that offer, but I was. Anyways, that's not why I'm calling. Bonnie and me, we're cutting a new duet, and I'm asking a few friends over to the session. It's gonna be a nice one and you're welcome to drop by and give us a listen."

"I don't know what to say," Pres said.

"Well, hell, say you'll come."

Pres laughed. "All right, I'll be there. Where is it?" Maybe Bonnie won't remember me. Christ, that was ten years ago.

"Studio's called Wolff's Lair, down Sixteenth Avenue, Skibo'll tell you. Day after tomorrow, and we'll start up about five."

"April fourth, then?"

"You got it, April fourth."

"Well, thanks for the invite. I'll see you there."

"Good, good. Our pleasure."

They rang off, and Pres, surprised and pleased, told Skibo what it was all about. Skibo laughed loud and said, "Damn, boy, you're in!"

"In?"

"Don't play dumb, Pres. Bo Talley don't invite just anybody to come by a session. Means he must be willing to help you out. Hell, you come back from that Billy Harmony session last week and Talley'd already said you could put a demo together out at his damn ranch. And you been in Nashville how long?"

"Not quite a month."

"You must of been living right, son. Montreat gonna be there?"

"So he said."

"Well, I'll be," Skibo said. "I'll just fucking *be*."


# BONNIE MONTREAT
## Spring and Summer, 1968


As far as Bonnie was concerned, she and Bo were riding pretty high. She'd mended quickly after her fall, and she had laid into Bo pretty severely for his daredevil stunt during the DJ convention and for gunning down that horse. She had threatened to leave him and his show if he wouldn't take more time for himself and for them. Bo Talley in turn swore off alcohol and pills, but his casual and massive overuse of those drugs seemed to have left a lot to be desired. Bo Talley was impotent.

At first it depressed them both, but he came back from a trip to the doctor's with a report that as his body straightened itself out over the next months, his chemical and hormonal imbalances should even out and his sexual ability return. She and Bo just mainly got on the professional track, and if the magic seemed to have gone out of things for a while it was just going to have to be that way. They were working too hard and making too much money to stop and worry about magic.

Then they were on the road and she got him interested a time or two, but nothing worked out quite right. So Bonnie stayed up late on the bus smoking Camels and having long heart-to-heart talks with her cousin Treat. Their one slip they never mentioned—it was like they'd agreed somehow that it never had happened and never would happen again.

"Wayfarer in Your Heart" was a song Bonnie and Bo had written over Christmas, while they were getting ready for their traditional big New Year's Eve show. It was a three-quarter song, weepy and blue, a song for beer joints and dancehalls, for faithless lovers and divorcees. They were going after an old-fashioned Smoky Mountain sound, so Treat McVaine would play fiddle. Both Bonnie and Bo Talley were leaving their guitars home and concentrating on the close-harmony singing, that aching sound the tune called for. It would be cut live.

Bonnie went by to pick up Treat and Bumper, and arrived at Wolff's Lair Studio twenty minutes or so ahead of Bo. She fixed herself an enormous Styrofoam cup full of hot tea with honey and lemon to warm up her throat and stood out in the studio drinking it. Bumper worked through a taut guitar part he'd play using a Kentucky choke style of picking, and Treat stood over at the piano with his fiddle, tuning up. He'd plunk a note on the piano and hold down the sustain pedal till he got it true, then move on to the next.

Presently there was a commotion beyond the tinted control-booth glass, and Bonnie saw it was Bo coming in behind some of his other players and that there was a younger fellow along that she didn't recognize. He had shaggy brown hair and a beard and looked like he might be visiting from some rock-'n'-roll band that was in town on tour. Bo came on in the studio, slapped Treat on the shoulder, and rubbed his hands together like they were cold as he got over to Bonnie. "Bout ready to roll, honey?"

"Yes indeed." She smiled. "Who's your friend?"

"Who? Oh, him. That's Pres Hewitt, new boy in town."

"Pres? *Preston* Hewitt?"

Bo nodded yes. "I think that's his name—he's a good ol' East Tennessee boy, Bonn, you all probably got a lot in common."

Bonnie felt herself getting red as an American La France. Mercifully Treat didn't recognize either the face or the name. *What is he doing here?* She put her tea down and said to

Bo before she headed into the control booth, "Scuse me a second. I used to know him way back."

In the control booth she walked straight over to him with her trademark wide smile and held out her hand to him. "Why, Pres, what a nice surprise. Why don't you and me go out in the next room and visit a minute while they're still getting set up in here?" It was spoken sweetly, but still it was more like a command than an invitation.

Pres Hewitt followed, and once they got out in the hall Bonnie turned on him, her green eyes narrowed and her voice like ice. "What do you mean coming here like this?"

"Bo invited me."

"Bo? Invited? What are you doing in Nashville to start with?"

"I'm a songwriter, Miss Montreat."

"You? You city-bred college-boy songwriter, now that is rich."

"Miss Montreat—"

"Oh, cut it out, you know my name."

"Bonnie, you never gave me no chance to apologize back then."

"Why're you bringing it up *now?*"

"You brought it up, Bonnie, yanking me out here like this."

He's right, she thought. Who the hell do I think I am?

"And since I didn't get to say it then, I'll just go ahead and say it now: I'm real sorry about what happened. I thought you come looking for *me* that night, that's how stupid *I* was."

She looked him square in the eye and failed to see the actor there. She softened. "Well . . . we was just a couple of kids lost in the woods a long time ago. No harm done, I reckon."

Pres Hewitt laughed when she said that. "Maybe not to you. But I had to go all the way down that hollow with a sprained ankle."

"Oh, no. You did?"

"That's the truth. But like you say, it was a long time ago."

Her eyes asked the question she couldn't bring herself to.

"I've never told anyone, Bonnie. Never."

The engineer stuck his head out of the control booth and called out, "Ready to run it down, Bonnie."

She shook her head as they walked back. "Still can't picture you writing songs. But say, you done a good job on Daddy's record. He's been right proud of that ever since it came out."

Preston grinned. "Me too. That record was real important to me—a big turning point in my life."

Why, he's all right, she thought. I mean he's just fine. He ought to be cussin me out the way I just acted. Life's full of surprises, for sure.

The group formed up in the studio, bass, drums, piano, pedal steel from Bo's band, and Bumper and Treat as leads. Bo and Bonnie stood at a pair of microphones angled toward each other. They each had a high music stand, so even the slight rustle of a hand-held lyric sheet could be avoided and kept off the big master tape.

"OK," the engineer's voice crackled over the talkback speaker in the studio room. "Everybody set in there? Bo, you want to run it down so I can get some levels?"

They ran the tune through twice, and the engineer—Bo as always being the producer—called in over the talkback, "Let's take one."

The red light came on and the drummer clicked his sticks together, setting the time they had all gotten comfortable with. "One, two, three, two, two . . ." and on the "and-three-and" of the second measure Treat McVaine laid into the fiddle, playing a short turnaround passage on the downbeat of the next measure. Then Bo and Bonnie sang, voices full of ache and conviction:

> *"I'll catch the train tonight*
> *I guess you'll see the light*
> *As it's cutting through*
> *The mountains and the dark.*
> *You said you'd set me free*
> *But I don't want to be*
> *Just a Wayfarer in Your Heart . . ."*

They all held their breath and didn't move till the last tones faded out at the end. "Want to listen to that?" the engineer asked from inside the booth.

"Won't it a take?" Bo said.

"Real close—couple of shaky spots on the bridge vocals."

"Which one of us was it?" Bonnie said.

"Both of you," the engineer said.

The musicians all cracked up laughing and hooting. The session felt good.

"All right," Bo said. "Let's nail it down this time."

The engineer spoke encouragingly just before switching on the red light. "Let the big dog eat."

Bo and Bonnie peaked right there. They got "Wayfarer" on the second take.

The single would be mixed the next day and released within a month. By the time summer was high and they had toured three months behind that record, "Wayfarer" would have sold more than a hundred and fifty thousand copies in the country markets, bringing Bo Talley and Bonnie Montreat almost ten thousand dollars in sales royalties alone— they got four and a half cents a record as recording artists for NRC, the National Radio Corporation, and two cents a record as writers. And that didn't count their BMI-monitored royalties for radio airplay and mechanicals, and pennies more every time the needle dropped on their record in a jukebox. And a duet hit always boosted sales of their solo albums, Bo's on the NRC label and Bonnie's on the smaller Cane label. Word would get back quickly that "Wayfarer" was being licensed for major releases in both the popular and the soul and rhythm-and-blues markets. They were bound to make a bundle off that tune, for, like Hank Williams before them, they had written a *standard*.

That night in early April, 1968, when the green light came back on and the group in the studio at Wolff's Lair rushed into the control booth to hear the tune played back over the big hanging speakers, everyone knew it was going to be a hit, a *big* hit. The air crackled with that feeling. There was much backslapping and whooping. Bonnie hugged them all and laughed and cried, she was so pleased, and marveled to herself, Who'd of ever thought that little song could be so . . . *powerful?* The engineer asked Bo if he wanted to dub in a chorus of background vocals.

"No way! I don't want to touch it—just come back tomorrow and mix it, that's all. Let's quit listening to it before we put a *hex* on it. Listen, all you—drinks at Trix's are on me, and that's a *order.* Come on, Pres, you can ride with me." Bo lumbered around the console to Bonnie and they shared a big hug and kiss. "Good work, Bonn, real good work. Let's go have us a big time. Get Bump and Treat and foller me downtown."

The Cadillac and the '57 Chevrolet screeched out of the back parking lot at Wolff's onto Sixteenth Avenue and up the three blocks to Broadway. At the intersection, Bo slammed on his brakes. Bonnie nearly plowed into his rear end. She couldn't see around the Cadillac what'd made Bo stop so sudden, but even over the throaty muffler of the Chevy she could hear a grinding and rumbling echoing up the street.

Bonnie Montreat felt a holy terror. Bumper started to get out to see what was going on, but she caught at his jacket. "Don't you get out—there's some kind of *war* going on." She leaned out her window and called to Bo, who was leaning out his, "What *is* it?"

Bo yelled back, "I don't know, but they's goddamn *tanks* down Broadway far as I can see."

Then, with the same speed and surprise of a state trooper coming out from behind a billboard and bearing down on you, an Army jeep roared up beside them with four heavily armed National Guard troops in it. The man in the death seat jumped out, waving an automatic pistol. "Get these cars off this street and get the hell out of here!"

Bomar Talley lunged out of his Cadillac. "You just hold your fire, soldier boy—I'm Bomar Talley and I been in a recording studio since five this evening. You mind telling me what's going on around here?"

"I'm *sorry*, Mr. Talley. I should of seed. You got to get out
of here. There's a curfew on. The niggers is threatenin to
tear this town apart. Somebody's gone and shot Martin
Luther King dead over at Memphis."
*Just a Wayfarer in Your Heart.*

She loved that new car.

It made her feel so damn good to put the top down and
just *cruise*. Bumper kept the Chevrolet, and she'd bought
herself a mint-condition customized powder-blue sixty-four
Galaxie 500 convertible with the big engine, the three-ninety
that could by damn go through one barrel after the next of
premium gas. Not only a convertible, but one decked out
with fender skirts and Lakes pipes and wire wheels. And her.
She felt an awful lot like a million bucks behind the dark-
blue leather-wrapped steering wheel, her copper curls swirl-
ing out from under her kerchief.

She'd been out on the road all summer. Now it was back to
Nashville and work and Bo after a week in Honey Run with
her folks. She fiddled around with the radio knob and found
the local Lebanon station, a thousand-watter, pouring out
the latest play-on-words minor hit of a stumblebum singer
who was an old friend of Bo's, a peckerwood Alabaman who
called himself and his act Billy Harmony and his Harmony
Grits. It was pure foolishness, but she had to laugh at his
chorus:

> *Habeas corpus, habeas corpus,*
> *You got the body, Sweet Thing!*

She knew what she'd do: just drive on out to the country to
Bo's, take a swim in the pool and cool off and come back in
the air-condition and make love with him—if she could get
him interested. Can't figure it, she thought, unless it's this
last tour's got him back on them damn whites and drinking
again. They'd had a few quick snuggles on the bus, but it
won't like it once was, quality *or* quantity. Things never did
get quite straightened out between them. Working, they still

had a right good time together and Bo seemed like his old self, except, Jesus God, he had a temper nowadays when he wanted to.

No matter, she thought. I ain't seen him in a week and only talked to him once. We'll make it right tonight.

It was balmy when she pulled up at dusk and parked out front of the vast split-level house. She put up the Galaxie's top to keep the dew out, and stretched a minute as she watched the rolling sky. An hour and it would be all gauzy along the long Milky Way from the thick summer evening air. The roar of the crickets hit up again as the car engine clicked and popped cooling down. The bullfrogs' *ga lunk ga lunk* coming up the long hillside from Old Hickory Lake caught her ear and made her smile.

She got her traveling bag out of the back seat. Damn, he's got his music up awful loud. There was a country version of "Let the Good Times Roll" she could hear from the driveway. Some demo he's listening to. Poor Bo. Maybe he's got lonely for me after all. I'm glad I cut it short at home even if it was nice there.

She sauntered up the flagstone path to the house between the dim lime-green lights here and there that were supposed to keep you from breaking your leg or neck while they kept the bugs away. The front door was unlocked. She stepped into the foyer, where she gave a listen and cocked her head and called out, smiling as she did, "Get ready, Bo!"

There was no response.

Just the good-times roll music booming out of the wall speakers wired all over the house. All right, then, she thought; since he's missed me driving up, I'll do something special. She skipped back to the car and grabbed the key out of the ignition. She unlocked the trunk and got her guitar out and tossed the big nickel key chain back up on the flat dash. There was a slide and a clunking sound. Lord, I hope it didn't get down in the defroster vent, she thought.

Back in the house, the song had changed, though it was the same voice. The air-condition was on, but it wasn't too chilly. She unbuttoned her madras blouse and hung it in the big walk-in closet there in the foyer, and she undid the little hooks on her skirt and stepped out of it and clipped it on another hanger and that was it.

She was naked.

Bonnie stooped down and got her guitar out of its case. The instrument was warm from riding back in that hot trunk, and she winced a little recalling Bumper's continual warning to be careful how she transported it—old as it was it might warp easier than she'd think. Oh, well. She strummed across the strings and smiled. It was still in tune from the singing they'd done last night up at the house in Honey Run. Not so bad for a forty-some-year-old guitar. She walked over to in front of the big plaster-and-gilt-framed mirror and pulled the strap over her head. Her breasts were squashed along the top of the guitar body, and she could see her stomach and everything below her navel. That ain't fetching, she thought. So she loosened the strap to where her breasts rode over the top of the body and rested easy on it. And the guitar itself was now slung low enough so you couldn't see anything but just a hint of her coppery pelt. That's better— now I'll hunt him up.

She glanced into the souvenir-filled living room, but he wasn't there. The two duck-in-flight end-table lamps were set to the low end of their three-way light. Probably laying up in bed drinking whiskey. She glided past the lute-strummers and up the nearer of the twin stairways that curved upstairs to a small balcony and then beyond back to the bedroom wing. Beneath its royal-blue velour canopy, the big bed they always shared was all unmade and a heap of clothes lay on the rug—but there was no Bomar. Well, goddamn. Maybe he's down in the basement shooting eightball by hisself, she thought. The lights were on there too, but the balls were racked and all the cues lined up in their holder on the wall.

I know: the pool.

As she climbed back up the steps and decided she'd go out belting "Big Heart," she cleared her throat and made sure she could toss off at least one or two good yodels. Across the living room the curtains were drawn over the sliding plate-glass door that led out to the hillside patio and swimming pool beyond. There was a switch on the speaker box right by the door, so she could turn off that demo, throw the open door and hit the patio singing, all in one quick movement.

> *"The great big heart from the little old valley's*
> *Gonna love you tonight."*

She got all of the way through the chorus as she strolled in time to the music across the patio toward the pool. It was a few seconds before her eyes adjusted and she could really focus again out in the lime-green bug light and the flickering kerosene lamps around the pool. Finally she spotted Bo over on the left side of the pool lying right up at the edge on a air mattress, and he called at her harsh and gruff and labored:

"Go on back to the house, Bonn."

But she didn't—she just kept singing as she walked toward him. Then she saw: Bo was naked, too, and he wasn't alone. He was lying on top of somebody else—she was stomach down with her face turned away so Bonnie couldn't see who she was. Bonnie quit singing and stalked forward real slow while Bomar disentangled himself. The two lovers were right there at the edge of the pool, like primeval slime come out of the seawaters to copulate and make new life on land. When Bo pulled himself out and loose, he lost his balance and fell awkwardly back into the pool. His lover turned slowly and stared up at Bonnie with a cold-blooded smile.

It was Preston Hewitt.

Flashes of faint and heat shot all through her. Pres didn't move, just propped his head up on his hand and watched her. Bo splashed and spluttered in the water. Now it was all clear as a McGuffey first reader: the Greek way. Roll over and I'll show you how it's Not there Yes there. The flashy clothes and jewelry. Boys that can't get girls get jelly and get boys. God. Bonnie reeled back. She felt sick like when Bo killed the mare.

She turned and ran for the sliding door while Bo swam toward the shallow end of the pool. She tore into the living

room, slamming and locking the door so he couldn't get in
after her. *Leave!* she heard the cry in her mind. *You've got to
leave!* She ran into the foyer and slammed her guitar into its
case. Her hands were shaking too violently to fasten the
buckles. She could hear Bo pounding on the door and
hollering her name. She yanked at the two clothes hangers in
the closet, and they snarled up with several others and fell in
a wiry tangle on the floor. She snatched up the whole bundle
and her guitar case and threw the front door open so hard it
ran down a doorstop and smashed into an unrecessed
stained-glass sidelight. She ran barefoot across the gravel
drive, struggled with the car door and threw the clothes and
the guitar beyond her in the front seat. She locked the doors.
There was no key in the ignition and she remembered how
she'd thrown it on the dash. She felt around with her fore-
and middle fingers down in the narrow defroster vents till
she found the big nickel key chain. It was stuck. Bo was
calling after her—he'd run naked all the way around the
enormous house. Tears were streaming down her face, and
her chest was heaving—every breath she drew became a low
desperate groan. She rolled her window up with her left
hand while she tugged at the big nickel with her right.

Bo reached the car. "Wait, Bonnie, let me explain!" He
reached in at her through the back window still part way
down, but she smashed his hand hard with her elbow and
rolled up the back window. He pulled out his arm and
started pounding on the ragtop roof. "Don't go, Bonnie," he
was screaming. "I can explain."

The key chain jerked loose from the vent and she somehow managed to jam the right key in the ignition. The three-
ninety roared to life. She dropped the gearshift into low and
peeled out, spraying gravel and laying rubber for forty feet.
She caught one last glimpse of Bo Talley in the rearview
mirror running naked down the driveway after her, still
screaming.

Explain, hell, she thought. One picture's worth a million
words.

# PART FOUR

# BONNIE MONTREAT
## 1968–1970

Quill and Bumper and Treat closed ranks around her. The tour Quill put together after Bonnie quit Bo and his road show and his television program all in one fell unexplained swoop did at least get her out of town. Bonnie simply told the three of them that she and Bo were through and that she could no longer work with him—and that she would not discuss her decision or her reasons for it with them or anyone. She lodged no complaint, public or private, against Bomar Talley. She kept quiet despite the intense curiosity of the writers from the trade papers and the Nashville press. In his own remarks to the press, Bo Talley took his cue from Bonnie. He echoed her comments, general and unsatisfying, about how the time had come in her career to try her own wings. Her fury and his terror about being unmasked—both went undetected by the world at large. Gossip over the breakup raged about Nashville, but it died for lack of sustenance.

Bonnie moved in briefly with Bumper, then bought herself an old refurbished homestead cabin on twenty acres of land out near Franklin. It was simple and rustic like she

wanted, with heart-pine floors and a big stone fireplace and a
tin roof that played the music of rainstorms to her as she lay
in bed alone. Outside a family of sycamores towered over the
creek from which she drew cold, clean, sweet water, the best
she'd had since she'd left Honey Run. Out at the hard-road
end of her long dirt-and-gravel driveway, she took a big
plain tin mailbox she'd painted white and stuck it into the
ground through a white ten-gallon milk canister. This was
where she lived now, and that was that.

After leaving Bo, Bonnie Montreat became a major headliner in her own right. Those who worked with her and those
who saw her show were amazed at the quality and intensity
of her performances. She was overflowing with personality.
Offstage, she seemed in a daze. She retreated to her private
compartment in the GMC bus they'd had upgraded at the
Dickerson Pike bus-customizing service north of Nashville.
She read. She read detective novels, magazines, trade papers, *National Enquirer*s, anything, it seemed, she could get
her hands on. She wrote bleak songs about lost love and
broken faith. She listened to the music of Bob Dylan. Even
within the tight confines of the touring bus Bonnie managed
to steer clear of everyone, and they returned the favor. Even
Treat.

She instructed Joe Quill *not* to let her be scheduled at the
*Opry* any night when Bo Talley and his songwriter protégé,
Pres Hewitt, were on. Between that and being out on the
road so much, she hardly appeared on the *Opry* for months.
In early 1969 the *Opry* management cited a minimum-per-
formance rule and threatened to drop her from the roster if
she didn't begin to meet the requirement. After that, she and
Quill worked harder at making the occasional Saturday-
night appearance at the Ryman. Bonnie missed doing the
show, the regularity of it she'd had with Bo, the familiar feel
of the old tabernacle and the generous worshipful audience
that filled it every weekend.

She couldn't afford to run afoul of the *Opry* management.
The publicity that would go along with getting kicked off the

*Opry* would be far worse than the press she had gotten when she left Bo. Nor could she afford to lose the exposure the *Opry* gave her, more than ever now that she wasn't getting seen weekly anymore as she had been on the *Bomar Talley Jamboree* program. The problem of reduced exposure worried her greatly, and it was uppermost in her mind by the time the next winter rolled around. She hadn't done a lick of television in all the sixteen months she'd been shut of Bo.

# PRESTON HEWITT
# 1968–1970

When Bonnie walked in on them, it was Pres's third or fourth time like that with Bo. Pres caught on the first time he was out to the Talley ranch. Bo had made a big deal of pointing out the sheep out in their pasture, and that led to a string of sheepfucking jokes and stories about how he'd done it with chickens when he was a little boy. "Didn't you, when you were a boy, you know, ever kind of just mess around, I mean when you were out camping or something, just mess around to see how it all worked, and what it was like?"

So that's his game. "Make a demo out at my ranch," my ass.

They sat talking in the big zebra-skin-rugged living room, drinking the double or more like triple Scotches Bo Talley was pouring. Pres parried. "Nah, never did. Never got much interested in any of that stuff. Bo, I tell you I think I really ought to get this stuff down on tape before I get too blasted." They were on the second round, drinking from silver cups that seemed wide as pancakes. Pres had his guitar case right there on the floor in front of him, and he opened it and unpacked the instrument.

"Yeah, yeah," Bo said. "Sure. Guess I kind of got to talking there. Whyn't you play me three or four that you want to record, that you think are your best shots."

Pres played, and after each song Bo was enthusiastic, and during each response he moved closer to Pres on the sofa. By the end of the fourth song, Bo had his arm around Pres. "Good work, Pres, real fine. Hell, I think *I* could record one or two of those."

Now, that would be something, Pres realized immediately. He hadn't even thought of that as a possibility, since his songs were a bit esoteric, or what they called progressive, lyrically.

"Come on, Bo, really? My songs ain't exactly your style, now, are they?"

Bo Talley squeezed Pres hard around the shoulder. "They *could* be, boy. I been in this game fifteen years and I done a lot of different stuff. So what if I never cut anything like these tunes here of yours? I can try something different and pull it off, if I got reason to."

"Ain't money reason enough?" Pres said.

"Money?" Bo laughed. "Pres, I got more money than I know what to do with. Things I do now, I do cause I want to. I want to write and record good songs, so I do. I want to work with Bonnie Montreat cause she's a fine singer and writer and the public loves us together. It's all money in the bank. But there's some other things I want that I got to be careful how I get em. I could spell it all out to you, but I don't know as I want to do that. I'll just say this: your songs are good, real good, I can hear that. And I know you know your way around a studio cause I watched you. So if you stick it out here and get in line and let some of the ones ahead of you peel off, you'll probably do all right in Nashville, producing, writing, whatever you want to do. Especially if not too many of the boys in the industry find out you ain't really no East Tennessee good old boy straight out of the hills with a song in his heart and a pint in his boot like you put on to be. College-educated professor's son don't exactly get it around here, you know."

"Now, Bo—"

"I ain't through talking yet. The thing is, see, I can smooth the way for you, open some doors. And it wouldn't be doing anything I won't sincere about or didn't believe in, cause you got the talent to back it up. But I need me a little something I ain't been getting, and that's some sugar now and again to keep things sweet, you see what I mean?"

Pres saw. "So that's the way it works, eh?"

"Sure that's the way it works: you be nice to me and I'll be nice back at you. Simple."

And what'll it cost me? Pres thought. Nothing but a little kinky sex, that's all. Who gives a damn?

"Well," Pres said. "You want me to make this demo, then?"

"Hell with the demo," Talley boomed as he stood up and clapped Pres again on the back. "Bonnie's staying in town with her brother tonight. Let's you and me have another drink and take us a swim."

Bo Talley was a careful man, so the liaisons that followed were infrequent but intense. Business doors did open. One of Talley's publishing concerns offered Pres a contract, and Bo Talley made good on his promise to record a Hewitt tune. When his familiar gravelly voice was heard singing the pain-drenched ballad drawn from the Eugene O'Neill play *Long Day's Journey into Night,* heads turned in Nashville. What the hell kind of a song is *that*? And who *wrote* the damn thing?

> *It's a crying shame to see*
> *That everyone's misunderstood*
> *And all these crucifixions*
> *Don't do no one any good.*
> *If I've a choice to make*
> *I'll waste it all on love and life—*
> *It's a Long Day's Journey into Night.*

After Bonnie left Bo, he began to bring Pres Hewitt onto his syndicated television show as a guest. Before a year was out, Pres got a recording contract, not with NRC or Carpathian or any of the majors, but with a small company named Stone Mountain that would carry him and let him develop. He toured some with a ragtag band of what he called country leftists, back-to-the-landers, good pickers who'd let their hair and beards grow. They were a new breed in Nashville, marijuana smokers in a whiskey-and-amphetamine town, anti-Vietnam sympathizers in a flag-waving town. With Bo's powerful support, Pres came to be a leader of these folk-rock country writers and performers who called themselves outlaws and progressives. Others on Music Row called them worse.

By mid-1970, Preston Hewitt could no longer be denied as an important figure in Nashville's music scene. To the surprise and shock of everyone involved, his hit single "Wide Open Sunset," produced by Bo Talley at Wolff's Lair on Music Row, swept the Country Music Organization's Silver Guitar awards for best song and best male solo vocal performance and best production. When Pres walked out onstage at the Ryman to accept his Silver Guitars, he was listing dangerously, so stoned he could barely stand up at the microphone and form a sentence of appreciation. Bo Talley was outraged. He caught up with Pres and his pals down the alley at Trix's Cat & Fiddle and blew up in an incoherent screaming fit.

Pres told him, "I won, didn't I, Bo? You can take your Country Music Organization manners and go fuck off."

Bo took a furious swing at him and missed. He careened into the table, scattering Budweiser and Blue Ribbon cans every which way and collapsing the flimsy table beneath him. When they pulled him up, his face was dark with indignation. He pointed his finger at Pres and leveled his parting words like a threat: "You're gonna regret this, boy. You're gonna regret this more than you know."

"Careful, Bo," Pres said. "Watch what you say."

Bo Talley turned on the heel of his snakeskin boot and was gone. Inside of two weeks, during the taping of the *Bomar Talley Jamboree Show*, which prizewinner Hewitt was to have attended and did not, Bomar Talley collapsed of extreme nervous exhaustion. Hospital press releases said it was brought on by steady overuse of alcohol and amphetamines. The lawyer Viggery from Talley's organization called Pres in what he knew was a blind panic. After hospitalization at Nashville General, Bo would voluntarily confine himself for an indefinite period of time at a drug-abuse clinic somewhere in Arizona. Pres must step in, Viggery insisted, and take Bo's place on the television show during his illness. There was a great deal of money at stake. The Talley show must go on, with quality talent and high visibility, in spite of Bo's absence, because—"and this is privileged information, Pres"—it was close to going network and had to be kept viable or the opportunity would be lost.

"What do I get out of it?" Pres said.

"You name it."

"I want what Bo makes for performing on the show."

"That's ridiculous, Hewitt. Bo *owns* the show. He doesn't get paid a salary."

"Then figure out what he makes as owner."

"That's blackmail."

"Sorry, Viggery. You want me. I want a lot."

"I don't have a dollar figure in front of me, Pres."

"Maybe you will by tomorrow morning. And one other thing."

"What?" Viggery said.

"I want a piece of the show when it goes network."

"Extortion."

"You come up with some nice figures and we'll make a deal tomorrow."

"Let me tell you, Preston Hewitt, this is a very disappointing conversation. I've got a list right in front of me of a half a dozen other candidates for this position."

Sure. "Fine, Viggery. Use it. Sorry you bothered me." Pres hung up on the lawyer.

As host and master of ceremonies standing in for Bo Talley "in his absence," Pres Hewitt did a surprisingly good job. He was upbeat, he was flip, he was ingratiating. He was many moods in a short period of time, and he was absolutely relaxed through all of them. As the weeks of Bo's institutionalization turned into months, Pres settled into the role. Network men who flew into Nashville to check on their project all but admitted that they found him even more appealing than Bo Talley. Overtures were made. They believed Preston probably had less appeal than Bo with the straight country-music crowd but that he had a substantially better chance at making an impression on the vast urban audience. The television men weren't sure how a Talley-Hewitt co-hosted show would do. "Probably too much split focus." Why not two different programs, then? Pres asked. No—it was a gamble to test the demand for any show at all. The situation was clearly one or the other. But then something happened that neatly cleared the way for Pres Hewitt to become a television idol.

Out on that alcoholic recovery farm, Bo Talley got up one evening and rode off into the sunset desert. The Ozark Cowboy was dead in Arizona.


# BONNIE MONTREAT
## 1970–1973


*Little bastard didn't even come to the funeral. Didn't even come to the grave.* Bonnie and Joe sat in Joe's car at the edge of the small old cemetery in Gallatin where an hour before they'd put Bo Talley in the ground.

"Sip?" Joe said.

She took the silver half-pint flask from him and turned it up. *Whiskey, whiskey.* An ironic smile she knew she wore of late came across her face. She could feel it. "Well, Joe, I guess we just run till we run out, eh?"

"Bo?"

"All of us. Bo's going is a real shock. So big it hasn't even hit me yet. But I knew it was bound to happen—he just lived too damn hard. Records, TV shows, franchise restaurants, touring, and then out carrying on half the night every night. I been missing that old boy. Now I'm gonna miss him the rest of my days. You and him, you two made me my career."

"You had a little to do with it yourself, you know, Bonnie girl."

"Well, you catch my meaning. Here." She passed the flask back to him.

Quill took a pull. "Why'd you quit him, hon?"

"Oh, Joe, even if I told you, you wouldn't believe me—and I ain't telling no way. It don't matter now. That last year we's together, we won't really. He didn't have time for me, in between. It was either all business or all wildhogging."

"I never could figure it, you just up and ending it like that—you two was so much in love."

"I tell you, Joe, I've thought about that a long time. I cared a plenty for Bo Talley, good as he was to me, and we had some fine times and a lot of fun—but I won't ever deep down in love with him, or him with me neither."

"Hard to believe, Bonnie girl."

"I been crazy in love before, Joe, but with only one man and I couldn't have him. Lord, but I'm tired."

Joe Quill took him a drink. "You need a good cry and a lot of sleep and a week or two off somewhere."

"It ain't that kind of tired, Joe. It's spirit tired. I can still crank up and do a good show, but I swear I ain't getting out of it what I'm putting in."

Joe sighed. "I'm glad to say that this don't come out onstage. To see you up there, folks wouldn't believe you won't having a ball and loving every minute of it. They *love* you."

"They love me from years ago. I've changed. My feelings are different. And that makes it real hard to go out and put on a act and be somebody onstage I feel less and less like in real life."

The whiskey flask went back and forth, and Joe spoke first after the silence. "I hate like hell to see you down, Bonnie girl, and I sure don't know how to tell you to get your fighting spirit back on a day like this."

He reached across and put his hand on hers. "Working on the road is one hard way to serve the Lord. You couldn't find a better band than the Green Valley Band, that's for sure. And you couldn't find a more loyal audience than yours. And I couldn't find a better talent than you to represent. So there you are. It's all laid out in front of you. Lot of folks'd be mighty glad to change places with you."

"I know, Joe. It's not I'm ungrateful either. Just tired. But I guess I'll run till *I* run out, too." She felt a deep grief washing into all the lonesome corners of her soul.

Quill must of known, because he spoke quickly with a strength and assurance she would never forget. "That ain't no time soon, Bonnie girl. No time soon."

She hit the road again with a vengeance.

Bonnie Montreat and her Green Valley Band logged a half a million miles over the next few years. Rhythm sections came and went, but Bumper and Treat stuck by her. In time, she was able to add a piano player and a pedal steel guitarist as well.

Some kind of corner had been turned commercially, and now country music's popularity was spreading as rapidly as it had a generation before between the Second World War and the coming of rock 'n' roll. There were hundreds of full-time country-music stations to court, far more than the handful that had been left carrying the flag back when she'd first gotten into the game. She made records, still for the Indianapolis label, hits every one, but some more modest than others.

She worked doggedly at her career, and for that she was amply rewarded: two of the foremost music trade magazines named her Top Country Female Vocalist, and a third proclaimed her Best Country Female Songwriter. Ironically, the year *after* Pres Hewitt won his awards, the Country Music Organization bestowed a Silver Guitar award on Bonnie as Female Vocalist of the Year for 1971.

She was lonesome inside, though, and she ached. But she told Treat late one night as the bus roared across Texas that it looked like she never would be lucky in love and that she was through with men.

Treat sighed. "Maybe we was wrong, Bonnie," he said. "Maybe we should of gone to your daddy and mama."

"And to your people? And Bumper?"

"No, I know."

"It won't never in the stars for us, Treat. It's like being punished for loving the one you was always supposed to from the very start."

"Sometimes I think I might ought to go away, Bonnie, get out of your way. Hell, you ought to be getting married. You'd make some man real happy."

It cut her deep, his saying that. She reached her hand up to touch him, and in the dim near-dark of the rolling bus she felt his cheek as wet as rain.

Bonnie was celibate.

She kept such an even keel during this lengthy period in her career that eventually she became troubled with the sameness of her music and life. She had a depressing, recurring thought: Things have leveled off.

The thought and the numbing repetitive work from which it sprang were like so many thunderclouds that boiled up of a summer's day and threatened to crash and rain and blow, but only rumbled and retreated.

It was a brooding time for her.


Bonnie had sold out the 5,800-seat college coliseum in Atlanta, and her fans were hanging from the rafters a half hour before the opening act even stepped onto the stage.

The hall looked larger than it was. Telescoping rollout bleachers were arranged below the upper tiers of fixed dark-green wooden seats, and the basketball court was filled with metal folding chairs which students had spent all afternoon setting up. The stage itself was an assembly of bolted-together platforms with one light-rack proscenium at the fore and another at the back; each had three dozen instruments of red and green and white and purple. Strung behind the rear lighting rack was an enormous black velour, providing a walk-across area behind the stage out of sight of the audience. There were wires everywhere. And Lord, the sound equipment.

On the floor at the front of the stage a line of trapezoidal monitors faced back toward the performers so the bands could hear what they were playing. A concert without a monitor system, even in a hole-in-the-wall club, would make more of a mess than a jackknifed watermelon truck. The drums took five microphones—two overhead, one on each of the two tomtoms, and a floor mike on the bass drum. The stringed instruments were played through twin Fender reverb amplifiers, which in turn were miked and played through the speaker system. Bonnie's keyboard player had both a Steinway grand piano and a Fender Rhodes seventy-three-key electric. In addition to the sound and light men running controls from out in the audience, there was an onstage sound man working a monitor control board set up behind the stage-left stack of speakers. It was a lot to haul around, the tools and the crew and wherewithal to fill up even a modest hall like this.

After the Green Valley Band's sound check at four o'clock, the Red River Ramblers showed up for theirs—the opening act always checked out after the headliner, in reverse of their performance order. In between shows, the stage would be reset for Bonnie.

Teaming up the Red River Ramblers with Bonnie had been one of Quill's ideas, and the combination had been drawing well for six months. The Ramblers were known for an eclectic show. They could roar through the East Tennessee and North Georgia string-band music of the late 1920s and 1930s, gear down into stump-pulling range for a Bessie

Smith blues, and then cinch up and pour forth an *a cappella* sharp-note hymn as austere and hauntingly beautiful as the brush-arbor original might have sounded a hundred fifty years before. Bonnie was right fond of them all—she called them the musical Marx Brothers. Her special favorite was the ginger-bearded banjoist, whose heart she knew was big as one of those West Virginia mountains he came from; he had been among those who sought out Daddy Montreat and learned to play clawhammer banjo from him.

Before the concert, the two bands mingled with each other and the crews at a dinner set up and served in an alumni meeting room below the permanent bleachers. To pass freely through official and unofficial security lines, everyone connected with the bands or the concert wore shiny fabric badges gumbacked and stuck on their clothes, on sleeves, on thighs, on shirt pockets. The badges read BONNIE MONTREAT ACCESS ALL AREAS with an illustration of the mountain flower that had become her symbol, the "fiery azalea." On the serving tables in stainless-steel warming pans were fried chicken, beans, dehydrated mashed potatoes, stringbeans, salad with big slivers of red onion, and apple cobbler that wouldn't quit. No one left the room hungry.

They relaxed in a smaller room on the other side of the coliseum after they ate. One of the Ramblers played an Irish song with Bumper and Treat. Another explained to a girl from the usher staff that he wasn't very good company the last hour or two before a concert but what was she doing later? Bonnie took an imported beer out of a trashcan filled with beer and ice. There was a discussion heating up over whether or not vibrating discs ought to be used inside Gibson guitars and mandolins. Bonnie winked at the crowd of musicians.

"Think I'll stick with my little Martin," she said. "It's got the tone."

She returned to her dressing room, where she stayed alone during the opening set, strumming the guitar and singing to herself to warm up her pipes, as she was fond of saying. Must be a good crowd, she thought when she heard the thunderous applause the Red River Ramblers were getting. There came a knock on her door.

"It's Joe."

"Joe!" She opened the door just wide enough for Quill to slip in. They had been on such different itineraries lately, she hadn't seen him for a couple of months. They hugged.

"You look good, Bonnie girl. How you feeling?"

"All right. Been working so hard I can't even find the time to get tired. I sure do like these sold-out houses—we must be doing right well."

"Doing fine. You gonna be ready to go back into the studio month after next like we were talking about?"

"Sure. You tell Indianapolis we'll have em a master by middle of summer."

"That's pretty fast work, Bonnie, even for you. You are *hot* these days."

It was true. But nothing led her to think that what she was doing right then, in public, represented the peak of her powers. She never really felt that, deep in her mountain-girl gut. She was writing songs now that she wouldn't dream of doing with the Green Valley Band. She would work hard until the time her ideas were firm and her reach trusty enough to take her where her stretch-out songs longed to go.

Joe Quill spoke and brought her out of her reverie. "Hell, I almost forgot. There's a fellow outside wants to meet you."

"Not now, Joe. After the show. Anybody I ought to know?"

"He's from Carpathian in L.A.—we been trying to get together on that Memphis band of mine, Whipsaw." She smiled. "He's a big fan of yours, Bonnie girl."

"Yeah? What's he do?"

"He's one of these rock-'n'-roll producers claims he likes country music. The *real* thing, don't you know? Aw, he's all right. I got to go kind of easy on him, since he's going kind of easy on Whipsaw."

"I'll go easy on him, too, then. What's his name?"

"Paul Flank. I'll bring him on back to the bus after the

show. He's *real* California, now, but I sort of think you'll like him."

"Bring him on, Joe."

"Guess I'd best let you get on out there. I took a look a while ago and everybody seems to be having a big time. Hell, it's always a good sign when the cops are tapping their feet."

They were resetting the stage now, and one of the road men was tuning up guitars with the stroboscopic oscilloscope tuner and earphones, not even having to hear or have sense of pitch, just tuning to the visible vibrations. Her talk with Quill had lifted her spirits. It made her smile to think as she walked in and among all that backstage activity and then up onto the stage to the thunder of approval from the crowd, she must of been radiant. That was the word he would use to describe her, looking back months from now, the way she was the night they'd met in Atlanta: "radiant." There she was framed by the proscenium light tracks and the treble radial horn speakers and the bass cabinets and the acoustic defraction lenses, all these tools working for her as she greeted the fans. When one old boy full up of his favorite party beverage hooted and hollered at Bonnie, she just beamed and called out, "Whoa, now, son—they's a *catfish* in the house!" Mammoth cheers.

The band cranked up and boomed into "Jodie Ain't Got Nothing on Me," and Bonnie Montreat onstage in Atlanta thought, I wonder where he is. I hope he's having a good time, cause I'm trying my best to show him one. Maybe Joe was right: "I sort of think you'll like him." I sort of think I just will.

Nashville
January, 1973

Bumper Montreat had been drinking with some studio session musicians in the backroom of Trix's Cat & Fiddle on lower Broadway. The place was packed as usual. All night

long the roar of talk and music was punctuated by the sound
of thick beer mugs breaking on the concrete floor. Waitresses
slammed out of the kitchen in twos and threes carrying beer
by the gallon pitcher, chili in bowls with saltines on the side,
and thick fried porkchops. Bumper and his buddies sat
listening to a nameless house band run through hopped-up
instrumental versions of songs like "Memphis" and "I Walk
the Line."

Trix's was the one true honkytonk hall of fame. Since its
backroom was a ninety-second alleyway dash from the Ryman's stage, it was the watering hole of the stars and all their
supporting casts, a nerve center in this town of dreams.
Managers, publishers and agents hustled each other; hang-
ers-on and has-beens drifted through. About everyone at
Trix's had either made it or was trying to make it in country
music.

Both rooms at Trix's were wallpapered with posters, bum-
perstickers and business cards, and promotional glossies; to
these, tourists had paperclipped Polaroids of themselves. As
he went to leave, Bumper's eye ran along the gallery of
autographed star pictures below the front room's black tin
ceiling. The cashier was on the phone. Bumper leaned
against the check-out counter staring up at a poster of a girl
who wore a lowcut green satin gown that showed off a good
deal of bosom.

A beefy middle-aged man with a porkpie hat in hand paid
his bill, got him a couple of Grenadiers, and nodded up at
the poster. "I'd kiss them pretty legs for a quarter if she *never*
paid me."

"What?"

"I'm telling you. Wouldn't you just like her to back that rig
right up—"

Bumper slammed him up hard against the heavy glass
case, which cracked from top to bottom, then yanked him
into the aisle and decked him with a roundhouse right.

"Cut it out, Bumper," hollered the cashier, her hand over
the telephone mouthpiece.

A dozen or so people from nearby tables stepped up to see

what the trouble was and whether it would go any further.
Bumper glared at them, then back at the stunned fat man on
the floor. He spat out his toothpick and jerked his thumb in
the direction of the poster girl.

"You son of a bitch," he said. "That's my sister."

Outside Trix's the neon of central Nashville's tawdry strip
made a fuzzy glow in the night. The drizzle had turned to
freezing rain, and the sidewalk and the street were already
slick with ice patches. Bumper winced as he stepped out into
the cold. He wore an unlined leather jacket over his flannel
shirt, and his whole right hand was smarting from that
punch.

What if I broke my damn hand? he thought. It'd serve er
right for me to not be able to pick.

He drifted on down to the Cum-Park security lot he'd left
his car in. The old red-faced ticket taker was asleep in his
steamy four-by-six Plexiglas booth. Bumper could see a small
red-hot electric heater on the floor working overtime and a
half pint of MD 20-20 laying over in a pile of ticket stubs. He
found his car without too much trouble, lurched up to the
exit and blared his horn. The old man woke up with a start.
He cracked open the booth door and just missed the ticket
Bumper let go a second too soon.

"Jesus God!" Bumper yelled as it blew under the car and
away.

The old man made a face. "I got to charge you the whole
day anyways when the ticket's lost."

Bumper considered ramming through the barricade but
remembered the broken glass counter at Trix's and paid up.

He pulled out onto Broadway, rolled down the passenger-
side window and put the heat on full blast. Fast-food debris
whirled around inside the car till he reached in back and got
a cushion to drop on it. The '67 navy-blue Camaro super-
sport, fitted out with a 327 engine, was hard to hold back. He
eased onto the interstate headed east, thinking about his
sister. He was heading out home, to Honey Run.

What the hell did Bonnie want in California, to call a six-week break and go out there on some kind of vacation? All they ever took off was two weeks, and they always worked right through midwinter. Bonnie had told her band this break was coming and that New Year's Eve in Tampa would be the last show for a while. That got him, too, how she told them all together, instead of him first—the bandleader—so he could tell the rest. Things had for sure gotten queer and nervous between them.

Bonnie was keeping them all on full salary, but that wasn't it—it was what it felt like to not have much of a say anymore. Hell, he had money he didn't know what to do with. He didn't have a wife, didn't even want a steady girlfriend. A little on the side now and then was all he cared about. What he wanted was to keep touring, to keep moving and playing.

At Lebanon Bumper picked up WWL, the New Orleans clear-channel truckers' station, which was playing a bunch of Johnny Horton's hits as a tribute to the late singer. God-damn, Bumper thought, here it's over ten years since Johnny died. ". . . in a tragic automobile accident," the radio said. He slowed from eighty to seventy.

Los Angeles
January, 1973

A chauffeured van met the four musicians in a downtown Burbank parking lot. The only thing any of them knew was that the evening session had been set up by someone in Paul Flank's office at Carpathian Records—and it was paying double scale. They were driven to a discreet cedar-sided Laurel Canyon home. A twenty-six-foot camper van parked on the street gave nothing away unless one's eye caught the thick black cable snaking up the hillside lawn to the house. A secretary none of them knew ushered them into a large room which had been made over into a studio. "Go ahead and unpack and get comfortable," she told the musicians. "Paul will be in in a minute." As she left she added, "It's cool to smoke here—but that's all."

Only a fireplace and mantel suggested the room had originally been intended for living rather than recording. Off in one corner was a drummer's isolation booth, with thick black baffles and a lowered pagodalike ceiling. In the other was a nine-foot Steinway grand. White acoustical tile lined the ceiling and walls, and the picture window was double-sealed with soundproof glass. Late-afternoon sun streamed in through a gap in the heavy deep-purple curtains and lit up a collection of chrome mike stands and booms. Below the window was a large metal box, the hookup for the snake cable, with inputs for sixteen lines. The snake running down the hill connected the studio to the camper van, which was in fact a sixteen-track mobile recording unit. The inside looked like the cockpit of a 747—it was fitted out with a Neve console mixing board, an Ampex tape unit, and giant Altec Lansing speakers. The producer and the engineer could communicate with the studio through a closed-circuit TV and talkback speaker system. It was a far cry from Phil McCracken's garage and 1962.

Musicians were used to waiting, often long periods of time, for high-handed producers and managers and stars. But Paul Flank, though fashionably laid back, was not the least bit wasteful of a performer's time and energy. He wanted every sound put down on tape sharp and crisp so he would have the most freedom possible later on in the mix-down— and he could not get clean performances from musicians whose concentration was shot. So before the drummer had even lugged all his cases in from the van, Paul Flank was in the studio to welcome them and explain the situation.

He was not a tall man, and wearing his dark-blue and silver Hawaiian shirt untucked made him seem shorter than five feet ten. His shoulder-length blond hair, thinning in front a bit, was parted in the middle and hooked behind his small, remarkably neat ears. Sky-blue eyes and a perpetual faint smile gave him the look of a man calmly floating above this turbulent world, but there was a commanding intensity to his hushed voice.

The atmosphere in a rock recording studio could be

volatile. Performers and players often got out of hand, but Paul Flank never raised his voice. He wasn't the sort of producer who would wrestle for hours with an unruly artist or musician throwing a fit because he or she wasn't being allowed to upstage the material. Flank characteristically spoke over the talkback about his need to "rethink his ideas about the piece." Then he came into the studio to say how disappointed he was that things hadn't gone as well as expected. The session was scrubbed and everyone sent home. It was the kiss of death—he would simply get someone else more attuned to the Paul Flank method. His reputation blanketed the L.A. scene. Very few musicians went to the mat anymore with Flank—you wanted to be on his side.

"Really nice studio, Paul," one of the musicians said.

"Yeah, man, beautiful."

"Thanks," Flank said. "I've been putting it together for a while with this project in mind. Go on and fill out your work cards while I talk."

Bonnie was waiting in the vestibule, out of sight of Paul's hand-picked musicians. Only she and Paul and Joe Quill knew what she was really doing in California during her six-week break. She had been so wary of Paul Flank's exploratory recording scheme—of its potentially devastating effect on her band, her friends and associates in Nashville—that she had resisted his overtures for the better part of a year.

But the idea had taken hold.

Bonnie Montreat had gone about as far as anyone could on the country circuit. At thirty-three she was part of the establishment. Her songs, good or bad, would get plenty of play from now on; she could grow old on the *Opry* stage beloved and respected by everyone. It had begun to trouble her, even before she met Paul Flank, that nothing more was going to be asked of her.

Paul wanted to sign her to Carpathian in a big way when her Cane Records contract was up in early April. He guaranteed her that no one in the company would know what his secret project was until he was ready for them to hear the work. And, as he and Quill pointed out from the start, if it didn't feel right after she gave it her best shot, she could always renew with Cane, nobody the wiser. It would take a half an album's worth of material—cut hot and sultry—to convince the California label to gamble on her. That was what they were going after.

Bonnie leaned up against the vestibule wall next to an ornamental lemon tree. It had been a long time since she made an entrance with a thumping case of stage fright. Dressing for this first session had been confusing. Back in Nashville, a star wouldn't think of going out without being all done up—here it seemed you couldn't dress down enough. She finally chose over-the-knee boots, a short denim skirt, and a shimmery white blouse; she pulled her hair back in a ponytail and toned down the extravagant makeup. Paul hadn't remarked one way or the other when he picked her up.

She closed her eyes and waited for her cue.

"This is a really special project for me, and the label," Paul was saying. "I want to do probably two dozen sessions over the next few weeks—one out of three I'll pay double scale. I have to have absolute secrecy and I want to reward you for keeping quiet. But if the first rumor gets back to me about what's going on up here, you're all through—and you won't work on another Carpathian project as long as I'm with the company. So no talk. No friends dropping by. Closed shop."

One of the musicians spoke. "Come on, man. Why're you getting so heavy?"

Paul sympathized. He didn't like having to start out with a big stick, but there was no way around it. "Sorry. We're having to work around some things here. I picked you all to back up someone you've been listening to a long time. If I can get the right blend between you and her—and I wouldn't have set this thing in motion if I'd thought otherwise—we're going to be breaking a great new name." Now he had them smiling. Something big was up—they could feel it—or Flank wouldn't have laid the heavy secrecy rap on them. He'd hooked them up with a star, a woman.

"Bonnie," he called.

Bonnie Montreat walked in wearing the wide smile that was her trademark. She needn't have worried whether or not she was in looks. They were floored. "Hey, fellows," was all she had to say.

The enthusiasm of this bunch of mellowed-out West Coast musicians was a sight. They clambered to their feet, tripping over one another to say hello and shake hands the old straight way—as opposed to the peace-and-freedom clasp— since she was from the country, from the real America. She was only a few years older than these guys, but she had been a legend in country music when they were still dropping out of Columbia and Berkeley and putting together their first rock bands. She was the real thing.

Paul introduced them quickly, perfunctorily.

"Little far from home, ain't you?" One of the players tried his level best to sound country for her.

"Well, I played the Palomino once and had a good time," she answered. "I been meaning to come back and take another look. So far, I like what I see." They laughed as one.

"OK," Paul said. "This is going to be hard and steady, but I feel like we can have a good time with it. Bonnie's got a bunch of new tunes and I want to cut them hot. I'd like to lay down a rhythm track, maybe two, tonight if we can get going. Bonnie, why don't you take the guys down the hall and start teaching them 'Deluxe Time' and 'Valdosta.' I'll work on the drum sound. Let's try to get started in an hour."

As they trooped out, each of the musicians made some remark: "A real coup, Paul." "This is gonna be a killer." "Knock L.A. on its ass."

Paul Flank smiled a faint smile. He was convinced he was playing a hunch right. He'd long felt that Bonnie had a funkier, more soulful style than she got from her boom-chucka country band, that her songs could easily handle a bigger beat and hipper production. The timing was perfect. Dylan's *Nashville Skyline* and the Byrds' *Sweetheart of the Rodeo* had paved the way, and already many rock artists had used a country sound. But up to now no one from the old-school

Nashville crowd had gone the other way. Bonnie Montreat would be the first to leave the country.

## Honey Run, Tennessee
## January, 1973

Bumper pulled up the Log Road Pike, as they called the highway that ran along the railroad that ran along the Tammabowee, and into Honey Run proper. It was dawn. Smoke from dozens of woodstoves curled up and knit together in a blanket even lower than the clouds which settled and hung on the ridges at night. Later the clouds would burn off and the smoke would disappear and it would be a bright day. He drove along the two blocks of blacktop, crumbling now, that the government had laid down when it helped set up the small World War Two boot plant there. There were a number of stores along that stretch, each with a two-story frame façade and no difference between the ones shut down and the ones in business except smoke coming from a stovepipe in the back where the storekeeper and his wife might be living. On one you could still read the faded legend MILLING SUPPLIES, and that store hadn't served the timber trade since before Bumper was born. He slowed and turned at the double Quonset hut that had been the original makeshift Army boot plant, then on past the one fancy building in town, Carson's white stucco gas station and grocery with the high-pitched blue-tile roof and the drive-under portico. Last of all was the old clapboard Mount Olive Free Will Baptist Church. In its steep graveyard one muddy April he and the three other pallbearers had almost dropped the coffin bearing the immense maiden lady Miss Wanda Furbee. He crossed the bridge.

A plume of woodsmoke was drawing slowly out of the chimney at his parents' home. Up on the front porch the flower pots were empty and the springy metal chairs were tipped up against the side of the house.

Ivy Montreat opened the door. Five years ago, she and Bonnie could of almost passed for sisters, they looked so much alike. Now Ivy was getting gray and silver in her own red hair, and the corners of her mouth were drooping a bit.

She took one look at her weary son and sent him straight off to bed. From the kitchen at the other end of the house, where she was setting up to bake, she heard his boots hit the floor.

Bumper slept all day.

The sun had set behind Eight Mile Ridge, and the crisp air was thick with the smell of woodsmoke. Bumper pulled on his clothes and headed down to the kitchen, where his mother was washing up the baking pans. Ivy wiped her hands and gave him another hug. "Much better, Hubert," she said. "I hope you're hungry. I got a ham all ready and we'll eat soon's I fry up these potatoes."

"Home cooking." Bumper grinned.

Just then Daddy Montreat crashed noisily through the back door with an armload of wood. He was a shorter man than his boy, maybe five-ten, and heavier set. The two shared the same close-set brown eyes, but where the father's winked and danced, the son's were guarded and full of suspicion.

They shook hands, and Daddy Montreat reached up to clasp his boy's shoulder. "Welcome home, Bumper," he said. "Come on in the parlor and I'll buy you some whiskey."

Bumper studied the gallery of photographs on the wall by the mantel while his father rummaged in the cabinet. Several of the old pictures showed signs of being eaten away at by silverfish; Bumper pressed on one of the frames, and a couple of the insects slid across the photograph like balls of mercury.

Daddy Montreat poured two glasses of bourbon and set the bottle back. "Early Times, Bumper."

"Early Times, Daddy."

They clinked glasses, and each took a healthy swallow. Daddy Montreat handed a postcard to Bumper.

"Look here," he said. "Your sister sent us this from California."

Bumper snatched it from his father's hand and looked at the picture side first. The card was glossy white, with two red block-style words on it that read: "OUT NOW!" The legend on the writing side said: "Anti-Vietnam sign, Berkeley."

"That girl," Bumper said. "Sending you and Mama this California crap. She don't seem to have both oars in the water these days."

DEAR MAMA AND DADDY,

Getting lots of rest and enjoying the sun—even working on a tune about (of all things for a mountain girl) the ocean! How about the sign—they're all over out here.

love, B.

Bumper looked up from the card and took another slug of Early Times. "Daddy, I'm worried about Bonnie. Here she calls this break and takes off for California, and now we're supposed to sit around on our ass for six weeks and wait for we don't even know what. Everybody's edgy." He sipped again.

In the kitchen, Ivy was heating some bacon fat in an iron skillet. Through a register in the kitchen wall, she could easily hear the talk her husband and son were having about her daughter, and the turn it was taking. She pulled a camphor-soaked handkerchief out of her apron pocket and pressed it over her mouth.

"Son, you so used to living in that bus and them motels, you don't know a vacation when you see it. Somehow I don't get the feeling the rest of the boys in your band are going to have much trouble with six weeks off. Especially when your sister keeps the whole mess of you on year-round wages."

"Jesus Christ, Daddy."

"All right, then—and don't let your mother hear that kind of talk—what's the trouble between you and Bonnie?"

The tall lean thirty-seven-year-old Bumper Montreat whose father still called him "boy" tipped way back in one of the rocking chairs. "She don't talk to me anymore, Daddy, or Treat neither, except through Quill. She's too busy."

"What kind of busy?"

Bumper exhaled noisily. "She's getting scouted by some major labels, Daddy, and I got no more idea than that ham in the oven what she wants to do."

Daddy Montreat snorted. "Don't tell me a few talent scouts got you upset."

"It's gotten different. Used to be just some fool sharpie working his way backstage after a show wanting to shake hands and rub shoulders. But this last year, specially the last six months, there've been three or four, the same ones, showing up, flying in to wherever we're playing. They're smooth guys, Daddy. Home-office guys, renting the biggest cars and wining and dining Bonnie every minute she ain't onstage." He added sarcastically, "Not a one of em wastes a lick of time on the band. Now, if you was me, wouldn't you be getting upset about things?"

"No, Bumper, I wouldn't," Daddy Montreat answered. "It don't bother me, what all you've said. You ought to be glad things're going well and your sister's a big-ticket item getting all that attention. I think you're sore about nothing."

"She don't need these guys from New York and California."

Daddy Montreat didn't answer for a long minute while the room filled with the sweet ham smell and the sounds of the ice cracking in their glasses and the steady *toc-toc* of the banjo clock. "Bumper, son, you never know where these things'll lead. I told you children years ago it was just a crap shoot without any rules and it'd change on you in a flash. You just play it out is all."

The three ate Ivy's ham and potatoes at the kitchen table without speaking much.

"Don't get many chances on the road to eat like this, Mama," Bumper said when he finished.

"I got these pies, Hubert, if you want dessert."

Bumper shook his head no and stood up stretching. He went back in the living room and turned up the radio.

Ivy cleared the table, putting the ham scraps and grease from the potatoes on a battered pie tin for Daddy to take out to the dogs. "It's coming, ain't it?" she said.

"I can't tell," Daddy said low. But when he looked her straight in the eyes he said, "Probably."

"Do something about it," she said. "Don't let em grow apart."

"It's already happened, honey. Them two grew up sleeping in the same room, undressing back to back. Now he can't believe that all of a sudden—but it ain't really all of a sudden—he ain't the most important thing in her life anymore." Ivy was near to tears. "Damn," he said. "I knew sooner or later this business was gonna hurt one of em. And I knew it won't gonna be her."


Los Angeles
February, 1973

For three weeks Paul Flank worked the copper-curled singer like a mule. He and Bonnie were in the Laurel Canyon studio two sessions a day, seven days a week. She went back to her room each night whipped, with barely enough strength to call Joe Quill in Nashville and let him know how things were going.

"You getting along all right with Flank?" he'd asked.

"Working for him, mainly." She laughed. "It's a whole different ballgame, the way they make records out here."

"You like the pickers?"

"Sure I do. They been listening to Nashville for years and taking our licks and rocking em up. You're in for some surprises."

"Oh, Lord! Just don't forget who you are, Bonnie girl."

"Don't you worry, Joe—I'm getting a real kick out of this."

The work typically began with Bonnie recording a scratch vocal, singing and playing to a metronomelike click track in her headphones to insure steady time. Paul thought the sound of her little Martin guitar was too thin, so he had her play her parts on a raspy round-back Ovation. Then he added bass and drum rhythm, followed by a piano track or another acoustic guitar—played not by Bonnie but by someone with a much heavier hand bashing across the strings. "It's too much, Paul," she worried at first. He would smile. "It'll be buried in the mix, Bonnie. You'll never hear it, but it'll help make the beat stronger and tighten the overall cut." She found herself relying more and more on his judgment.

It was her voice, her songs, and occasionally, deep down in the mix, her guitar; but the sound of the music itself was the best that American technology could produce. In California, far more than in Nashville or New York at that time, recorded music was moving from the realm of artistic creation to that of a sophisticated manufacturing process.

On one song, she did something quite new to her—she sang a set of close-harmony parts to her own lead vocal. The blend was seamless. "It's so much me." She laughed as her multitracked voices cascaded over the chorus like a waterfall.

"That's what we're selling," Paul replied. He had her vary some parts on different tracks so that he could pick and choose between them and then mix them stereo so one track would seem to answer or inspire the other. "People who listen to their records with headphones go crazy over stuff like this," Paul would say, and she could sense the glee brimming behind his faint smile.

Bonnie Montreat marveled at the wizardry of it all. At first, she'd wanted to stay late for every overdub session and for every session in which Paul worked alone on a given cut experimenting with effects. But the close quarters of the mobile van made her restless. Her concentration flagged beneath the weight of all the gimmickry and the incessant high-frequency garble the signal-laden tapes made when rewound. And she found Paul Flank provoking company—he was charming and considerate, but wholly absorbed in his work. It was a job just to get that little smile out of him. Bonnie found she missed the loud-laughing, liquored-up atmosphere of studios like the Lair back in her earlier days in Nashville, back before everybody there quit taking chances and learned what not to do.

The record began to take shape.

Paul and Bonnie had carefully conceived an approach to the music. They would sacrifice a certain amount of her mountain-valley style for raw contemporary energy. There were cuts that they agreed should sound rough and sweaty and steamy and make folks think she'd come barreling right out of the Delta instead of a plaintive ballad sort of place like Honey Run. The rest of her old style they would convert into towering popular ballads.

When Paul told her that three weeks more or less would produce the tapes he wanted, he hit it just about right. They had taken only two days off and driven up the coast road to San Francisco. He was his usual remote self, with nothing more of a touch than offering his hand as she stepped from the Porsche or giving her a light kiss on the cheek when they parted. Years of men's gawking and fussing over her made this apparent lack of interest unsettling. Maybe he was one of them like Bo. She asked him in for a drink when they got back to Burbank, but he merely smiled and reminded her of the long day ahead. "Get your rest, Bonnie. We'll toast when it's done."

Bonnie had her doubts, but he showed up for the last session, a review of the six mixed cuts, with half a case of champagne. She and Paul and the four key players jammed into the van and listened to the new Bonnie Montreat boom out of the Altecs. After twenty minutes, four bottles of champagne and a handful of joints, the little party was euphoric. "Time for you to meet the brass, Bonn," Paul said. Then, including the players in his confidence: "With tracks like we've laid down here, she can cut a wide swath."

"Like Moses parting the waters," one of the fellows said.

It was a short party, as it seemed to her he meant it to be. He reminded the musicians, she thought unnecessarily, that it would be a while before they could take the wraps off the project. They shook hands all around. "You'll be hearing from me," she said by way of goodbye, and the players were gone.

"There's more champagne," Paul said.

She cut her eyes at him. "I hoped so."

"It's up at the house, though. Before we lock up I want to listen to that last tune once more." It was a rocking gospel song about a woman hellbent on getting back to her lover:

> *You know I'll burn up the highways*
> *And I'll tear up the tracks*
> *And I'll do what it takes to get you back.*

The song finished and Paul smiled. He packed the sixteen-track work tapes and the half-track stereo mix-down into a couple of boxes, then shut down the tape players and power amps inside the van. "Shall we?" he said. He wore his faint smile as they walked up the steep driveway.

"What've you got that funny look on your face for? What're you thinking now?"

"Well," he said, "it always hits me listening to 'Burn Up the Highways' just how much of a departure this record is, how much it's going to change your career. Your image too, as far as I can see."

"What?"

"Just look at you." He gestured at her, at what she was wearing: trim leather sandals, white silk slacks and a green-and-blue dashiki she'd bought soon after they started recording.

"It's true," she said. "I'm getting pretty comfortable with all this, for a mountain girl." She threw back her head and laughed. "They'd *shoot* me in Tennessee for looking like this."

In the house, Paul locked the work tapes in a wall vault and got another bottle of champagne and a couple of glasses. They went out through the kitchen onto a redwood deck built to catch the sunset. He lounged across a cushioned sofa, and she rocked gently back and forth in an oak glider.

As he was untwisting the little wire around the cork, she looked off at the sinking orange sun and said, "Seventy degrees in February. Know what it's like in Nashville right now?"

"I can imagine," he said. "That's why I'm here." The cork exploded out of the bottle and landed on the other side of the deck. He poured the two glasses full.

"Well," she proposed, "rock 'n' roll."

"*Country* rock 'n' roll," he answered. For a minute or two they sipped in silence, not looking at each other.

"Still leaving tomorrow?" he asked.

Bonnie nodded.

"I'll drive you to the airport."

There was another pause. She couldn't believe how matter-of-fact he was being with her, even now when the pressure was off. She stepped over to the sofa and held out her glass. He filled it again and smiled up at her.

"What's the matter?" she asked. "Won't nobody come over and set by you?"

"Well, I don't know. I haven't asked anybody."

Bonnie took a big gulp of the champagne and waved her arm, gesturing at the deck and the lawn beyond. "Now, if you could ask any girl at the party here to come set and talk to you, who would it be?" She cocked her head and smiled, waiting for his answer.

He seemed to give the question some thought before saying, "You know, I'd give about anything to get introduced to Bonnie Montreat." He slid aside just enough to give her room to sit down.

"Well, I happen to know she's been wanting to meet you,

too," Bonnie said, taking his hand as if to shake it and then not letting go. "But you might not want to set by her—she's got a deep dark secret."

Paul Flank slipped his arm around her shoulder and moved over to where they were cheek to cheek. "Why don't you whisper it to me so no one can hear?"

She leaned away from him just enough that she could look him in the eyes. "What would you do if I told you she never wore any underwear?"

He shook his head gravely. "I'm afraid," he replied, "that there would be nothing to do but ask her to prove it."

It was a week and a day before Bonnie Montreat left Paul Flank's home in Laurel Canyon and flew back to Nashville.


Indianapolis
April, 1973


At two that afternoon, the International Harvester Lode-star 1600S bumped up against the rubber pads of the loading dock, and work started for the last show of the tour.

The South Indianapolis Armory was a mildewed old hangar of a building. They'd played it many times. Along the hallway leading in from the dock to the arena floor were open storage rooms heaped with tarps and musty flags and banners brought out for the college- and industrial-league ballgames played there. Water from exposed pipes dripped down the pale-green block walls and rolled in no particular hurry across the bare concrete floors into little drains.

The load-in was not going well. A cranky old Eaton forklift broke down right off, and they had to call in an overtime crew. For the next two hours, the roof girders shook to the steel clatter and rattle of half a dozen red handtrucks ferrying the drum boxes and stacks of amplifiers in to the temporary stage. The Green Valley Band's lighting man had to be sent to an Indianapolis hospital for observation after a power cord ripped loose from the Trooperette follow spot he was setting up and shocked him, knocking him off a ladder onto the floor. And the star of the show, Bonnie Montreat, hadn't showed up.

Bumper sat way off in one of the lower bleachers and chewed on a mint toothpick. It made him uneasy and mad that they hadn't heard from Bonnie yet. Every so often he'd stand up and stretch and go out to the mezz and get a drink out of the old silver-handled Coca-Cola machine. The other fellows in the band had found a basketball and had gotten somebody from the armory to crank down the goal so they could shoot some. Bumper wasn't interested. He sat and fidgeted and watched his buddies get out of breath playing Horse.

It was the first tour in ten years where Bonnie hadn't traveled with the rest of them in the GMC bus they still called Road Hog Heaven. She'd kept apart and stayed with that California dude Paul Flank. How she could take up with a dope-smoking rock-'n'-roll producer was beyond him, but it was just one more thing gone wrong. Hell with it. By four-thirty, when the stage was pretty well set, Bumper began to feel sure something had screwed up and she wasn't going to make the five-o'clock sound check. Not that it mattered much: it would be the same show, the same dozen-and-a-half songs most of the audience already knew by heart. The lousy acoustics in the South Indianapolis Armory would more than offset any problems with the band's sound.

He went back out to the mezz and found a pay phone; the girl at CentrAir told him the airport had been closed since noon because of heavy ground fog and it would be six before any planes could be cleared for landing. Bonnie's flight from Cleveland had gone on west to Terre Haute, where it would refuel and wait. Bumper hung up. Goddammit. It was easy enough to think he minded about the sound check. Getting annoyed at his sister was about the only protest left to him, short of quitting. A wad of chewing gum stuck to his boot sole as he came back down the aisle.

"Jesus!" he shouted, and the musicians playing Horse

turned and looked up his way. "Come here," he said, waving them over to him. "You boys go on. Her plane's real late—there ain't gonna be any sound check. Her plane's late."

"You want to do it without her?" one of them asked.

"Can't. When that cord come loose on the spot it blew a bank of fuses or some crap—they got a lectrician fiddlefucking around with it. Sound board's on the same line, I already asked. This hall makes it sound like you playing inside a whale anyway. So go on and have some supper."

He'd waited another half hour or so when Quill stepped up and gave him a poke in the ribs. Bumper whirled around.

"Keep off me," he said.

"Aw, come on, Bump. Why don't you quit stewing?" Quill said kindly. "You ought to be celebrating—it's the last show. Quittin time."

"Shit. Since when have we been in the custom of six on and six weeks off? It's a pussy schedule and you know it."

"We been over this—"

"She's singing good as she ever did."

"Hell you say. I'm out in the hall these nights, and I'm telling you her pipes are shot. You got a short memory, son."

"Go to hell, Quill."

"No," Quill replied, trying to keep it light. "You go to hell, Montreat, you sour-ass hillbilly."

Bumper Montreat clenched and jerked his fist back like he was ready to take a swing at the manager, but Quill held up both hands, palms flat, in a Why bother? gesture.

"So you deck me, and I swear out an assault warrant. Why don't we just do a show and go home?"

"You riled me, Quill," Bumper said accusingly.

"Yeah. Come on, Bump. You're just hanging around waiting and hoping for somebody to rile you so you can start in swinging." Quill put his arm around Bumper's shoulders. "Why don't you just tune up and go on to supper? I'll wait on her."

"I'm tired of talking to my own goddamn sister through you."

"Bumper, can I help it if there's a new guy in her life taking up all her time? Hell, I didn't hear from her but once the whole time she was out in L.A. You're the one got the postcard and shared it with several hundred daily newspapers."

Bumper Montreat looked at the concrete floor and scuffed his foot on it. That postcard interview had made him look pretty damn foolish, all right, and Bonnie had been plenty mad about it. She hadn't mentioned it in the last couple of weeks, but then she'd hardly mentioned hello or goodbye either. It was "OK, boys, one more time" as they went on, and "Thanks, fellows, see you tomorrow" as they finished up the encores. He couldn't even get to her to say "What's up?" or "How you feeling?"

"I'd better check my guitars," Bumper said.

"That's the boy."

Bumper went on down to the stage, and Quill watched, his face drawn up with concern. "Poor bastard," he said under his breath.

One of the stagehands was unpacking Bonnie's little Martin guitar when Bumper reached the stage to put new strings on his Gibson. He should of done it earlier in the afternoon, or, better, last night after the show in Cleveland, so the strings would of had time to stretch out. Now they would be ready to start drifting out of tune about the time the band cranked up, and he'd be tuning and retuning all night. What the hell, he thought, I ain't the only one getting slack around here.

The stagehand stepped back from Bonnie's guitar after he laid it on its stand, and whistled. "Damn, that's one beauty."

"Yeah," Bumper said as he loosened the old strings on his Gibson.

"Single ought-forty-five, isn't it?" the stagehand asked. "I hadn't seen one of them in ages."

"That one goes way back," Bumper said.

"I sure would like to play a tune on it," the stagehand said, glancing sidewise at Bumper. "But it's hers, ain't it?"

"Yeah, it is, but go on. I'm her brother and I was there when it was bought."

"No kidding?" The man picked it up and strummed across it.

"Where'd it come from?" he asked Bumper. "Some old-timer, I bet."

"Nope. It was a guitar shop in Nashville," Bumper said. "My daddy bought it for Bonnie the morning after Hank Williams first played the *Opry*. She was only nine years old."

"Damn, ain't that a Buick!" They both laughed.

The stagehand went through a handful of stock runs, flatpicking the little Martin, while Bumper finished up tightening the new strings on his Gibson.

"Would you make sure it's tuned up when you're through? Damn thing won't be right for a couple days." The stagehand nodded yes and Bumper walked off, stopping near an exit where someone had slapped up a poster for that night's show. There were two warm-up acts—one a sports comedian billed as "The Rambling Wreck"—which meant the Bonnie show wouldn't be over till ten-thirty or eleven.

From the empty hall he had just left, Bumper Montreat was surprised to hear the stagehand—faintly, but clearly, even in that acoustically lousy armory—strumming Bonnie's guitar and singing:

> *"Life is like a mountain railroad*
> *With an engineer so brave . . ."*

Damn, he thought, Daddy used to play that same song. Bumper stood staring at the poster as the stagehand sang:

> *"We must make the run successful*
> *From the cradle to the grave . . ."*

"Hey, Montreat, you still here?" It was Quill, calling him from down the corridor. The stagehand kept singing in the distance:

*"Keep your hands upon the throttle . . ."*

Quill was walking toward him, Bumper knew. He didn't look back, but slammed through the exit door and into the early-April Indianapolis mist just as his eyes filled and the tears began to stream down his cheeks.

Outside the window of her eighth-floor suite at the Hotel Calumet, the National Bank tower clock read eleven-twenty.

Bonnie lay propped up on the hotel bed pillows. She had taken off the big elaborate wig she wore onstage and shaken out her own copper curls. Beside her on the bed was an untouched bowl of cherrystone clams. Across the room two men were arguing.

Bonnie Montreat wasn't listening. She was puzzling over the flat, let-down way she felt. She'd expected to be all torn up at this moment, tonight's show being her last with Bumper and Treat and the Green Valley Band. Instead, though she had missed the sound check, everything had gone pretty much as usual.

She sighed and looked over at Paul Flank and Joe Quill. It seemed like they'd never finish. She watched them awhile, remotely marveling at the difference between the two.

Joe Quill might have been the man for whom short-sleeved shirts were invented; he was most at home on a county fairground getting a stage set up on a dusty lot. To Bonnie, he looked just the same now as when they'd met, a short fleshy man of uncertain age, his soft pale face permanently worried. After years of success as an agent and manager, the only changes she could tell were that he carried his clipboard in a briefcase and that he could afford nice suits, which he still wore rumpled and mismatched. There was nothing slick about him, not even his line of talk.

When she had started hinting to Quill over a year ago that she wanted a change, he responded with savvy and intuition. He could see she was restless and he told himself, "You don't argue with your meal ticket." Now that the secret California sessions had been a success—though the tracks were not exactly his style—Quill was prepared to see the whole thing through.

Together he and Paul Flank worked out the details of the five-year, five-album Carpathian deal. He had to keep reminding himself, though, that they were on the same side. To him, Flank seemed like a visitor from another planet, a place where show business was an easy-monied, stressless affair. No one had been more amazed than Quill that this man had made his way into Bonnie's heart and bed.

The smooth, soft-spoken younger man lounged comfortably on the hotel sofa while Joe Quill sat on a stiff chair and strained to hear.

"Goddammit, Paul, *speak up.*"

"Quit yelling at him, Joe," Bonnie said from the bed. "Why can't you two talk later? I can't keep my mind on it now."

"This can't wait, Bonnie girl. I got to be back in Nashville tomorrow morning about the time you two are waking up."

"Relax, Joe," Paul said. "Just relax." Then to Bonnie, "It'll just take a few minutes." He reached for his kitbag on the side table, pulled out a wad of cellophane and some papers, and rolled a joint. Quill shook his head and muttered. Paul brushed a bit of spilled marijuana off his sky-blue Hawaiian shirt and back into the cellophane bag. He lit the joint and smiled at Quill. The eyes behind the Polaroid glasses closed. "OK, Joe, go on."

"All right," Quill said. "What I want is to keep our ass covered over the next couple months—we can't just hold back booking till you get that record out. By June we'll have already lost the festivals and it'll be high time to let the state fairs know for fall. You people got to let me book enough dates to keep this operation going, especially if that record just lays there." He stood up and shoved his hands in his pants pockets. Paul opened his eyes and offered the joint to Quill, who looked back at him like he was crazy.

"This *is* the operation now, Joe," Paul said. He gestured slowly to himself, Quill and Bonnie. "And you know as well as I do 'Double Shuffle' is not going to just lie there—the only question is how fast it goes gold."

"Don't it make you nervous, Bonnie?" Quill turned to her.

"Why should it, Joe?"

"Honey," he began, "*I* know you're terrific. I even know the record you've come up with is gonna be terrific, and I'm backing you and Paul right down the line on this deal. But I got to admit it makes me nervous that a major artist under my management is going to sit back with no future bookings at all and wait for the release of a first album on a new label in the popular market where she is *completely* untested." He sat back down, red in the face and out of breath.

A swell of gratitude and fondness took Bonnie by surprise. Quill had been watching over her like a broody hen since she was a wide-eyed twenty-one. She came over and sat beside him and took his hand. "You told me this'd be a gamble, Joe. Now we just got to wait for the cards to turn up." She smiled at him. "I don't mind sitting out for a while, believe you me. I'm just going to write and take it easy and get all this behind me."

"I don't like it."

"And advertising," Paul said. "There's a whole photo campaign to do—it's not like it's a waste of time, Joe."

"I still don't like it."

Bonnie gave him a big hug and dropped her head on his shoulder. "I sure will miss you, Joe. You'll call, won't you?"

"Probably every day," Quill said. "And I aim to keep after you on this booking business."

Paul removed his glasses and offered Quill a mild, friendly handshake. He stayed behind in the room while Bonnie walked Quill to the elevator.

The corridor smelled like it had just been vacuumed—an odd clean smell she associated with hotels. There was a young black man putting fresh sand in the stand-up cigaret receptacle by the elevator. He gawked at Bonnie and looked quickly away.

"You hadn't talked to Bumper yet, I take it," Quill said.

"No. I tried a couple times, but soon as he heard the word 'California' he'd just go off and sulk. We barely said three words to each other the last half of this tour. I mean to tell him tonight."

"This'll break his heart, you know."

"How you think *I* feel, Joe?"

"I know, honey, but it's different," Quill reflected. "You can go on, almost no matter what, with your voice and looks and reputation. But Bumper, something about him's stuck in the past. He'll get work, no trouble. It's just I imagine he'll end up like your daddy—a great picker from a time that's dying out."

The elevator arrived, and the black man stepped in ahead of Joe Quill, rolling his sand cart. "I'll get up with him back in Nashville," Quill said. "Take care of yourself, Bonnie girl."

"Sweet old Joe." She smiled tearfully. "Thanks for everything."

When Bonnie returned to the suite, Paul Flank was lighting a second joint. He held it out, but she shook her head no, as she most always did, and crossed back over to the bed.

Paul drew another lungful of smoke. Any minute now, he thought. All through his talk with Quill he had been watching her watch the ceiling and waiting to see how she would handle this last night. He was ready.

"How was the show tonight?" she asked.

"So-so," he answered evenly. "Nothing to write home about."

She hugged one of the pillows and shook her head. "Funny how you can fool yourself. I got to feeling, just a few songs into the first set, that it was going pretty good—that it was a good one to go out on." Bonnie slipped back down in the bed and sighed deeply. "Goddammit to hell."

Paul waited awhile before speaking again. "Bonnie, are you still planning to say something to your brother tonight?"

"Yes," she said weakly.

"And you know what you're going to say?"

"No."

He waited again. Bonnie Montreat had touched Paul Flank. He liked all her sass and salt and he admired her hard work. It didn't surprise him when they got involved—in their setup it was almost a matter of course—and it never occurred to him to separate his professional and private concerns. They were the same.

"Bonnie, I don't think you're in any shape to drive across town and talk business. Why don't you let Quill handle this?"

She didn't answer.

"Bonnie?"

She turned to look at him, her green eyes brimming now. "I sang my heart out."

She wore herself out crying. Paul had seen this sort of career shake-up many times, and he was used to the show-business saying that some continue and some get discarded along the way. Bonnie took it harder than most, but then her case was complicated. She had to cut her own brother and cousin loose. Paul had watched it gnaw away at her until she could hardly look Bumper or Treat in the eye anymore. Once or twice, he wondered seriously if she was going to be able to swing it. If not, Carpathian would be stuck with a pretty expensive load of dead wood. But now that they were down to the wire, he was sure of her—it was all over but the crying.

When she was finally quiet, he helped her out of the tight satin vest and the matching pants and into one of his loose-fitting Hawaiian shirts. He suggested once again that she turn the business over to Quill and call Bumper later from California.

"No, Paul," she said. "I can't do that." She sat up and took a Kleenex from the bedside-table dispenser. "It wouldn't be right for me to not go. I owe them."

She slipped on a pair of bluejeans, then sat back down on the bed to pull on her sneakers. "Don't wait on me. It's a ways out there and this may take a while, I don't know." She slapped her hands on her knees and stood up. "Well," she said with a brave smile, "here I go." At the door she blew him a kiss.

Bonnie drove the rented apple-red Impala out to the edge of town, to the I-465 beltway where the band was holed up at the Slate Motel. That was how she thought of them this tour—holed up, under siege in a way, separate and removed from her like never before. She hadn't gotten any closer than to show them her back onstage at four or five concert dates a week—an hour and a half apiece of apparent harmony and common purpose. Show business, she thought bitterly.

The sky over the motel parking lot was bright with shrimp-colored urban light. Bonnie could see the bus parked beside a little picnic area with pecan trees and a couple of tables. She pulled up beside it and turned off the car, cursing as she broke a nail on the unfamiliar dashboard. Her heart was thumping.

For months now she'd been dreading this moment and the way it would slice her life in two. Treat was one thing—he'd be hurt, but he wouldn't blame her. It was Bumper who would see what she'd done as the deepest kind of betrayal. To hide her misery she'd acted distant and allowed Paul Flank to take up all her time. Now she could see that she'd cut Bumper off to the point where he wouldn't even try to understand. She stood before Room 19 feeling panicky and raw.

Inside, a Western was blaring on television—she thought she made out strains of "Do Not Forsake Me, Oh, My Darlin' " and guessed it to be *High Noon*. A roar broke from the room. They were hooting over a hand of poker, Night Baseball, most likely, and there was the light sound of women's voices.

Bumper Montreat tilted his chair away from the card table and reached in the cooler for a cold Iron City beer. He scowled at a picture of the Pittsburgh Steelers on the can and popped it open. He and the boys had had a bit of a set-to after that night's show. Bumper still wasn't able to tell them what the agenda was for the Green Valley Band. They all knew that Bonnie's contract with Cane Records of Indianapolis was up for renewal, but nobody had the first idea when they'd be back in the studio or out on the road again. It put him in a hell of a spot.

Bonnie gave two raps on the door.

"Hoosit?" Bumper called out, and everyone got quiet the way they always did when it might be the manager come in person to shut them up after four or five phone calls from the front desk didn't work.

Bonnie didn't answer. Finally Bumper jumped up and yanked the door open.

"Just me."

"Well, hey, just you," he said, backing away so she could come in. One of the other three—she didn't see who, because she and Bumper were locked in a staring match—yelled, "Hello, Red, you good-looking thing! Come on in!"

"Yeah, stranger, come on in," Bumper said, still holding her eyes. He was thinking how she hadn't come around once for a beer or a pizza or a laugh or anything the whole six weeks of this tour.

Bonnie stepped into the room. It was long and narrow and pine-paneled, with ancient cracking linoleum floors and putty-colored covers on the two double beds. She must've been in hundreds of rooms just like this and had wonderful times, after shows, with folks crowding in and drinking whiskey and smoking cigarets and carrying on till the sun came up.

"Got a beer with my name on it?" she asked, and Pick reached in the cooler for her. She looked around. A card table was pulled up to a crumpled daybed where Treat was all sprawled out wearing a Midas muffler T-shirt and boxer shorts. He had a beer in one hand and a couple of cards in the other. Over on the far bed, Joe Sam, shirtless and barefoot, was trying to slide his hand out from under his teenage girl's blouse. The girl looked horrified like Bonnie might be her mother come looking for her. In the bathroom another girl was retching loudly.

"Whose date is that?" Bonnie asked and took a big swallow of beer.

Pick answered, "She was kind of sweet on old Treat here."

"You sure can pick em, Treat," said Bonnie, and the others laughed.

"Ain't it the truth, sugar-britches—and they's some of em just can't take the torque." She could barely return his smile. "Come on, set down." He brushed the ashes and cigaret butts from a spilled ashtray off the daybed.

"No, no, I hadn't got a prayer of catching up to you boys. I just wanted to get a beer and talk to Bumper." She could see him in the doorway looking impatient to go on outside. "You'll do fine without me." She waved and left the room, and Bumper shut the door behind.

The air outside was reeking with a chemical smell from some nearby industrial plant; it made a harsh acrid taste in the back of her throat. She leaned up against one of the picnic tables.

"Well, what brings you around, Bonnie—your boyfriend kick you out?" Bumper seemed to tower over her with his arms folded across his chest and hands jammed up flat in his armpits.

"I got something I want to explain," she said. "I'm going to California."

"You already been there."

"I don't mean for a vacation, Bumper."

"What're you getting at?"

She looked straight at him. "I'm going to California for good, to live and work. I'm leaving Nashville—this was my last tour on the country circuit."

Bumper turned his bitter hawkface up to the sky. "Jesus God."

For a moment it looked like that was all there was to it. She went on. "I didn't come here to cry or carry on. Or to talk business—Quill can tell you about it. What it comes down to is I'm not renewing with Cane Records. I'm signing with Carpathian. Nobody knows about it but Quill and Paul and me—and now you. I'm leaving tomorrow, so I came to say goodbye. I tried to tell you before now, but you never seemed to want to hear any of it."

"Hear any of it?" he said. "You got a great career in Nashville and that son of a bitch's gonna put you on the rock circuit and screw it all to hell—you're forgetting that all you got to do is walk out on the *Opry* stage every so often for the next twenty years and you got it made."

Again she looked up at him square in the face. "You said that right, Bumper—all's I got to do is the same thing over and over for the next twenty years. Well, I'm tired of it. I want to not get jumped on for every new little thing I try out. I want more money and a better time of it."

"And you think you'll get it, just like that? Don't be a damn fool, Bonnie. In California you can go down the tubes with one record." He spoke bitterly. "I ain't interested in that bullshit scene."

"Well, I am, Bumper," she said, turning on her heel and walking toward her car.

Bumper thought he would choke. His voice, when it finally came, was all strangled up. "You just hold it right there."

She stopped and closed her eyes and listened to him crunching over the gravel in his boots. He jerked her around and dug his fingers into her arms. "Who do you think you are?"

She began to cry, and he realized how rough he was being on her and let her go.

"How come?" he said. "Just like this, how come?" His big hands throbbed from gripping her so hard.

"You like this grind so much and you're so strong and good at it, you never looked around to see what it was doing to me," she said. "Wearing me down, never enough time to enjoy life or settle down or anything. I hate it anymore."

"Think what you're throwing away, Bonnie. Thirteen years. Think how we worked."

"I know, Bumper. I'm sorry."

"It's that California bastard, isn't it?"

"Oh, Bump. I was going that way in my mind on my own. He just helped me to make the change."

"Well, you said something there: you sure as hell *have* changed. You're my sister and I'll never deny it, but as I stand here right now I swear I hate you."

She had quit crying, and she looked down and nodded. "Yeah, I reckon you do." She went on back to the Impala, and the last thing she said to him before she got in and drove away out of his life was, "So long, brother. Guess I ain't the big heart from the little valley anymore."

# JOHNNY REX PACKARD
1973

The riot had started in the long corridor that led from the dining hall back to the cellblocks during a shift change for the guards. It'd been whispered back and forth among the inmates for a long time. The leaders were a group of Klansmen doing time for the bombing of a South Alabama black church some years back. They'd long been saying that being in hell was one thing, but sharing it with niggers was another. Time would come they won't gonna take it no more.

Johnny Rex Packard stood at his window staring blankly out on the empty prison yard listening to the howling from the other sections. He was housed in the east wing of the prison, the only section the administration had had time and security enough to cut off from the mob. The center and the west fell. Against all warnings Johnny Rex stared straight into the setting sun. When I come here, he thought, I had me some sunglasses.

Across the yard two Klansmen appeared at a fourth-floor

window and threw down one and then another decapitated body. Their hands and arms, he could see even at this distance, were covered with blood. Too much blood, he thought.

The yowling and screaming were getting worse. Johnny Rex's thoughts were confused. He remembered Karintha in the river, and his vision of leading the singers was coming back to him. Fourteen years it had been, but his need was a window in time through which he might search for his black angel. He heard the cannonfire again in the gunshots echoing down the prison corridors. The yowling of the mob in the other cellblocks merged with the roaring in his temples, the old roaring. He craved tobacco and whiskey together. He wanted to change that cacophonous roar into something harmonious, into something not just wild but wild and beautiful. There had been a time when he knew how to do that. He closed his eyes and pictured the keyboard of a piano in his mind. He tried to recall the feel of running his finger over it, and he felt the phantom missing first joint of his left forefinger at work on the ivory.

Suddenly he called out for a guard.

"They need somebody to help em quit doing that way," he said.

"What?"

"You tell the warden I want a piano."

It was the warden who years before tried to get Johnny Rex to play for the prison religious services. He hadn't wanted to play or sing then, but now, hearing that wild roar, he wanted the warden to let him set it to right. Johnny Rex wanted them to sing right, to sing together instead of against one another. He needed the warden. He needed a piano. The terrified guard got him both.

Johnny Rex went with the warden to Birmingham and sat in the carpeted, chandeliered room listening to the talk of respectable men. Vance Garland sat across from the warden, and that gave him comfort and strength.

There had been nothing like the Packard case in all the annals of the Alabama parole board: the albino's tremendous fame, the spectacular wife–mistress murder case that came close to getting him the chair, and now his role in the recent Caldonia Prison riot. He was appearing before the board with a parole request that was backed by the prison's warden, by leading evangelists, and by three quarters of the South's major daily papers. The *enfant terrible* became the *cause célèbre*.

The warden tried to explain what had happened that day. He told of the Klansmen who started the thing, and how, strangely enough, they had a number of blacks in league with them, desperate men bonded in hate for one another and by a fury at the stench and overcrowding of the ancient prison. He testified under oath how a guard from Block J got a message to him that Johnny Rex Packard had some secret plan to stop the riot. At that moment it was only barely contained. The prison was thirty miles from anywhere. If the mob broke through before state troopers or National Guard arrived they could all be dead in ten minutes. Of course he let Johnny Rex come forward.

The warden told how Johnny Rex never had said a word to him. "There were a lot of men who thought he couldn't talk at all—but that night it was like he knew where he was for a change. He was like a man waking up out of a deep sleep, or coming out of a coma or a trance or spell."

The warden was an educated man, had been through the state university and gotten his master's degree in criminal sociology. This day in Birmingham, he spoke like a song leader at a high-school youth camp, zealous, excited, all caught up. He described how Johnny Rex wanted "to lead the singing" and asked for a piano, and how for two solid hours without stopping Johnny Rex sat at the piano and sang, sang songs the warden had "never heard anybody sing that way," "O God Our Help" and "Walk in the Light" and "Rock of Ages." And all the while, the singing was being carried through the riot-torn prison by an aged intercom system, little tan wood boxes high on the walls and other speakers mounted behind the ceiling grilles, until the yowling began to subside, to die down, till there was a quiet eerie calm, but not for long, because then voices began to join, from away off in the prison so there was an odd delay like there were people singing on one side of a great stretch of fields and being answered back in song, the same song, by people on the other side. Or like voices coming across a distance of water—clear and muted and precious as river pearl.

And that was it.

Eighteen men were butchered that day, and dozens more injured. But the fury of that mob dissipated and fell away as the voice and piano of Johnny Rex Packard played on, distracting more and more of the men, till there really was nothing left but the Klansmen with their empty guns stolen off the guards and their crude knives, and a much bigger bunch of toughs, black and white, staring them down. Someone joined in, repeated from the back of the mob the words the albino was lining out, and others picked it up, till the cacophonous yowling had become an enormous unison chorus, song after song. The handful of Klansmen retreated deep into the west section of the prison, to the room where they were finally captured, crying and screaming and fighting pitifully among themselves.

The riot was over.

They practically gave Johnny Rex the run of the joint after that. And what he really wanted he got: he auditioned nine tenths of the prisoners and formed a choir, an organized version of what had begun so weirdly during the riot itself. He got permission for two dozen or so of his leading choristers to perform outside the prison and on television and for large religious and civic groups in Birmingham. His parole proceeding was being taken up steadily at meetings in the capital, the warden assured him, but the board was moving cautiously. Johnny Rex scarcely gave it two thoughts.

He was alive again through the harmony and brotherhood of this music.

Winter came, and signs were positive that parole would be granted, that it was just a matter of a few months. But even before the warden picked up this news, Johnny Rex received a visitor from California, a blond bespectacled man who introduced himself not through crisscrossed diagonal wire but in the warden's office because that was the kind of respect and latitude they now accorded the singer. The man said his name was Paul Flank, said he was a record producer. And would Johnny Rex be interested in a project to record his gospel chorus there in Caldonia and distribute the album on Carpathian Records?

Johnny Rex didn't have to think long. He had made records and signed contracts and done all that before. "Just don't bother me with details," he said to the Californian. Then he stood to leave and gestured toward the warden, who became by that gesture a negotiator between a choir of prisoners led by a convicted wife-killer rockabilly piano player and one of the country's largest broadcasting and recording corporations.

Two and a half weeks later Paul Flank showed up at Caldonia with a mobile recording unit. He set up his equipment in the dining hall and recorded and mixed on sixteen-track Ampex equipment the music of Johnny Rex Packard and a hundred black and white voices. With great fanfare, Carpathian released the album: *Johnny Rex Packard and the Caldonia Gospel Choir: Songs That Stopped the Riot*. It was January 15, 1974, two months to the day before Johnny Rex's parole went through and he was driven to an airstrip for a flight back to Tennessee. It all happened so fast Johnny Rex didn't know what hit him: he was invited to appear as the featured final performer the last night *The Grand Ole Opry* would ever be staged in the Ryman Auditorium in downtown Nashville. The *Opry* was moving to a big amusement park ten miles away, Opryland U.S.A.

"They want *me*?" he said over and over as he and Paul

Flank and the warden waited in the warden's office for the call that would tell them the parole board had stepped up the procedural pace. Due to the unique combination of circumstances relating to Mr. Packard's career and the closing *Opry* show at the Ryman, the parole would be granted three months early and would become effective at noon of Friday, March 15, 1974. Just in time.

"After all the hell I been through they want me to sing the last *Opry* song on the Ryman stage. Life's a damn crazy thing, Paul. *Damn* crazy."

But there was no real mystery about the invitation: after all, Johnny Rex's prison-choir album had shipped *gold*.

# PART FIVE

# BONNIE MONTREAT
March 15, 1974
Afternoon and Evening

"Do you a world of good," Quill said when he and Flank sprung the plan on her to play the Ryman's last night in front of Johnny Rex Packard. "Put you back in good stead with folks in Nashville, and you don't got to give up a thing."

In the year since her dramatic move from Nashville, Bonnie Montreat had enjoyed a phenomenal success with her album, *Double Shuffle*. There'd been a national tour behind the album during the summer and fall, and a number of major network television appearances and oceans of press. She was the new darling of the national media. In Nashville it was a different story. In the trades and in the gossip she picked up from Joe Quill, she knew how bad her career move sat with the country-music-industry people. They saw it as one more great and hateful mistake made by the woman who walked out on Bo Talley. First Bo, now her own damn family. More than fifty hard-line country stations refused to play the singles off the *Double Shuffle* album. She felt like she'd been crucified.

"Somebody'll shoot me if I show up to play the *Opry*'s last Ryman show," she'd told Quill.

"I don't think so, Bonnie girl. The *Opry* management wants you—they think the record and the film wouldn't be the same without you."

"Oh, that's *business,* Joe. I mean the folks who'll be there—it'll be a mighty hard crowd for *me* in particular to please. I don't know if I'm up to it."

"Stand up there and take it, girl. They loved you then and they love you now, but they got to see you being brave enough to come home and do this one thing before they're going to admit it. You'll regret it forever if you don't."

Bonnie knew he was right. She agreed, but she let both Joe Quill and Paul Flank know in no uncertain terms that she would *not* be available at the Ryman until virtually the last minute. No sound check or light call, no press interview beforehand. They assured her there would be no problem with the details.

Carpathian Records was sparing no expense on this package. An independent film crew from Atlanta—credited with the astounding cinematography of Hud Vonder's 1969 filmed-in-Georgia cult hit *Hard Drifter*—had been hired to get down the cinema-verité footage of the concert. It would be the Inchon landing for the rockabilly MacArthur, a homecoming for the Tennessee mountain girl whose dreams were bigger than Nashville, and a fond farewell to all that as far as the Ryman went. A red-letter day in country-music history: the Ides of March of '74.

Bonnie went by herself to an old inn she knew of over in Flat Rock, North Carolina. A couple of days off in the Carolina Hills to think about it did her good.

She prepared herself to face the audience, and to see for the first time since the break Bumper and Treat and Daddy and Ivy, who were performing together earlier in the evening. She reflected on how a woman could be so fortunate in the world of music and money and so unlucky in that of love. But for a circumstance of birth she might have had her one true love.

If her affair with Paul Flank had cooled considerably, their working relationship was like a fine fluid drive. He had proven to her that he was shrewd, if manipulative, and efficient; he had always encouraged her to try new and different things in her singing and writing, and in the production approach to her songs. She found after all that she was glad Paul had gotten Carpathian involved in documenting on film and record the last Ryman *Opry* show—and that she felt proud if anxious to be included, especially since the evening marked a forgiveness and appreciation and acceptance for Johnny Rex Packard as well.

She took a deep breath and lifted her spirits up and drove west toward Nashville to ring out the old.

Crowds and traffic swarmed all over lower Broadway. She parked way off down Fourth Avenue and pulled her coat hood over her head so she'd not be recognized. She weaved through the mob at the Cat & Fiddle and out the back door and up the alley to the Ryman the way she and Bo had done, drinking a quick one or two and then hustling the ninety seconds it was from the back door of Trix's to the stage of the most popular radio show in the world. At the stage door she raised her outsize sunglasses to show the security guard who she was and then asked where to find Paul Flank.

"The Californian? He's holed up in that blue box yonder." The guard pointed to Paul Flank's command trailer in the parking lot back of the Ryman.

He was set up next to the mobile recording unit monitoring what was going on inside the Ryman on closed-circuit video. The show had been going two hours now with the bluegrass and string bands and quartets and honkytonkers and honkytonk angels. Bonnie had a moment of difficulty getting in to see him.

"Sorry, miss," said another security guard at the door to the trailer. "He can't be disturbed."

"I'm Bonnie Montreat."

"I know. I'm sorry, but he said *nobody*."

"Get out of the way."

Bonnie went on into the trailer. "Some welcome this is."

Paul waved her to be quiet and pointed to a small ladder-back chair with a cushion in its seat. He had the trailer monitor turned low. A telephone was cradled between his ear and his shoulder, and there was a small mirror balanced on his knee onto which he was tapping out a couple of lines of cocaine.

"Are you *crazy,* Paul? This is *Tennessee.*"

He shushed her and motioned toward the telephone to show he was listening. "All right. Sure, we can see to all that. You're a saint to do this."

Bonnie glanced at a wall clock: eight-fifteen. Damn, she thought, on in a hour.

"Fine, but hurry. You'll go on just after nine—it's all clear with the management. Thanks." He rang off, and Bonnie lit into him before he could say a word.

"I thought *I* was going on then."

"You were."

"Well?" she snapped.

"There's been an accident."

# JOHNNY REX PACKARD
March 15, 1974
Afternoon and Evening

It was small talk, mostly, during the half-hour drive from Caldonia to the industrial-complex airstrip where Johnny Rex was to be met and whisked away to Nashville. It was just the driver and the warden up in the front seat and Johnny Rex in back with the black briefcase they'd give him with his initials "J.R.P." on a brass plate on top. The briefcase was full of press clips about his release, about the welcome home and

*Opry* last-night show at which he and former Nashvillean Bonnie Montreat would be featured.

The singer gripped his parole papers tightly, and his knuckles whitened. The prison car turned down a red-clay road with ten-year pines along one side and a tall anchor fence along the other. Beyond was the five-thousand-foot airstrip where his ride was waiting. They pulled up at the tie-down area and got out, Johnny Rex's grown-out white hair, long for the first time in fourteen years, whipping about in the high breeze like cornsilk.

Nearby a couple of men leaned up against a small Kingair jet. The bleached-blond younger fellow came forward to Johnny Rex and shook his hand with a strange arm-wrassling grip and said, "Far out—I'm Cy. Henry over there's the pilot. Got any luggage?"

Johnny Rex nodded over toward the prison car, but the driver had already got his things out of the trunk. The pilot hung back, his eyes hidden by thick sunglasses, chewing on a toothpick. Johnny Rex turned abruptly back to the warden.

"Guess this is it."

The warden extended his right hand. "You made it back, Johnny Rex," he said. "And I don't mean you just pulled your time and got out. I mean you been somewhere in hell and you made it back."

"Got to get going, Mr. Packard," Cy said, "if you want to have a chance to lie down before the show tonight."

"You'll be all right, Johnny?" the warden said.

"Long as they got my piano tuned."

"Good luck to you." They shook hands again, and then the driver shuffled around and looked down at his feet as he reached out and shook hands goodbye with Johnny Rex. "See you, Johnny."

Johnny Rex looked back at the warden, whose eyes now were luminous and teary. "Warden?" he said.

"Never seen anything like it," the warden said. "Never have and don't ever expect to again: it was a miracle."

Now Johnny Rex scuffed his heel and looked off into the blue. A puff of white smoke from a manufacturing plant nearby blew into his field of vision and disintegrated like a cloud into vapors. Johnny Rex tried to think of the right thing to say. He wanted to be well thought of and remembered. "We'll do us another record with the choir, real soon. I'd like that."

"OK, Henry," Cy called, glancing one last time at the men from the prison before ushering Johnny Rex into the King-air's rear compartment.

Henry yelled, "Clear!" out the left portal and fired the jets.

Cy Legare, Paul Flank's advance man, was talking nonstop about how Flank had spared no expense arranging for the recording and filming of this last *Opry* night at the Ryman, how national press coverage as well as a massive publicity campaign were being planned around the release of the record and the film, planned just right to take full advantage of—

"Sounds real good, Cyrus," Johnny Rex said as the aircraft lifted off. "But I'm fourteen years dry. You got anything to drink in this damn place?"

Cy Legare seemed to look at him warily before reaching forward and opening the imitation-wood-grain door of a small refrigerator. There looked to be a dozen or more cans of soda and beer inside. Johnny Rex jerked out a Blue Ribbon and popped it open.

"You shouldn't drink too much of that," Cy Legare was saying. "Altitude doubles the effect of alcohol, you see."

Johnny Rex smiled. "I know how much beer I can drink, boy, and that's all you got."

He swilled down the entire can and crushed it and reached in the icebox for another and drained it too. He turned back to the window and looked out on the industrial park, the new Southern landscape that could no more have produced him than his own, forty years earlier, could have produced Mozart. He saw the small prison car moving away from the airstrip on the red-clay road and stared down as the ground disappeared behind afternoon wispy sheets of haze and clouds, and it just then hit him like a rock wall hits a car that it was the first time in his whole life he'd ever been up in an airplane.

*I'll be goddamned if there ain't a bolt loose in my head somewheres. Still.*

They were flying north, high above Birmingham, then on like the route of the L & N north from the gulfport bays at Mobile and Pensacola. It was somewhere thirty, forty miles below Huntsville, below the Tennessee River, that they ran into a line of storm. Too high, the tower at Huntsville radioed, for even the high-flying Kingair to climb over. And too broad to the west, over to the Mississippi line as far south as Columbus, for them to get around that way. Fly northeast, the tower advised, and get clear around Chattanooga.

Coming up that way you can follow the ridges, those trailings off the Appalachians, flying up them longwise to the north and east. If the great late-winter storm keeps bearing down, you can skip over one ridge to the next like a swimmer trying to get past the breakers. But if you failed to keep count of the ridges, or counted wrong because bulges in the storm cut visibility to nothing while blowing your aircraft easterly, then you could get too far over, into the wilderness east of Sand Mountain, east of Lookout, the wilderness where the states of Georgia and Carolina and Tennessee come together and face each other off in a jump-up country full of laurel hells and raging gorges and blue boars and black bears and hardly any people. It would be a terrible place to end up flying over when you discovered that a defective fuel gauge had been reading deceptively high and that the fuel line to the auxiliary tank was blocked.

Maybe the pilot figured that what he was seeing when he came in, all cockeyed and shook up, was a highland meadow, a hilltop field of winter wheat or something—good fortune, a rare place to set her down—instead of a three-acre block of feldspar laid out by the hand of God at a better than forty percent grade up top of a big cresting mountain above some hog farmer's ramshackle house and farm. The last thing the pilot and his passengers would have seen was the western sun glinting off the mica in the spar like diamonds in the heavenly crown, one quick glimpse from right at the near side of Paradise.

The hog farmer heard it come apart and blow, he and his boy both. "Heard it? Hell, a piece of wing, numbers on it and all, come slamming down in the mudyard out back, come within a bristle of flattening my prize Poland China boar."

His boy raced down the mountain in an old beat-up International Harvester jeep to where there was a phone line. He wrote the number off the wing with charcoal on the back of a shingle and called it in to the sheriff, who said he'd be up with a rescue squad. When the boy got back he found his father up in the barn loft looking out at the burning wreck. Too steep to get up there without hooks and ropes, he said. Too hot, too. So the hog farmer and his boy dragged the wing out of the hog lot and into the barn, where they could figure out later what use they'd put it to.

Three quarters of an hour later the sheriff and half his deputies and both the valley's four-wheel-drive rescue-squad vehicles got there, along with the editor and photographer of the *Three Counties Herald* and another fellow with a pad of order forms who kept saying he was "wire service." That was when the hog farmer and his son found out just whose plane it was had got so far off course and come apart on their isolated slab of spar.

The boy got a idea.

He hightailed it to the house and found the gallon of yellow paint left over from when they'd painted the kitchen before his ma died, and carried it to the barn. He made him a brush by crushing and splaying out and fraying the end of a cornstalk. And when the crowds arrived to gawk at the rescue work, they saw the boy standing hands in pockets by the barn door looking like he'd found something good to hock so he's for a few seconds got a leg up on the world. On the barn door was the yellow scrawl, big as he could get it with his cornstalk paintbrush and still not run out of paint:

HERE THE PLACE JON PACKIRD PLANE
GON DOWN
SEE THE WING     25 CENT

## THE RYMAN
March 15, 1974
Night

"The plane went down way the hell off course over in East Tennessee a couple hours ago. It blew up—almost nothing left of it, apparently. They identified it from pieces of the wing some farmers found right after it happened."

Bonnie wept quietly. Paul Flank snorted the cocaine.

After a couple of minutes, she looked up. "Who were you getting to play?"

"Pres Hewitt."

Son of a bitch. Bonnie quit crying in an instant.

"He's the only one I could think of to step in and play before you."

"I'm to be *last?*"

"That's right. I think it'll work out pretty well."

"I don't believe this, Paul. I can't believe this is happening to me."

"Well, it's happening to all of us, Bonnie. We're all in the same boat. There's been a horrible accident and we've got to deal with it. We've just got to live through tonight and then clear out of here in one piece."

"I suppose you're going to use my band to back him up, since that's what we were going to do with Johnny Rex?"

"Yes."

"Have you told them?"

"Yes, they know."

"They'll do it?"

"Of course they will. Come on, Bonn. You're above acting like this."

Bonnie walked to the trailer door and leaned there a moment. "Paul, I'm going out for a walk. Figure out whatever you got to do so I don't get within twenty feet of that little bastard. One other thing. I want you to find me some bourbon and chill it down cold as you can get it. That's all I ask. I'll do my part. I'll try and sing like a bird."

"No problem. I've never seen so much bourbon as there is floating around here. What kind do you want?"

"Early Times, Paul. Early Times." She left the trailer.

After a short walk she went backstage and found Daddy and Ivy and sat in a corner talking quietly and stiffly with them. She'd telephoned them maybe once a month during the year since her break with the Green Valley Band. That way she'd managed not to lose complete touch with home, and to keep up with Bumper and Treat. They were touring as a string-band revival act playing colleges and the network of small folk clubs and festivals around the East and the South.

The bourbon in her jelly-jar glass was cold as the creek water of Honey Run during spring thaw. She sipped on it during the long silences in their conversation and now and then reached back under her copper curls and squeezed the muscles in her neck, trying to get them to loosen up a little. Ivy spoke of people who'd died and gotten married and had babies back at Honey Run. Daddy spoke of his machines, breakdowns of his tiller and his power saw, the trustiness of his Super-A tractor. And, like always, he spoke of the dogs.

"Looks like Penny Lee's done gone for good this time," Daddy said, rubbing his hand nervously on his knee. Bonnie noticed how his knuckles were swollen with arthritis, and how the wrinkles had gathered in her mother's cheeks. God, she thought, they're old.

"Not Penny Lee," Bonnie said. "She's got the go in her, but

she'll come back. Always has, Daddy, you know that." Ivy was shaking her head.

"It's four weeks tomorrow, honey," Daddy said. "That's a long time for a dog to get gone and still make it back, even Penny Lee."

"Well, I ain't giving up no way," Bonnie said. She knocked her fist on the wooden arm of the blue deck chair she was sitting in. Penny Lee had been her dog, even though she was a hunting hound, a black and tan, that ran with Daddy's pack. Bonnie had picked her out of a big litter she went with Daddy to look at not two years before she left for Nashville. "Why that one, baby?" Daddy had asked. Bonnie had held the pup in her hand, its stomach cradled in her palm, and said, "She's the only one in the litter that'll really look at you. She's got the deep eye." Twelve, no, sixteen years, she thought. All that time and now here I am with my folks that I'm practically strangers to, waiting for a man I hate to show up and open for me in a welcome-home show turned into a wake. The Ryman was full of ghosts for her. She could see Bo wherever she looked. She could picture Ivy asleep in the chair by the light box while Bumper auditioned banjo and Hank Williams came out and spoke to her: Don't forget Old Hank, now.

"Where's Bumper?"

Daddy and Ivy glanced at each other and shrugged. "Around here somewheres," Daddy said. "Said he wanted to see you."

"Did he?"

"That's what he said."

I wonder, she thought. There was another pause in their talking. She sipped the bourbon—couldn't get Daddy or Ivy to take any—and waited as the sound of banjo and dobro came from the stage. The crowd didn't know yet what had happened, but word was flying around backstage. She saw the engineer Skibo run up and tell a smiling colored fellow with a tambourine who was supposed to play along with Johnny Rex. The colored fellow turned to the wall, his shoulders shaking. A high thin wailing sound started up from the distance outside beyond the nearby stage door.

"You hear a siren?" Daddy said. The sound got louder and louder. Bonnie sipped again, not drunk in the least, but aglow. The siren became louder still, and she got up and looked out the stage door just as the squad car pulled up at Paul Flank's trailer and cut both the horn and the engine.

Bonnie's flesh crawled.

It was the State Patrol delivering Pres Hewitt.

Preston had turned the *Opry* down when he was first approached to be on this last show. He wasn't interested. But this, now, was something else, to step in before the huge emotional crowd at the last moment and lead the mourning for Johnny Rex Packard. More than that, it was a great opportunity to show up Bonnie Montreat. As far as he could tell, she had never used what she knew about him and Bo Talley against him, but she had let her dislike for him be known first all over Nashville and, more recently, around Los Angeles as well. Fine, he thought, if she wants to play it that way. But if I ever get a chance to bareknuckle the bitch right out of the ring, I'll sure as hell take it. And this was it.

Paul Flank and the *Opry* manager and *Opry* emcee Efland Oaks were in the trailer deciding how best to break the news to the crowd. Oaks would say a few words and allow time for it to sink in, and the show would continue with the introduction of Hewitt. Pres thought to himself as the others talked, figuring correctly that Bonnie would have been severely unnerved by Johnny Rex's death, especially when it meant she became the show-closer, the Ryman-closer.

Pres's notion was to make his set so outrageously *hot* that Bonnie would have a hard time topping it. And the masterstroke was that he'd be using *her* band, a hot bunch of L.A. session men if there ever was one. She had very carefully crafted her sound and used the players in a very controlled way. Pres would turn them loose. He had just enough time with them in one of the cramped pine-paneled dressing rooms to find out which of his songs they were familiar with. "Let it fly," he'd said. "I'm here to help give the crowd a feeling of release. I want to do my best to warm them up for her."

Efland Oaks went out onstage and said his piece, and Pres Hewitt walked out onto the great stage to a stunned audience as Efland Oaks introduced him as "the closest thing I know to being the next Johnny Rex Packard, the progressive outlaw Pres Hewitt!"

Bonnie went back out to Paul's trailer and watched on the monitors as Pres Hewitt, wearing a buckskin suit, played through his set, going on between songs about him and Johnny Rex this or him and Johnny Rex that. I'll be damned if Preston Hewitt ever spent any time with him, she thought. I'm the one saw him twice, of us two anyway, and there was damn little to that. And now he's selling himself to this crowd as Johnny Rex's blood brother and them crying every time they hear his name.

And I can't believe that's my band, she thought. Out there playing like a bunch of cavemen, banging on their instruments instead of playing em, all the amps turned up to ten. How the hell am I gonna get em back?

*They're with you, Pres.*
The applause grew louder after each song, building up to where it was like a roar now. *Take it down a bit.* A slow poured-on version of "So Lonesome I Could Cry." *You got em now, you got em.* Then to the band he shouted, "OK, boys, let's give it to em."

There followed thirty minutes of "Amazing Grace," the whole crowd singing with Pres Hewitt leading and yammering on like a bad street preacher between the lines about Brother Johnny Rex and his trials and his sin and his women and his love and his gift of love and life through music.

> *"I once was lost . . .*

*(Goddamn, every lick of this*

> *But now am found . . .*

*is going down*

> *Was blind but now . . .*

*on film.)*

> *. . . I see."*

Thirty minutes of "Amazing Grace" and he had them howling, country people, Music Row publishers, Woodstock vet-
erans, all ready to believe in the Resurrection not of Jesus
Christ but of Johnny Rex Packard.

Pres looked around to thank the band, but the players
weren't there. How weird. That's how big he guessed the
sound of this audience singing was, that the players had gone
off and he couldn't tell the difference between doing it with
them and doing it without. But the audience wasn't just
singing, there was a howling in it, and now he heard anger in
the tears and voices. It frightened him. *Maybe they feel cheated
by Johnny Rex dying. Hell, they got his records—he's part of the past,
let it go, hell with it. They ain't been cheated by me, no sir.*

*Take the applause, Pres.*

*Take it.*

*Take it.*

He soaked in their adoration, their fury, their fire, held his
guitar with two hands high above his head. And just before
he walked off the stage, he took one last good look and
thought, *Fools.*

At a point just past midway in the long singing of the
hymn, Bonnie saw her band members stare at each other in

amazement over the frenzy Preston Hewitt was whipping up.
The din from the audience singing was so great that they
couldn't even hear themselves in the monitors. She could see
and hear that they'd lost their places, like the poor little
sheep of song. One by one, they shook their heads and gave
it up. Hewitt didn't even notice.

Bonnie left Flank's trailer. She wanted to see this backstage, up close for herself. Her drummer was the first to get
to her. "It's *crazy* out there, Bonnie." Daddy and Ivy were still
there.

And Bumper was with them.

He was over near the gaping hole left when the *Opry*
management had had a circular section sawed out of the
Ryman backstage floor and carted away and built into their
television-studio stage floor down center way out at Opryland in the Cumberland River floodplain where Captain
Tom Ryman would of never built because he *knew* that river
and he *knew* what made sense and what didn't.

Bumper was leaning up against the backstage wall chewing
a toothpick, with his Martin guitar by his leg, his hand on its
neck and its strap knob on the floor. When she looked over at
him, his expression didn't change, nor did he say anything.
He just nodded and worked the toothpick.

"What do you want to do?" her steel player asked.

A familiar hand lay on her shoulder, and a voice she'd
loved since childhood spoke softly from behind her. "I been
meaning to ask you that myself, sugar-britches, but you just
ain't been around."

Bonnie wheeled around and faced her cousin Treat, and
in his eyes she saw her future clear as the waters of Welsh
Girl's Creek back home. "First," she said, "I mean to kill
somebody." She threw her arms around his neck and whispered, "Then I mean to settle down with you." They kissed
good and big like the long-lost lovers they were, right there
backstage at the Ryman in front of her family, her band, in
front of God and everybody.

Preston Hewitt, guitar still above his head, backed slowly offstage, still absorbing the strange wild applause of the mob audience. He turned offstage right and saw Bonnie, and his smirk fell away. "Well, well, we meet again."

There was a palpable freeze there backstage. "You're one more sorry son of a bitch," Bonnie said.

Out front, the crowd roared on. Pres laughed, and jerked his head toward the stage. "You try and follow *that*."

Bonnie stepped squarely in front of him. "I been wanting to do this again for years." She slapped him hard and sudden and he reeled back, startled.

"I'll sue every red hair on your ass, woman."

"You do that, Pres. And I'll tell the whole truth under oath, so help me God." This time she drew back a fist. The blow threw him off balance, him in his high-heel cowboy boots, and he stumbled backward a few steps and fell, right through that hole in the Ryman stage floor four feet down on top of his guitar.

Without missing a beat, she turned back to her band gathered there watching the fracas. "Boys, I don't exactly know what kind of program to do. I think maybe they don't need to hear a big rhythm section just now. Maybe something quiet, old-timey. I don't know." Someone handed her her little Martin, and she lifted herself up and went out onto the Ryman stage alone.

It was an eerie moment. At the sight of her, the crowd went precipitously silent and people stopped moving in a way they almost never do at great public gatherings except maybe for a split second or two during the National Anthem.

What could she say to them? She hadn't known Johnny Rex, had only seen him when the tent revival came to Honey Run and then again that time in Knoxville. She really didn't know him at all.

And what could she say about the last Opry music to be sung and played in this great old tabernacle, the Ryman? It moved her to be standing there at the microphone where the great ones had stood and sung, to be standing there again herself and know that she would be the last one. She looked in one swooping glance high up at the high white slatted ceiling and the Delft-blue walls that came up to it smooth and curved, at the Coca-Cola and no-smoking signs on the walls, at the mass of people leaning forward in the close-thrust Confederate Gallery with its two dozen globe lights along its front. The only sound was from the steampipes that ran all around backstage and from the silver radiators down front of the stage and along the back wall.

As her eyes filled, the globe lights at the front of the gallery seemed to sparkle just long enough to make her think of the moonlight dancing on the mica in the white rock high on the mountain the night she spent in the hollow oak, and she could hear her own small voice singing to that tusked blue boar, and she could hear Miss Mary Liza: "*. . . You done had a miracle happen to you up on that mountain, and it just could be you been marked for another. If it comes I aim to see you're prepared for it.*" And, hearing, remembering, Bonnie Montreat in one of the most graceful and honest moments of her life stepped back several paces from the microphone and bowed her head, then half knelt, her arms extended as if to embrace not only all those before her but also all those of her own people, kin or no, who had gone before her, who had given her a name, a speech, a music, a home, song and symbol and clues that'll help you cipher something sometime and a memory as old as her hills. And she knew that the old country music she'd come up on was dying here tonight, dying like the old country gospel shouter she knew Johnny Rex to be, dying when the last crowd to sit on the hardwood pews left Tom Ryman's honest-to-God tabernacle tonight for the air-condition and soft seats of a state-of-the-art television studio out on the floodplain at the edge of nowhere not related to nothing. And she who had already left knew it was ending, the thing called country music that meant just that because it came from the heart of the country, where people like her had known the dirt. It was ending crashing down like Johnny Rex's airplane and the Ryman's last curtain.

But in that moment she knew, too, that there was something more important, something that came long before the radio and the record and the Ryman had created this thing now ending, and that something was the music that knew no author, the ancient airs that came from across the great waters, carried quiet and still in the steamboat banjo and in the Welsh Girl's guitar up into the hollow above Honey Run, and come to life and handed down to her, the high lonesome-sounding tunes that had time and trouble and sorrow and glory all woven in them.

And this was her second miracle, that she knew not only what was at the heart of this moment, but what to do, how to sing and what to sing. As she bowed, there came the start of an applause from the crowd, but it died aborning as if its sponsors understood late but not too late that the fragile moment could bear neither weight nor interruption. First by ones and twos, then in clusters and in moments from all over the hall they raised lighted matches, even lighters. A hand at the light board dimmed the house lights and brought the spot up on Bonnie, who looked beyond and backstage to where Bumper and Treat stood in a pool of blue light.

"Bumper, Treat," she whispered toward them. "Please come join me."

She watched as Bumper looked down at his feet, then off in the other direction. She saw him put his hand down in his pocket like he always did before he shambled off and away from you. She saw Treat start toward her and then hesitate. Her heart fell at her feet. She looked forward again into the sea of flickering light and wondered that her miracle could of come and gone so suddenly. I reckon I deserve it, she thought. To hurt him like I done. The both of em. They got every right to refuse me now.

"How about 'The Parting Hand'?" Bumper said, approaching her and pulling his fingerpicks out of his pocket.

"Oh, Bumper," she said. "I thought you wouldn't."

He nodded. "Go on—I'll be right behind you."

"Beside."

"Beside, then," Treat said as he stepped up with his fiddle. The three of them stepped forward to the microphones together, and Treat drew his bow across an A-minor, and Bonnie began to strum and Bumper to pick. Treat said, smiling like a possum cat, "Do what you do best, Bonn."

Like never before, Bonnie Montreat sang.